# THE SILENT WOMAN

# THE SILENT WOMAN

## MONIKA ZGUSTOVA

TRANSLATED BY MATTHEW TREE
FOREWORD BY NORMAN MANEA

THE FEMINIST PRESS
AT THE CITY UNIVERSITY OF NEW YORK
NEW YORK CITY

Published in 2014 by the Feminist Press
at the City University of New York
The Graduate Center
365 Fifth Avenue, Suite 5406
New York, NY 10016

feministpress.org

Originally published in 2005 in Czech as Tichá zena by Odeon in Prague; in Spanish
as La Mujer silenciosa by El Acantilado in Barcelona; and in Catalan as La dona silenciosa by Quaderns-Crema in Barcelona.

This project was made possible, in part, by the New York State Council on the Arts
with the support of Governor Andrew Cuomo and the New York State Legislature.

This project is supported, in part, by an award from the
National Endowment for the Arts.

This project was made possible, in part, by multiple grants from the
Institut Ramon Llull.

First printing March 2014

Cover design by Faith Hutchinson
Cover photo by Jordi Folck
Text design by Drew Stevens

Library of Congress Cataloging-in-Publication Data

Zgustova, Monika.
The silent woman / by Monika Zgustova ; translated by Matthew Tree.
    pages cm
  ISBN 978-1-55861-841-1
I. Tree, Matthew, 1958- translator. II. Title.
PG5039.36.G87T5313 2014
891.8'636dc23
                                                    2013045005

FOREWORD

## Solitude, Duplicity, and Resilience in Dark Times

## NORMAN MANEA

MONIKA ZGUSTOVA BRINGS TO THE AMERICAN LITER-
ary lanscape her Czech and Central European upbringing, her
adolescent years in the United States, and her current Spanish
citizenship. This rich life and her culturally diverse roots are
enhanced by her refined talent—an acute critical knowledge and
approach to literature, recently iterated in her novel *The Silent
Woman*, which may be seen as a global narrative (moving back
and forth from Prague to New York, Sarajevo, Boston, Moscow, Saint-Petersburg, and Detroit) during a large and essential
period of the brutal twentieth century and its aftermath.

At the center of this novel is an appealing and complex
female character, the "silent" Sylva, seen first in Prague in 1974,
not long after the promising Prague Spring and the Soviet invasion that followed. At that time:

> This woman is not the old Sylva, the one who lived in Paris,
> where they called her Madame l'Ambassadrice. No, she isn't
> the muse of the surrealists, not anymore, she is no longer

Mnemosyne, the goddess of memory; this seventy-year-old Sylva, whose age coincides exactly with the year of the century, is somebody else. Who is that solitary woman who wears a bunch of white narcissi on her head, with a lace veil woven so thick that it seems to have been engraved on her face? It is she, Sylva, and it isn't her. We swim in the same rivers and we do not, we are and we are not.

Her troubled life—as troubled as the century itself—includes tough moral and psychological tests and traumas, hardships typical of life lived within an oppressive system, be it Nazism or communism. Giving in to the pressure of the sly and brutal agents of power, after prolonged and painful hesitations, Sylva signs opportunistic agreements with the German invaders and with the communist police state.

The cynical adjustment imposed by a hideous governing power under German occupation, and then under the pressure of the communist dictatorship, was for her a tribute of affection and solidarity with her loved ones. She rightly will later remember, "when the going gets rough, it is difficult to see things clearly. It is easy to make mistakes that you'll regret for the rest of your life." It wasn't easy for her to compromise her own moral ideals. Her regrets are authentic and lasting, indeed, and also forcefully challenge the simplistic and opportunistic way a lot of postcommunist and postfascist rhetoric are selling out now, in our apparently safe environment, in contrast to that bloody historical past, that overwhelming nightmare full of ambiguities and gray zones and of silent human suffering of heroes and villains.

Zgustova adds a valid warning about the questionable sides of the new pragmatism in the late capitalist free world, which has its own cynical agents of power—the power of money, this time, of course. More trivial and common, and apparently harmless, this trap is still not a spiritually rewarding alternative.

Sylva's son, Jan, had his own troubled experience in the communist dictatorship, due to his father being sentenced to the gulag and the dubious social standing of his mother. When he had finished university, "the political authorities hadn't allowed him to enter the Academy of Music because of his family origins." Now a cybernetics scientist in America, confronting the temptations of financial improvements by gradually giving up his real identity, he is also obeying, in his own way, the pressure of a new time. Again, it is about trying to satisfy family, this time his Russian wife. The dealers representing the new ubiquitous power of money have their own strategy: "Your salary . . . wow! It'd be finger lickin' good!" The potential new captive in a free society is hesitating, as his mother did. Yet, Jan does finally sign up, as his mother did in much more difficult times. "For some men a time comes when they have to give a big Yes or a big No. Over and over, I told myself: No. But then I thought to myself that if I worked for the Ford Motor Company from my university, I wouldn't be betraying my big No, and Katya would stop her nagging. I nodded: 'OK. Fine. I'm in.'"

IN HER Czech refuge, Sylva said, "During the darkest periods of our recent history, the times of Hitler and Stalin, our moral values began to deteriorate. That process is continuing now, nobody knows the difference between good and evil." Monika Zgustova's intense and acute questioning of the contradictions and conflicts of the social-political environment and of the individual's traps doesn't stop at the "end of history," what some fashionable commentators called the collapse of European communism.

The novel summons mainly exiles and focuses on a generalized estrangement in our current modern and mercantile society.

Sylva feels more and more exiled in her own country, where she was born into an aristocratic family of mixed ethnicity (Czech and German), under her father's name, von Wittenberg; where she spent her childhood in a magical chateau in northern Bohemia and married a bizarre German diplomat—the cultivated, polite, impotent, jealous, anxious, count Heinrich von Stamitz—who committed suicide; where she was assiduously courted by her French teacher nicknamed Beauvisage; and where she developed a tense, erotic, and affectionate relationship with a Russian modernist painter, the sensitive and arduous Andrei Ivanovich Polonski. Andrei also came from aristocracy, first engaged on the side of the Communists, then with the White Army, and ending up as a marginal expatriate in Prague. He returns to his homeland, only to be immediately arrested by the Soviet secret police and sent to a concentration camp in Siberia, where he works in terrible conditions. Sylva's son is the result of this profound and sad relationship with Andrei, shattered by the frosty and criminal Soviet exile that followed his Czech exile.

In this novel, Zgustova creates a significant group of interesting and memorable characters. She describes them with a nuanced understanding of the inner life and with a lucid, intelligent scrutiny of the never simple choices human destiny offers in such bleak, hostile circumstances. All inhabitants and wanderers of this remarkable novel live in the Kingdom of Shadows that dominated the planet and its calendar for too long a period.

*The Silent Woman* is the work of a sensitive, cultivated, skilled, and original writer who deserves our full attention and admiration.

# THE SILENT WOMAN

# I

# SYLVA

AT SEVENTY, YOUR LIFE IS OVER. OR A NEW ONE BEGINS. That's what I thought not long after hitting seventy, which is when I got his letter. I had never received a single letter from him before. Not even back then, years ago. Twenty-five years ago, or more.

The very idea of a quarter of a century suddenly makes me smile. A young mother passing by with a pram looks at me where I'm sitting, and, not seeing anything worth smiling about, acts as if I don't exist.

Through the steam filling the station I can make out a glass door. A woman is reflected in it. The skin on her face resembles fine cobweb, a tangle of slim snakes covers her hands. This woman is not the old Sylva, the one who lived in Paris, where they called her Madame l'Ambassadrice. No, she isn't the muse of the surrealists, not anymore, she is no longer Mnemosyne, the goddess of memory; this seventy-year-old Sylva, whose age coincides approximately with the year of the century, is somebody else. Who is that solitary woman who wears a bunch of white narcissi on her head, with a lace veil woven so thick that it seems to have been engraved on her face? It is she, Sylva, and it isn't her. We swim in the same rivers and we do not, we are and we are not.

Rather than feeling old, I feel immortal, and I feel like laughing.

Some elderly people can offer no more proof of their having lived than their own death. That is not my case. But I have often envied that kind of person.

Yes, my new life started half a year ago, when I received his letter. How I had waited for that letter back then—a thousand years ago. Yet it arrived much later, long after I had stopped expecting it. When I turned the envelope over to see who the sender was, I paused upon reading the name. I thought: at last! He took his time. Holding that letter I felt as young as when I wore my hair long—sunset colored as it then was—when I had my life ahead of me. A life in which he would be a part. A new life is about to begin, I thought.

He had taken twenty-five, no, thirty years to get in touch with me. Meanwhile, imperceptibly and unexpectedly, as silently as a ballerina advancing on tiptoes, old age had slipped inside of me.

"Wait, don't rattle the door like that; I'll give you a hand," I say to that young mother. The train is rusty and the platform, deserted.

A railway employee came out of an office door and, as soon as he sees two women making futile attempts to open a train door, he slips straight back into his office. At that precise moment, a male voice, sounding like it's coming from a better world than the one the station belongs to, can be heard: "Attention, please! Train number one four two from Benešov, Čerčany, Říčany will soon be arriving at platform three, line twenty-two. This train line terminates here."

"You know what we could do?" I suggest to the young mother, "We could each try to open one panel of the door. If you pull on the one on the left, I'll pull the one on the right. One, two, three!"

She thanks me profusely as I help her get the pram and the baby into the train, and I detect a flicker of guilt on her face. Just a moment ago, she was probably thinking, that old woman is completely gaga, smiling to herself for no reason at all. Now she is waving to me from the other side of the dirty glass and I would bet anything that she thinks I am a kindly grandmother. She's wrong. Nothing is as we imagine it. I am neither kind nor gaga. I'm only old. Old age is a sickness and it has to be fought. She knows nothing about that yet. She doesn't know why I behave as I do. I only helped her because I'm waiting. Do you know how a person feels when she is waiting? When she's waiting and she doesn't really know what she is waiting for? When she doesn't know what the awaited one will be like? Have you ever had to wait for a lover you thought you'd lost ages ago?

At seventy, can one start a new life? And what if doing so depends on another, unpredictable person?

※

LAST NIGHT I GOT THE SHIVERS. I LIT THE STOVE AND cozied up to it with a glass that I'd poured a couple of fingers of beer into. They say it soothes the soul. Behind the books on the shelf, I'd hidden the typed pages of a samizdat novel; tomorrow I must pass it on to the next reader, I told myself. But I dwelled on the clothes that I would put on tomorrow. I only had a few items to choose from. In such wet weather I'd put on a raincoat, of course, and a light brown scarf. I have a pair of shoes the same color, though they are badly worn out. I took a pair of earrings from the lacquered Japanese cabinet. They were a gift from him. With the sale of his paintings, I imagine, he had bought me real pearls. I haven't put them on in thirty years. I never had occasion to do so. No, come to think of it, I did put them on once! Yes, one single time, some seven or eight years ago.

They match the color of my hair, I told myself. Before they stood out, but now they melt into it. I gathered my hair right up to the nape of my neck: perfect, an elegant, modern style. The raincoat is the same color as the earrings; it is old and battered, but those pearls shine and gleam.

A new life, isn't that too much to expect?

It was when I began feeling weak yesterday evening that I remembered I hadn't any supper. I placed a couple slices of bread on a side plate, having cut off the crusts; the glass, with what was left of the beer, stood next to it. My supper was lit by a small lamp, and I suddenly lost my appetite, so busy was I gazing at that still life with a painter's eyes. Even after thirty years, once again I was looking at the world with an artist's eyes. Two slices of bread and a glass of beer, lit by a feeble bulb hidden behind a coffee-colored cloth.

Such is the world. My world, my world entirely. Two slices of crustless bread, a half-finished glass of flat beer. I require nothing else.

I live as I see fit, which is the reason I am not poor. When I lived surrounded by luxury, fitting myself into other people's scheme of things, I was not rich.

Every day bears me gifts. Today, it has offered me this still life. Now, at seventy, I have my little pleasures and no longer expect any grander ones.

Yesterday the plumber came, and could hardly squeeze past my large upholstered cupboards, the helmets, lances, and suits of armor that decorate my little living room and hall. Lady, he said, "you live in a tiny apartment on the outskirts and you've got it bursting with furniture that's fit for a king. I answered, in all honesty, Do help yourself if you like anything. I don't need them anymore. He didn't want anything—the items wouldn't fit into his place either, he told me.

No, I don't need them. They are mementos of what was. Right now I want a couple of slices of bread and a glass of beer. And that's it. Nothing else, nobody else. But is this enough to be starting a new life with?

This morning, at the crack of dawn, I don't know if it was the light or the birdsong that woke me. I placed the crumbs of the leftover crust on a saucer on the windowsill and offered it to the sparrows, taking care to make sure the saucer was out of the wind and sheltered from the rain. The geranium was soaked. I closed the window and drank my morning tea with the bread left over from supper.

Finally, when I left for the day, the prefabricated walls of buildings— usually so threatening, like a row of armed, gray warriors—were hidden behind a gray veil of dampness. It started to drizzle as soon as I sat down on my bench, the red one. Immediately, a sparrow flew over to me. I threw it a few crumbs and that little sparrow walked right up to the toe of my shoe. Then I realized that I'd put a stocking of a slightly different shade on each leg. And that my hands were shaking.

On the way to the metro, I grinned at my stockings. People turned to look ill-humoredly at me. And that made me laugh all the more.

ONE DAY, it must have been half a year ago, I received a letter. Someone was looking for me. I answered coolly; I didn't want him to understand how I felt inside. And I got a reply:

Dear Sylva,
I am so pleased that you answered my letter! Your answer has given me reason to believe you also remember me and the happiness that we shared such a long time ago. "Dear," this standard term of endearment, strikes me as

so wonderful when coming from you, or rather, from your pen. When I read the word, I felt a kind of physical warmth.

You mentioned memories. For my part, I assure you that the times I spent with you were the most beautiful I have ever experienced in my life. Back then, I thought I would always feel as good as I did during those moments.

Do you remember the present you offered me? You don't? I'll tell you about it: One evening, in a café, the Café Louvre in Prague's city center, I was admiring your black lace glove, and you, too, as you toyed with it. For many years I have kept that glove, which was my only possession; over many decades, whenever I felt like it, I took out your long, black lace glove with its bloodstained fingers, and laid it out before me. Whenever I see that bloodstained black lace, I hear you, Sylva, I see you and feel your presence.

I would like to know about your life in more detail, and, of course, I hope to see you again. I would meet you anywhere, no matter how far I had to travel.

Please do not get lost again. I beseech you with all my heart.

Yours,
The Old Tree

P.S. The old tree no longer has any leaves or branches, and yet the spring winds have shaken its roots and it has flowered. Both the red flowers and the yellow ones will soon disappear without a trace.

When I read these words, in the royal garden of my old age, a white flower budded.

THE TRAIN isn't here yet. The only thing I can hear is a young man's voice over the PA: "Attention, attention! A freight train will be arriving shortly at platform nineteen!" Its locomotive breathes and whispers and snores. What time is it, in fact? One doesn't want to miss the train, after all. That new, square-shaped clock hanging over platform one must be slow. It says half past eleven. It's stopped. It's new and yet it's stopped. I need to ask the time and look for the platform where his train will be arriving.

The mother with the pram waves to me from the train and signals me to come over.

"There's something I have to ask you. I really have to!"

"Look, no, I really can't. Any moment now the train I'm expecting will . . ."

"Please, I'm begging you . . ."

On that train he will arrive, the one who is coming to see me. At seventy I've started my new life, I wouldn't miss that train for anything in the world, I am about to say, but the mother has managed to sit me down next to her.

"I want to ask you," she says breathlessly, "it's my grandmother, my grandmother's making my life impossible."

As soon as a new announcement has been made over the PA: "Attention please, a warning for the driver of the locomotive," I answer her, "Tell your grandmother that young people need to be with those their own age. And give her a piece of advice: every day she should feed the birds and water her flowers. And no matter what, spring will come. And . . ."

Then I realize that the railway worker has signaled with his little red flag and I hear his whistle blow. I jump out of the train, which had slowly been getting underway. I land unsteadily. I'm dizzy and feel I'm about to fall under the train: Anna Karenina. The wheels turn, huge, threatening. I'm falling, but an inner voice orders me: You mustn't fall! You have to get your balance back, you have no choice! You must go over to meet the other train! Maybe it is entering the station right now—right this instant! Everything is hanging on a thread, you must do this if you don't want to lose everything at once!

Then the railway worker runs over and helps me back to my feet. He takes a large, brown check handkerchief out of his pocket and wipes the sweat from my forehead.

"If I were you I'd go have a stiff drink to get your strength back!" He tells me and taps his forehead as if to say, crazy old woman, jumping off a train like that!

But I had to jump, I absolutely had to jump because a train is coming, bringing someone. Outwardly, I simply smile with a mixture of gratitude and guilt.

I feel dizzy. I remember that I haven't had anything to eat all day except a couple slices of bread and a few sips of tea.

I AM sitting at a table, drinking hot chocolate. The warmth spreads through my body, right down to the tips of my toes. For a long time now, I have learned to ignore cigarette and cigar smoke, and the reek of piled-up ashtrays in the Prague cafés. But noise is quite another matter. I can't escape seated men with their glasses of beer in their hands, shouting. The only soft voices here in the café are those of lovers saying goodbye to each other. The noise is so deafening that I can't even recognize music they're playing. I can only hear mad, pounding music. Again, I savor my warm, comforting potion.

My hair! I am flustered. My bun must have come apart when I jumped from the train. I pat it, everything seems to be in place. Now I run my fingers over the pearls adorning my ears and my body fills with joy. I adjust the raincoat collar, caressing the fabric, which has grown old with me. It is too light for this April weather, but I don't care. It's so elegant! I run my fingers over it once again: the pearls and the hair and the raincoat, my beloved things . . .

The café is as jam packed as my own head. Snippets of sentences and smatterings of sensations and some piecemeal images swarm, all taken from my life, which has lasted a thousand years. Two young girls sit at my table and whisper into each other's ears. I keep smiling: they are pretty, they must be exchanging secrets about men, and I could surely compare their experiences with my own memories of the time when I was as young as they are now.

But my train! What if I were to miss the train I'm waiting for? I am horrified. But the possibility that I might overhear the girls' conversation is so tempting! Just a second and then I'll be off, I promise myself.

The girls talk in whispers and I can't catch a word of what they say. They murmur into each other's ears, then burst out laughing. From time to time, they look at me. I do not attempt to read their lips; they would notice that.

This art deco café is as old as I am. Maybe I'm older, even. It's covered in huge mosaics from the period of independence, representing flowers and girls. This girl over here is spring. And that one? No, she's not summer; she's Phaedra, the enigmatic one, like these two young ladies, like I had once been, and as I perhaps still am for the man who—while I savor hot chocolate in a café and listen to the romantic secrets of two girls—is racing toward Prague in an express train, combing his hair, if he still has any, who at all events is standing up and sitting down again and standing up once more. Oh, how restless he is! I smile.

All men used to get a little nervous in my presence. They're dead now.

We lose, and then we are lost to our loved ones. My loved ones have died. As someone once said, the dead live only in the memory of the living if, when they were alive, they proved themselves worthy of being remembered. Is that true? No. I don't think so. Their memory will live as long as I do, no matter what kind of people they were.

They have died, the women and men in my life: my mother and grandmother, my husband and my father, and the elegant Bruno Singer. Did they think of me before they died? Maybe they did. Or perhaps not. Does it matter at all? The only thing worth knowing is that in my own memory they have remained intact. The lives of the dead live on in the memory of the living.

And the living? There are only a few left to me. The man in the express train is racing toward the sign that reads, Prague Central Station, which I can see through the window. The man is perhaps entering Prague right now. It is time to go and see if his train has arrived. It is due at platform six which is quite a walk from the station café. With all this noise I can't hear the loudspeakers.

WHAT'S HAPPENED? Has the sun come out?

A velvety baritone voice has made its presence felt and is now spreading through the café. It expelled the reek and noise and bad language. This male voice is dancing a mazurka on tiptoes. It descends all of a sudden to a low register, then floats up again like summer clouds over a meadow, only to descend once more to melancholy depths.

"Your hot chocolate, madam," a waiter is smiling at me.

I don't remember having ordered another one.

"Where did it come from . . . the music?"

"Schubert, do you mean?" the waiter says, so softly I have trouble making out his words, "I put it on just for a little while. It's 'An Sylvia,' which I like a lot," and he smiles apologetically, or so it seems, and I have a feeling he's blushing.

# II

# SYLVA

I TAKE ANOTHER SIP OF THE HOT CHOCOLATE; IT REMINDS me of the touch of my grandmother's fingers. My gaze slides down to the floor, to my feet in two differently colored stockings. One light, the other dark.

I'm in such a tizzy. Like that day, a thousand years ago when I was a young girl in the chateau garden, the garden of my home, on the path by the riverside . . .

ABOVE US a blackbird happily chatted away. I looked for it among the branches to see if it might be carrying a worm in its beak. And then I sank down into mud. Petr took my high-heeled shoe out of the muddy puddle and cleaned it. When he'd finished he made me sit down on one of the low branches of a hawthorn or a plane tree so he could remove the mud from my foot with his handkerchief. He spent a considerable amount of time rubbing away at it. Then suddenly, as if making an offhand remark, he said, "Sylva, she's a poor woman. Your mother is."

My mother? Madame la Comtesse? I didn't understand.

Petr cleaned the mud off my foot right up to the ankle. Then he wrapped the handkerchief around my foot and kept rubbing it. Like a mother swaddling a newborn, I thought. When the handkerchief was all dirty, he scraped the mud from between my toes and wiped the sole of my foot. There was something in that mud that couldn't be cleaned away.

On the way back from the convent to the chateau, we laughed about my feet, one belonging to a little white girl, the other to a little black girl.

AN ELDERLY person likes to sing the praises of the past.

One black foot, one white one. That was fifty . . . no, fifty-five years ago. It's as if thousands of years have passed me by. The thousand-year-old woman remembers. That could be a title for my memoirs, assuming I should ever want to write them. Clouds of steam have covered all the platforms, the only thing shining is the glass on the stopped clock near the ceiling.

I taste the hot chocolate, again, I feel my grandmother's supple fingers, the only fingers able to make me feel safe and sound in that haunted chateau . . .

ON THE way back to the chateau, which belonged to my parents, the sides of the path were lined with yellow and white daisies and poppies and chicory and apple trees. Memories of my return trip come to mind, as do the reasons why I left my home for the convent. There is a single main reason for this, which I've never confessed to a soul. My mother often went to Prague to a ball or to the theater, to the opera or to a concert. She would put on her blue theater coat, the one with white ermine fur at the collar and the cuffs, and if she was going to a ball, she would put on the olive-green lace dress, or that sleeveless, pink satin one, and gloves so long they reached beyond her elbows. Often she wouldn't even say goodbye. I waited for her under the big archway of the entrance gate on the far side of the bridge, and threw myself at Maman's neck. I smelled her pompadour rose perfume and cried and shouted at her not to go. Maman always disentangled herself from me coldly, "What a pampered child! Back home with you!"

And then there was the case of my father's house slippers. I embroidered them with little blue flowers with orange stamens and green leaves on a black background. It was a lot of work; if I didn't get one of the leaves right, I had to unstitch the entire flower. After a few months, everything was ready. The shoemaker put the finishing touches on them. I placed the slippers in a box that I wrapped in silky green paper. The following morning I handed my father the gift, tied up with a golden ribbon. Papa tried on the slippers and thanked me for them, but remained aloof. In the evening, when everyone was asleep, I was feeling hot, so I opened the door that led onto the corridor. Then from papa's room, I heard his voice answering some question of my mother's, "What a ludicrous thing, giving me slippers! They're too small. I like best my usual ones, those really light fur ones!" I hid myself under the eiderdown so they couldn't hear my sobs.

When I left home for the convent, the night was dark, moonless, but the sky was splashed with stars. We passed through a silent landscape, the only sound was the neighing of the horses and the clip-clop of their hooves against the stones of the unpaved road. From one village to the next, the dogs greeted each other with barks, as our squeaking, creaking carriage moved on. In the sleeping villages behind dark trees and bushes, white houses glowed and I said to myself that on a night like this everybody ought to feel happy. The starry sky above and the unreachable horizon ahead made me ponder my future at the convent, and I imagined it full of veneration, beauty, and tolerance, brimming with magic, silence, and mysteries.

The return journey to my parents' chateau: a coffee-colored automobile, complete with chauffeur, drove over an asphalt road, with poppies and lilacs growing along the edges, and the apple trees wrapped up in billowy white clouds. From afar I looked at the ruins of a little castle on the hill, two fingers trying to touch the spring clouds, and suddenly our chateau appeared. Years had passed. From a distance, my parents' chateau looked like a wine-colored glass box, decorated with white ornaments, like one of those boxes that ladies keep in their boudoir for perfumed hand-kerchiefs and love letters. When we got close, I saw that during my years of absence the plaster had flaked as if it were the surface of a croissant. We entered through the main gate, the arch, and crossed the little bridge where the servants bid me welcome. Well, no, not exactly. Rather, they acted as if they were bidding me welcome, whereas in fact they were watching me as if I were an ogre from a fairy tale.

Maman wasn't at home, Papa wasn't either.

In my room, they had placed a big, shiny piano with golden letters on it: PLEYEL.

In the evening, my maid passed on the message: they were waiting for me upstairs. So I went up the palace stairs, up, up, and ever up. Then I climbed a spiral staircase and when I was so high up I couldn't climb any further, I saw the silhouette of a mature, well-built woman. This lady turned her back to me and walked away to the right. Not knowing what to do, I followed her. The lady entered a room, and I was right behind her. She circled around a long table, I did the same. We skirted that table more than once, more than twice.

The lady went up to the window, and opened it. Then I saw that wonderful thing.

Against a background of darkening turquoise blue sky, doz-ens of volcanoes could be made out, their mounds both great and small like a row of dusky pyramids, and those volcanic hills were spitting clouds of fire and sulphur and lava into the air. The lady positioned herself so that her face was not visible, all of her was in shadows, and from her hair snakes of fire raised their heads. An Egyptian goddess. The queen of fire.

Then a young man came into the room.

THEY SERVED me dinner at the table of my apartment. I was very hungry and there was only a tiny handful of rice with prawns on a huge plate. I was ashamed to ask for more. Then the door opened and the room filled with the smell of chocolate. My grandmother stepped from behind this aromatic curtain holding a silver tray with a cup and a few books on it. I took the cup of hot chocolate from my grandmother's supple fingers. In silence, I savored the steaming chocolate.

My grandmother watched me with her opal eyes. She gently stroked my hair with her smooth, soft palms. Although I preferred sitting on my own and in silence, I talked to my grandmother about all the things that I'd once longed to find in a religious place like the convent, but which, when it was all over, I hadn't found at all.

My grandmother sighed, "Sylva, very few things in life depend on whether we long for them or not."

By way of demonstration, she told me some of the myths of ancient Greece, and in the books she had just brought she showed me illustrations of classical heroes and heroines, old engravings on silky paper. Before going to bed, she gave me the sign of the cross. Her fingers gave off the smell of chocolate.

Once in bed, I felt strange in these surroundings. I thought about the goddess of fire. Her image would not go away, a beautiful, voluptuous profile danced in reflections of burning lava. I started to play Schumann's *Arabesque*, but it didn't calm me down.

In the morning I awoke at the crack of dawn, and went up

the winding staircase in silence to the room where the evening before I had been led by that luxuriant woman who had showed me the beauty of her figure against the foil of the stormy sky. But there was nothing unusual now in that room. Though on the round table, next to the sofa, I did discover a pair of small, decorative combs, the kind used to hold a coiffure in place; their inlaid jewels shone like dewdrops in the brightness of dawn.

CLOUDS OF steam have covered all the platforms. An elderly person is an adorer of old times, I say to myself, and aren't my memories old? I raise the cup to my lips. The steam has covered all the platforms, the only thing shining is the glass of the stopped clock near the ceiling. What time must it be now? Must make sure I'm not late when the train I'm expecting finally pulls in.

IN THE silence and darkness of the convent I was astonished by the paintings of biblical scenes; almost all of them were examples of obedience to the will of God or of punishments of those who failed to abide by it. Those images disturbed me. I found it difficult to understand them and I balked at the idea of making them part of my life: God orders the angel to expel—rather rudely, in fact—Adam and Eve from paradise. Why? For having disobeyed an order and eating an apple. Or the flood, what horror that was! The little children who drowned in the waves were guilty of nothing but being born! Why did God punish them? Or Lot's wife, who was made into a pillar of salt simply for turning around to look at her home. Orders and bans. Must one always obey orders, no matter how cruel?

The story that struck me as being more brutal than all the others I couldn't get out of my head. God said to Abraham, "Abraham! Take your young son, your only child Isaac, who you love and for whom you have waited so long, and offer him up in sacrifice." Abraham was prepared to do as he was commanded. Why? For the simple reason that the order came from his god. And God, when he saw that Abraham was so obedient, was happy and rewarded him. Is this kind of blind obedience a good thing? Is it good that, in order to satisfy his god, a man should kill the one he loves more than anything in the world? Is it good to obey a god as egocentric as this, a god who is capable of giving such a brutal order and putting someone to such a cruel test?

There was nobody in the chateau I could talk to about this. I tried to talk with the stable lad.

The young groom, Jakub, was the only person I could spend a little time with and get everything off my chest, talking non-stop, there in front of the stables.

"Why did they send you to the convent?" he asked me one day, with a sardonic grimace that I didn't really understand. "You aren't the type of lady who wants to be spending time enclosed with nuns, a girl as pretty as you . . ."

And he laughed again, with those half-closed eyes that made him look like one of the Chinese people on my parents' tea set.

"Why did they send me to the convent? Nobody sent me there. I was the one who asked to go there," I told him, without giving a thought to his strange behavior. "I was looking forward to seeing life in Prague, walking along the side streets of Malá Strana, spending time on the benches on Kampa Island."

All this I said to Jakub, a strong, tanned man who smelled of horses. I was well aware that he wasn't listening to me, and I didn't tell him the truth anyway, not the real truth as I saw it. How could I tell him that before I sought refuge in the convent, my mother, the Countess von Wittenberg after her marriage, had been going to the balls and theaters of Prague, and that my father, who had always been Count Wilhelm von Wittenberg, was spending whole weeks at a time in Germany, while I felt quite alone in that huge chateau? How could I tell him that I used to sit in a chair staring at the wall, hoping that someone would come, anyone, even Death if necessary, who would carry me off to his kingdom?

Jakub smoked a cigarette while I told him that I had gone to the convent, to a school run by enclosed nuns, filled with hopes that my new teachers would answer my questions about the meaning of things, that they would show me what the world was and what I was doing in it. I told Jakub that I had gone to all the Masses, praying through the winter with my bare knees on icy stone, wanting my suffering to freeze over my questions, but question after question kept popping up in my head, like spring air that slips through even the smallest gaps into cold, sealed-off rooms. I said to Jakub that I had wanted so much to help the poor and the sick, but had realized that at the convent nobody wanted any help from me, that the only things the sisters were after was my father's money.

"I wanted the convent to help me think things over," I told Jakub, finishing the conversation, "but the church asked only for my blind faith. And I didn't want to grope my way around like a blind person."

I know that the chateau's young stable lad had no interest whatsoever in the story of my disappointment in the convent. He kept smoking and ogling me with those Chinese eyes of his.

"Come on, let's go to the stable, I want to show you something," he said in a voice so shaky I could barely make out his words.

He opened the stable door.

I abandoned the sunlight, entering a darkness redolent with animal stench.

"*OH LÀ LÀ*, what is he teaching you, this young man who has just left your chambers with a pile of books, *mon enfant?*" Mademoiselle Lamartine was notable for her incapacity to hide her inquisitiveness. In fact, she was really called Mademoiselle de Lamartine. She would correct us, and most emphatically, every time we dropped the "de." Madame de Lamartine, my tutor in French language and literature, had a weakness for perfume. She would wear navy-blue dresses, tie her hair up in a bun, her gold-framed glasses would dance about on her nose, and her whole body would give off a greenhouse aroma.

"Do you like that boy?"

"*Mais ça alors!*"

"I can see that you're falling in love with him!"

"The things you say, *mon enfant, c'est honteux!*"

"Ahem, I also rather like this Monsieur Beauvisage."

"Is he French, *comme moi?*"

"Monsieur Beauvisage, Mr. Handsome Face, is called Petr, and he's teaching me about the French poets, especially Baudelaire."

"*Mais non!* That's not possible! I am the one who is introducing you to the French language and the French poets, *ma fille!* But not a word more about Baudelaire, he is not a suitable poet for young ladies. Tell me about him!"

Her tone was like the ruler that she just used to slap me on the back of the hand.

I had no wish at all to turn that ruler into my confidant. What business was it of hers that Petr, or better said, Monsieur Beauvisage, was my tutor in world literature and the Czech language, and that my mother had found him for me? By the way, my mother also rather fancied Monsieur Beauvisage, without a doubt. How she narrowed her eyes when she led him to my apartment!

"What has *votre instituteur* taught you? *Dites-le moi!*"

The ruler was now striking the table.

"What has he taught me? Listen carefully," I said as I began to recite in Czech:

> Come to my heart, soul mute and wild,
> adored tiger, nonchalant monster;
> I want to sink my trembling fingers deep
> into the grave thickness of your mane.

I added, "But you don't know Czech, Mademoiselle Lamartine, oh, pardon, de Lamartine. How long have you lived in this country? A good ten years, isn't that right?"

"I communicate in German, I do not require Czech."

"And what is German to us! We've been an independent country for three years now. Do you want to hear how these verses sound in French? Listen," I said, and recited them in their original language.

"*Mais quel horreur!* Such rudeness! Does your mother know what kind of thing this shameless fellow is teaching you?"

"Not only does she know, she is in full agreement with what he is doing."

"I must talk to her about your education. What else have you learned from *votre instituteur?*"

"Now we're getting somewhere! You liked that poem, you really liked it!"

"I have to tell your dear mother about this whole affair, and I need to be informed of every single detail of your studies."

Mademoiselle de Lamartine was pacing back and forth, stiff as an inquisitor.

Biting her lip, as if wanting to hold something back, she gave me a furtive look and said, "Today we shall practice the past perfect."

THE AFTERNOON before the ball that my parents were giving at the chateau for their friends and acquaintances, I went out into the garden for a stroll. I sat close to the lake's fountain and the nearby rock, the coziest and most poetic place in the entire park. Like Narcissus, in silence I watched my reflection broken into a thousand pieces on the water's surface, there where the stream from the rock splashed onto it. This is me, I thought; me, shattered, me, smashed like a water jar on paving stones.

I remembered that on one particular day, with my fellow students at the convent, we went for a walk in Prague; I must have been about thirteen then, and I saw a throng of people burning the Austrian flag in the street. I ran over to the blaze as fast as I could—I, who had grown up in the Austro-Hungarian Empire, I, the daughter of a German aristocrat—to save the flag from the fire. The crowd hurled insults and shouts of revenge and reprobation at me, and shooed me away. But there was a most kindly gentleman who said to me, "Listen, girl. Listen, you soppy thing," and he explained that things had changed, that the war had ended with the defeat of Austria-Hungary, and that we, the Czechs, no longer formed part of that empire, but lived now in an independent state, in the Republic of Czechoslovakia.

I didn't understand a word he was saying.

But soon I realized that everything was changing: the names of the streets and the signs on the shops were now in Czech. On the postage stamps, the old man with the cross expression, Franz Josef, had been replaced by a gentleman with a beard and ruddy cheeks, who was also old and looked like my grandfather when he was still alive and would sit me on his knees and play that game There Go the Gentlemen, There Go the Ploughmen. My grandmother told me that the man with the white beard was our president and that he was called Masaryk, and that he was a philosopher and a wise man, and above all, he was Czech. "Like us," she said.

Overnight, my mother began to speak to me in Czech. Not like before, when she mixed a couple of Czech words into her German, together with the odd exclamation in French, as if she were adding spices to a sauce. Now she spoke nothing but Czech. My mother also started to learn to write Czech, and became an actress in a Czech amateur theater company. My father spent little time at the chateau, for weeks on end he was in Germany consumed by work.

I looked at my face, deformed by the water's flow: that was me. I, who had confessed all to the stable lad and followed him into the stable. Afterward, without saying a single word, I washed my hands, sat in front of my Pleyel piano, and played Chopin's polonaises. That was me, Miss Countess Sylva von Wittenberg.

One day, after I had come back from the convent, my mother asked me to go up to her chambers. She received me as she might a friend, as an equal. Then I knew for sure: the enigmatic Egyptian woman that day in the dark room had been my mother. Over the years that I had been away, she had put on a little weight, and now seemed to me more feminine and better looking than before I had left for the convent. And the mountains behind her? They were volcanoes, it is true, but extinct ones, and above those distant volcanic hills, on the horizon, dozens of lightning flashes had drawn zigzags on the sky. My mother had prepared an unusual spectacle for me. Was it really for me? Or maybe ...

"Do you know, Sylva," she said to me, steeped in a cologne that I didn't recognize, as fresh and gentle as the singing of angels, not like the reek of the stuff Madame de Lamartine used. She was wearing a rather sporty white, pleated skirt, and a sky-blue shirt in a gentleman's cut. It was an effort for me to concentrate on what she was saying because I was watching her in silence, entranced. "Do you know, Sylva," she was saying, "you come from a distinguished and eminent family, your grandfather was not only a great violinist, but also a great Czech. It is due to him that Czech culture has not fallen into oblivion and has not died under the pressure imposed by the Austro-Hungarian Empire, that is to say, the pressure of German culture. You are from an eminent family, Sylva, and that makes you different from other people. Your origins make you elevated and noble. You must assert yourself, daughter, you must assert yourself both before the eyes of those around you and in your own eyes, because if you know how to show what you are worth, if you are clearly aware that you are elevated and noble, others will respect you and treat you like a great lady. I once read about a beautiful and proud aristocrat who lived over one hundred years ago, a Spanish woman who was the muse of the painter Goya. She said that whenever she entered a soiree, the musicians had to stop playing. They couldn't help themselves; they were so stunned by her beauty and comportment. Look at these flowers, if I had filled this vase with a bunch of daisies of the type that grow on the roadside, or with a posy of poppies and other wildflowers, my visitors would think I was vulgar and tightfisted. This is why every day I make a fresh arrangement of two dozen magnificent orchids. You too must be like an orchid, beautiful and noble, cold and inaccessible, a flower that does not give its scent away to the first comer, but rather keeps its perfume to itself."

I was watching my mother. She was like a Meissen porcelain cup, a prodigious object whose signature was marked in gold: two swords and the hallmark. It was this distinction that made Meissen cups different from the other tea and coffee sets that were used at the chateau: the set from Vienna had a crossed, closed V on it; the one from Sèvres, two LLs; the one from Berlin, two bars. My mother paused, paying attention to the orchids in their large vase, and then went on.

"Life has taught me the secret that I shall now go on to share with you, Sylva. Listen well, daughter: the woman who wishes to have the respect of both society in general and that of her immediate circle in particular must possess the ability to become as exquisite as an exotic flower. In the morning, in the dawn's first light, you must be like a white flower, fragile and innocent. Throughout the rest of the day too, for that matter, you must continue to be like a bud that the gardener has just cut from his favorite orchid—a flower as white as marble, which the painter would place on a tablecloth of cream-colored damask, the folds like baroque angels, the sun's rays playing with them, dying them the tenderest shades of pink. And in the evening? In the evening and at night you will transform yourself into a flower that is dark, but no less exotic. Yes, daughter of mine, at night you must transform yourself into a flower that exudes a scent of sandalwood and poppy, a poisonous flower placed in a slim, blood-red vase. Like serpents of paradise, the most exquisite and antique jewels will be wrapped around the vase, and their rubies and diamonds shall project their inscrutable and enchanting luster onto this flower."

I didn't take my eyes off the huge vase full of delicate pink orchids.

"To ensure that others respect you," my mother went on, "we must start with your appearance. What you need is a new coiffure and a brand new wardrobe. And a new way of addressing others. You're stilted; you speak very little. I don't want you to turn into a silent woman. Starting tomorrow, you will be given lessons in Czech and world literature by a student who is on summer holiday and can teach you these subjects."

"THE EXPRESS train from Ostrava has been delayed," announces the man on the PA, interrupting my recollections. This voice is clear, friendly, and despite the urgency of the warning, gentle. A sensitive man, no doubt. The trickle of water from the rusty tap on the wall has reached my feet. People would hardly notice that. A gentle dribble, thin as a snake, that goes where it wishes and takes possession of anything it wants, quite unnoticed. This is the only truth I know: old age. It came in on tiptoe without knocking, and ever so lightly, rested like a snowflake on a chair, and stayed with me.

THE TIME came when I couldn't take the convent anymore. My father had me released without uttering a word to me. When I got back home, neither of my parents were in. And in the evening, the Egyptian goddess and a young man. In silence, the convent schoolgirl left the room.

I always leave, everywhere I go. I flee. Silently, so as to pass unnoticed.

Who am I? I asked myself, staring at the water. Who? A German or a Czech? A countess, or the progeny of a musician—a man of the people? A little daisy like the ones people press into books to dry them out, or a proud orchid, like my mother wanted me to be? A future Carmelite nun or a coquettish, young woman? The daughter of an aristocrat, or a lady pianist specializing in Chopin's nocturnes, which she and she alone can play like an angel? Girlfriend of the stable boy or Fräulein von Wittenberg?

I am all of this, I think, and I continue to contemplate the uneven surface of the water in which I can make out the fragments of my face.

AT SIX in the evening, a lady with a white, rococo coiffure arrived. The coiffeuse. Not our usual coiffeuse, but the one who would create something special, worthy of the ball to be held at our home. She would have to curl mine and Maman's hair, so she said, but my grandmother would have none of it; it went against her principles, she insisted. I saw the disdainful look my mother gave her. The curling tongs, those pliers for frizzling one's hairdo, left our hair dry and burned and brittle; our hair was so curled we looked like a pair of ewes. The coiffeuse had given my mother a Greek chignon, as she called it, that hung down over the nape, and she ran around her with a hand mirror so that Maman could see it from different angles. All the while the coiffeuse screaming at the top of her lungs, "Oh, what a profile, you look like the empress, Madame von Wittenberg! Yes, you're the spitting image of the Empress Elizabeth!" When she'd finished, she burned my hair again, and then my ear, and tied the hairdo down with such force my eyes nearly popped out of my head. I felt I looked a fright, with two different ears, one ending in a point, and the other hanging too low.

The modiste brought me my dress for the ball, which was as yellow as a dandelion. Once it was on, I couldn't breathe. The modiste added a lot of ornaments that made me look like a caricature of Madame de Pompadour. Blushing from shame, and my eyes red from crying, I made my way to the ballroom.

WHAT BRILLIANCE! I couldn't make out the girls' faces, blurring as they did into the lights and candelabra. The brightly colored dresses seemed to dissolve into huge bunches of exotic flowers. I had the impression that a shining treasure had been put on display before me. Seated on my chair, I watched all those fireworks and floated on the waves of Strauss's waltzes. How could I have spent so many years on my knees, praying in the shadows of the convent!

Seated silently in the midst of all that musical commotion, I realized I had never once danced with a gentleman. Only with other girls in my lessons, but they didn't like dancing the part of the gentleman and would tread on my feet. My mother flew from one pair of arms to the next. My aunt and my cousin, too. I was the only one still sitting. As always, my parents paid no attention to me. I ought to have complained, given that this was my coming out in polite society! Yes, I would complain, but to whom?

I saw myself as a tall tree, a slender palm tree in the desert. Everybody could see me, everybody could see how ashamed I felt.

I was scrawny. Not thin, but rather bony. My mother was svelte and feminine, and tanned from so much tennis playing and swimming. I was as white as a drop of milk. My hair was a light chestnut color; it wasn't blonde or brunette. Altogether, I was poorly outlined. Transparent.

Each of the girls dancing around me was different, unique. Their shoulders and arms were rounded, their cleavages were cut from alabaster, their hips and breasts were well delineated, their waists flexible and their smiles, alluring. I, on the other hand, was just a piece of wood, like a stick or a shelf, a dull little girl. Like a page, like a little boy dressed up as a girl. I was proud. I tried to convince myself that I was a cold and distant orchid. But around me everything was joyful, only I was waiting for something else.

I'm going to go, I told myself. From here, too, I will flee in silence. I will sit at the piano and play one of Bach's sarabandes. But where would I end up? I would have to go back to the convent. I would go with my face all covered up and would live for an ideal, nothing else.

"THIS IS your first ball, is it not?" a curly-haired man asked me in German. He was shorter and much older than I was, and his tummy stuck out. He was looking at me through thick glasses set in a gilt frame.

Our dancing was lackluster. It didn't matter. At last somebody had asked me to dance.

"How did you know?" I asked in surprise, but mentally corrected myself: a noble orchid should not have reacted in such a way. I decided to say something cold and elegant.

"It's obvious," he said with indifference.

"I do not understand you, sir."

He danced on his short legs with sureness and aplomb. He pressed me closer. When I said something to him, he didn't look me in the face but fixed his stare on my cleavage. That made me feel both piqued and proud. He was the only man who had shown any interest in me. He held me firmly. I found him repugnant, and yet reassuring.

"As I said, you could see it at first glance." He sighed. "How warm it is! Shall we take a seat?" He bowed before me. "Farewell, my lady, may you have an enjoyable evening."

I wanted to go home!

At home? But I am at home!

I wanted to go home to the convent.

The corners of my mouth sagged downward. Quick, to the powder room! Or better still, I'll flee to my chambers.

I made my way through the crowds.

All of a sudden, he took my hand and put his arm around my waist. My fat little waltzing partner! I smelled cigar smoke and sweat. That little man stood on tiptoes and leaned into my ear. He didn't look at my face. He was staring at the cleavage of my ball gown.

"What is your name, silent Miss?"

"Sylva."

"Sylva, from Latin. It means forest. Yes, that name suits your personality."

I hadn't known my name had that meaning. I smiled.

He went on, in a low voice.

"You are still very young, but one day you will turn into a bonbon, all chocolate outside and cognac on the inside, remember that!"

A woman with more experience would have slapped him then and there, not only for being impertinent, but for the ungraciousness of his metaphor. I, a foolish convent girl, stared ahead of me, thinking, he's German, he's just spoken to me in Czech with a heavy accent. Does he know what he's saying? I felt like hitting him with my fists; I felt so powerless. It was this same powerlessness that made me burst out laughing.

"IS IT too warm for you, Miss Sylva?"

I stopped laughing. Why was everybody going on about the warmth?

I turned around, bad temperedly.

Monsieur Beauvisage!

We danced the next waltz. Monsieur Beauvisage was telling me something and asking me questions, but I wasn't listening. I let him lead me to the rhythm of the waltz. We spun around and around, and the lights and the brightly lit candelabras were burning in the beaming faces of the girls and the flames of the gladioli in the vases turned into long ribbons that floated around us, fanning us and linking us together.

With ice cream confections in hand, we walked through the

chateau garden. I led my companion over to the artificial lake, with its fountain set in rock. Then I realized a couple was already sitting there and that we might be bothering them, but we had already taken our seat.

I had never seen so many stars in the sky. It was as if I'd asked Saint Peter for them and he had arranged for an entire army of little angels to light tiny lanterns in the sky, and to keep on lighting more and more.

As soon as we sat down, Petr started to talk a blue streak, then recited:

> To exist in shame, spindly, fearful
> shadows, sprawling and feeling the walls;
> nobody waves to you any more, ill-fated ones!
> Leftovers of humanity, forever past your prime!

"Do eat, Petr, your ice cream will melt," I interrupted him.

He pushed the saucer away. He was lost in thought.

"Petr," I said, "why did you recite those verses about spindly shadows on such a marvelous night?"

"For just that reason. Old ladies are marvelous too, more so, even."

"I'm sorry?"

"They have an admirable inner life. All that suffering. Because there are so few people who are able to grasp the beauty of it."

"Look, Petr, is it really necessary to talk of spindly old ladies, precisely now, when we have flowering gardens at our feet and the starry sky above our heads?"

I wanted us to continue in silence, without talking.

"What you're talking about is the kind of beauty that anybody can comprehend. A banal beauty, which bad poets and young ladies' private diaries have thoroughly trivialized."

I blushed. Petr went on, "Read the works of Baudelaire and

Božena Němcová, Miss Sylva, and you will find that true beauty lurks in the humblest of things, in everything that at first sight seems so poor and unflamboyant."

I thought to myself that I too, should look for the hidden beauty that Petr so admired. I couldn't take my eyes off the bench where the young couple embraced each other. The young man was caressing the arms, shoulders, and breasts of the girl. She wasn't moving, or even breathing, so as not to spoil the magic of the moment. I looked away.

My eyes turned to my own cleavage. I'm still a little girl, I thought; and lightly, as if without meaning to, I rested my head on Petr's shoulder. He didn't move, but he stopped reciting poems.

I looked once again at the couple on the bench, on the side of the artificial lake. The girl had also rested her head on her sweetheart's shoulder, as if she were my mirror image. The young man went on caressing her. His hand was deep in her cleavage.

I looked at Petr out of the corner of my eye; could he, too, see what was going on? He was sitting with his eyes closed, as if he were asleep, but he wasn't sleeping.

I could hear the frogs croaking.


A WHITE ghost shifted in front of us. It moved fast, almost at a run.

"Sylva, home with you! That's enough, I don't want to see you here."

Petr's eyes opened wide. We heard a horse whinny, followed by a dog barking.

In the distance, a waltz started up. Petr sat up. I stood up slowly, then Petr did the same.

"May I accompany you, Miss Sylva?" he said in a low voice. These words were addressed to me alone.

I was about to say yes.

"No thank you, Petr," my mother broke in, "Sylva knows the way back home perfectly well, in fact it's just a moment away. Go and dance for a little bit longer, darling." Soothing words expressed with an icy voice.

Petr was looking at me. He followed me with his eyes as I walked away.

When I was at a distance, I turned around. I could see nothing but the gigantic, black trunks of the beeches and oaks.

The bench was empty.

THE DAYS went by, arid as a dried-up riverbed. I had to do something. I didn't know what.

I requested an audience with my father. He made me wait for quite a while before receiving me in his study, which smelled strongly of cigars and musty air. He wore a shiny, silk dressing gown that changed color every time he moved.

"I didn't want to waste your time, Papa. Please, would you be so kind as to let Monsieur Beauvisage know . . ."

What was I about to say? And why?

"Monsieur Beauvisage?"

My father came to an abrupt halt in the middle of the room and looked at me with hard eyes.

I didn't have time to think.

"It's a nickname, Papa." I gave a nervous laugh.

"Monsieur Beauvisage? So you also find him attractive?"

Also?

"I didn't know he was a writer," I said aloud.

"A provincial scribbler, I dare say."

"Papa, could you . . ."

"You haven't answered me."

"I'm sorry, but what is it I haven't answered properly?"

"Well . . . It doesn't matter. You are the apple of my eye, Sylva."

"I don't want to waste any more of your time, Papa. Would you be so kind as to tell Monsieur Beauvisage that I will not be requiring any lessons from him for some time."

"I will indeed inform him, word for word."

I heard a creaking noise. My father was stretching his fingers to ease the tensions in the knuckles. I noticed that sound, so typical of my father, and wasn't sure I understood my own message. Why didn't I want to see Monsieur Beauvisage? What would life in the chateau be like without my tutor?

"Sylva," my father said in a low voice, as he lit a cigarette, "don't you think it's absolutely crazy, this thing your mother's got about the Czech language? Although it was the last thing anyone would have expected, she gets it into her head to take private lessons. But as she's a Czech from a family of musicians, she must speak the language well enough."

"I wouldn't know, Papa."

"I've no idea," I repeated, "because my father kept on watching me with an enquiring look on his face. "Perhaps she's unsure of her grammar, or maybe she doesn't know how to write Czech properly, remember that she went to German schools. You won't forget to forward my message, will you, Papa?"

"Of course not, *ma chérie*." He caressed me.

"Sure?"

"Very sure."

For a little while, he drew circles on the carpet with a leather-slippered foot, staring at the window. Finally he said, "Wait, don't go just yet. There's something I wanted to say to you."

I wasn't going anywhere. But I realized that this was a cultured person's way of saying, one more thing, and then you can go!

"Listen, Silent Woman," said my father in the direction of

the window, as if addressing his message to the apple and plum trees in the orchard. "Remember what I am about to say to you, 'Whereas all other creatures walk with their heads bowed, looking at the ground, Man has a face at his disposal, with which to observe the horizon, and a head, with which he can look up at the stars.' That was written by Ovid, a lucid poet, whose life ended sadly, in exile."

I STROLLED through the village next to the chateau, looking for the things that were in the poems Petr had quoted to me.

I saw elderly men and women. I saw beggars. I saw cripples, both male and female. I saw huts full of destitute people, run-down cottages, wretched hovels. I went in, leaving a couple of coins. The inhabitants eyed me, both surprised and suspicious.

I saw a man whipping a horse. The beast was standing stock-still, its head bowed, and its eyes full of woe. The horse could not defend itself as the carter whipped it with all his strength. I rushed over to the horse and hugged it. I kissed it. In the deep, sad gaze of that fine beast, in its tears, I saw the eternal suffering of the universe. In those horse's eyes, I saw the misery of all those who were born only to be beaten.

I walked over to the chateau garden. I wanted to summon Jakub, so that he could buy up all the whipped horses.

TWILIGHT WAS falling. The crickets were singing, but the croaking of the frogs was louder.

I headed over to the river to see them. As I ambled along the bank, my feet sank into the mud more than once. The mosquitos were buzzing, there were whole clouds of mosquitos. I saw a blackbird carrying a clay-covered worm in its beak. The worm twisted about, trying to get out of the beak that trapped it, but the blackbird had a firm grip. All the frogs jumped into the river.

As I walked back home, that blackbird was singing on the branch of a beech tree.

It was getting dark. I was afraid I might get lost. I started to run, my face lashed by branches.

I finally found a path that led to the chateau garden. It took me directly to the fountain. I would have liked to avoid that artificial lake, I don't know why, but there it was, right by me.

Nightfall.

A couple was sitting on the bench, like the last time.

I felt a sudden desire to rest on my bench, to examine the surface of the lake and look at my face. Maybe in the milky light of the half moon, I would discover a change in the image I saw, in comparison with the last one I saw there that had been smashed to pieces. Perhaps I would find those pieces now stuck together with the glue of my new experiences, my new thoughts.

I sat at the edge of the little pond. From their bench, the couple couldn't see me, there were bushes between us. I looked down at the water: I saw the shiny surface and, on it, a dark stain. My head. None of my features were distinguishable. Only a hole as dark as the night itself.

I moved away. Out of the corner of my eye I saw the couple on the bench, the man embracing the woman passionately; she was responding to his caresses. This was doubtlessly a couple from the village; the garden had recently been taken over by the state, and anyone could enter as they pleased.

The frogs resumed their croaking. I left. I smelled a whiff of jasmine.

In the morning, as I was taking a walk with Mademoiselle Lamartine, repeating my lesson, I stepped off the path. On the bench, I found a pair of little combs, the kind used to decorate a coiffure and keep it in place. Encrusted with precious stones that shone brightly in the light of day, they seemed to be gleaming. Then I remembered the night of the volcanoes that spat fire, and the bright morning that followed, which was so like today.

I KNEW that Jakub wasn't listening to me, but I so wanted to get it all off my chest!

"I saw a man whipping a horse," I kept explaining to the stable lad, "That animal was standing stock-still, with its head bowed and its eyes full of suffering. A horse can't defend itself."

The stable lad looked at me, unconcerned.

"Couldn't we do something? Maybe buy that horse? I've already told my parents, but . . ."

"But?"

"But nothing. I mean, you love horses."

"We'll see," he answered, nonchalantly.

I noticed that now, apart from indifference, the stable lad felt a sort of abhorrence for this capricious little lady before him. I had seen that expression before on the faces of those I had visited in the wretched hovels in the village.

"You will try and buy that horse, won't you?" I insisted.

"We'll see."

WE USUALLY dined from twelve to two. The maid laid the dining room table, and we all sat down to lunch, even my grandmother, who usually preferred to spend her time in her chambers. That summer my mother often turned up for lunch looking fresh, cheerful, youthful, her eyes full of optimism.

Every day, from two to four, Petr came to the house to give my mother lessons. My mother kept her door locked during the two hours that Monsieur Beauvisage spent in her chambers.

One day I walked past Maman's apartment. I couldn't hear a thing. No dictation. No creaking door. Not a word. Silence. The following day, I did the same thing again. Nothing. As if there were nobody at all behind that door.

The third day, I forbade myself to walk past Maman's door, but I couldn't hold out: I went past on tiptoes, barefoot, back and forth, time and again. Nothing, just a heavy oak door.

Then one day I came across my father outside Maman's door. He too was pacing in silence, back and forth, again and again.

ONCE I had to walk along that corridor at four in the afternoon, on the dot. I saw Monsieur Beauvisage closing the oak door behind him, heading for the staircase, his head bowed.

"Petr!" I whispered.

He didn't turn around. He only bowed his head a little lower.

"Petr!" I repeated, a bit louder.

The back of his neck was disappearing around the curve of the staircase.

When I reached Maman's door, this time, for the first time, I heard something. My mother was crying.

I FOUND the stable lad at the entrance. I reminded him of the incident with the whipped horse and of his promise.

"We'll see," he said once again.

We walked over to the stables.

He opened the door. I was swallowed up by the darkness, and overwhelmed by strong animal smells.

The stable lad came up to me. I was getting used to the dark. I looked into his eyes. They were green and glinting like a cat's. Through the reek of the horses, I could smell his sweat. He took me into his arms—thick and strong as tree trunks. I pressed my body against his.

He felt me up, roughly. So this is what it's like, I thought, as his expert fingers ran over my body. Like this, and nothing more? I remained silent and still.

I pushed him away.

In a hoarse voice, he said, "Go away, I don't want anything to do with you! First you get me all worked up and then you go cold as a dead fish. You know where to go, you pampered, little girl! I've had enough!"

Puffing, he pushed me out of the stable.

The sunlight dazzled me. I felt dizzy.

I patted a dog as it wandered along the path. That smooth skin, that tender warmth, but the dog responded with violent barking. I felt like a stranger in my own home.

I TIED my hair back into a ponytail and sat down on the bench in front of the house. It wasn't yet four in the afternoon.

Monsieur Beauvisage. The only person with whom I wished to speak. In his presence, I felt the way I did when I changed out of my party dress and tight-fitting dress shoes to put on some casual clothes and comfy slippers for wearing in the house. Although this meeting with Monsieur Beauvisage was making me feel uncomfortable. I didn't take my eyes off the belltower clock.

The bells were ringing.

Together we left the chateau garden and stepped out into nature. On the bank, the frogs and birds were silent, it was a muggy day. Only a sparrow chirped feebly, as if welcoming us into his green kingdom. We found all the splendor overwhelming. The weeping willows rustling above the water, the century-old beeches standing in two rows, their branches spanning the space over our heads. Above us, a blackbird began chatting. I looked for it among the branches to see if it was carrying a muddy worm in its beak. Then my feet sank into the mud. With difficulty, Petr removed my heeled shoe from the puddle and cleaned it. That done, he made me sit down on a low branch of a hawthorn, or perhaps a plane tree, to rub the mud off my foot with a handkerchief. Like a mother swaddling a newborn child, I thought.

✳

I CLOSED THE DOOR BEHIND US, GENTLY.

In silence I led Petr to the bathroom. He stopped at the threshold. "We will wash my foot," I repeated more than once, tugging at Petr's sleeve.

He stepped away.

"Sylva, I can't go in there. The only person who could do that would be your husband."

"Husband?"

Petr was silent.

"And I am not him," he said in a low voice.

The parquet floor of the antechamber looked black now. Night was falling.

In the distance, in the streets, the sound of a funeral march could be heard.

We were silent. The light was fading.

The funeral march grew closer. It was purple in color and filled the entrance. The drawn-out sound of the trumpet, a melody that came to an end, started up again. We stood still. Bewitched. Only the trumpet continued singing its grief.

From the door came a light sound; we turned our heads.

Maman, all fresh, was shining on the threshold of the room. Madame la Comtesse, the Queen of the Night, was watching us with a haughty, scornful expression.

"Sylva, there's something I want to tell you immediately, that's why I've barged in like this. But . . ."

At this point, my mother opened the door wide and in an icy voice that clashed with the cloying and falsely friendly tone that she had used with me, "Monsieur Beauvisage must get out of here. Right this instant. What I have to say is not for his ears."

Maman ignored him. She addressed only me, once more with her saccharine voice, "A gentleman, a most well-positioned and wealthy one, as it so happens, the Czech ambassador to Budapest, has asked for your hand in marriage, Sylva. After a close analysis of all the pros and cons, your father and I have given our consent to the count. Count Heinrich von Stamitz has already requested a formal transfer to Prague, to the Ministry of Foreign Affairs. I know that in all probability you will be, if not happy, though I would dearly like you to be, then at least fortunate with the count, who, after the creation of Czechoslovakia, uses the Czech translation of his name: Jindřich. You are a flower that must be cared for in the most luxurious conservatory of them all."

My mother repeated the gesture of holding the door to the corridor wide open.

"Goodbye, sir."

With heavy feet, slowly, Petr headed for the door.

"Say something, Sylva," he stammered, his voice faint, as if he were sick. In his confusion, he had addressed me using the familiar form.

Still I said nothing. The Silent Woman, as my father had called me the other day.

"I don't even know him," I said, finally, to my mother.

"But you do know him, Sylva," she assured me with that sugary voice, "You danced with him, *ma petite*. It was after our ball at the chateau that he asked for your hand in marriage."

I smiled at Petr. The look I gave him said, I only danced with you! Surely my mother is doing a bit of playacting, and has prepared a surprise for us.

But Petr didn't react. He had gone pale.

"Fare thee well, sir," said my mother. Snowflakes fell from her words, landing onto my neck and shoulders.

Petr gave me his hand and whispered a few words into my ear. Even when he whispered, his voice sounded like an old man's.

"I want you to be my wife, Sylva. I'll write."

The door shut behind him, hesitantly.

"You are a flower, Sylva. I will not allow you to marry the first comer, a beggar, a vagabond, a third-rate scribbler," said my mother. Then she repeated, in a metallic voice, "You are a flower which must be cared for in the most luxurious conservatory of them all."

The doorknob clattered behind her, clearly and decisively.

ALONE, I gazed down at my feet, one black, the other white. I turned to look at a huge vase full of orchids that were coldly white as if sculpted from alabaster.

I shut my eyes, full of hate. I saw a carter whipping a horse in the middle of a street in our village.

I felt like vomiting.

I decided I had to get out of here.

# III

# JAN

*FLIGHT 2901 PRAGUE DELAYED 9 P.M.* READS THE AIRPORT
display, the one that is announcing arrivals.

It doesn't matter, I tell myself; I've waited for Helena all my
life, two more hours aren't going to make any difference. And
you, mother, have you ever waited for somebody with this mixture of patience and impatience?

When I was little, mother, you waited for my father. You
waited for him even though you knew he would never, ever
come back. Or maybe you didn't know, did you? Perhaps you
pretended not to know, you didn't want to admit it. You preferred to live in hope. You listened and in a soft voice you sang
the sort of music that made you think of my father. I remember
our silent walks, the quiet suppers. We remained in silence, like
an elderly couple that has said everything they ever needed to say
to each other, so who in the end words are no longer necessary.

You sent me to take piano lessons. Why, in fact, didn't you
teach me yourself, if you were a piano teacher? You might have
done so if we'd actually had a piano at home. The flats assigned
to us by the government got smaller and smaller. During the
piano lessons I liked the smooth touch of the keys. I sat next to
the mysterious teacher and breathed in her honey scent as her
silky hair occasionally brushed against my fingers, which used to
happen when we played duets and her fine hair grazed the key-

board. What I most loved about music, apart from the harmony and the theoretical precision, were the scores, those pages full of staves and notes, those complex arrangements that determined the whole feel of the piece.

BE MOVED reads the sign hanging on the wall of the concert hall in the university town where I work. Orpheus first seduced Euridice with music. Later it was his languorous melodies that moved the drunken, unbridled women to kill him by tearing off his head.

Is it a coincidence then that Helena's a violinist?

Once, I remember starting a new year at school, and as soon as I entered the school I was filled with a feeling of revulsion. Nothing had changed, everywhere the same posters, the color of ripe strawberries, proclaiming eternal friendship with the Soviet Union. The bald pate on the bust of Lenin shimmered in the morning sun. Only one thing had changed: the math teacher. Last year's, young and irate, had been popular with the girls at school, but the new one seemed old and silly and the girls despised him as a relic from another age. He wore an old-fashioned suit, a white shirt, and a thin tie, his hair was Brilliantined and combed back. He smelled of pipe tobacco and his teeth reminded me of potato peelings. The new math teacher was different from the rest of the teaching staff, maybe because he had lived in Argentina, where, as he put it, he had lived like a monk. Our nickname for him was "The Monk," everyone made fun of him.

The Monk was quirky: a poet. Math, for him, was a sort of art form, or a musical composition. When he explained the laws that governed mathematics, he never stopped hearing music, like when my piano teacher, whose long hair smelled of honey, played a Mendelssohn sonata. In mathematics, axioms are the basis of everything, and the truth of an axiom is unquestionable, said The Monk. In the same way that a building is constructed on its foundations, the construction of the science of mathematics begins with axioms. This is also true of music: musical compositions are created with the aid of only seven notes. In mathematics, these notes are the axioms. And if the arrangement of musical notes creates different melodies, the configuration of axioms makes new knowledge possible.

"How?" we would ask.

"How?" The Monk would laugh. "Nobody knows that. It is here that the talent of the mathematician lies, his imagination, his gift for hearing a brand new melody," he'd say, waving his arms about as if he were conducting a one-hundred-and-twenty piece orchestra.

The Monk would open his textbook, then shut it again suddenly, exclaiming, "Yuck! How boring!" Then, in the way a painter filled with inspiration will use wide brushstrokes to fill the canvas with images dictated by his imagination, so The Monk would draw all kinds of parabolas, hyperbolas, and ellipses on the blackboard, which the mathematics textbook could only present in a thoroughly tedious fashion. Back at home, I pored over the textbook, but quickly put it aside. I spent whole hours looking for unusual solutions to mathematical problems. Our new teacher would have explained that what I was looking for were aesthetic solutions. When I showed him my geometrical drawings, The Monk shook his head and made me understand that not everything was a question of aesthetics, but neither was it simply a question of only rational thinking. With this attitude, he instilled in me the ability to analyze according to the rules of the strictest logic. I will never forget how this teacher would run from one end of the long blackboard to the other, sometimes jumping up or squatting down, forever repeating that quote from Einstein about true learning, only sticking in our heads once we had forgotten everything we were taught at school.

MAMA, DO you remember that small bedside lamp in the room where we lived when I was little? You hung a lace cloth over it, and then that tiny room, which served as both our study and living room, our bedroom and kitchen, would fill with a gentle, golden glow. While I tried to solve mathematical problems, that glimmer of warm light blended with the music of Chopin, Schubert, and the liturgical chants of the Russian Orthodox Church, those albums that you selected and placed on the black platter of the record player. That atmosphere helped me to create a new harmony and a new melody, my own, geometric, mathematical melody. I feared the chaos and instability that surrounded me: while you made me doubt the official ideological dogmas, the teachers worked to make me believe, eliminate any doubts, which they treated as if they were sins. So it was that I grew up surrounded by paradoxes, though I badly needed a feeling of security.

Years later, after the Soviet invasion of our country, when I took advantage of my stay in Yugoslavia to request political asylum from the United States, and they offered me a place as a teaching assistant in a prestigious university, you sent me that piece of cloth, Mama. As if you sensed that death would take you away before we could meet again. I, on the other hand, tried to convince myself that all I wanted in America was to acquire experience and return to you and Helena. Or, if our country continued to be ruled by a foreign power, I would invite both of you over to the United States.

I said goodbye to Helena . . . no, in fact, you can't really call it a goodbye. Helena vanished. She evaporated like a drop of water on a baking hot stone, like those next to the Bosnia river in Sarajevo.

Looking back, I was simply putting off the time when you could be with me here at the American university. At that time,

I had more work than I could cope with. I'd invested myself in a whole new field of research: as a mathematician and engineer, I was becoming interested in electric cars. What's more, for the first time in my life, I was teaching classes at the university, and I was doing all this in a foreign language that I hadn't quite mastered.

One day I received a letter from the Czechoslovakian embassy. It informed me that the judicial system had declared me guilty of having abandoned the country illegally, and had sentenced me to jail.

I tried not to think about it too much. The fact is that that letter, when it came down to it, guaranteed that I would never see you again, not you, or my friends, or my city, and, above all, it obliged me to abandon my mother tongue.

At that time I was convinced that my work would make up for the loss of my country, my mother tongue, and a much-loved woman. Now, years later, I can say that I fully subscribe to what Bertrand Russell said about science offering us the causal skeleton of the world, while it leaves out all the colors and variety and singularity of those things which make up the world.

However, I didn't know that, not back then. I went from one lecture hall to the next, from one class to the next, without looking at the time or even what season we were in. I spent the nights looking for solutions; I can still remember one of them:

$$u = -(GB)^{-1} Gf$$

I published the first article based on my research in the *IEEE* transaction on *Power Electronics Journal*. I then received a summons from Professor Benjamin Fortner, a celebrated mathematician and world specialist on the theory of differential equations.

"Sit down," he said in a tiny voice, "you're probably wondering why I've asked you to come. One of my colleagues told me about the article you published in *IEEE*. You make use of a method that is not in the least bit traditional, and this interests me. I would like to go over certain aspects of the text with you. However, I haven't got a clue about all that electronic stuff you wrote about."

Professor Fortner picked up my article and took a close look at it.

"'The right-hand side of the equation is a discontinuous function of system coordinates,'" Fortner read aloud. "In the situation you describe, current theories cannot be applied. I'd like to hear how you would go about solving this problem."

I could scarcely believe that such a prestigious mathematician was unaware of Filippov's method of solution continuation. And I told him so, adding that I personally found that the solution lays in the convex set.

Fortner replied as if he were a schoolteacher, explaining something that everyone else already understood to a not-very-gifted student.

"Yes, I know Filippov's method, of course," Fortner said slowly, disguising his impatience, "but if you look at this piece of research from 1958, you will realize that Filippov developed his method using just one discontinuity surface, whereas you, in your article, employ an arbitrary number! This is why I have some objections to your article, at least those of a formal nature. Of course it is possible that in practice, things might actually work in this way, but in our branch of science one must speak with greater precision. Indeed, I am almost tempted to tell you that you should treat mathematics with more care, with tenderness!"

He added, icily, "Your heuristic approach probably works in engineering, but it is not acceptable for mathematics. Not only that, remember, if you please, that you are teaching in Boston at one of the best mathematical schools in the world."

He was choking with rage, and I understood that from that moment on, I was not welcome in his study.

I set myself the goal of finding a solution to the problem Fortner had posed; I would wake up in the middle of the night, leap out of bed, and sit down in front of a huge pile of papers, all full of equations. During the day, I got through my classes mechanically; my head bursting with whole waves of calculations, involving all kinds of discontinuity surfaces, differential equations, and coordinate systems. When a friend of mine pulled me out of my office for a beer, I could talk to him of nothing else. I couldn't contain myself and, with a beer glass in one hand, I grabbed a pencil and filled napkin after napkin with calculations.

And then, one fine morning, I found the solution. I called Benjamin Fortner. The mathematician was busy.

Nonetheless, I went to see him. There was no way I could not.

He looked at me wearily, and sighed.

"Professor, the results of my scientific inquiry are now correct. I will demonstrate this to you using my own method, the method of equivalent control."

I imagined that Fortner would be left speechless.

The mathematician, however, said with impatience, "What do you expect me to say? I'm glad that after all my objections you didn't give up, but . . ."

But from the sound of his voice it was clear that he didn't think my work could be of much interest to him. He glanced fleetingly at the pages on which I had written down my results.

"Leave it here with me," he said, "I'll take a look at it later." Then he pushed my work away, placing it on top of a pile of paperwork.

That mathematician was already thinking about other things, a bit like me when I said goodbye to my students at the end of a class.

A MONTH passed before he called and invited me over to talk. When I knocked on the door of his office, I was ready for yet another show of indifference.

Benjamin Fortner grumbled, "You see . . . how can I put this . . . this work of yours . . ."

He stopped himself, quietly grousing, then continued, "Your work has been a pleasure to read. You proved the theorem confirming the validity of your absolutely universal discontinuity method, because it doesn't depend on the number of surfaces."

"So . . ." I said.

He turned his suddenly animated eyes to me, "So I retract my objections."

"Really?"

"You must publish your findings in a peer-reviewed journal. I will help you."

An unusual thing happened to me then: not only my engineering colleagues, but the mathematicians too, began to treat me with respect. One day I got a call from the Ford Foundation. They had read my article, and had spoken to professor Fortner. They invited me to give a lecture at their Detroit headquarters.

I noticed that the Ford specialists listened to my conclusions with respectful attention, but without any real interest. Even so, when I explained the relevance of the control of electric automobile motors, they sat up in their seats, craning their necks forward.

NOT LONG afterward I received a letter on Ford Motor Company letterhead. They'd found my lecture stimulating and wanted to invite me back to Detroit to discuss certain matters, they said, that they and I might have in common.

I was greeted by two top-ranking Ford executives. Both wore impeccable navy-blue suits and ties. Those limber, athletic gentlemen had bronzed, closely shaven faces, though one of them had a goldenish hue— probably because he'd spent time at the beach—and the other one was darker—probably because he'd been skiing, even though Detroit is as far from the sea as it is from the mountains. My shabby, gray corduroy jacket, and my unkempt, unstyled hair both indicated that I was a completely different category of human being. We sat down in the meeting room and the two men were cracking jokes and laughing. We were brought some extremely thick sandwiches made with sliced bread, which the rules of etiquette dictated had to be eaten with one's hands.

"Let's talk about you maybe working for Ford," the one with the golden tan said.

"In the future, that is," the skier clarified.

"Right now would be impossible," said Golden Tan.

"On the other hand, why not in the future? You could do that for sure! No doubt!" said the skier, laughing and raising his glass of coke.

I didn't say anything. I waited. They watched me attentively. I remained stubbornly silent. There was nothing to discuss, so I waited to see what would happen next.

Finally I replied, "I've never considered leaving the university or my academic work."

They looked at me like I was some kind of exotic animal.

Golden Tan said, in a low voice, "Think about it carefully, John. We're not forcing you to do anything, it's a free country. But do think it over. The best university in the world couldn't beat the offer we'd be making you."

IV

# SYLVA

A BLACK VEIL. THE DAY I WAS MARRIED MY MOTHER wore a black veil that covered her face and sealed her off from the world. My white veil was draped over my indifferent eyes. Indifferent? No. Rather, they were curious. When I observed that white, aristocratic bride in the mirror, through the mesh of the veil, my face seemed to have been sliced into tiny, little pieces. The girl reflected back to me did not desire the man she was to marry. She was merely a silent young woman, who felt a certain curiosity about the world that her future husband, a man of standing, would reveal to her. She hoped that such a grand world would thrill her and, above all, that she would find her place in it.

The black veil made my mother look even more noble than when her face was uncovered. Since my father's recent death, my mother never removed the veil whenever she was outdoors.

And my father? I know nothing about him. I hardly remember a thing about him. My father . . . yes, now I see him . . . "Listen, Silent Woman," he said to me one day as we gazed out at the apple and plum trees in the orchard, "Remember what I am about to say to you: 'Whereas all other creatures walk with their heads bowed, looking at the ground, Man has a face at his disposal, with which to observe the sky.'"

AFTER THE wedding, my new husband and I climbed into his black car. It was a Hispano-Suiza. We headed for the wedding reception, held in the palazzo he owned in Prague. The chauffeur was wearing livery, like a waxwork figure. I didn't look at my husband. I grew afraid when I saw him sitting absolutely still so as not to spoil the cut of the black suit into which he had squeezed himself. When I had peaked at him out of the corner of my eye during the wedding ceremony, he looked to me as if he were preparing to blow out a candle, his cheeks were so puffed up.

As the car pulled away, my husband looked me over. Or rather he looked my body over. All of a sudden, he placed a hand on my breast, and squeezed it. The first thing I thought of was the chateau cook when she squeezed the tomatoes and cucumbers to make sure they were ripe. My husband watched me as he fondled me. I made an effort not to show surprise. Or fear. I thought that this was the way things had to be, and waited in horror for what would come afterward. He plunged his hand into my cleavage, the way our cook dug hers into a pile of potatoes in the market so as to find the biggest one.

"Given your age, I find them too large and heavy," he said, staring me in the eye.

He used the familiar form of "you." And as he fished for the best potato in the pile, he said, as if we were alone, "Did he caress you . . . like this? And like this? Or like this?"

"Who?"

"That boy, your teacher. Your mother told me everything. I want to know what your face looked like when that boy caressed you."

He watched my face as his hand continued searching furiously. He pressed his other hand into service too, to help the first one out. His mustache twitched like a puppet's.

I remained silent, unable to move.

Then he retrieved his hands and rested them on his belly. He sat back in the seat, whistling an aria from an operetta, and watching the passersby in the street.

I buttoned my dress up.

He said, as he looked out at the street, "And what about you, what did you do to him?"

"'WHEREAS ALL other creatures walk with their heads bowed, looking at the ground, Man has a face at his disposal, with which to observe the sky.'" He repeated Ovid's words to me, and other ideas that he found in the works of classical poets and philosophers . . .

I knew these philosophers personally, had talked to them face to face, asked them for advice. For a happy person, philosophy is complementary to life; he has already achieved his aims. For an unhappy person, philosophical ideas help one to keep on living. They are instructions, a promise of survival.

AT THE wedding reception, my husband put his hand in my lap.

"And which place did that boy like best, this one or that one?"

He wasn't looking at my face but at my chest, like the time when we danced together, the night of the chateau ball.

THE WEDDING banquet lasted until the small hours of the morning. When I least expected it, everybody left, both the orchestra and the dancers.

We were alone.

My husband took me by the hand and showed me around the palazzo. Paintings hung on every wall, grim, uncolorful ones, dark and dim, not at all like those in our chateau. These paintings were either black landscapes or portraits covered in dust, from which the spectator was only too happy to flee.

"This is the bathroom," he said, and showed me the only bright room, covered in white tiles and all kinds of shining taps and showers and washbasins, and a bathtub that was whiter and shinier than everything else.

"Take off your clothes," he commanded, and closed the door behind him.

I turned the taps on and hot water came from one and cold water from the other. The shower felt like April rain, ever so fine. The bathroom filled with steam.

The door opened and my husband walked in slowly. I saw him through the mist: he was wearing a vest and short pants, as if he were at the beach. He looked as if he'd walked out of a film. A bizarre film.

"We'll have a bath, we'll have a bath," he repeated, drawing out the words as he undressed me, "we'll have a bath."

He held my breasts in the palms of his hands and murmured, as if reflecting on something disagreeable, "Oh God, how big and heavy they are, breasts so full and weighty that they cannot satisfy a man with a refined sensibility. At twenty you'll sag like an old woman."

As he said this I thought of Plato's *Symposium*. Agathon says to Socrates . . . "I do declare that among all the gods, happy as they all are, the happiest of them all is Eros, being as he is the handsomest and best among them."

My husband didn't take his eyes off my breasts, not even when I removed my skirt. He ordered me to sit on the edge of the bathtub with my feet in the water. He wet my chest, my belly, my thighs.

And I thought about Plato's words. There is no pleasure greater than love: all pleasures, all of them, are surpassed by love. I thought, hopefully, in silence.

My husband soaped me as I leaned back against the white, tiled wall. I liked the cold of the tiles on my back, it kept me tense. My husband soaped me as if he were a nanny and I, a little girl. He covered me with soap completely then took his time working the lather over my skin. He made soap bubbles on my body, blowing at them and playing with them across my skin. I sat quietly, repeating Plato's words to myself, "As regards the mastery of the arts, do we not know that he of whom Eros becomes the master, will become famous and renowned, whereas he who remains untouched by Eros will be submerged in darkness?"

And my husband whispered, "You're dirty, we have to wash you properly, until you're as clean as a whistle. So much dirt! My God, it's so disgusting! Look, here there's still some here, look, look, and here too, I can't take this anymore, how revolting, so much dirt!" With one hand he soaped my breasts and with the other my thighs, spitting out words like "Ergh, ergh, this is too disgusting, ergh, ergh, I think I'm going to throw up." He continued with the yellow bar of soap, spreading the lather and making bubbles. Then he took off his spectacles that looked like they were made out of the bottoms of beer glasses and, his eyes wide open, he stared at me closely, observing the lather he was spreading over me as if he was buttering a slice of bread. He would say "ergh, ergh" from time to time, and I had the feeling that the more he examined me, the more revulsion he felt, that it was only through sheer willpower that my husband could overcome the disgust he felt for my body, and that only with a tremendous physical and moral effort could he continue soaping me. Finally he pinched me and scratched me and hit me, shouting, "Ergh, ergh, filthy, sordid, repulsive, ignoble, abject, indescribable little girl!" And when he was fed up with the sound of his own shouting, and when his blows and his pinches really began to hurt, I yelled, "That's enough!"

Then he took handfuls of water and rinsed the lather from me, carefully, deliberately, with all five senses on full alert to ensure that not a bit of lather was left anywhere on my body. He wasn't shouting anymore, he simply made small noises of disgust. And his mustache shifted from one side of his face to the other, like a doll in the hands of a puppet master at the village fair.

Then, with the same fastidious care, those same heightened five senses, he dried me with a towel so that not even the most concealed area was left wet. He put me to bed, and with another towel, dry and white and soft, and made of cambric. He went on drying and massaging me. With the tips of his fingers and the palms of his hands he penetrated into my body's remotest places so as to dry them, always with an expression of repugnance and aversion and horror in his popping, feverishly shining eyes.

I thought about the words of Aristophanes in Plato's *Symposium*, "When we celebrate Eros, we are celebrating the god who in the present can furnish us with the greatest benefits and who, in the future, can provide us with the greatest of hopes, that will make us fortunate and favored . . ."

When I had had enough of the massages, of the towel, and my husband's fingers and hands, when I'd been dry for some time, I repeated, "That's enough!"

And, at once, he stopped touching me.

He put the towel back in the bathroom. Once he'd done that, he got into bed next to me, and immediately began snoring.

In the dim light, I got up, left the bedroom in silence, and hurriedly got dressed.

ONE DAY, the modiste came to show me the dresses and the jackets and the skirts and the corsets and the waistcoats that she was making for me. When I was trying on the final item, a sand-colored dress, my husband burst into the salon. He wore a dark blue suit with little, vertical stripes that were all but invisible. He had a distinguished air about him, quite a different person from the one I had known in the brightness of the bathroom. He reminded the modiste not to forget what he had already told her, that all the evening dresses should have a generous cleavage.

"That's ever so fashionable now, and I don't want my wife to wear anything that isn't the very latest fashion." As he spoke, he watched me as if we were back in the bathroom, and the longer he looked at me, the sterner his expression became.

As soon as he had left, the modiste and I looked at each other and burst out laughing. When our laughter had subsided, I said, in a serious, grave voice, "This is very fashionable now and I want my wife to dress in only the very latest fashions," and again we doubled over in laughter.

Once we'd calmed down, I told to the modiste, a girl who was the same age as me, "The dresses should be comfortable, and none of them should have a cleavage that would make it impossible for me to bend over."

The modiste winked at me as she gave a discreet smile, her lips full of multicolored pinheads.

ONE EVENING, at a reception for high-ranking diplomats, my husband made me sit on a solitary chair in a corner, while he flirted with sylphlike and coquettish ladies and conversed with elegant gentlemen. With a glass of champagne in his hand, he went from one little group to the next, blinking and raising toasts and laughing. From time to time, he brought me a saucer with some canapés or a small cake. I sat in silence and drank in the surrounding feast of lights with my eyes. Then, however, I grew self-conscious, like that night of the ball in the chateau. I asked myself: Why did my mother force me to marry this man?

I WILL go. From this place too, I will flee in silence.

Yes, but where? To the convent? To my parents' home? All of those places were behind me now.

"As if he were a stranger unworthy of respect," I had read this line in the *Iliad*. More than ever in my life, I felt like a stranger.

✳

THAT EVENING, MY HUSBAND BADE ME ENTER THE BATH-room, giving me a little push.

"Get undressed!" he ordered as he left.

Is this what is meant by matrimonial duties? I asked myself as I took my clothes off with a feeling of deep abhorrence. I was afraid.

After a moment, my husband returned with a brush for scrubbing the floor, one of those with horsehair bristles, to clean me properly. As soon as he hurt me, I said, in a loud voice, "That's enough!"

And something incredible happened: my husband left the bathroom and went to bed.

"FREEDOM, SIR, is as difficult to cope with as obligation."

This is a *cri de coeur*. When I read those words of Masaryk, I thought about my life. I was just twenty years old. I knew all about taking orders, I'd spent my life obeying the orders given by my parents and the nuns and Mademoiselle de Lamartine and my husband, just like a dog would have obeyed its master.

Yes, I knew all about honoring my obligations: having to pray, having to play the piano, having to be dutiful daughter, not marrying Monsieur Beauvisage, having to marry the honorable ambassador von Stamitz, having to be a good wife.

My husband was sleeping restlessly, beside me. I stayed awake reading.

A dream, like a flower blossoming within me, was born.

THE FOLLOWING day, the telephone woke me. It was my husband calling me from his office at the Ministry of Foreign Affairs; he wanted to know if I'd slept well, what I would do today, where I would go, and with whom I had appointments. I didn't feel like making any confessions, so I said the first thing that came into my head, that I would visit a cubist exhibition with a woman friend. When I'd finished he told me that in two days' time, on October 28, the national holiday, we were invited to a reception at Prague Castle, as guests of the president of the republic.

Masaryk! I had to sit down. I would get to see the author of the *Pensées* I had been reading and rereading time and again! Perhaps I would even get to meet him in person?

"I want you to wear that new dress."

"Which new dress?"

"How can I put this . . . the one the modiste just made for you, the one with that generous cleavage!"

"Won't I be cold?"

"In the castle? Not at all!"

It seemed to me that that dress wasn't decent enough for such a solemn occasion. I said as much to my husband.

"Sylva, with that dress on, you'll look like Aphrodite. You'll make me happy. Do it for me!"

But I didn't want to look like Aphrodite.

"So at midday you'll be at home?" my husband wanted to know.

I had no idea. I couldn't stop thinking that I had absolutely no wish whatsoever to look like Aphrodite, that the dress he had in mind would end up in the garbage can. That very day, I would buy myself a new one. I answered as vaguely as I could.

My husband wouldn't give up. "I'll come, we can have lunch together."

"I don't know if I'll be back in time."

"Come back home, Sylva. You'll make me happy."

For the second time, instead of firing off an order at me, he'd said, "You'll make me happy." He said it in an imploring tone. I hadn't expected that. But then immediately I thought, my husband wants me to waste my day! When he hung up, I scowled, then made an oh-forget-it gesture and asked my maid to get me some breakfast. Quickly!

On the dark, hand-carved, baroque dining room table, it was impossible not to see a page that I'd torn out of my notebook and that read, "Don't wait for me, I'm dining out. Sylva." In no time at all, I was out in the street.

IN THE evening my husband, armed with a mitten, washed my breasts and once they were wet, he twisted them with his hands as if they were a pair of towels he was wringing out, as he whispered, "Ergh! Ergh, you dirty, impure, foul thing! You grimy, filthy, disgusting thing!" While he busied himself cleaning my body, I licked a chocolate ice cream and read some of Masaryk's philosophical reflections. When my husband's shouting started to interrupt my reading, I said, "Enough!"

And off he went to bed.

ON THE evening of the twenty-eighth of October, hanging on my husband's arm, I entered the reception hall of Prague Castle, which was festively lit. My husband had grown thinner and his black suit made him seem even more slender. When we entered the hall, we were met by several inquisitive looks, and dozens of ladies and gentlemen rushed to welcome my husband. I sensed that behind his diplomat's mask he was disappointed not to see me in my new dress with its plunging neckline. Imagine if he'd known that for the last couple of days that dress had been the main item among other equally unfortunate items in the trash bin in our yard! I don't know if my husband was made more disconsolate by the absence of that dress or by the fact that I hadn't done what he'd said. I'd decided to wear a simple, white tunic, inspired by the attire of the ancient Greeks. My dangling earrings were also in the Greek style. My coiffeuse had bunched my hair into a discreet chignon at the nape of my neck.

This time too, my husband made me sit in a corner. From my solitary chair, all unnoticed and blushing, I devoured that magnificent soiree with my eyes. As I allowed myself to be dazzled by the hundreds of lights and thousands of jewels shining on all the ladies' necks, I thought back to that morning. I had woken early and headed for Václavské Square. Although it was very early, it was all I could do to catch a possible glimpse of him through a crack in the packed crowds, and then only if I stood on tiptoes. I'd started to get impatient with all the waiting. I had woken early to find only Czechs in the throng. Where were the German and Jewish citizens, why hadn't they turned up? Then some shouts interrupted my thoughts; all heads had turned to the left in unison, like sunflowers. An elegant, imperturbable man was crossing the long square on horseback, dressed in riding gear and a cap. There was the philosopher president, and behind him, like a bridal train, the long procession of civilians followed him. I'd noticed that even the children, on their fathers' shoulders were behaving themselves; nobody was in a hurry to have lunch or an aperitif; everybody was as quiet and solemn as if it were some kind of ancestral ritual.

But now, in the evening, my husband made me sit in a corner of the room. When he came to see me, to bring me a platter with some canapés, he didn't find me there. I decided that on my own and of my own volition, I would do what everybody did: move from one group to the next. All by myself, I chose the canapés that I found most to my taste and from silver trays borne by waiters in evening tails, I took my own glasses of champagne.

Nobody knew me. Nobody asked me any questions. Nobody paid any attention to me.

At one point, as I walked away from one of the little groups, I heard two men ask each other who I was.

"She's an actress," said the lanky blonde one, "I saw her perform at the National Theater."

"Now I know who she is, she's Pandora!" said the other man, who was short and bald.

"Of course! With that hairdo and Pandora's box under her arm. The box is full of diseases; let's move away from that woman, let's go!"

"Don't be ridiculous," said the short bald one in a serious tone, "she might be dressed up like a Greek priestess, but that woman's no actress."

I would never become an actress. It is not dignified for an aristocrat to work, my parents had always told me, and they had forbidden me to accept any paid work whatsoever.

And then I saw him.

His tall, slim figure, his white hair radiating light. Did others too see the aura that gleamed around our president? I shared my impressions with a lady who happened to be close by. She smiled and nodded, but then shot me a furtive look, as if to see whether I was really and truly mad.

I looked around for my husband. He was watching me. He invited me over to where he stood with a smile. I did no such thing. When I saw that he was heading toward me, I moved away in silence.

The president of the republic was greeting guests, shaking hands with some, exchanging a few words with others, chuckling now and again.

When he came to where I stood, he was about to greet someone who was just behind me. Then I gathered all my strength and introduced myself, "I am Mrs. von Stamitz, the wife of Mr. von Stamitz, ex-ambassador, an important civil servant in the Ministry of Foreign Affairs."

"Excuse me, Mr. President," I added, "but I recently read that sentence of yours, 'Freedom is as difficult to cope with as obligation.' I can't get it out of my head. Do you really believe that to be true?"

"Yes," he answered, seriously. "Have you read Dostoyevsky's *The Brothers Karamazov*? Freedom? It is a burden," he said, essaying an apologetic smile.

I didn't really understand. Next to me a lady in a black lace dress fluttered her fan in my face, even though it wasn't hot. That fan came between me and the president with the force of a windmill. The president introduced me to her.

"Mrs. Olvido, the wife of the Spanish ambassador."

"Excuse me, but is Olvido a surname?"

"Olvido is the lady's Christian name. It means 'oblivion.'"

Olvido . . . oblivion. Wouldn't it be nicer if she were called Memory? I thought. But the president interrupted my thoughts.

"Do you have a profession or are you still studying?" he asked me.

Blushing, I shook my head.

"You could teach something, perhaps," and quickly said his

goodbyes. He waved with that expression of his that was so typical, so distant.

Soon afterward, I heard the president in conversation with the Spanish woman, "It is necessary to understand the state and politics, and everything else in life, sub specie aeternitatis."

He was leaving. At that moment I felt as if I'd been stung: I urgently needed him to answer all of the questions that were piling up inside me!

Sub specie aeternitatis, I repeated to myself as our Hispano-Suiza took us home along the dark and winding streets. From somewhere, some very distant place, I heard my husband asking me for details of my conversation with the president. But all I could do was to go on repeating to myself, as if hypnotized: sub specie aeternitatis.

THE DAY after the reception I woke up asking myself: A Trojan woman or Phaedra? Or Pandora, perhaps, or a drunken reveller? I looked at myself in the mirror, and gave a violent shake of my head, "No!"

My hair fell down to my waist.

As I stepped into the Hispano-Suiza I asked the chauffeur to drive me to the center of Prague, to Na Příkopě Avenue. I got out of the car and told him not to come back for me until the evening.

I headed for a fashionable hairdresser. The hairstylist, Giuseppe, whose real name was Josef Svoboda, put my parasol away in a cupboard and removed the needles from my chignon. My hair spread out over the chair like a waterfall.

"Shall I wash and dry it as usual, dear madam?"

With a hand as straight as a ruler I made a rudimentary gesture across my neck, as if to say: cut off my head!

"Mikado!"

Giuseppe's teeth shone.

As he got to work, I entertained myself by reading a poster in a frame on the wall:

> Ours is the era of youth, par excellence. Whatever one's age, one must seem young. Nowadays there are no old ladies. A woman does not consider herself old even when she reaches sixty. The world finds this idea acceptable and admires women who struggle valiantly against the implacable march of time. To keep themselves young is the obligation of today's women!
>
> Therefore, to dye one's graying hair is comparable to the work of a modern painter who reinterprets the canvas of an Old Master.

I left the hairdresser with my hair cut to just below the ears and with a straight fringe at eyebrow level, but also with a few locks of hair dyed bright blonde. Giuseppe even gave me some final touches: he darkened the brows and lashes, and pressed coral-colored lipstick against my lips.

At the door, he brushed my dress and handed me my parasol.

"Madam is quite dazzling now, fascinating!"

I smiled.

Giuseppe quietly added, for my ears only, "You look as tasty as a bonbon, Sylva . . . Yum!"

I was already on my way out, ready to get rid of my long dress.

In a modern boutique selling prêt-à-porter clothing imported directly from Paris, I chose only the most up-to-date items, which were also the most comfortable, a skirt that reached down to just below the knee, a boy's shirt, and a jacket made of Scottish velvet, also cut in a masculine style. And shoes with not-too-high heels and a bag that hung from a strap. With a decisive, final gesture, I threw all my old clothes away, together with the parasol.

When it was time to pay, at the silvery till that made a ringing sound like a horse's bell, some thick, lilac-colored lettering on a large, framed poster hanging on the wall caught my attention. The lilac letters said: GIRLS TRANSFORMED INTO BOYS. I ran my eyes over the text signed by one Milena Jesenská:

> A dress mustn't hamper me when I move. I want to breathe deeply, I wish to live without limits and I ask of my clothing that it allow me to do so. The feverish activity of modern man, a direct result of the modernity, in which neither women nor men have time to sit still in the same place for very long, in a period in which we dedicate every minute we have to open air sports . . .

Before I had finished reading it, I, too, was already throwing myself into feverish activity. I walked up Václavské Square, my short hair flying. With one hand I swung the bag on its long strap. My new, comfortable shoes made my waist and hips sway with each step I took. My short skirt fluttered, caressing my legs.

During my long walk, I realized something I'd never had reason to notice before. I was the center of attention for most of the other pedestrians. The men gave me brief looks, some smiled flirtatiously, others glanced at me involuntarily, their eyes drawn to me instantly. Women gave me looks of admiration and curiosity and, of course, they observed me carefully. I glimpsed myself in a shop window: yes, I looked different from the other Czech girls from well-to-do families, locked up in their traditional world, dressed in long skirts of dark blue, wearing a blouse of the same color, embellished with a white embroidered or lace collar. Nor did I look anything like the stout Jewish ladies, covered in gold bracelets and necklaces, walking along Na Příkopě Avenue. In a sports shop, I bought some skates, a racket, and six tennis balls, and comfortable clothing so that I could practice both of these sports. I had the packages delivered to the palazzo in Malá Strana.

Once I was back on Na Příkopě Avenue, in a shop specializing in telephones, I ordered my own private telephone line for my chambers and my personal use only. I also ordered two of the latest models of telephone, black and rounded, shiny. I made myself comfortable in a chair at the Arco Café and ordered a Viennese coffee and a chocolate cake, all in German; in fact, I had come to this German-speaking café because I felt like hearing my own pure, German accent. Most of the customers who were having a cup of coffee and a glass of brandy were Jewish, elegant, and bohemian, but their German was the kind spoken in Prague; I winced with distaste because my German was better, of a higher category than theirs, and, after I'd eaten my cake, I left.

On the way to our Hispano-Suiza I made time to drop by the House of the People, that magnificent Art Deco building, where a huge exhibition of contemporary photography was on. I spent so much time looking at those Cubist compositions that I arrived late at the appointment I'd made with my chauffeur; I ran to the car as fast as my legs could carry me and my new skirt flew up until it covered my back. From a distance, I signaled to the driver of the Hispano-Suiza; he didn't respond. He hadn't recognized me. At home, my husband looked at me, speechless.

A DARK veil hid my mother's eyes, making her gaze seem noble and mysterious. Some time had passed since my father's death, but my mother had still not removed her black lace veil.

On the days that my mother left her home for Prague and decided to see me, we usually dined together in the French restaurant at the Rococo Savarin Palazzo. That's how we celebrated the advent of spring, but also of autumn and winter. In the summer we preferred to have supper on the romantic terrace of the restaurant on Sophia's Island, the breeze off the Vltava caressing our bare shoulders.

During one of our lunches at the Savarin, a tall, slim man dressed in black came up to me and greeted me in Prague German. "Herr Singer," he said. I introduced him to Maman. For a fraction of a second, Herr Singer looked straight into my mother's eyes; he then immediately wished us an enjoyable lunch and took his leave. His elegance had impressed my mother. I understood as much when she asked me, "Who is he?" in a voice more detached than usual.

I didn't answer her at once; I went on talking about the film I'd seen the previous day.

"Who is he?" she interrupted me in the same tone.

I didn't break off my description of the film, as if I hadn't heard her question.

"Who is he?" she asked for the third time.

"He is the father of one of my pupils."

"Pupils?"

"That's right, pupils."

And I shrugged, as if I had said nothing untoward.

"You . . . teach something?" she said with infinite horror and disdain.

I was savoring the chicken à l'orange, washing it down with a Burgundy, a Mercurey La Framboisière from 1919. I was so engrossed in it that again I didn't answer at once. Only after a while did I say, nonchalantly,

"Yes, I teach. Why do you ask?"

"Might I know what you teach?"

I wiped my lips with the napkin, busying myself. I didn't like her judgemental tone, the tone in which she ordered me to do some things and forbade me to do others. By now I was used to it, my husband also used it when he talked to me. But the president, that day we had spoken, addressed me in a very different fashion. And if *he* hadn't ordered me about, who was anyone else to do so?

"I teach piano. Why?"

"Ever since you were little I have tried to drum it into you that a woman of our social standing does not work. Must not work. Cannot work. You must let it drop, at once. Do you understand me?"

I felt anxious, just like when I was young, as if I were guilty of something. I became the silent little girl of my childhood days.

I met her cold stare, her icy, haughty eyes.

Her lack of understanding did wonders for my lost self-esteem.

I remembered the pretty, naughty girl in the film I'd seen the day before.

"Maman, tell me, what is Monsieur Beauvisage up to?" I asked in honeyed tones.

Now it was my mother's turn to busy herself with her plate. She didn't answer my question, but she held forth on two of her historical favorites, Madame de Sévigné and Madame du Châtelet. I didn't hear her comments; they bored me. I wanted to tell her: you're not even an aristocrat by birth, you're nothing but a plebeian! But I remembered that I had to obey orders: Abraham, take your child, your only son, Isaac, who you love, and go and offer him in sacrifice! So I didn't say a word.

We left the restaurant, and the avenue was shining in the rain. My mother then told me off. "I never want to hear about any job of yours, or anything else you might do for money. Nothing at all, is that clear?"

I said goodbye to my mother as she was waiting for a taxi. I myself was staying in the city center because I had a driving lesson scheduled. Maman, light as the lace veil, which covered half her face, half-shut her eyes and said, "Monsieur Beauvisage is in Prague. Your old teacher has becomew a high-ranking civil servant in the Ministry of Culture. And he has already published two books of poems."

She winked at me, conspiratorially, and was off in her taxi.

THAT EVENING my husband had invited a few important civil servants from the Ministry of Foreign Affairs and their wives over for supper. According to his exact words, this was to be only a little homely celebration, during which he would present a surprise. Aside from our usual servants, we hired four waiters to serve us. After supper, we went on to sample a wide assortment of wines and cheeses. The bottles of Chambelle Musigny and Aloxe-Corton were finished in no time.

This was when my husband revealed the reason for his little party: "I raise a toast to the health of my friends present here today, who have helped me aspire to and eventually achieve the great honor which I have just received. To your health, my good friends. And above all I would like to raise a toast to the health of my wife, Sylva, whose beauty will soon be radiating divinely amid the luxurious elegance of Paris."

Paris? The first thoughts that went through my mind were about the tickets I had gotten to see Voskovec and Werich next week, that with considerable effort I had managed to set up my music school, and that in the winter, I had planned on skiing in the mountains of Krkonoše.

On top of which, in Prague there was . . .

"Are we going on a trip?" I was making an effort to show that I was pleased.

"A trip? No, Sylva."

My husband took a long sip of a very special Burgundy that he had just uncorked, a La Romanée Grand Cru, 1915. He gave a smirk of satisfaction, and then he, whose entire life had been spent in diplomatic circles, disregarded etiquette and served me first. Only then did he pour a few drops of wine into the glasses of the ladies and gentlemen present.

As he did, he said, slowly and precisely, stressing each word, like a teacher of foreign languages, "You will be the wife of the Czech ambassador to Paris, my dear."

I pretended to look enthusiastic. It didn't come off, I know. When I caught a glimpse of myself in the huge cut-glass mirror hanging on the wall in its baroque frame, I noticed that my effort had twisted my lips into a completely unexpected type of smile, laden as it was with disappointment, disdain, and vanity.

My husband had finished eating the *fondant au chocolat*. On his lap, he was crumpling his napkin with his left hand. Not long afterward, the guests stood up from the table. He too stood up. The crumpled napkin in his left hand.

When the guests left, he hugged me.

"Come to the bathroom, my love. There's something I want to talk to you about."

"Let's talk about it here."

My husband looked guilty and dispirited. With bent back and bowed head, he said, "I do not wish to insist, Sylva, I have achieved this long-dreamed-of position thanks to you. Your presence in my life has inspired me in such a way that I am receiving more and more recognition for my work."

I poured myself a soupçon of Charmes Chambertin into a cut-glass goblet. As I drank, I heard him say, "Come to the bathroom, my love."

I savored the wine, not deeming my husband worthy of a single look, much less a reply.

Timidly, he put his arm around my waist.

"Are you not pleased, my love?"

I remained silent.

"You never tell me anything, but now you don't answer when I ask you something. You are a silent women, an enigmatic woman."

By way of an answer I stayed silent without turning toward him.

"Are you pleased, my love?" my husband repeated, placing a hand on my hip.

I looked at myself again in that huge mirror with its baroque frame. A silent, enigmatic woman?

THE FOLLOWING evening, when I came back from a concert, gently and with care, my husband made me sit down on the sofa next to him. He told me that since he had married me, he had changed a great deal: he was active, sociable, enterprising.

"We will be leaving for Paris next week. Start getting your things ready, Sylva."

I thought of my mother, light as the lace veil that covered half her face, of how she had winked at me as if we were in cahoots. "Monsieur Beauvisage is in Prague . . . he has become a high-ranking civil servant in the Ministry of Culture. . . he has published two books of poems."

I answered my husband, "Next week I'm going to the theater. I already have tickets."

Today too, he was crumpling up a handkerchief in one hand.

"Sylva, there is somebody else in your life."

"I had a lot of trouble getting the tickets, they're for Voskovec and Werich, just imagine! I don't want to miss their performances, that's all. If you want to come, all you have to do is try and get another ticket."

"I know you're seeing someone."

"Don't be absurd! I have tickets for the theater and that's it. What is more, I have obligations toward my students. I, too, now have duties to perform. I will join you in Paris a little later."

"I can see through you well enough. You sometimes have such a strange look on your face. Don't say one more word."

We fell silent. I myself even began to believe that I must be seeing someone, if my husband was so convinced that was the case.

"Not one more word, Sylva. I wouldn't believe you anyway."

He pushed me in the direction of the bathroom.

"Get undressed," he ordered, and went out.

As on other occasions, he soaped me and I leaned back against the white, tile wall. I sat and said nothing, and my husband whispered, "Sylva, I want you to tell me, how did he touch you? Like this, or was it perhaps like this? Where did he caress you, here, or, perhaps, here? And you, what did you do? Did you let him do as he pleased with you? Did you like it when he did so? You didn't, did you? Sylva, I beg of you, just tell me, how many things did you let him do? This too? Really, my dear?" He whispered in my ear and gasped and stuttered, and went on. "Sylva, this too? But not this, I imagine! Or this too? This too! My dear, that cannot be!" He was almost in tears and I felt guilty and wanted to restore his confidence, even though I didn't know what he was talking about. "How did he touch you? With his fingers, or with the palms of his hands as well? Or with his face? Like this?" And he looked at the lather spreading over every inch of my skin, and moaned. "I see the traces of male claws, of fingers and palms and nails and teeth and lips. I do not tire of washing you and cannot help but see all the vestiges and marks and signs of a man and his desire, his desire for you," thus did my husband snivel and howl, and when I saw him like that, I too started to cry. Then he repeated in that pleading tone of voice, "What was it like? Did he do it to you like this, and also like this? But not this, surely? You wouldn't have allowed him to do that. Or did you allow him? Perhaps you even liked it when he did that to you? No, you didn't, did you? Tell me, darling, I beg of you. Or perhaps you did?" And I nodded and said yes, yes, yes and wanted only to cease existing. This time I didn't tell him that it was enough, nor did I eat ice cream, because I pitied my husband so.

Early in the morning, I heard him open my bedroom door wide. I didn't need to see him to know that he was standing next to my bed, watching me. I shut my eyes tight. When I opened them, he was no longer there. But for a long while afterward, I heard his voice whispering in my ear, "Sylva, don't leave me, stay with me . . ."

I DIDN'T think about Paris. I often had visions of mother's half-shut, metallic eyes: noble, cold, haughty. Her lips, under the black lace of her veil, slowly enunciating the same words, "Monsieur Beauvisage is in Prague . . ."

I developed the habit of taking a daily walk, just after breakfast, around the Valdštejn Palace, where the Ministry of Culture had its offices. It was very close to where my husband and I lived.

At night, I had strange dreams. In the dark, my husband would appear, looking at me, crumpling a napkin in his fist. His expression was redolent with anguish, and a spark of hatred. And also weakness. Sometimes he turned up with a white lace handkerchief in his left hand. A revolver was hanging off the loosened fingers of his right hand.

On the days after these dreams, I bumped into furniture and people, having slept little and restlessly.

I bought myself a powder compact and every day, before heading off to the Valdštejn Palace, I covered up the bags under my eyes with face powder. I was dizzy with exhaustion and lack of sleep, and by this stage neither the philosophers nor Masaryk's pensées were able to keep a feeling of oppression and asphyxiation at bay.

ONE MORNING on my walk, just as I entered Malostranské Square, I saw him. He was waving his arms about in the middle of a passionate conversation. Monsieur Beauvisage. He seemed more mature and more interesting than before. He wore an unbuttoned black coat, with a perfectly cut dark blue suit underneath. He was walking in the midst of several men who were dressed as elegantly as he was. I started to tremble and turned toward the wall so he wouldn't see me. I was ashamed of my own exhausted appearance. And I wasn't ready to meet him.

In the evening, I walked into my husband's study without knocking.

The room was dark. I headed for the desk, and opened the first drawer on the right. There was a pile of papers in there, which I couldn't make out very well in the darkness. I was about to switch on the table lamp. Then I heard something move inside the room.

My husband stood up. We were smack opposite each other in the darkness, but couldn't see the other's face.

There was a creak from one of the cupboards filled with books.

In the street, a car stopped suddenly.

After a long silence, I said, "I won't be coming with you to Paris."

My husband said nothing.

We could hear a cheerful group of young people walking down the street. In an instant, their voices became inaudible, but they had increased the tension in the room.

"Or at the very least, I won't be coming with you right now."

The silence made me afraid, and I was afraid of breaking it too.

"I know the reason," my husband said in a low voice.

The gaslight on the street corner flickered a little.

"I know the reason," my husband repeated. "Just as I know the reason for your long morning walks."

The gaslight flared up again, then went out. We were now in total darkness. I couldn't even make out his silhouette.

He gave a brief laugh, deep and uneasy.

"I know the reason," he repeated yet again, "and I know why every morning you do yourself up and comb your hair with such care, why every morning you follow the same route. I also know that you have seen him today."

I stayed silent.

"And that the fact of seeing him has greatly impressed you," he said in a faint voice.

I had the very definite impression that this was a dream, a nightmare from which I would soon awake.

That laugh again. Grave. A grave and heavy laugh.

I felt that it couldn't be me standing there, because I would never have put up with this, no, I wouldn't have been able to take it, so enfeebled I was by such scenes. I felt that it was another young woman there in that room and that I was watching her.

Suddenly he came up close to me. Or rather, he came up close to that other girl, the one I was watching. He whispered something into her ear. At first I couldn't make out the words, but he never stopped repeating them. Finally, I heard him plead with that woman, "You have to do it, do you understand me? You have to describe exactly what happened. How he caressed you. Were you dressed or naked? I beg you to tell me. Everything I do, I do only for you. It is for you that I work, I have no other purpose in life. I beseech you to tell me. I have lost thirty pounds, can't you see that? I can't sleep, I have not slept one single night, every time I switch off the bedside lamp, I see you right in front of me . . . with him! What was it like? How did he do it to you? Let's talk about it and perhaps then I'll get him out of my head."

I couldn't stop watching that young woman as she stood in the middle of the study, in silence, motionless.

"How did he do it?" the man pleaded in a whisper, "How, Sylva? How did he caress you? Were you dressed or naked? Tell me, can't you see that I am suffering?"

The girl was trembling. Then she said, without thinking, "I was dressed." She said it to break the silence.

I saw her husband take her by the hand and pull her away somewhere. She let herself be taken away in silence, she didn't defend herself. She looked like a rag doll.

He made her go into the bathroom. He filled the tub. And he closed the door. I know nothing else.

I ARRIVED in Paris about six weeks after my husband. The first thing I took out of my case was a large padlock with a key. I called for a locksmith to attach it to my bedroom door.

I felt rested, strong, full of energy. I was becoming myself again.

In the Paris apartment assigned to the ambassador, right underneath the Eiffel Tower, I organized a music school with the help of other teachers. I gave piano and chamber music lessons, with emphasis on teaching Czech music: Smetana and Dvořák, of course, but also Janáček, who was, most undeservedly, less well known. I had ten trunks sent to me from Prague, full of books by Czech authors, mainly Božena Němcová and Karel Čapek and Jaroslav Hašek, but also works by Czech avant-garde poets. I invited the most important French publishers to dinner at the embassy and talked to them about Czech literature. So it was that a number of Czech authors ended up signing contracts for French editions of their books. Once the books were out, the embassy organized literary salons. My Parisian friends and acquaintances started to address me as Ambassadrice. Madame l'Ambassadrice.

One night, after a reception with the Minister of Education, I was waving away a clinging layer of cigarette smoke. Suddenly the door opened and my husband peeked at me through the gap. I slammed it shut and fastened the bolt.

That night I was woken by some strange noises. A kind of sighing from behind my door.

The maid I questioned the following morning shook her head, flustered.

At the chemist's, they assured me that the best brand of earplugs was Quies. I bought three boxes containing ten each. I slept better than ever.

My days were full of feverish activity. I never forgot Masaryk's words about organization being, when it came down to it, a form of politics. I felt that I was not living in vain.

✳

ONE DAY I RECEIVED AN ENVELOPE THAT HAD BEEN delivered by a diplomatic courier. It was from Prague, from the Ministry of Culture. I quickly broke the wax seal:

> Gracious Madam,
> We know of your cultural activities in Paris, which are so praiseworthy, and we would like to express our appreciation for everything that you are doing.

This was written on a typewriter. Then there were a few lines written by hand:

> P.S. Thank you, Madame l'Ambassadrice. We are proud to have people like you working for us abroad.
> With my warmest regards.
> > Yours,
> > Petr or Monsieur Beauvisage

I had trouble breathing from the happiness I felt. I had to go out. I took off over the Champ de Mars.

THAT NIGHT, despite the earplugs, I heard a light but persistent knocking. Then there was silence, and I went to sleep. But after a while it came back. Knock-knock-knock.

The maid I questioned the following morning opened her eyes wide in surprise. She obviously thought that this lady was going crazy.

Knock-knock-knock, I heard it every night.

With thick layers of face powder, I once more covered up the bags under my eyes.

DURING AN official dinner at the embassy, a foreign diplomat praised my coiffure.

"But you don't look too well," that gentleman added, attentively.

"She works too much. She should stop being so active, it exhausts her," my husband answered.

The Minister of Health suggested a thorough checkup. The following day, he said his secretary would call me and introduce me to the head of a reputable clinic.

My husband thanked him warmly. I, too, showed my gratitude for his suggestion.

That night I packed my luggage and ordered a taxi.

Twenty-four hours later I arrived at Prague's Wilson Station. This same station where I am now drinking the cocoa that reminds me of the cup of bedtime hot chocolate that my grandmother used to bring me.

I arrived the next day at Wilson Station, at platform three, I think, with my face black from the soot of the train and a smile as fresh as snow.

From the bedroom of our palazzo in Malá Strana, I made preparations by phone to continue my activities as cultural ambassador in Paris, but from Prague. It took me a few hours to sort out my things, and then I wrote a letter to my husband: I told him that I preferred to be attended to by my doctors here in Prague. I went to Jan Neruda Street to buy a stamp, and, as I was posting the letter in the blue postbox on Valdštejn Square, just opposite Valdštejn Palace, people turned to look at this woman laughing to herself.

Returning, I closed the door and lowered the blind.

I slept until the afternoon of the following day, and then again from early that night, through the following midday.

Then I filled the bathtub with piping hot water and lowered

myself into it. I soaped myself all over with a rose-scented soap until I was like the queen of the bubbles that were spreading all the colors of the rainbow around me. I blew at bubble after bubble, tossed them into the air with my hands, and made them fly over my nose and mouth and breasts and belly. My world became a fragile paradise full of pastel colors that changed hue every fraction of a second.

I wasn't thinking about anything in particular, snippets of images and thoughts fluttered through my mind like butterflies in high summer, and Mahler's "Song of the Earth" echoed in my head, a contrast to the cities around me, bursting with clouds of smoke and soot and pollution and filth. The beautiful fog of modern capitals: the fog that requires us to cleanse dirt away, reminding us of the benefit and comforts in this act. I remembered how that had to be done in earlier days and what many people still had to do. Whoever wanted to be clean had to go to the public baths: to make the trip there, on foot or by train, and then wait in a long queue until their turn was called. I stretched myself out further in the tub, sniffing the moist, rose-scented air.

I breakfasted on a cheese omelette made with three eggs and toast with honey and jam, and a huge teapot full of black tea; once I'd finished, I slung my coat over my shoulders and caught a moving tram. The girl sitting next to me was reading *The Illustrated Weekly*. As she turned the pages, my eyes ran over the print, pausing at words or sentence fragments that caught my attention. I especially liked that "the writer Joseph Kopta is playing nursemaid to his son Petr" and also that "the emancipation of women, within the context of marriage, in their professional lives, and in the way they dress." I let these new ideas flow over me.

The tram reached the Prašná Brána stop and I jumped onto the pavement. I bought a washing machine with a built-in spin dryer, the latest model, a labor-saving device for both me and my maid. That's also a way of emancipating women, I thought. In several shop windows I looked at hats whose design was inspired by African hairstyles; in Paris, these little hats were all the rage, designed and created by Agnès. I entered a shop, the salesgirl proffered trinkets and earrings "of a type favored by the cannibals," as she put it. So, together with my purchase of a suit with a skirt that barely reached to the middle of my knee, I also bought a wide leather belt, decorated with African-inspired feathers, and a small sweater with a geometric pattern. Giuseppe fixed my mikado so that it took on a more angular shape. Everything was getting shorter: distances and hairstyles, skirts and marriages, *chacun à son gout.*

I bought tickets to see a new opera, Leoš Janáček's *The Makropoulos Affair*, and also some for the Russian ballets.

Prague at night was delivering light from streetlamps and bright advertising and lit-up shop windows and colored signs and lightbulbs and blinding flashes. Elegant crowds filled the center of the capital, heading for the theaters and the concert halls and the cinemas and the jazz dives and the dance halls, to forget, albeit just for that night, the recent financial crash and the economic depression that had come in its wake. Prague seemed to me to be new, surprising. I saw a pair of men who had dyed their hair green.

I ate dinner on my own, sitting at a round table in the Café Louvre, which was painted a dark pink with neoclassical motifs on the ceiling. I had trouble getting a table. I noticed men were looking at me. I finished my glass of wine and after I'd left, I devoured my city with my eyes, from the seat of a taxi. The headlights lit up a huge S, and we were already hurtling, my young driver and myself, into that suicidal S. Then came a bridge into a never-ending space, and my taxi driver and I conquered it at high speed, with our wheels and lights, and all of this spurred my desire to fly, to throw myself at the unknown, into infinity.

THE NEXT day, after skating in the open air in Grébovka Park, I went back home; I tossed the skating boots into the air, out of sheer euphoria. An icy wind was blowing and I tucked my white ermine scarf right under my chin, protecting my neck and nape, and setting off my long, white woollen sweater. Despite the icy wind, I walked along the street with nothing on my head, so eager was I to show off my new boyish hairdo. The icy wind made me walk faster, but, cold though I was, on the way I took a detour: I felt an urge to cross Valdštejn Square.

From the gate of the Valdštejn Palace a little group of elegant men was emerging, they wore long, dark winter coats, with hats pulled over their foreheads. One of them separated himself from the rest, a good-looking man. A young woman was waiting for him with a pram. The man took the pram and pushed it in front of him with one hand, putting his free hand around the woman.

I stopped. It was Petr.

He was talking to his wife. Then I felt his eyes on me. He came to a halt and stopped talking.

I stayed where I was.

We looked at each other in silence. I noticed, for the first time, that Petr's eyes were gray.

After a second, I reacted, turning around so as to continue walking. Again, I tossed the skating boots into the air, as the mood took me.

WHEN I got back home, the phone was ringing. I picked it up; whoever was calling hung up. This happened three times.

Two or three days later I woke up at night, suddenly alarmed. My husband was standing in front of me. Wearing a winter overcoat, a scarf, gloves, he was holding a hat in one hand. He was lit only by the faint reflection from the streetlamp.

"You're here?" I made an effort to talk in a light tone. Fear had puffed the last white feathers of sleep out of me.

"I'm taking a holiday."

"A holiday?"

"Yes. Because it does not look at all well, for the wife of an ambassador to go all alone."

"Are you such a stickler for etiquette?"

He began to tremble a bit.

"Sylva, I know everything," he said with a grave air.

Like the murderer in a cheap detective movie, I smiled.

"What do you mean by everything?" I asked ineptly.

It was the worst of all possible replies. Despite the seriousness of the moment, I realized that, when someone determines that you are guilty of something, no matter how innocent you might be, you end up feeling guilty anyway.

"What do I mean by everything, Sylva? You know perfectly well what I mean!"

"I don't know what you're talking about. My conscience is quite clean."

What an idiotic thing to say, yet again!

"I am talking about what happened on Friday evening in Valdštejn Square. The looks you gave each other. Well, at least now I am certain as to what is going on."

He was gazing at the gas lamp through the window, as if that muted brightness were going to bring him comfort.

"No, Sylva, don't look at me as if I'd lost my mind. Although it is true that this is driving me insane. I think of nothing else but you."

In the light of the gas lamp he looked like a corpse that had emerged from its tomb to say its piece. All of a sudden he took a few heavy steps toward my bed, on which he ended up stretching himself out, awkwardly.

"All my efforts . . . everything . . . for you, Sylva. Everything, I have done everything for you."

I saw his all-but-lifeless expression. I wasn't listening to him. I could learn more from reading his thin, exhausted face and his feverish eyes, instead of concentrating on his words.

He stood up. He spoke in such a low voice that I only caught the last few words.

"Sylva, I have no other way out."

What was he referring to?

"I have no other way out," he repeated, "the only one left is this."

He took a revolver out of his pocket.

I froze. An absurd idea went through my head. Why, in novels, is it always, "The man took out a gun and the woman screamed until she woke up the entire household?" Now I knew that was impossible. Instead, you go all soft. Incapable of the slightest movement, let alone of saying anything. I didn't move. I didn't breathe. He wasn't moving or breathing either.

"This is my only way out," he whispered, "I have to kill it. What's inside me."

Kill what? I asked myself. Kill what?

I couldn't understand. He was talking to himself, "Kill him . . . him? If I do that, he will go on living in you and me . . ."

We were in darkness. For an entire century we were in darkness. Then daylight broke. He got up slowly and went out. He didn't look at me again.

IN THE morning, he wasn't at home. Nobody had seen him. Not the maid, nor the cook, nor the chauffeur. Had he really been here?

Once I'd dressed, I headed for . . . No, I gave the Valdštejn Palace a wide berth. I walked toward Petřín Mountain. Every few steps I turned to check if anyone was following me. I made an effort to watch the leaves that had fallen from the trees, and were now mixed up with the snow.

AFTER A few days, the Minister of Foreign Affairs called me on the phone. He wanted to see me right away, he said in a grave voice that brooked no dissent.

The tea I'd ordered from the maid still hadn't arrived when he called at the door.

This man, who was usually so friendly and smiling, was serious, stern, almost severe. He came straight to the point. A moment earlier he had received the following letter.

Most Honorable Minister, my dear friend,
The recent economic crash and the economic crisis that it had brought in its wake have ruined me completely. I am bankrupt. I have nothing left on the stock exchange, and my once considerable properties have vanished as if they were smoke. I cannot bear to show my face to my acquaintances or my wife, who, because of this situation, no longer has any protection. I did not want my wife to incur any debts. Everything that has happened has occurred against my will.
I place my post at your immediate disposition.
Above all, I ask of you, from the bottom of my heart, to explain all this to my wife in the most delicate fashion possible. I am unable to do so myself.

I finished reading. Or rather, I finished running my eyes over those lines, unable to take in their full meaning. I sat in silence. The minister said, "Whether you believe the reason stated here by your husband, to wit, the financial crash, or whether you do not ... at all events ..."

That normally decisive man could say no more.

In a barely audible voice, he added that my husband's dead body had been found that morning in our Paris apartment. He had died in the night from a single shot from his revolver. "Who knows why," said the minister sadly, without looking at me.

A few days later, together with other letters addressed to me, I received an envelope containing a bill for a very large amount of money. It came from a detective agency. After reading the description of the services rendered, I understood that for all those years, my husband had me followed around the clock.

I WALKED back to Petřín Mountain. I don't know why I turned around to see if anyone was following me.

Under the soles of my boots, the snow, mixed with fallen leaves, squeaked from time to time. After a little while, I turned around again.

No, nobody was following me. I was alone.

Only the leaves beneath my feet were making a muted snapping sound.

# V

# JAN

I'VE BEEN WALKING AROUND IN THE AIRPORT. ON THE first floor of the international terminal, I sat down in a café, at a table with a pink tablecloth. In my mind, I was looking for a solution to an equation, drawing figure after figure with my finger on that same tablecloth.

I was distracted for a while by a quarrel between a foreign visitor and an Asian waitress. I tried to concentrate, but the voices in the café got disrupted with my figures; the noise kept me company, lonely as I was.

For many years in the United States, after a long workday I would return to a dark, cold, and empty house, a house that was not a home.

Every evening that damp, dark silence would grab hold of me. That silence drained my energy and filled my arteries, veins, and blood vessels with a mixture of revulsion and anguish and shame. That silence paralyzed me, right there in the house. Only after a while could I start to distinguish those sounds that are so typical of American houses: the creaking of wood, the scraping of window frames, the cracking noises coming from the ceiling, the knocking in the pipes, the sighs of the central heating. Which is why America is the only country where Edgar Allen Poe, who wrote so much about houses full of ghosts and spirits, could have been born. Don't you think so, Mama? The fridge would raise its voice with its catlike purring and, once the reloading process was over, you could hear several kicks from it, as if a fat, sour-faced man had become frustrated working on the fridge's motor and *wham!* was giving it a good kicking. As I took in those familiar sounds, little by little my anguish dwindled and I could start to move around freely. I left the dishwasher humming away. The central heating brought a crowd of naughty children who wouldn't stop hitting the pipes in the rooms and corridors.

I had only liked silence when I was with you, Mama. Because with you, the Silent Woman, I didn't need words to communicate. With you, I never felt alone.

Every evening I switched on the TV just to hear some human voices. Do you remember how, in Prague, we used to make fun of that very same habit when we saw other people do it in their own homes? But automatically I put on one of the TV channels—which all more or less have the same name, WTHA, WTRD, WBAB, WBRJ, WFTY—and each one is specialized in something: one is a news station, another covers sports, yet another deals with newborn babies. Yes, Mama, on one channel children are born twenty-four hours a day in front of a TV camera. From the TV came those clipped, self-confident voices shared by so many Americans, voices giving opinions and verdicts that are far too brief, and conclusions and pronouncements that are so often too firm, too resolute. The TV would keep me company while I got my supper ready.

Mama, you ask if I sought out any female company? Yes. To be honest with you, I get on just fine with women. I had a few relationships. I would love to introduce these ladies to you but of course I can't. But I'll write you some brief descriptions of them, as if they were snapshots or postcards.

## DAISY

She vaguely reminded me of Helena, especially because of her long, swinging earrings. I invited her to restaurants several times just to be able to look at her and project the features of my Czech girlfriend onto her face. Eventually I stopped doing that, having become interested in the girl herself. One day she asked me, "What are your intentions as far as I'm concerned?" I didn't understand the question. She explained, "You Europeans are too enigmatic for us plain-speaking, practical Americans. You never talk about your plans for the future." But I didn't know my plans for the future, or my intentions toward her. Nor did I want to think about them and neither did I want to know her intentions toward me. When there's no mystery involved, a relationship just becomes humdrum. During one of our dinners, Daisy revealed her plans for our future together. I know it was a cruel thing to do, Mama, but I never called her again.

## WENDY

Wendy, a fellow student at the university, invited me to a café for lunch one day. As we ate, she unbuttoned her jacket, cold though it was, and I couldn't help but notice that she had a prominent cleavage. I even found it a bit vulgar, aggressively provocative, so to speak. Wendy told me that her husband had gone off on a business trip, and invited me over for coffee and dessert at her place. I got out of it by saying I had work to do. She asked me to drop by in the evening, adding that she'd never been with a man from a communist country before.

## CINDY

Cindy, who wore her hair down to the waist, invited me to a dinner party at her place. There were a couple of friends and acquaintances of mine there. Cindy was a considerate, tactful hostess, very attentive to her guests. By the time the main course was served—chicken teriyaki—different kinds of social and political stuff were being discussed. On the subject of the death penalty, Cindy said, "Whoever kills, deserves to die!" Nobody paid any attention. When the dessert came along, we were arguing about what had to be done with countries that actively supported terrorism. Should we wage war on them? Would that be advisable? Or would it be better to avoid that? There was a wide range of opinions, backed by an equally wide range of different reasons. Cindy waited until everyone had their say to share her view on this subject, "Any country that supports terrorism should be bombed outright!" One of the guests objected that a country's inhabitants did not necessarily agree with their government's decision to support terrorists. But Cindy wasn't having any of it, "Bomb that whole damn country! Destroy 'em all!" Spotting my alarm, she immediately changed the subject. She spoke of nothing else but ancient and contemporary art and classical music for rest of the night. But I didn't accept any more of her invitations.

JOANNE

"Liar," Joanne yelled at me on our first weekend together, when she caught me in the act of writing a letter. "Liar! You told me you needed more time to dedicate yourself to your scientific work!" She looked crestfallen. I'd spoiled the weekend. "You look really great," I told her one day, after a dinner she'd prepared for the two of us. I was looking at her thoughtful profile, though Joanne was no textbook Hollywood beauty. "Liar!" came the harsh accusation. From her expression, I realized that this was the worst crime anyone could commit in her worldview: to affirm something that did not correspond to an objectively provable truth. A week later, I told her over the phone, "I've been trying to get hold of you all afternoon." I said this to cover up an oversight of mine, not wanting to hurt her just because I'd forgotten to get in touch with her for a few hours. "Liar," she said knowingly, "I haven't had any phone calls at all up until now." Her voice sounded like that of a prosecutor addressing the bench. Then it finally dawned on me that I didn't belong to her culture. I was unable to behave according to its rules and, even worse, I was offending my girlfriend by ignoring them. I liked Joanne, with her intelligent face and thoughtful expression, but she drifted away from me.

SAMANTHA

We met at a party, where I didn't know anybody except for the hosts, and she probably didn't either. Samantha sat in a corner sipping Lambrusco from a glass that would have been better suited to a gin and tonic. I sat next to her with a bottle of beer in my hand. She introduced herself, saying she was a theater critic. Later on, she would invite me to various Boston theaters. After a performance, we would sit cross-legged on the carpet of a Turkish restaurant, cast into shadow. As we slowly sipped red wine from the Turkish coast, we would analyze the play we'd just seen. It fascinated me to see the way Samantha lived her job, the way she spoke about the actors and directors, the things she would tell me, such as how stage fright had been the driving force behind a good performance, or about the inspiration that can fire up an actor once he's stepped onto the stage, or how a negative review can destroy an actor's self-confidence. Between us the candle's flame would tremble, as its dry light would illuminate our fingers and lips, which seemed to float in the shadowy atmosphere. Samantha invited me to the theater more and more often, but even so, every single one of our evenings together still felt like a celebration. After one performance, she asked me if I'd like to have some coffee over at her place. Like a chess player, I imagined the consequences of this move: I envisioned drawn curtains and dawn light filtering through, an unmade bed, Samantha's hair, tousled, spread over the pillow and her smeared makeup. I said yes. But I left before I could see that woman's face puffed up by sleep; I wanted to keep her in my mind in high heels when she walked along the carpeted corridors of the theaters, or with her lips painted the color of wine in the half shadow of the Turkish restaurant. That was the last invitation I got.

MEI

Mei, a small Chinese girl, had an important job in the Chicago headquarters of Citibank. She told me to come visit, so I took a week off and ended up spending an entire sabbatical year over there. While Mei was getting herself ready to go to work, I would prepare breakfast for both of us and serve it on the kitchenette counter in her small apartment. We'd sip orange juice, me in my pajamas, she in her gray pantsuit, with her short hair combed to one side, like a boy dressed up as a banker. A little white handkerchief stuck out of her breast pocket, like a spruced up gangster from Chicago in the twenties. Before she left, Mei would give me a kiss and ask about my plans for the day. Mei suffered from a baseless, illogical, and destructive jealousy. At the end of every working day—always a long one, like those of most high-ranking executives—as we had a glass of chardonnay in a bar, Mei would track my line of sight, making sure it didn't wander over any of the elegant girls and ladies gesticulating with glasses of dry martinis or manhattans or margaritas in their hands. If I decided to check out the headlines of the *Chicago Tribune*, Mei watched me like a hawk to see what news items I was *really* interested in. From the bar, or a restaurant, we would head back home in a taxi. Then too Mei would be on the alert in case my eyes drifted over to the sidewalk and settled on any of the pretty women who might happen to be walking there, with their long hair caressing their backs and breasts.

One windy, sunny day I entered a shop on Rush Street that sold Asian products to buy a bottle of soybean oil that Mei and I used for wok cooking. Afterward, a Japanese woman asked me where I'd bought the bottle. We started up a conversation and continued it with a glass of wine in an Italian café next to the shop; the Japanese woman gave me some promising looks.

That evening, I ate Chinese dumplings at Mei's place. She asked me for all the details of what I'd done that day. I was in a bad mood, said little, and wasn't hungry. Soon I realized that I was angry with myself, not with Mei. I was sorry I hadn't asked for Kyoko's phone number back there in the Italian café. Dinner with Mei dragged on. The next day I discovered I just didn't have the stamina to keep on putting up with short, attractive Mei's jealous scenes.

KYOKO

I had a tough time finding Kyoko. On the day of her piano concert at the McCormac Center, I had a front row seat. At the end of my sabbatical year in Chicago, we got married.

When I had to go back to Boston, Kyoko decided to move to her parents' home in Tokyo. A month later, I took a holiday as to visit her. She stayed at her parents' house, and reserved a room for me in a hotel in the Ginza neighborhood, in central Tokyo. I didn't miss a single one of Kyoko's concerts: I always bought a front row ticket, and after each performance I'd bring her a bouquet of flowers. Afterward, she would head back to her parents' place. One day, and this was unusual for her, she asked me to have a coffee with her. She unfolded a petition for divorce over the café table. I didn't understand. What had happened? Was it because I knew nothing about the way Japanese people thought?

Kyoko was stunned by my lack of comprehension. I signed the document, paid the bill, and walked Kyoko to the door of her parents' house. I continued living at the hotel in Ginza and, as before, I went to listen to each and every one of her concerts, sitting in the first row and watching Kyoko, so slim, with her long hair, dressed in black clothes that clung to her well-proportioned figure. I admired her there on the stage in front of me, when she played Beethoven's "Moonlight Sonata." At the end of every concert I brought Kyoko a bouquet of white chrysanthemums. After one Sunday concert, I took a plane home and throughout the entire flight, I kept on seeing a fragile woman, her hair hanging curtainlike, as she bent over a black and white keyboard, concentrating, barely stroking it with her fingers. I knew then that I had married Kyoko because of this frangible, black-and-white image.

ASSIA

We met on the train from Boston to Washington DC, where I'd been invited to lead a seminar on the discontinuous function of coordinates. I was looking forward to perhaps spending some of my free time, maybe even a whole day, in the Library of Congress. Assia was looking for the smoking compartment; I tried to help her to find it, but the entire train was nonsmoking. So when we got to Washington we went into a restaurant, right there in the station, which made me think of an ancient Greek temple, a refurbished one, to be sure. There Assia smoked stealthily, placing the ashtray on her knees. Her fingers trembled when she told me that it must be very amusing to be a foreigner and that without a doubt my life was more interesting than that of other people. "That depends," I replied, "it can also be difficult: your customs and habits are different from those of the country in which you're living. A foreigner always calls attention to himself because he stands out. You don't get people's sense of humor, they don't get yours." Assia said that she was a foreigner too; she felt that other people didn't understand her, and she didn't really understand them either. "But," I said to her, "English is your mother tongue, you can make yourself understood." "I can't," she said, "I've already told you that I don't understand other people and they don't understand me." "But Assia," I said impatiently, "there's a huge difference between not being understood and not being able to use your mother tongue, like me." Assia looked at me as if I'd whipped her favorite dish away from under her chin. I started to explain my point of view, "The effort of learning English, which I have had to make, has meant that I've forgotten much of my Czech, my mother tongue. I'm even ashamed now to write letters in Czech and that's why I don't even write to my ex-girlfriend. And my English is worse than broken, as you can hear for yourself." I said to Assia, "Scientific English is the only type of English I've mastered properly, and that has a limited vocabulary and simple grammar because it's based on a few formulaic sentences." Assia nodded. Thinking that she had understood me, I said, "Exile, among other things, means that you never really master any language." Assia went on nodding, and answered, "Yes, that's me all right." "Why, are you a foreigner as well? Your name, Assia, sounds foreign." "My parents were born in the US; myself, I only really know the area around Philadelphia. But I understand your trouble just fine, I'm an emigrant, just like you." I didn't say a word more. With the car I'd rented at the station, I gave Assia a ride to the address she gave me, declining her invitation to go in for a drink. Then I went for a spin in the car: the city at night, its long avenues, so wide and spacious with a boulevard running down the center, surrounded by buildings held up by Doric columns, and their Greek staircases, facades, and frontispieces, all of this emerged out of the night, dressed in white. It was like a kind of Acropolis: like gigantic temples with white marble colonnades, and they rose up from the water and shone against the night sky, all white and shiny like stars, or the moon on a summer's night.

ALL THOSE women, girlfriends, fiancées . . . They didn't realize that a foreigner's life is nothing if not restless. Anything that a foreigner does is an event, because it involves decisions, choices, adaptation, painful surprises, rifts. They never realized that a foreigner always feels uprooted, and that to put down roots in another country turns out to be an impossible task. He is left floating in the air, always on the move, always subject to change. As an immigrant, he has no political rights and is excluded from any kind of public office. His loneliness leads the foreigner to identify with a cause, an activity, or a person, to which or to whom he becomes violently attached, because it is there that he has found a new country. Those women friends of mine didn't realize that a foreigner, a human being who feels constantly humiliated because of his poor knowledge of the host language, and because of the lack of comprehension he encounters wherever he goes, suffers from depression, as well as resentment, fury, and even hatred. Foreigners seek refuge in their resentment, they live in it, they turn it into their sanctuary and their flag. Resentment is something palpably present in the foreigner's volatile universe.

And then, Mama, I grew tired of casual encounters. Within myself, I went on feeling I don't know what, something like when Brahms's concert for piano and orchestra bursts out in the middle of dead silence, with its noisy, relentless beginning. But when it came to sharing this feeling, to sharing myself, I couldn't find a soul. So I preferred just to go on dreaming.

Then the day came when I found somebody. One of my students. That, Mama, is to court severe punishment. If you fall in love with a student, they can put you on trial and throw you out of the university.

Would you like to know how it came about? I'll begin at the end. This story is longer than the others, because it's so important to me. Listen ...

LESLIE

One day, her husband came to see me in my office. He was smoking. The smoke covered him the way mist covers a mountain peak. I imagined, in fact I was sure, that he'd come to give me a piece of his mind, after which he would hand me over to the authorities for having succumbed to temptation and sexually harassing his wife. The man talked and talked; I didn't listen to him, I knew what his monologue was going to be about. Instead of her husband I saw her, Leslie, sitting in his place. We were talking about who knew what, anything to avoid a silence falling between us which would have been too dangerous, too tempting. We talked about hybrid cars, about voltage modulation. Then, later, we chatted about this and that.

I remembered that one day in 1968 in Prague, on Charles Bridge, I had seen two girls, a slim, dark-haired one, and a voluptuous blonde, both in miniskirts. The dark-haired one was hefting a violin case, but that didn't stop her from walking at a brisk pace. I followed the two girls over the Charles Bridge and Kampa Island over to Malá Strana, to the U Glaubicu tavern, where they ordered a draught beer each and something to nibble on. The two girls had been aware of my presence for some time and were making fun of the situation. While I was thinking of a way to start up a conversation, the blonde one got up to go to the bathroom and on the way, asked me out on a date. But the one I fancied was the dark-haired one—it was because of her that I'd followed them! All the same, I went out on the date with the blonde one. In the cinema I spent the two hours that the film lasted caressing her breasts and belly and thighs. I got to meet the dark-haired one a week later, when she came over to her friend's house for a visit. Then, tying a towel around my waist, I took advantage of the fact that the blonde one was taking a shower to ask the dark-haired one out to the cinema. I spent the film sitting there like a piece of wood, and only toward the end did I dare to briefly caress her hand with my fingertips.

She was a violinist. In August I accompanied her to Sarajevo, where she was performing at a music festival. One evening, Helena's music excited me in an extraordinary way. During the Bach concert, it seemed to me that her violin was trembling with a hidden, contained grief. Helena played with lowered eyes, her chestnut hair flowing toward the floor. That was the last time I saw Helena. At the break of dawn, news came that the Soviet army had invaded our country. Helena wasn't in her room. I looked for her all day in vain. Desperate, in the evening I climbed up onto the mountains surrounding Sarajevo, to see if I could find her. A few dogs came up to me, snarling and showing their teeth, in that moss and pinecone-scented twilight. But Helena wasn't there. I looked for her for days and days, everywhere. I plunged myself into an academic life here in America, but never stopped longing for Helena, and to look for her in all the women I met. Her, Helena, who had disappeared one day from the banks of the river Bosnia like sea foam, pulled away from the beach by a retreating wave.

Until I found Leslie, a student who came to see me to ask for help with her doctorate courses.

And now her husband was sitting in my office. He was smoking. Any moment now, Leslie's husband would report me to the university authorities for sexual harassment.

As her husband went on, I only saw Leslie, my friend, coming in to tell me how her scientific research was going. I listened to her melodious Boston English with pleasure, that mezzosoprano's voice, and, not really aware of what I was doing, I found myself looking at her breasts. Leslie noticed. She smiled, with goodwill, with joy.

And I thought about her. My mind was tainted with the memory of my search for Helena, that August of 1968 in Sarajevo. I'd gone to look for her in Ilidza Park: Helena, I assumed, must have gone to the Bosnia River Springs, a place that was sacred to Bosnians, to tell them of the pain she felt because of the attack on our country, there where the water springs forth. They didn't let me go into the park, night was already falling. But I had to find Helena! When it was dark, I vaulted the fence. The water from the springs was falling over the stones, and, as other streams fed into it, it grew broader and sang its sad song, its litany full of grief, there in the middle of the night.

I brusquely interrupted my train of thought to encourage Leslie to talk, "Tell me something about your childhood!"

She told me stories about her and other boys, when they were little. In the summer they visited barns and deserted houses in the woods, and played there, watched each other, exposed themselves mutually. In that very moment, I couldn't get the image of being in a dark barn with Leslie out of my head: we'd stripped naked, I wanted to feel her warm skin against my hand but didn't dare touch her directly. I picked up a handful of grain and rubbed it on her body, through the grains I felt it was loaded with electricity, her skin, with the grains I was rubbing around her waist, and over her breasts, then I made her lie down and with my palms full of grain, I massage her belly, her thighs … I reached out a hand. I touched her body. No! I didn't want to imagine the end. I got scared.

"You're scared," Leslie said with a laugh, "What happened to you?"

I didn't look at her. She didn't stop laughing, in little fits of giggles, as she looked at me with shiny, moist eyes. Then she stopped; she too was in some place outside reality. She opened her eyes wide, staring at me in complete seriousness. I knew those sparks in her eyes. They indicated desire.

I got up and accompanied her to the door.

"Goodbye," I suddenly became aware of my voice. And was surprised to find myself adding, "I won't have any time tomorrow, nor the day after that, nor the one after that."

And now, her husband was sitting in front of me. He didn't stop smoking, sighing. He was saying something about his wife, his wife's behavior. I made an effort to listen to him.

"Recently, my wife has been behaving strangely. During the time she used to come over here to ask you for advice, she lived in a state of euphoria. Now she's fallen into one of desperation. I took her to the California beaches for a few days and she wandered around there in the same dejected mood, like she was sinking into mud."

I started to think about myself again, I didn't want to hear that man's laments. But his words couldn't help but brush past my ear, "I'm worried that my wife is seeing someone. A love affair which, at the beginning, had made her very happy and which is now making her terribly sad." I didn't really hear what Leslie's husband was saying. I was thinking about myself: To whom could I explain my hapless life? To whom? To Helena? She'd gone from the picture a long time ago. To Leslie? I'd got rid of her myself. Yet, even so, I really needed to talk!

"You know . . ." I started a sentence, but I was speaking to Leslie's husband. There was nothing I could do about it though, I just had to talk. "You know . . . Exile may well be a mind-broadening experience, but deep down, it's an incurable illness," I began. And the words bubbled up from inside me like the Bosnia River streaming over the stones. I couldn't stop talking to the husband of my woman friend, about my two women friends, Helena, and the other one, Leslie, who I didn't mention by name, but simply described her. All of a sudden I found there was an expression of surprise, consternation, on my listener's face; he'd even stopped smoking. The smoke had melted away and I could see his eyes. They appeared to me to be suddenly relieved.

"So it's because of you!" sighed Leslie's husband, unruffled, cordial, steady. "I was suspicious of other men, but this would never have occurred to me. A foreigner! A professor from who knows where . . . from the East! A stranger!" he said to himself, looking at my fair, graying hair, and unconsciously patting his own thick, black mane. "So there's no danger, then, and there never has been," or that's what I think I heard, though I'm not entirely sure. But the smile spreading over the whole of Leslie's husband's face was a clearer expression of his sense of superiority than anything he might have said.

Leslie's husband leaned back happily in his armchair, he didn't need his cigarettes anymore. While I went on talking, he listened, then he got up and cheerfully headed for the door.

I didn't stop talking, addressing myself to the empty chair.

# VI

# SYLVA

THE DAY AFTER THE DEATH OF MY HUSBAND, MY MOTHER arrived. She loaded me into the Hispano-Suiza as if I were some kind of parcel and took me to Prague's main shopping area. She made me go into a very large shop and had me wrapped in black fabric: shoes, blouse, skirt, coat, gloves, everything was black. She dressed me. I stood there silent and still, with that flag of grief. At the end she plunked a hat over my short, blonde hair. A hat that covered my head from my eyebrows to below my ears. Sort of like a priest's bonnet.

Then I realized. All of a sudden, I understood that I missed my husband. Now I thought only of his polished manners, of his pain and anguish, of those eyes that had so often pleaded with me not to abandon him.

I went home and asked my mother to leave me on my own. My grandmother arrived to replace her.

But that unique word . . . Oblivion . . . Oblivion. The sweet lullaby.

A word I repeated when I left my husband's palazzo for good, and when our ever-so-luxurious Hispano-Suiza turned up, and when I dismissed the chauffeur, and when I counted my money to see if I could buy myself a little secondhand, chauffeurless Skoda, and then when I reached the conclusion that I couldn't afford it. When I put my things in order and left them packaged up, ready for the move, I repeated to myself: Sylva, the woman who demands that both society and her intimate circle respect her, must possess the art of making herself as exquisite as an exotic flower!

My huge debts obliged me to sell the palazzo in Malá Strana. Even my own family felt the effects of the Depression. My mother kept only the east wing of the chateau, where she continued to live with my grandmother; she left the rest of the building to the state because she couldn't afford the upkeep. After my father's death, I inherited a small mansion, also in the Malá Strana District, on the Kampa Island side; we used to call it the Pink Palace. I turned the first floor into my living area, and converted the rest into rented apartments. So now I had neighbors: Jewish families who, like so many other people, had gone bankrupt after the Wall Street crash.

I filled my apartment with furniture from the chateau: I wished to surround myself with the atmosphere of my childhood. The apartment was so full, there was hardly any space left in it, but I walked past the mirrored cupboards and the corner pieces and the credenzas, the buffets and the sideboards, the side tables and the glass cases and the Japanese jewelry boxes, and with the tips of my fingers and the palms of my hands I felt that piece of exquisite wood and this item of cut glass, and I caressed the lacquered furniture with its encrusted pearl and ivory, and I embraced the lances and pikes and javelins and the rest of the medieval weaponry as if they were tree trunks in the middle of a forest, and I hugged the cold metal of the suits of armor and the helmets that knights had worn centuries ago. Every day I strolled around the apartment, which was permanently submerged in half shadow, because the sun's rays never managed to penetrate that first-floor apartment in a narrow street in Malá Strana. But I wouldn't have wanted such sunlight, or too much brightness; I preferred that cold darkness. And the silence: I even played my music quietly, making the piano do little more than whisper. Some evenings I didn't even switch on the lights, finding that a gas-powered streetlamp, here too, could provide me with enough light. The piano didn't fit in my room, which was full to bursting with all the furniture I'd put in there, so I had it placed in the living room, next to the window. I played it at twilight; Brahms's Piano Sonata no. 3 op. 5, and Chopin's mazurkas tinted the falling shadows, the music that my grandmother, more than my tutors, had taught me to play. My grandmother, who, like my shadow, only seemed to appear when I needed her. When that was not the case, she lived in the east wing of the chateau with my mother, who needed her much more than I did. My mother was alone.

I was, too. For the first time in my life, I was completely free. Nothing had any meaning anymore. The only pleasure that brightened my days was the music I played when it began to grow dark.

I developed a habit of strolling on Kampa Island, where I found both nature, and manmade encroachments on her territory. I found living water and dead water; the dead water of the canals and the living water of the Moldova River.

The Silent Woman, I would hear occasionally when passing a bench full of elderly women. The Silent Woman, my neighbors in Malá Strana used to call me.

Maman came to see me, as she'd done before. We had season tickets for the concerts at the Rudolfinum and a box at the German Theater; before or after the music, we would lunch or dine at the Savarin Palace.

ONE EVENING, at the Savarin, we'd finished dinner, but it was raining outside and neither my mother nor I had brought an umbrella. Someone called my name and greeted me in German. I looked up and saw the father of one of my former students. Herr Singer was smiling at me, but under that polite layer of a melancholy smile—melancholy, together with elegance, was one of the characteristic features of Jewish men in Prague—I discerned a different emotion. Herr Singer was taken aback, I would almost say startled, by the change he saw in me. I understood from his look that I had got thinner, that I was pale and looked the worse for wear; Herr Singer found it disagreeable to be a witness to this metamorphosis. In the expression of that attractive man, with his olive skin, who was certainly not slow to appreciate beauty in a woman, I saw my own transformation: death had made me look like I myself was on death row.

Mr. Singer turned his gaze to my mother and in an instant, he forgot about me. I introduced them to each other once more: Herr Singer, Frau von Wittenberg.

Mr. Singer said, "In comparison to the light you ladies radiate, this luxurious French restaurant is now nothing but a vulgar tavern."

Although a man as courteous as Herr Singer took care to look at both my mother and myself, it was quite clear that this homage was addressed to her.

Herr Singer invited us to dance, "If your state of mourning were to permit it, it would just be for a very little while, right next door, in Venceslau Square, I know a cozy little place where they play jazz music." Maman looked at me questioningly, her look said, "Come on! You've spent enough time in mourning." Her eyes were shining. At age forty-eight, she was slim, youthful, and enigmatic in a way that only mature and experienced women know how to be. They took me home in a taxi; Herr Singer asked about the possibility of his son taking piano lessons from me once again. Oddly enough, this time my mother didn't protest. I got out, Herr Singer moved from the front seat to the back, next to my mother. I waved goodbye, but they were so deep in conversation that they didn't see me.

I went straight to my piano, I played Brahms's intermezzi. The music enveloped me and, as always, cut me off from the outside world. But on that day, it didn't satisfy me the way it had at other times. I thought about the conversation in the restaurant. Mr. Singer smiled at me, but in a way in which I knew that he didn't see me as a woman, but rather as a creature to be pitied.

Why had death changed me so much? Was my husband's death really such a great loss to me? The marriage, from my point of view, had not been at all satisfactory. I would surely have asked for a divorce, given time. But the death of my husband had changed something in me. I thought about his pleading look; his sort of passion; his jealousy, through which he revealed his love. His sudden death caused by his having gone bankrupt? Or was it rather . . . A voice inside me said: Isn't it your heavy conscience that's making you think about all this? All this theatricality, what with the mourning and the dark rooms and the longing for eternal night, is all that not just a pile of sand with which you are trying to put out the fire of your guilt? I answered the voice: Guilt, you say? Guilt for what reason? Back came the voice: For what reason? Why, it's obvious! For living! You are alive, he isn't. I said: but you can't call it living, really. And the voice: too right, now you're starting to get the idea. This is the last battle between us and the dead, the last struggle for power and at the same time the final vengeance of our dead ones: to make us feel guilty, to make us sad, to make us not live or to live just a little, to live insufficiently.

The following morning I woke up early, took one of my new brightly colored skirts from the wardrobe—it smelled of mothballs—a pair of transparent stockings, and a chalk-white blouse.

I got on the phone and made an appointment with Giuseppe. He cut my hair below the ears, leaving some locks of hair blonder than ever, and then added the final touch: a sinfully red piece of ribbon; the very latest fashion. I didn't go back home until I'd had dinner in a smart restaurant. I switched on all the lights and called Mr. Singer. We arranged for his son to take piano lessons with me again starting the followingMonday.

THE PIANO was next to the window. When I taught my students—most of them the children of wealthy Jewish families, like that of Mr. Singer himself—I used to open the curtains to make it easier to see how the pedal should be used. As my students practiced their exercises and I listened with a view to correcting them, I stared out at the house opposite mine, on the far side of the street. I did this unconsciously. The house was as gray as a raincloud, and thoroughly uninteresting. But one day I noticed a hand raising the blind and opening a window. A woman leaned out and sniffed the fresh air, summer was almost upon us. She glanced out at the street, only to vanish a moment later back into her apartment. The next day, this scene was repeated. The woman leaned out of the window to look down at the street, then very cheerily she waved at somebody, and closed the window. On yet another day, as the woman was looking at the street, a man stood next to her leaning on the windowsill, and whispered something into her ear. The woman bit her lower lip. A gust of wind came along and the couple closed the window. That gust heralded several overcast days full of wind and rain. The window remained closed and I forgot about my neighbors on the far side of the street.

Afterward, when the stormy weather had passed, I drew the curtain back to see the woman leaning out of her window again. At first glance she seemed to me to be rather ordinary, but later I saw that wasn't the case. The fact was she had makeup on, and all of the makeup had started to run: from her lips, eyes, and cheeks, and her hair was dishevelled. She must have been a lot older than me, but still a bit younger than my mother. The woman wiped her nose with the back of her hand . . .Oh! Now I saw it: she was crying! Miluška, one of my students, was playing Beethoven's "Moonlight Sonata." I opened the window just a touch to let some fresh air in. The woman peered at us; she must have heard the music. What's more, Beethoven must have caught her husband's attention, as he, too, appeared at the window. Surprised, he looked at his wife and caressed her tousled hair. He went away and came back with a large handkerchief, all clean and ironed. He cleaned up his wife's face . . . yes, just as, long ago, Monsieur Beauvisage had wiped my muddy foot in the park at the chateau. Now the woman burst into fresh tears. The man, who looked concerned, disappeared back inside the apartment. She was crying uncontrollably . . . Where did all those tears come from? Gradually she stopped crying. Very gradually. Now she only let out the odd sob. Once she'd calmed down, the man returned to fetch her. He hugged her, kissed her hair, her forehead.

"Is that love?" I asked in a low voice.

"I'm sorry?" asked Miluška, who hadn't heard me properly. She looked at me, not understanding a thing.

Hugo, my next pupil, took no notice of my mood, and played Haydn without paying attention to anything else.

If someone cries, it's because they are weak, I told myself. The one who consoles them then is the stronger person. The weak hate the strong: they resist, they seek revenge. They want to feel stronger, but their struggle only gives further proof of their weakness. Hatred, therefore, has no strength to it.

Hugo handed me an envelope with money and left. The relationship between a pupil and a teacher is straightforward. Like that between parents and children, or between an entrepreneur and his employees. But, what about the relationship between a woman and a man?

A week later I saw them again at their window. They were silent. Miluška was playing a Chopin study at full tilt. When she finished, the silence sounded to me deeper and truer than the music that had preceded it.

Goodbye, Miluška, see you next Tuesday!

I CLOSED the lid of the piano and put on a new dress. It was black and white, tight fitting, with a little skirt that came down to just above the knee. The black gloves came to just above my elbow. The new sandals, white and high heeled, hurt me. So what now? I'll go to a café, I thought, or to the cinema or to visit some friends. Or I'll go dancing, and break these new sandals in! I just had to flee, to get well away from my home.

"A glass of red wine, please!"

Red wine didn't appeal to me as much as white, but I wanted the wine to be deep burgundy, so that everything would look right. On the little café table there was a small glass vase in the shape of a tube, with a blood-red rose in it.

Over the reflections of the wine on that white tablecloth, I projected mental images of yesterday's party: a few poets had read their surrealist verses . . . and on a wicker chair, a single leather glove had been left behind.

On the first chord
the dancers shook wings made of girls' arms
like moths at the first light of dawn . . .

One of the poets had been reading some of his work, and when the applause died down, he continued:

> . . . the knees,
> lean knees
> like two skulls with silky garter crowns
> from the desperate kingdom of love . . .

I stared at that leather glove. I noticed a hole in the glove, as if someone had skewered it with a knife.

All that evening I had felt stabbing pains in my index finger, as if the knife hadn't been thrust into an empty glove, but into my own flesh.

"What a surreal still life!" laughed one of the young poets who I'd met in Paris. He was trying to start up a conversation with me, about the latest tendencies in philosophy. But my finger hurt and I didn't feel like chatting.

Now I was projecting images of yesterday's party on the reflections from the wine. I ordered another glass. When I'd drunk half of it, I said to the waiter, who was flying past me, "Bring me a knife. I don't want one with a round blade. It's got to have a point and be really sharp. A knife for cutting meat!"

I took another sip of wine. With the tip of the knife I cut around the shape made by my splayed fingers on the table, my hand and my arm sheathed now in the black lace glove that reached up to above the elbow, where a kind of wainscot of white skin separated the black glove from the edge of my sleeveless dress.

I noticed that the men at all the surrounding tables were watching me.

I stuck the knifepoint into one of the spaces between my black-gloved fingers. Then into the space between the fingers next to it. I repeated this again, and yet again. Several men tensely got up from their chairs and stood, stock-still, as if they were all set to rush to my assistance. I sped up the stabbing. The knifepoint jabbed the wood of the table, again and again. Several pairs of eyes hung in the air, motionless, alert . . .

What beautiful evenings,
when the city looked like a clock, a kiss, a kite
or a sunflower, bending . . .

I was singing the poems from yesterday's surrealist party as I played with the knife, which was flying through my fingers. Its point scraped my ring finger. No matter. Then it cut my thumb. I didn't care. More and more men were jumping out of their seats. Once they were up, they didn't move. Drops of blood were filtering out through the black lace of my gloves. I increased the pace, singing . . .

What beautiful Sundays,
when the city looks like a ball, a letter, a mandolin
or a bell clanging
in the sunny street
the shadows of the pedestrians were kissing each other
and people went on their way strange and anonymous . . .

A man came up to me, without daring to interrupt my game. I didn't see him. I sensed he was there, but I was concentrating on the knife that was thrusting itself between my fingers all on its own. My black gloves were now embroidered with blood. Silence reigned in the Café Louvre that evening, though it was chock-full.

Suddenly everything around me started to dilute, then vanish into the heavy fog that thickened the more I sunk into it.

I CAME to in my bed at home. Somebody was bandaging my fingers and a male voice said with a drawn-out, sing-song foreign accent: "Wine and blood, and the virgin point, black though it is with desire, everything under a pink flag . . . You will fall in love with someone, you foreign beauty, and then you will kill your beloved, or you will send him to death or to the auto-da-fé, convinced it is the best thing for you both"

The song melted into the night.

My grandmother was sitting next to my bed when I woke up.

So my nocturnal adventure had been a hallucination, a dream fashioned from that recent surrealist party, I reasoned.

But . . . under my bed sheet, unmoving, lay my left hand, disfigured by thick, white, bloodstained bandages.

ABOUT A month after I'd played with the knife, I was coming back one night from a party at the home of some friends, who were distinguished architects. The sky was becoming light, I was humming softly as I walked, a little unsteadily. I stopped in front of my house to look for my keys. Then a man stepped out of the house opposite—I wasn't expecting that, and it startled me. The man's hair was long and unkempt, and he wore an unironed shirt that flapped wildly about him. He was dragging along some packages, or rather enormous bundles, the kind that Gypsies or farmworkers carry with them. He was walking slowly; the bundles were heavy. Although it was warm, the man was trembling. I don't know why I was reminded of the ill-treated horse of my childhood.

I found my keys and went in, banging the beech-wood door shut. Then suddenly, I realized: that man was my neighbor. Yes, he was the one I'd seen at the window opposite. I'd never seen him properly, and besides, he'd always been with his wife. That man was leaving for good, I knew it. I don't know why, I had the feeling he was leaving me as well.

A few weeks later, a short-haired gentleman with sunglasses appeared at the window opposite. He was kissing my female neighbor's bare back.

But with the dances and the dinner parties hosted by Prague's intellectual elite, I soon forgot the man with the bundles, and the woman at the window.

"WAITER, BRING me a glass of white wine, please!"

After having placed the book I'd brought—Dostoevsky's *The Idiot*—on the café table, I lit a cigarette.

A few steps away, next to the window of the Café Louvre, a man with a shabby briefcase in one hand was observing the café as if searching for someone in particular. He looks familiar, I thought, but I couldn't recall where I'd met him. Probably at some party or other. When he caught my gaze, I blew out cigarette smoke.

"At last!" he said, as if we'd had an appointment.

I took a sip from the glass the waiter had brought and quickly paid the bill before the man could beat me to it.

He'd sat down opposite me, having put his briefcase on the floor, and was now watching me in silence. I pretended to read my novel. I thought about how all the men I'd ever met had tried to start conversations. This one remained silent and looked at me with curious eyes.

I drank quickly, wanting to leave. The wine went to my head.

The man picked my glass up by its stem and took a sip. I looked at him, surprised and offended.

"I'm sorry if I've bothered you in any way," he said.

I didn't say a word. After a pause, he said, as if to himself, "An elegant woman reading Dostoevsky's *The Idiot* . . . that's something you hardly ever get to see."

He had a bass voice, like an opera singer's, and spoke with a strong foreign accent. All the same, the implied judgement in what he had said made me look at him disapprovingly. But he paid that no mind and went on. This time he addressed himself directly to me, "It's quite a coincidence you are reading Dostoevsky's *The Idiot* because the other day somebody showed me a reproduction of a Holbein painting of a dead Christ taken down from the cross. Dostoevsky must have seen that painting, and been so impressed by this painting that he wrote some reflections on it in *The Idiot*."

"I haven't reached that part yet," I said apologetically.

"With reference to that image of Christ, Dostoevsky says that after seeing the painting a believer could lose his faith."

"Why?" I asked.

"I've asked myself the same question. Dostoevsky doesn't explain why. Later, when I was able to look carefully at the painting, I understood: the dead Christ is more human than divine, in fact Christ is simply a man steeped in misery, shorn of his hopes and aspirations, without questions or doubts. He is bereft of any kind of greatness, even the greatness conferred by freedom. He is a man lonelier than the Christ in Haydn's *The Seven Last Words*, who is afforded the ultimate consolation of tragedy. Holbein's painting is neither a majestic tragedy nor a pleasant drama in *adagio e cantabile*, but an absolute vacuum. Holbein's Christ is a man stripped of all attributes save that of insignificance. It is as if the painter were telling the spectator: this is you. Then the spectator will become aware of his own terrestrial misery, so far away from the solemnity of the divine. He might lose his faith: his god has died when what he needed was an immortal god."

My companion picked up the book and leafed through it for a while. After a silence, which to me seemed long, he said happily, "We shall now have dinner."

"I haven't got time for dinner," I answered sharply.

I didn't know why he looked at me with such alarm. You could read his eyes like a book. Like the eyes in the stable at my parents' home.

He got up and helped me up from my seat.

"I'm going home," I said, as sharply as before.

"Fine, fine." He drew out the vowels.

He walked me along the streets of the Old Town. We came up to the riverside docks.

"Here, please do go in."

He leaned back against the wall to let me pass. In that dark street, his face was a shadowy chamber with two windows behind which stretched a green, transparent sea, lit up by the rays of the sun.

He took me by the elbow and led me into a small basement restaurant with a gothic arch. The place was full, I noticed with relief, but the restaurant's owner seemed to know my companion and managed to fit a little table for two from somewhere, covered by a white tablecloth.

"I'll stay, but only for a little bit," I said.

The owner placed a bottle of red wine between us, followed by a huge portion of roasted meat and mountains of rice garnished with fresh parsley.

I noticed that this good-looking man, so different from the glasses-wearing intellectuals with their pale, weak faces, ate in the most exquisite fashion.

He held the ends of his cutlery in his long fingers; slowly, he cut away little pieces of meat, placing them in his mouth like a swallow feeding its young. When he raised his hands they seemed no more than the wings of a bird. He ate slowly, with pleasure, but his main concern was for my own comfort. He was aware of every move I made, he served me wine and water. He got up to help me sit more comfortably. He served me pieces of meat, and lettuce leaves, and did all this with the utmost discretion.

"You are a Polish prince."

"No."

"A Hungarian duke, then."

"No."

"Then you must be a count."

"No."

"But you *are* an aristocrat."

"No."

"I have noble origins and I can detect them in others."

"In Russia, there has been a revolution."

He made his hands fly up then let them fall, sliding, down to his sides. Russia . . . the revolution . . . an explosion . . . chaos . . . many things destroyed. It was a simple, clear, eloquent gesture. And beautiful. An expressive watercolor sketched with only a couple of brushstrokes.

"Your father was a prince, then?"

By way of reply, his hands flew up again, only to fall straight back down again, like the broken wings of a swan. It occurred to me that I shouldn't be asking this sort of thing.

Should I never again ask then? Did I imagine there was supposed to be some kind of a future for us?

"His name was Ivan," said my companion, "So mine is Ivanovich."

"Ivanovich, that sounds like it came out of some Russian folktale."

"My childhood was a bit like a Russian folktale. My parents took me to the churches. To the Russian Orthodox churches."

"To pray there, I suppose. I know about all that! The saints, God!"

"God, yes, expressed as beauty. And beauty expressed as God. My parents took me once a week. It was there that I discovered true beauty. Spiritual fathers with endless white beards in black tunics that reached all the way to the floor. They spoke the words of the mass in low, melodic voices. When I came out of the church, I found myself in the middle of a stunning white silence, the silence of endless Russian solitude, blinded as I was by the icy sun, by snow and ice."

I took large sips of the country wine from Mělník, my companion served me some more rice. After having spoken about the icy solitude of Russia, he fell into a long silence; he was clearly in a world of his own. Bit by bit, this enigmatic foreigner's silence, his absence from my world, started to bother me.

"Mr. Ivanovich, do you have no intention of asking me who I am?"

"No. I know who you are. You are Venus, born out of silence."

His words affected me deeply. I'd never heard anyone speak like that. Perhaps words that were similar, but none said in this way. The men in the intellectual circles that I frequented, invented poetic metaphors and hurled them into women's laps as if they were bouquets of violets. But they did so because they were enamored of their own cleverness. When they addressed a woman, deep down they were really only talking to themselves. Yet this man spoke in such a simple, frank manner, and his words were addressed directly to me.

He excused himself and went over to the owner of the restaurant. They argued for quite a while. The owner shook his head obstinately: no, absolutely not. My companion pointed to the paintings on the walls; his eyes shone as he did so. I realized that those paintings were made by him.

At first glance they seemed abstract. A chaos of colors and shapes. But looking more closely, I could see there was a hidden order and harmony to them. I could see the leaves and branches of a forest in them, in purple and violet and mauve and blue, and I could make out the roots of the trees, the moss and earth-colored stems. These paintings were not done merely by the painter's hand, but by his inner self. An inner self that was, no doubt, chaotic and turbulent and tempestuous, but also, ultimately, idealistic and pensive, searching for its center. All this ran through my mind in a fraction of a second and I can't say for sure that I was right. But those paintings transmitted strong anguish, and a need to find refuge in a world other than the real one.

The restaurant's owner, a young man, continued shaking his head. No, no, and again no. My companion lowered his eyes. On my way to the bathroom, I took a hundred crown note from my bag, and slipped it discreetly into the restauranteur's hand. I gave him a look that indicated he shouldn't let on. He gave me a look that meant OK, and patted my companion on the back, saying, "OK, Andrei! It's a deal, you old rogue, but my restaurant will go to the dogs thanks to you!"

When I returned from the bathroom—I'd been about to refresh the coral color on my lips, but this time the habit struck me as useless, unnecessary—Andrei was waiting for me with my black coat in his hand. He helped me to put it on.

Outside, it was raining. The drops wet my face and filled me with joy. On Charles Bridge we broke into a run. It was raining cats and dogs. We stopped, breathless, halfway across the bridge. We were alone. We looked for our saints. I wanted mine to be serene and sensible. Andrei chose weirder, more eccentric saints, whose arms were pointing up at the sky.

Suddenly, he got up onto the paving that lined the bridge

and froze into the same position in which the saint he had chosen was twisted.

I was dumbfounded.

In the end, I said, inadvertently, "Get down, don't do this to me!"

"'Don't do this to me,'" he repeated enthusiastically as he got down, "It's a beautiful language that allows one to express oneself so. Fantastic!"

The rain had turned to a drizzle. I felt exhausted, as if I hadn't slept for a week.

"I'm going to bed."

We crossed the bridge, tired. We stopped to look at the reflection of the strange lights on Petřín Mountain in the Vltava River.

"Where do you live?" I asked him.

The man stood in front of the statue of a baroque saint, his fingers opened wide, his belly sticking out, and his head leaning coquettishly to one side.

I was busy looking at a luminous dot on the waves of the flowing river. That's my star, I thought.

"Where do you live?" I repeated, insistently, weary, "I mean in Prague. You must live somewhere, surely?"

He looked at me, suddenly silent.

I got irritated.

"Tell me where you live!"

The man was trembling a little.

"Do you want me to leave?" he said.

"I want to know where you live, that's all!"

"A long, long way away."

"Where?"

"Do you want me to leave?"

"Shut up and follow me," I said, sternly.

He gave me a frightened look.

Maybe he hadn't understood. I turned my back to him and repeated the order. My tone sounded positively military.

I don't know what was happening to me. Was I enjoying playing games with this man's evident fear?

He watched me with his eyes wide open.

I was enjoying this game more and more.

The man was blinking fast, an anguished expression on his face. I felt like a general.

"I'm a general," I shouted at the man. I had entered completely into the spirit of the game.

He shut his eyes as if he were about to be hit. Even in the half-light, I could see he'd gone pale.

"I am a harsh, cruel officer," I was walking noisily along the bridge's pavement.

The man didn't dare breathe. His fear spurred me on.

"Let's march," I shouted at the top of my lungs, "March, and keep your mouth shut!"

I marched a few steps ahead.

I heard a muffled cry, like that of a wounded seagull.

I turned around.

The man was leaning on the edge of the bridge. He looked at me, his eyes filled with horror.

A moment later, he turned and disappeared into the mist.

Again, I heard that cry like a wounded seagull.

I don't know how long I stayed there, staring out at the night and trembling. After a long while, at the edge of the bridge I found the briefcase, left behind by that man who had just lost himself in the darkness.

THE FOLLOWING day I went to the Café Louvre. I found a friend there, who was celebrating a new role she'd just landed at the National Theater. She couldn't stop exclaiming, "I'm going to play Nora!" and sent a glass of champagne over to my table.

The day after, I put on a pink jersey and woolen skirt of the same color. To read, I brought poems by Nezval and Seifert to the Café Louvre, of course. I smoked an entire pack of cigarettes. When mine were finished, men at neighboring tables offered me theirs.

On the fourth day I told myself that I wouldn't go back to the Café Louvre for at least a week, and went to the theater to see my friend play Nora.

On the fifth day, I attended a dinner thrown by a well-known journalist and translator. People there were talking about the short stories of a Czech writer in German, one by the name of František or Franz or Frank Kavka or Kafka. An actor read a few out loud, from the German original. It sank in: Odradek, that's me all over.

On the sixth day I couldn't stand it any more and went to the Café Louvre for a drink. To avoid staring obsessively at the door, I read the text hanging on the wall in a red wood frame:

> Got problems that seem unbearable? Go to the café!
> He's stood you up and you feel like hell? Go to the café!
> Shoes worn out? Go to the café!
> Always scrimping and saving and never treat yourself? Off
>   to the café!
> None of the men you know cut the mustard? To the café!
> About to kill yourself? To the café!
> Hate and despise people, even though you can't live without
>   them? To the café!
> Got debts here, there, and everywhere? To the café!

On the seventh day I thought: Do you long for something and not yet know what it is? To the café!

On the eighth day Miluška and five other students turned up. In the afternoon, I was having tea with my mother and Mr. Singer, and I realized that the two of them saw each other every day.

At midnight I couldn't resist it anymore.

The briefcase contained a few coins, a pencil, a white hand-kerchief, clean and ironed, and a little pad full of drawings and addresses and phone numbers. It also contained a train ticket to a far-off city in the mountains, and another to a village the name of which meant absolutely nothing to me. And one thing more: a small package wrapped in a white napkin and tied with light blue ribbon.

You can't do this! I said to myself, you're sticking your nose into another person's private life. I unwrapped the package: it contained a black piece of cloth. I spread the cloth out on the bed. Before me was a long, black lace glove; there were dark stains like clay on the fingers: dried blood.

I STEPPED off the bus that brought me to the skirts of the high mountains, carrying that leather briefcase worn by time and use. Two elderly ladies with black scarves on their heads, after recovering from the distaste my presence had evidently caused them, gave me the directions I needed.

The sky was very low, drops of humidity were forming pearls in the air.

An ancient carriage was coming down the unpaved mountain path, heading straight for me. Next to it walked a Gypsy patriarch wearing a black hat, and behind him two elderly Gypsy women were swaying along. One of them wore a purple scarf around her head, the other one's scarf was electric blue; they didn't try to hide their curiosity as they stared at me. When they came close, the carriage stopped and they asked me in harsh, foreign Czech what I was up to in this area where many of the people born here had left because there was nothing left but hatred. The Czechs against Germans, the Germans against Czechs, or of both Czechs and Germans against the Gypsies. I mentioned Andrei's name. They looked at each other. One of the women shrugged and pulled the blue scarf from her face, saying, "Oh! Oh!"

I stared first at one and then the other, visibly perplexed. The Gypsy woman with the purple scarf said, "Do you really have to go there? Are you sure you can't give it a miss? Had any children by him, have you maybe?"

I blushed.

The Gypsy man waved from the old carriage, full of boxes and bundles and sacks and paper cones. I noticed that on top of that pile of bundles, there sat a violin and a kind of puffed out mandolin.

The blue Gypsy woman repeated her guttural "Oh! Oh!" again.

The purple Gypsy woman gave me a long farewell wave and said, "He's a good man."

And the Gypsy man hissed, "You be careful!"

They left, following a turn in the road and waving and nodding goodbye. The carriage swayed and the Gypsy women headed down to the valley, moving like dancers.

He's a good man. Be careful. These words echoed in my head.

Then three woodcutters passed by; they also looked askance at me, the intruder.

Then a farmworker, whose trousers were covered in patches, overtook me on the path. He was leading a goat by a piece of string. He shot me a venomous look before disappearing around a bend.

Next a tall, blonde man came down from the mountain. He

suddenly abandoned his cart in the middle of the road and ran toward me.

"Venus born out of silence!"

He hugged me as if we'd known each other all our lives. In silence I handed him his briefcase; he made a gesture as if to say forget it, the same gesture the Gypsy patriarch had made a moment ago, as if to say that I shouldn't have come such a long way to bring it to him. He took me by the elbow, the way he'd guided me through the streets of the Old Town that night in Prague.

He showed me the bushes and trees of the area, and invented new names for each and every one of them.

He showed me the tumbledown house where he lived.

It started to rain. He thought it an ideal moment to take me for a walk in the surrounding countryside. The forest was steeped in the odor of that pouring icy rain. When the rain started to come down in thick curtains, we hid ourselves away in a cave that Andrei knew as well as he had known that underground restaurant in Prague. He spoke about the stones, he picked them up and showed them to me, and I could see clearly the paintings hanging on the walls of that Prague tavern. We sat down on a wide stone. My fingers slid over the wall of the cave as we looked out at the forest that the frozen rain had dressed in cut glass.

Andrei, in a voice from another planet, said, "Let us think no more of the glory and shame of the world. We have everything!"

Yes, we had everything we could have wished for then. We said nothing. In that silence, our closeness grew and grew.

Andrei asked in a soft voice, "Perhaps you're hungry?"

Without waiting for a reply, he took out of his pocket a piece of bread wrapped in a handkerchief. With those long, fine, white fingers he broke it in half and gave me the bigger piece.

His eyes sparkled when he saw how hungry I was. When I'd

finished my piece of bread, he carefully put the crumbs that had fallen from his own piece into my mouth, slowly, one by one. He caressed my lips with the tips of his fingers as he did so. When we'd finished, we drank from the icy brook that came down from the high mountains. That sip of water filled my body with a deep cold, and my spirit, with peace and freedom.

"Would you like to stay with me? Stay! Please, stay!" he repeated, like a child begging for a toy.

I wanted to stay, he knew that.

"I'm going to look for the bus," I said as I watched a white cloud against the background of the darkened sky.

Andrei followed my gaze.

"That cloud is like human life, ever changing, fleeting, and free."

I forgot the whole world. I waited for Andrei to ask me to stay, again. I had the words "Yes, I'll stay" on the tip of my tongue.

"I'll take you to the bus stop," he said. His voice was full of sadness.

After a short silence he said, "Time grips the curves of the mountains, deep and untameable."

Under the chains of rain we reached a wooden shack: the bus stop.

"Goodbye."

Why was he saying goodbye to me? I wanted him to stay with me.

"Goodbye," he repeated, and we shook hands.

No. Andrei, the mountain man who sometimes talked as if he lived in a world other than this one, didn't understand that I didn't mean what I had said; I wanted to stay.

A moment passed. He said, in a low voice, "Look, the dark pools reflect the mountains, and above them floats the cloudy sky. You, the woman born in silence, are leaving, and everything will be the way it always has been. Yet there are so many things I would like to tell you. You are leaving, and if we meet again some other day, amid the darkness of the clouds, I know that you'll listen to me. I know it."

And he walked slowly away through the pearly rain.

HE SPOKE and behaved differently than most people. But here in the middle of nature, I didn't find it odd. The wind made the mountains and the forests echo, and the twilight air, lit by the shine of the rain, felt fresh against my cheeks and plunged me into a state of nostalgia.

"Sylva," Andrei said, standing in front of me once again, "why do people go to sleep just now? And why would you leave now when the rainy evening is full of such sad beauty?"

"I'm glad you came back here, Andrei."

"There was something I forgot to tell you. Do you recognize this?" He started to recite something in Russian, softly, taking long pauses during which I had the feeling it was silence itself that was speaking the lines. I listened more to the melancholy of his Russian than to the actual meaning of the words. The poem was something about snow, prison, a bell.

Mountains surround the jail. As does an ocean of snow.
The blanket is as cold as iron.
The dream has turned to ash.
All the same, not everything can be chained down:
From where do the peals of that bell come?

After a long while, I asked, "Where did they come from, Andrei?"

He said nothing.

The downpour was thick. The wind stirred yellow and green leaves into the rain.

A pinecone fell onto the roof of the shack. It shook Andrei out of his thoughts.

"I served in the Red Army. In the cavalry, you know." He was narrating this slowly, reflectively, remembering.

If I had paid careful attention to what he was saying, I would have realized that those events were of the utmost importance to him. But the only voice I was listening to right then was that of my own curiosity. The revolution, the war . . . What did war mean to me? War is death. With my lack of experience, it didn't occur to me that for someone else, war, imprisonment, and death could be closely linked to life.

"And what was there before? I mean before the Russian War?" I asked.

"Nothing. A vacuum."

"The life of a young aristocrat is a vacuum?" I laughed.

"Look at that stream," he said, changing the subject.

Why did he always change the subject? Why did he avoid talking about his past?

"What do you see there?" he asked.

"Stones and water," I answered.

"Yes. The stones last, but the water flows, the stones are silent, but the water makes a sound. Where is it heading?"

"I don't know."

"Toward the distant sky, I think," Andrei said, following the direction of the stream.

"What kind of life would a young aristocrat have led, in the Russia of the czars?" I grimaced.

"When I was little, I longed for Sunday to roll along, when my parents would take me to church. Long Orthodox masses, enigmatic and emotive, full of liturgical chanting, the light given off by the candles, and the gold on the walls, and full, too, of the lively colors of the painted icons, the strong smell of incense, full of half shadows and mystery."

"And after that kind of childhood?"

"My parents' palazzo overlooking the Fontanka canal, and in the summers, a chateau in Repino. After that the Academy of Fine Arts in Saint Petersburg, and then the Berlin Academy of Arts, and when that was over, back to the Saint Petersburg Academy."

"What did you learn there?"

"In Berlin, I discovered the art of the oldest civilizations in the world. I learned how to admire the sculpture of the ancient Sumerians. The Sumerian ruler Gudea, who lived roughly two thousand two hundred years before Christ, was a whole revelation to me: he seemed to me to be the personification of spiritual beauty as I'd known it when I was little, in Russia."

He stopped and said nothing: he was mulling something over.

"The Red Army. The cavalry division," he said after a while, in a serious voice.

"Tell me how a young aristocrat and a refined artist from Saint Petersburg ended up with the Bolsheviks in the Red Army."

"That is easy enough to explain: I believed in the ideals of the Bolshevik Revolution," said Andrei, without a trace of irony. His eyes were fixed on the darkness of the forest.

I longed to continue teasing him, but was starting to listen to something inside me, "I too, a long time ago, believed in—"

"I wanted to help the revolution. I volunteered for the Red Army." Andrei cut me off.

I was happy now, because I could identify with that; I, too, had wanted to help the world, when I was with the nuns in the convent.

"Of course, just as I did, living with the nuns in the convent!"

"It would be easier to flatten these mountains and dry out the stream from which we've drunk than to satisfy the hearts of men," he said, very quietly.

He ran his long fingers over his forehead. Looking at his white hands, I tried to imagine how that young and refined aristocrat must have felt in combat, he who had been used to hunting for sport and the museums of Berlin.

"You were already an experienced rider, that must have been an advantage," I smiled at my image of a slim, elegant horseman, riding through the parks that belonged to the summer palaces of Peter the Great.

Andrei was lost in thought. He hadn't heard me.

"The wind fills the vacuum of the mountains," he said finally.

"How did an intellectual from the nobility go about joining the revolution?"

"In the cavalry regiment?" Andrei paid no heed to my irony, he continued seriously, forthrightly. "We Reds were waging war against the Whites, then I found myself in the middle of a large group of Cossacks. They knew how to do just about everything: kill a sheep for supper, skin it and disembowel it, roast it. They practically flew along on horseback, like Ilya Muromets, like mythical heroes. At the beginning, for me, a city intellectual, a Cossack was like a fairytale firebird, beautiful and all-powerful. The Cossacks knew how to seduce women, how to sing and dance. They knew how to carry their guns as if they were leading beautiful ladies off to dance a polonaise in a ballroom. They knew how to kill: they knew how to kill sheep, hares, goats. And ultimately men."

"Have you known death?" I asked, sighing.

He didn't hear me. The colors of the autumn were playing a nostalgic melody.

"Have you known death?" I asked again. "I have," I said with a sigh. We were back on a subject I knew something about.

The wind was combing the thick branches of the fir and pine trees. The mountain range shifted in the distance and melted into the horizon.

"One day my commander ordered me to follow him. We rode for over fifty versts and caught up with the Thirty-Third Division in a small Ukrainian village. My commander knew as well as I did that the soldiers of the Thirty-Third Division, who were almost all Cossacks, traveled everywhere completely drunk, and wherever they arrived they ransacked the village and rumor had it, murdered all the inhabitants. My commander burst into a house that was low to the ground; I followed him in. A wounded man was moaning on a bed. He was Jewish—those Ukrainian villages were almost all Jewish. In a corner, a woman was sobbing and covered in blood. They'd raped her. On the floor I saw a dozen corpses. And in the middle of all this, two of our own soldiers from the Red Army, and a nurse, were filling sacks and trunks and washtubs and boxes, whatever they could, with the belongings of these dying people."

"What happened to the two soldiers and the nurse?"

"The commander shot dead the Cossacks who were ransacking that house. The nurse fell on her knees before him pleading for mercy, not for herself, but for her children. The commander let her live. He got out of there as fast as he could, with a bunch of drunken Cossacks at his heels. I stayed behind. During the attack on that house, our soldiers, some of whom were after my commander, broke into the other rooms. In one, a Jewish family squeezed into a dark corner, trying to hide there. They pulled a man out of that group. They told me to finish him off. The man trembled like a leaf; he was short, stout, a typical family man with big eyes behind metal-framed glasses. I could see nothing else except those eyes full of terror."

Andrei fell silent. I didn't take my eyes off him. "That little man trembling with fear said, 'Kill me, but spare my wife. Sir, I beg of you to make sure that nothing happens to her, but shoot me dead right now,' and he pointed to his chest."

"And then?" I asked softly.

"I didn't kill him. I couldn't. But I saw the pogrom that they launched afterward."

"They?"

"They, the Red Army. Our people. The Cossacks. I saw the whole thing. Everything."

"And then?" I asked after a long stretch of silence.

Andrei said nothing.

The bus came and left.

Eyes full of terror. I knew them. In that instant, I saw them again in Andrei's face.

The heavy rain didn't let up, but I could see in the distance a single white cloud against the dark sky.

"Then? After many other similar massacres I fled from the Red Army. I hid in the forest. I became familiar with its secrets. But I couldn't stay there forever, so in the end I joined the White Army."

"The Whites believed you were sincere?"

"The same evening I turned up, the Whites had condemned a young boy to death. A deserter, like I'd been. That boy was full of panic. They led him over to a tree, and tied him to it. He kept begging for mercy. He talked about his mother, who had no one else in the world but him. He was crying so much, sobbing like a little child. They killed him anyway; five men shot him dead."

"And you? What happened to you?"

"In the beginning, the Whites wouldn't trust me. Then, when they saw I was ... "

"That you were what?"

"After that they did what they could to be rid of me."

"That you were what?" I repeated.

"Eventually I also managed to flee from the Whites. I made it to Prague, where Masaryk's government gave me a grant as part of the Czechoslovak government aid program to support exiled Russian intelligentsia."

"So you lived in Prague!"

It had stopped raining, we stepped out of the hut. Behind Andrei's head, over the dip in the hills, a bright cloud flew. Andrei turned and followed my gaze.

"That white cloud, free as it is, is pushing the wind," he said.

He turned up his coat collar, then did the same with mine. He smiled.

"Yes, it was in Prague that I discovered my Venus born of the rain. And of music. You played the piano and sang. I watched you through a curtain of rain."

His face was soaked by the wetness in the air. Two rows of mountains protected Andrei from the outside world.

Stepping away from me, he said something that surprised me. At that moment I remembered the Gypsy woman in blue, who could only say, "Oh! Oh!"

Andrei said, "I pray to the god of the mountains that he carry away all sadness. And that he fill us with warmth to dry out all the evil and pain in the world."

"A god who fled Prague for the mountains." I tried to smile when Andrei came back to where I was standing.

I tried to fill him with light, just as he wished. But above all I wanted to get rid of that image of the woman at the window, the neighbor opposite, who until recently had cried and laughed standing next to this very man. Now I knew why Andrei's face was so familiar to me.

"How do you know I ran away?" Andrei was stunned. "Who told you?" he roared.

This change of behavior frightened me.

"Have you been spying on me?" Andrei asked, beside himself.

I remained silent, scared.

I didn't understand the sudden change in this man. His face had gone dry and white.

"What are you, an informer?" he went on howling.

"Are you a spy? Always on the lookout for me?" Andrei bellowed.

I stepped away from him. The Gypsy's words ran through my head, "You be careful!"

"Have I got it right, then? Were you running away from something when you came here?" I made an effort to smile.

Andrei himself was shaking.

"Tell me everything, Andrei, if you want to," I whispered to calm him down, "I'd like to hear it, your story really does interest me."

Another transformation took place. Now, Andrei watched me the way the horse from my childhood looked at the carter.

I took his hand. At first he flinched, then he gradually quieted.

Once he had calmed himself, he stroked my hand, so delicately it was as if he weren't touching a human hand, but rather the white fluff of a dandelion.

His gaze fixed on the distant peaks. He said, "These mountains are black without their knowing it, the night is gray but doesn't realize it. And I, unthinkingly, am tottering through the empty darkness. My soul follows, flying, at a distance."

After a moment, he said, "Did I run away? I walked along a Prague street until I reached the city limits; then I walked along a very long road. At the feet of the mountains I found an unpaved path that led me here. Is that running away?"

He flinched again, jerked his fingers out of my hand, and sprang to his feet. He kicked at a stone.

"So now you are going to report me, to tell them everything!"

I remembered my "That's enough!" that had such a strong effect on my husband, all that time ago. With him, it had been like a magic word.

"That's enough!" I shouted.

Andrei stood stock-still.

"Enough! I'm fed up with all of this!" I was letting off accumulated steam.

With a long, pained howl, Andrei vanished into the forest.

I set off after him. The trees calmed me. In the forest, the rain only whispered. Nothing broke the silence, no footsteps, no sighs. Only the song of the rain, sliding through the branches.

I pushed myself forward through the wet forest, bumping into the tree trunks. Trees stay stiff and upright, I thought, they don't dither the way people do, who twist about, deform themselves, make contortions. The rain caressed my face and hair. It was almost dark by now. Nothing stirred. The only thing I heard was another bus, arriving and then departing.

IN THE street, the snow was mixing with rain. It was Christmas.

I was watching the window of the woman who lived across the street; the candles were flickering on the Christmas tree. A bald man with a thin line of a mustache, like a bank clerk's, was having dinner with her. Yes, maybe my neighbor's new friend was nothing but a clerk, but she had a Christmas tree in her home, and the atmosphere was warm, cozy, and gay. My neighbor and the man with the thin line of a mustache were keeping each other company. Although I had company for the holiday, I was alone.

"Now that your grandmother is dead," my mother mentioned this fact—which I found so difficult to accept—so casually, so without sentimentality, "we will celebrate our Christmas dinner at your home, Sylva, and we will decorate the tree here too."

Mr. Singer, the father of one of my students, and my mother's new husband, gave a discreet yawn. Not a single move made by Bruno Singer escaped my mother's notice. She straightened up fast as a cat.

"Bruno would prefer to celebrate Hanukkah. Wouldn't you, Bruno?" I said jokingly, although I knew that my mother's husband didn't celebrate the Jewish holidays.

Bruno Singer stroked his thick, shiny, chestnut mustache.

"You know perfectly well, Sylva, that I am an atheist."

I poured more tea into the old, Chinese porcelain cups.

"A good thing Grandma can't hear you," I said, as if Grandmother were in the next room.

"Your grandmother has not lived to see these terrible times," sighed Bruno Singer as he picked up his cup by the handle. As he moved I could see how much thinner he'd become. I remembered just how astonished he'd been, a few years ago, at the change he saw in me after my husband's death.

At that time I could only think of the past: it had become an obsession of mine. Bruno Singer, on the other hand, only had eyes for the future. It scared him. Would his Jewish firm withstand the Nazis' lack of self-restraint? I looked out at the street and at my neighbor's window through the slush. Her Christmas tree was glowing.

BRUNO SINGER went pale. Who was that knocking at the door? Since the Germans—the ones from Germany, of course, but also our Germans, the ones who until recently had formed part of our own country—had begun shouting hostile slogans in the streets and raising their right arms while they slammed their military boots to the ground, and clenched their teeth in puffed-up expressions of disdain and proud violence, since then anything at all would send Bruno Singer into paroxysms of fear.

The knocking at the door grew louder and louder. My mother took her husband's hand. I quickly went to answer it.

On the landing in front of the door, Andrei leaned against the wall. I hadn't seen him in a long while.

I hastened to put my mother and Bruno's fears to rest. With a wave of my hand, I told them I had a visitor, that there was no cause for concern.

I introduced Andrei to my mother and her husband. They looked at him, surprised. There they were, both with cigarettes in holders, their shoes shined to perfection, shoes with square toe caps, in accordance with the latest fashion, both of them were wearing French colognes. They stared at this bearded stranger who had come down from the mountains as if he were a genie that had just popped out of its lamp.

I asked my mother to accompany me to my room. There I told her that I needed time alone with Andrei. I suggested that he and I could take a stroll around the neighborhood, and that she and Bruno could finish their tea undisturbed.

She bowed her head. In a very low voice, she replied, "There's going to be a war. I can smell it in the air. I've already been through one and I know how the atmosphere grows saturated with war fever. Sylva, during war, you come to realize what is most important to you: your children. The lives of your children are the most important, more important than your own life."

Maman went on talking. Her words sounded something like the litanies recited by the nuns of my childhood. I didn't listen to what she was saying, I knew she was having a go at my relationship with Andrei.

ON KAMPA Island, Andrei was chasing after the falling snowflakes.

"Why have you come? What did you want to say to me?" I asked.

"I'm here with you. Isn't that enough? Do we need words?"

"What did you want to talk about? I'd like to know."

"I haven't seen you in a long while."

"Just tell me, don't keep me in suspense!"

"I haven't seen you in a long, long while."

From the Bridge of Legions we walked down to Hunters' Island. We went right across it, then circled to Kampa Island. I remembered when my husband and I sometimes had dinner on Hunters' Island and that during the meal we had listened to a quartet playing Dvořák. That kind of dinner struck me as being impossible these days.

The snowflakes drew thousands of milky ways against the darkened sky.

"Is your father Jewish?" Andrei asked me.

"He's my mother's second husband. My father is dead. Bruno Singer is Jewish, yes."

"As was my wife."

I didn't say anything. The snowflakes had ceased their dancing and now fell lazily to the ground, heavy and lethargic. In the midst of the snow I imagined a young, dark-haired woman arm in arm with Andrei, coming home from a concert; it was snowing softly, the night was brilliant and icy, yet the girl wore her ermine coat open so that her long pearl necklace glimmered in the golden brightness of the streetlamps.

"She died in my arms," Andrei said.

I leaned on the bridge railing. As if on a huge movie screen, the dark-haired girl's face unfolded before me, pale and intelligent even as she died. This evening is ruined, I thought.

"Was that long ago?" I asked, not really interested in the answer.

"She died in my arms. With her dying breath she asked me never to forget to recite her Kaddish. And I haven't been able to do that," Andrei said quietly, "That was seventeen, maybe sixteen years ago. And I haven't recited her Kaddish in a very long time. She died in my arms," he repeated, as if talking to someone who couldn't hear him.

I didn't say anything.

Andrei went on, "The Reds hated the Jews, the Whites didn't care for them either, and the Czechs . . ."

"Czechs and Jews live together in peace!" I said, defensively.

"Maybe. But the Czechs hold a grudge against the Germans."

"Does that surprise you? They're taking over our country!"

"That animosity already existed, I saw it on the mountain where I live."

In the fragile, naked, black branches of the island's park, I saw Bruno Singer's face, distorted by a grimace of fear. And I saw my mother's hands clasped together: What would happen to her Bruno? What would happen to me?

"No!" I shouted, fighting off the embrace of Andrei's black anguish, "No! You're a very strange man, Andrei! You see everything in the worst possible light, please go!"

I saw lightning bolts in his eyes. Andrei leaped onto the edge of the bridge. He took hold of a streetlamp and knocked his skull against it. There's impotence for you, I thought.

"I see everything in the worst possible light?" Andrei said, hoarsely, "But everything is terrible, horrifying! Everything is truly hellish!"

"What is it that's so bad?"

"This world! What else? This whole world!"

The figure standing on the balustrade of the bridge turned to face the river.

"If even you can't understand me, then who—"

"Andrei, please, forgive me! Come down here, I beg you."

There wasn't a soul in sight. Just the snowflakes and the mist.

When, after quite a while he raised his head, I realized that the clouds had broken. The stars were shining light on our desperation.

Andrei was calming down. He sat on the balustrade, one leg in, the other out. The mad song of the massacre had stopped ringing in his ears. But can anyone who has heard it once, ever forget it? When he spoke his words came out weighted with pain.

"Do you remember I told you the story of that day during the Russian Civil War? When the Cossacks tried to make me help them ransack the houses? I refused. One of them told me: 'For centuries these cursed Jewish landowners have exploited us and grown fat and rich at our expense. Now it's our turn! Comrade Lenin tells us to steal from he who has stolen from you! All the revolutionary leaders teach us to hate the class enemy and to seek revenge against him.'"

I thought that all revolutions were spawned by hatred. What else could they lead to if not more hatred and violence?

"In one house, I could hear weeping. I rushed over. Three of the Cossacks jumped on me then and one of them threatened me. 'Are you wet behind the ears, you idiot? Who do you think you were about to help, you young fool? The enemy of the revolution! The kulaks! The Jews! Not one step more, if you don't want me to smash your face in, you snake!'

"But I could still hear that weeping, those screams. I wanted to go in and find out what had happened.

'Damn it!' another Cossack yelled at me, 'Here's what you

wanted. Don't go telling anyone, you scheming bastard!'

"He opened the door of the house with a key and pushed me inside. He locked the door again, from the outside.

"I couldn't see anything, everything was dark. The weeping and the sobbing and the screaming for help was all in pitch darkness: to say that was hell, Sylva, is not to say enough. Slowly, I adjusted to the shadows. What I found there was horrifying. Corpses thrown one on top of the other, the moans of the dying, the cries of the wounded: all of it . . .'"

Andrei jumped off the balustrade and shook me.

"All of it was in a huge pool of blood, you understand? No, you don't understand! You can't begin to imagine it, you'd be a monster if you could. And there was also . . .'"

He began walking quickly along the bridge.

"What?" I asked as I ran after Andrei.

"There was a woman. A girl. Our men had raped her. Before her father's eyes. The girl told me she had begged them to do it in another room, not there where her father was lying in a pool of his own blood. They ignored her. They raped her: a dozen men, right there in front of her father!

"Many of the wounded started away from me in fright: I was wearing the same uniform as their killers. Others took my hand and asked me to help them and their loved ones. That night I discovered I was in the very heart of hell. All night I stroked the cheeks and soft hair of that Jewish girl. At the break of dawn she took my hand and said, 'I am your wife.' Then she died. That was my wife, who died seventeen years ago."

Andrei was walking briskly, waving his arms, and talking to the stars. He sat on a snow-covered bench, which gave onto the Vltava. The silhouettes of the poplars and the chestnut trees were chasing the stars on the river.

Andrei spoke as if talking to our footsteps, "I believed in the ideals of the revolution because I was drawn by the dream of equality and justice. I believed that those crimes would be investigated and that the people who had committed them would be tried and punished."

"Did they punish them?" I asked, ever so quietly.

"A government commission traveled from Moscow to investigate the killings and the pillaging perpetrated by Red Army soldiers all over Ukraine. Ukrainians, Poles, and Jews had all been the victims of these attacks. These commissars, a few ministers of our new country, arrived in Ukraine. They investigated, and then, by way of conclusion, Comrade Kalinin, one of the leaders of the revolution and of the new government, said, 'Comrades, it is our pleasure to state that all present have spoken with the utmost frankness and sincerity. We will now leave for Moscow, where we will make a final decision on these matters.' That's how they dealt with the whole affair. Not one more thing was done."

The Vltava flowed dark and solitary.

"Don't you get it, Sylva? I'd believed in their slogans!"

"What did you do?"

"I had to flee, I didn't have any choice."

"From the Reds to the Whites?"

"Yes. And don't mock me, although you are right to mock me. The Whites were no better than the Reds. But I didn't want those people who were betraying the dreams of so many to stay in power."

"So since then, you've done nothing but flee, is that it?"

"You're right, after that I fled from the Whites to Prague, as I told you. A good woman took me under her wing when I got here."

I offered my face to the snowflakes, which were pouring once again from the black vacuum of the sky.

"And then ... For days at a time, I sat next to the window and stared at a red geranium. Jaroslava told me I was full of terrible anguish. You know Jaroslava, don't you?" Andrei waved at what I supposed to be my neighbor opposite, "She was the one who insisted that I should be seen by a doctor. After some arguing, I agreed. I went to see the doctor."

He stopped and stared at me. He was trying hard to use his eyes to express all that he wanted to say. As if now he didn't even trust the spoken word.

I didn't understand. I longed to comprehend it all in the silence of that stare, but I didn't know how.

"What did the doctor say?"

"He was a neurologist. He told me that I had to start treatment immediately. That I couldn't go home, that they'd keep me there. He said something to the nurse and the door opened. Two men walked in. Each of them took one of my arms, and they held me down by force. I knew I couldn't shake them off, so I didn't offer any resistance."

"And then?"

"I asked calmly to go to the lavatory. Those two waited in front of the door, but they waited in vain."

"Don't tell me you escaped?"

"Someone who is forever on the run always knows how to escape. It's like a sixth sense. I escaped through the window. And I went on escaping: on foot, by train, on trams, by bus, and when there were no other means of transport left, I went up into the mountains."

"And in the mountains?"

"There I stayed. I found refuge there."

I saw a scene from my childhood: my father is riding at full tilt, chasing a fawn. I saw that fawn and the huge dogs that were after it.

MY MOTHER and Bruno Singer had left my apartment a while ago. The gaslight in the street lit the icy flakes that fell and broke against the paving stones.

I was playing Chopin's Nocturne in E minor.

The music was my way of meditating, of relaxing myself, or of calming someone down. Andrei lay on the sofa, silent, motionless. His fit was over. I had cleared away the broken crockery and swept the entire apartment. I'd done it quickly, without making a noise, while he slept, worn out. Shards of glass and porcelain were everywhere, the floor covered with them, as in *A Winter's Tale*. Now everything was neat and tidy, nothing would remind him of how . . .

Later when he woke, Andrei made strong, Russian tea. He took it without sugar. I also drank that bitter tea. *We* drank. After so many years of being alone, I'd lost the habit of speaking in the plural. Or even of thinking in the plural.

We drank the bitter tea.

Chopin's Nocturne in E minor.

I closed my eyes, playing it from memory. I thought back on what had happened: Andrei had come looking for me in the bathroom. It was the only room that his frenzy had spared. I was sitting on the edge of the tub, covering my ears with my hands. He kissed my eyes, but didn't seem to be aware of what he was doing. He took me into the bedroom. He'd caressed me with his fingertips, without looking at me. He kept my eyes shut, as I did, later, when playing Chopin's "Nocturne in E minor." Andrei had moved away from me only once. He removed the white lace curtain from the rail at the window, and he wrapped me up in it, all of me, from my hair down to my toes. "You're a bride," he whispered into my ear, "you're a bride."

Then he kissed me through the holes in the lace. When he reached my feet, day had already broken. And it was nighttime once more when he took me in his arms again, all wrapped up in white lace. "You're a bride," he said again and again until he fell asleep.

I'd fallen asleep after him, only to wake up before he did.

Half asleep, I swept up the splinters of glass and the shards of porcelain and pottery. Once everything was clean, I covered my ears again. In my mind, I'd never stopped hearing that deafening racket. I locked myself in the bathroom with my ears firmly covered. My tears had cleansed me from within, carrying off with them all that uproar, all that madness. And then . . . bride . . . bride . . . I heard this word inside myself.

I'd felt I needed to see him most urgently.

In the bedroom, I spotted the blood at once. In the night Andrei's nose had bled. Without knowing why, I covered my ears again. With my hands on my ears, I looked down at that sleeping body.

I hid the blood under a white towel. Andrei had stopped bleeding by now. I lay back down beside him. I put an arm over his sleeping body. He has to be protected, I told myself. Asleep, he held my hand and made himself comfortable under my arm as if it were a warm eiderdown.

And now we were drinking bitter tea. I was playing Chopin's Nocturne in E minor.

The phone rang. I ignored it.

THE PHONE went on ringing for quite a while, before falling silent.

I desired nothing, I needed nothing, I wanted nothing. I was full, like a pitcher full of sunlight. Full of his eyes, full of his warmth, full of music.

The phone started ringing again.

"Bruno has gone off to fight the Germans," my mother's voice said over the receiver, "He's just left with a friend on a motorbike, they're going to look for weapons."

"To look for weapons," I repeated mechanically. It seemed logical enough to me.

"Yes, Sylva, to look for weapons. There's going to be a general mobilization."

Maman spoke in a strange, almost solemn way.

"The weapons," I repeated. "The Nazis have started to occupy Prague. It seems to make you happy."

"They all, we all, want the same thing: to defend our country," she answered vaguely.

I said nothing. I was thinking that Andrei had left too soon. He'd left. And I was thinking about something else too: the week before, an entire Jewish family had committed suicide, one of the families renting an apartment in my building. I remembered again that Andrei wasn't there and that I didn't know when I'd see him again.

A moment later, I heard Maman's voice on the receiver again.

"Am I happy that the Germans have started to occupy Prague? No I'm not at all happy about it. But now Bruno knows what he wants. The time of uncertainty has passed, the months and years of fearing things yet to come, are over. The time of passivity is over. Now Bruno is going to look for weapons with which to defend the Czech people against the Germans."

"But his mother tongue is German." It was true.

"Sylva, what's wrong with you? Does it matter what his mother tongue is? Of course it doesn't! Are you still asleep? You sound like Verdi's *La Sonnambula*, the sleepwalker!"

Before my eyes swam Bruno's swarthy, intelligent face, but now it was hidden by the shadow of an army helmet, one of many helmets belonging to the Czechoslovakian army. No, I couldn't imagine the refined Herr Singer as a soldier.

I moaned inadvertently, because I didn't know what to say.

On the other end of the line, I heard a squeak like the badly oiled wheels of a cart. It was my mother, answering with a laugh that echoed her own mood.

When people have no words, they emit only sounds. Like animals, so they say. Like objects, in fact. Instead I started to play Brahms's last *Intermezzo*, *Opus 119*.

I had no words.

MONTHS LATER, my mother called to let me know that there wasn't going to be any mobilization.

"Right now the Minister of Defense, Jan Syrový, is on the radio. He's said that this is the most difficult moment of his life. Do you want to listen to him, Sylva?" and she placed the receiver close to the radio. I heard a grave, broken voice:

"Everyone has abandoned us. To retrace our steps and accept the situation as it is today, now that the three Great Powers have betrayed us, cannot be considered a dishonor. So we wish to call out to our people, to ask them to overcome their heavy heart-edness, their grief. The most important thing is that we are all united. It is vital to ensure that foreign elements do not impinge on us. Do not succumb to confusion."

Then Syrový said, with greater emphasis, "Do not stray from the correct path. Now, within our new borders, we will strengthen our community and our national identity. All this is in our hands, and in yours. With your help we will achieve this. We trust in you, so do trust in us!"

My mother pressed the receiver back against her ear.

"Our leaders have decided not to fight the invader. You know, Sylva, by doing this they have taken away Bruno's only feeling of freedom, and his power to decide for himself." She added, in a low voice, that both she and Bruno felt their country no longer belonged to them.

"I haven't left the apartment for days," I whispered back into the receiver.

"Prague is now full of Nazi uniforms, Sylva."

All of a sudden, she said something that made me think of the words spoken by Defense Minister Syrový, "Sylva, I don't know what to do. The only thing I know is that in all this chaos and uncertainty, I'm going to be at Bruno's side, no matter where he goes."

"I understand," I said in a quiet voice.

"Sylva," my mother went on, "life has taught me that there are three commandments. Sadly, I haven't always obeyed them. I'd like you to remember them. Always have the courage to take risks. Think everything over to see what lays on the horizon. As long as you are alive, do something that will be useful for the generations to come. You won't forget this little legacy of mine, will you, Sylva?"

I DIDN'T leave my home. Why would I do so? Andrei wasn't in Prague anymore. How could he get back to me now, when the Germans were strutting through the streets, humiliating all those who didn't belong to their nation?

For the first time I understood something that I would never before have been in agreement with—that a personal concern can be more important than a collective sense of grief.

The fact was, Andrei had gone.

But he existed!

A white geranium was blooming in the flowerpot on the windowsill, illuminating the world around it. In the breeze, the geranium's white petals mixed with the snowflakes.

# VII

# JAN

A PHONE CALL EARLY ONE MORNING CHANGED MY LIFE abruptly.

That day in my hotel room, my hair still wet from a recent shower, I was impatiently tying my shoelaces so as to get downstairs in time for a hasty breakfast, when the phone rang.

I was in Moscow for an international conference of scientists. Back then I lived in airplanes and hotels, in Sydney or Tokyo, London, San Francisco, or Johannesburg. All the hotel rooms were huge, and identical, as were the conference centers, with their headphones and their international audiences. I went from one capital city to the next, without seeing anything of them outside of airports and taxis, hotels and auditoriums. On my transatlantic flights, equations and questions concerning Bellman's dynamic programming danced about in my head.

In the evening, after a long day in the lecture hall, my colleagues and I would usually enjoy a drink in the hotel bar and laugh until the small hours. Even so, I reckon all our heads remained full of formulas and axioms.

I enjoyed living like that.

So, I was hastening to tie my shoelaces when the phone rang. My first impulse was to ignore it, to make sure I had time for a coffee and bite of something in the hotel restaurant. But the phone went on ringing and ringing, it just wouldn't let up. Its insistence both irritated and intrigued me.

"You've got the wrong number," I said, when a certain Yekaterina Somebody introduced herself. I was about to hang up, thinking only of my coffee and the lecture that was going to start in ten minutes' time. As I was hanging up, I heard the words, "I have not got the wrong number!" coming from the receiver. "Please! I never dial the wrong number!" The lengthy, rapid-fire explanation that followed put me in a bad mood, the lecture of a colleague from Amsterdam was about to start any moment, and I wouldn't have time for my morning coffee. Then little by little, I realized that I did indeed know this Yekaterina, or rather, I had known her some time ago.

As I stood there on the phone in my open dressing gown, I recalled an incident at an international conference, back when *perestroika* and *glasnost* were making their first timid appearances in Moscow. The Russian organizers had assigned a girl to act as both interpreter and guide for our scientific group: a student named Katya. This was about ten years before the phone rang in my room. I remember that the girl dressed differently from other young women in Moscow: she wasn't wearing a transparent blouse or high heels—though she did complain that her father wouldn't let her wear that kind of stuff—and what was more she played tennis and went water-skiing, and one day, a huge black limousine with a chauffeur had given her a ride to our hotel. I immediately figured out what kind of background Katya came from. I found it funny just how easy it was, in Russia, to spot anyone who was from an important Communist family. None of us took Katya too seriously.

One day, Katya brought her father along to our end of the room at the conference reception. None of us had ever seen anything like it. The arrogant heads of Moscow's scientific institutes bowed to Katya's father like servants before His Royal Highness the Czar. The more that sun-tanned man ignored them, the more they fawned over him, humbling themselves at his feet. It was like something out of that Chekhov short story "Fat and Thin." I was laughing to myself, thinking that although Russia had gone through decades of Communism and Stalinism in the last one hundred years, nothing had changed: everything went on just as before, even under a different flag. Katya introduced her father to her group of international scientists, but he shook his head; he didn't speak a word of English. When it came to my turn, Katya announced to her father something that one of my colleagues must have told her: that my father was Russian.

"What does your father do?" that thoroughly uninteresting man then asked me in Russian.

I'd muttered some vague comment. In English.

Katya then said to her father, in Russian, "Professor Stamitz's father was a political prisoner sent to Siberia."

How had she found out? I was upset that my colleagues had been so talkative. But the fault was mine alone, and that of the scotches drank in the bars of hotels where fellow conference members were staying.

Katya's father swivelled that bulldog head of his toward me and with his eyes fixed on some distant spot, he answered, his voice threatening, "Well, for a few years, in our country certain injustices took place, just as they did everywhere else. The history of any nation is full of dark moments. However, all that is in the past now. These are different times. There's no point in airing our dirty laundry, in dwelling on old misunderstandings. Katya, dear, what else were you thinking of showing our guests in Moscow? This is a wonderful capital city, all things considered."

I had excused myself, saying I was off to get a drink. I needed it. I took a glass of whisky off a passing tray and, going against all my usual habits, downed the lot in one go. Immediately I picked up another one and joined a group of Australian scientists cracking jokes about their mothers-in-law.

After the conference Katya sent me a Christmas card every year, which I answered mechanically, as I did dozens of others.

Now I was standing rigid in a Moscow hotel room staring at the wall, with my left shoe unlaced. The wallpaper was peeling. It surprised me that the newspapers visible in the cracks were written in Cyrillic, though that was logical given that I was in Russia. The woman's voice on the receiver was telling me something in an overdone English accent. Katya said she found out about the conference and had tried to find me. She was inviting me that evening to a concert in a church, performed by a choir in which she sang. Just to get her off the phone, I said I'd try and make it.

WHEN I arrived, I was trying to determine a way of calculating the speed of hybrid vehicles, but without expensive and unreliable measuring instruments. However, the atmosphere of that Orthodox church soon stopped me mulling over my calculations. In that church, so different from the pomposity of its baroque counterparts, everything was beautiful, everything was pure and delicate, everything was dark and comforting. My eyes went from one candelabra to another; they were round and the candles in them burned with flickering flame. The more I became absorbed in the music, the more my childhood came to mind, the parks of Prague with their lawns full of daisies and dandelions, where I used to play when I was small.

I remembered what you told me about my father, Mama, and what he had told you: that once a week his parents had taken him to church. It was there that my father had discovered the deepest beauty, you said.

At that moment in the church, Mama, I saw all that, and was able to recall my childhood, bit by bit. That evening, I soaked up the music you had once listened to so often, the chants of Orthodox liturgy. I didn't spot Katya immediately. I thought that maybe she wasn't singing that evening. After a short while, I recognized her as one of five angels with long hair, all of them dressed in dazzling silver tunics. That music took me back to our house on Francouzská Avenue. Yes, it was the first time since I'd emigrated that I really felt at home.

After the concert I went to see her in the vestry. She'd changed her clothes and was now chatting with some friends. I wasn't sure what I was supposed to do now. Katya was busy conversing with her colleagues and her eyes passed over me with the most absolute indifference, as if she hadn't recognized me. I felt ill at ease. I was drumming my knuckles on a tabletop: Would it be too daring to ask her out for a coffee? She'd probably reject the offer.

But Katya got there first: it was she who invited me to have a drink at a late-night bar on the corner. I don't remember what she was wearing, I still saw her in that silvery tunic, surrounded by celestial chanting.

After a long preparatory ritual, during which I drank two glasses of whisky, and Katya drank three French cognacs, she, seated on a red velvet sofa, started to tell me her life story. In a sad voice she told me how she'd been married three times, to a Russian, a Hungarian, and a German. "From East Germany?" I asked her.

Katya gave a little shiver of abhorrence, "No way! No! From West Germany, of course!"

The late-night bar struck me as a nice place, exciting, full of hidden sensuality and exotic music. At that moment I felt that the world was my oyster. It was in this happy mood that

I remembered Katya's father, who as from the lofty heights of a Roman Caesar, observed his servants as they fawned at his feet. I was so happy and relaxed that I laughed out loud.

"You're laughing at my misfortunes," Katya said, indignantly, while, slowly, she removed the brown shawl that had wrapped her body until then.

Only now did I realize that Katya was dressed, perfumed, and made-up with tremendous care. Her fine sweater, the color of a latte, clung firmly to her most feminine body, her golden jewelry glimmered in the bar's shadows, although hardly less than did her hair, nails, and glossy lips. Her makeup heightened the smoothness of her skin, unmarred by spots and wrinkles. The features of the sheltered little girl she must have been now mirrored the eyes of the young woman she was now, who so far had seen only a little of life, even if she had had three husbands. But in her look, I couldn't help but see certain qualities that put a brake on my enthusiasm: there was something cold and calculated, as if she had set herself an objective and wouldn't give up until it was achieved. Katya was no beauty, but her hothouse-flower movements, the care she'd taken with her appearance, the clothes from top European designers, gave her the look of a pretty, well-cared-for young woman.

I made a flattering comment about her hands. She laughed, saying that what she most liked doing was stretching out in the bathtub and painting her nails. "But you're laughing at all my misfortunes," she said again, irritated.

I was still under the spell the church had worked on me, which helped to protect me against the too-dark shadows of that vulgar late-night bar, as I now saw it, where I found myself conversing with a girl who used her clothes to accentuate her physical attributes, convinced of her own sophistication.

"No, I'm not laughing at your misfortunes, Katya. In fact, I want to invite you to stay with me for a few days in the States, if you'd like that."

Her eyes sparkled. She told me her heart was palpitating and she placed the palm of my hand over it by way of a demonstration. Some men sitting at the bar noticed this, and couldn't take their eyes off us. I was burning up under those masculine stares and wanted to remove that hand quickly, but Katya held it down firmly. After the men tired of looking at us, and when Katya lowered her eyes in an especially seductive fashion, I tried to caress her. It seemed to me that was what she was after.

"Only when I come to the States," she said, laughing and slapping my hand, not so much because she felt abashed, but rather because she wanted to make things more difficult for me. Finally, she invited me to Saint Petersburg to spend the summer, which was just beginning. This invitation cheered me up because, above all, it opened up the possibility of living in the city where my father was born.

IN SAINT Petersburg, Katya stayed at the place of some friends of hers, whereas I took a room in the Astoria Hotel. My stay there grew longer and longer. The feeling of being at home that Katya had stirred up in me, tied me to the place more and more. That is also how I felt during Katya's twenty-seventh birthday party, which was a kind of midsummer night's dream, vulgar and cruel.

May I project this party before you, Mama, as if it were a film?

KATYA'S BODY flew over the water, doubting for a second whether to fly higher or fall happily headlong into the waves.

A geyser of water droplets broke through the surface. Under the Nordic pines, some colored smudges began to shift, to form groups and scream and shout. The falling woman's body had disappeared under the surface of the water, only to emerge and quickly return to the riverbank.

Katya dried herself hard with a towel, but still not well enough to stop the goosebumps from appearing on her skin. The sun was frozen at a great height over the horizon, but had now acquired a twilight pink color. It hadn't moved for a while, it was difficult to know what the time was.

"What time is it?" Katya asked.

One of the smudges, the blue one, what I discerned was the color of a young Italian man's T-shirt, showed her the time on his cell phone.

"A quarter to ten?" Katya burst out laughing and couldn't stop.

"What are you laughing about now?" asked the green smudge, a woman.

"We'd arranged to meet Jan at eight, in the wood between Komarovo and Zelenogorsk."

Katya combed her hair with her fingers and looked at the gray cloud shaped like a cluster of baroque women. And like Rubens women, this cloud also had a luminous aura. It looked as if it was about to rain.

Katya tapped a number and waited. A long beep could be heard, followed by a mechanical voice asking her to leave a message. Abruptly, Katya snapped the phone shut.

I WAS trying to light the fire, but the smoke kept getting in my eyes. By contrast, the group of people one hundred feet to our left had made a bonfire that was burning beautifully, as was another fire made by the party to our right. I got to the forest over half an hour before our agreed meeting time, and chose a pretty spot under four tall birch trees. From there we had a view of a little bay with a small, sandy beach that seemed to have been hurled down from the sky. When I arrived, the forest was empty, but my presence must have attracted other visitors: one after the other they appeared on the scene, parking their cars not far from my birch wood oasis, before preparing their *shashlyki*. To make matters worse, some of them left their car doors open and switched on their radios. Really loud! To my left, a man sang in a hoarse bass voice, and to the right some fashionable little song was being howled out in looped refrains.

I looked at my watch: Katya and the others should have been here by now. Maybe they got caught up someplace else, chatting. Let Katya have a good time with her friends, it's her birthday! I unloaded all the food I'd bought at the market that morning. I had taken special care choosing the cheeses, the spices, the fresh herbs, the red cabbage and all the other types of greens for the salads. And the wine! I spread a white picnic cloth on the grass and laid out plates bearing pomegranate-colored Georgian salads, some ivory-colored Georgian cheese, Georgian mint and basil, pickled garlic, and yet more herbs for the meat. I looked at my watch: they should have been here a long time ago! I inflated the mattress and placed it next to the cloth.

It was time to gather firewood. I looked at my watch again: they should've . . . a long, long time . . . I took a handsaw and headed off into the forest. The deeper I got, the deeper I sank into the mud, and the wood I found was damp. I kicked the pinecones out of my way, while whistling Beethoven's *Sixth, The Pastoral.* Pastoral symphonies, I thought, could only have been written two centuries ago, before all the city people started to picnic on the banks of the lakes and on the beaches. Beethoven's undulating melody filled my head and I imagined Napoleon with his three-cornered hat and Josephine in her hoop skirt both sitting in the forest on inflatable mattresses, with cans of beers in their hands, next to a parked pink Lada from which a rap group bellowed. I raised a lonely toast to Napoleon and Josephine, posthumously to their health, then looked at my watch once more. I quickly picked up the wood I'd found and went back with it to the laden picnic cloth. I made the fire, I blew on it. Nothing. I looked at my watch. Smoke and still more smoke. I felt like putting out the whole bonfire with a single kick.

"WE'RE HERE, darling!" Katya shouted from the car window as she pulled to a stop, and then ran over to me with strawberries in one hand and raspberries in the other. She covered my mouth with her hand so I couldn't complain about her being so late.

The sun was slowly approaching the horizon, dying the diners' faces, first yellow, then an apricot color, and finally the color of wild roses.

"The last bottle!" announced the man in the red T-shirt, reaching out for the bottle opener. But Katya didn't let him open the bottle.

"And the *shashlyki*? Jan, with all this seaweed it'd be a miracle if you could get a fire going," she pointed at the smoking wood "Let's go to Repino and have them roast some *shashlyki* for us at the beach restaurant!"

I folded the cloth and placed the empty basket in the car, and Katya, paying no attention whatsoever to the parcels containing her birthday presents, stepped away from the multicolored group and turned to the Italian dressed in blue, "Tommy, lend me your cell. No silly questions!"

After a moment, she left a voicemail recording in a different, tender voice, "It is now eleven o'clock or quarter past eleven at night. We're going to Repino. to the beach, to roast some *shashlyki*. I'm just mentioning it because if, by some coincidence . . ." and then she hung up abruptly, like a naughty little girl.

I took the packages containing the presents to the car, and packed them carefully in the trunk.

ALONE IN the car a couple of hours later, I looked at the time, though there was no longer any point in doing so. It was as if the watch were my only companion. Katya certainly hadn't strapped herself to my wrist. In the thick, gray light of that almost phantasmagorical night, I could clearly make out the dial: ten to one. So I had ten minutes to cross the Neva before the bridges split into two halves that would rise up into the air, to allow the big ships to enter the city.

When I arrived in the Saint Petersburg suburbs, at a neighborhood of cloned buildings, I glanced once more at my rearview mirror: the reflection showed a plump woman in an apron, coming out of the gray edifice to the left. Again I recalled the sandy bank of the Repino Sea, and quickly tried to erase the image. But I couldn't help it. I saw myself walking along the beach toward the sea, in the west the sky was taking on a dark orange hue; it must have been around midnight. I was carefully carrying a platter with *shashlyki*, skewers of lamb that a restaurant nearby had roasted for ten roubles and then poured hot sauce on them. I saw Katya with her friends, sitting on parallel benches at a long wooden table. A night wind was blowing and Katya was curling up on herself against the cold. I approached her. Katya's teeth were shining pink in the twilight, even at that distance. Suddenly she got up, clapped her hands, and screamed, "Hurrah! Wonderful! Bravo!" and the rest of the group joined in. I felt like the main character in a movie, the one with the red sports car faster than his enemy's, the one who shoots the bad guys before breaking through the glass door, leaving a glittering cascade of shards behind him. I got closer and closer, with a big Formula One champion's smile on my face, but when I was almost there, I realized that neither Katya nor her friends were looking at me, that their enthusiasm was for something going on behind me. I turned around. Behind me was Il Mammone, the tubby, bald Italian who Katya had introduced to her crowd not long before. I put the grill with the roasted meat on the table. But nobody paid any attention to me, that multicolored swarm's attention was focused exclusively on the bald man, who was giving his daughter a piggyback ride. Then, shrieking like a pack of hyenas, everybody dove into the meat.

Katya was trembling from the cold. I was already unbuttoning my jean jacket to give it to her, but Il Mammone had also started to pull off his yellow sweater. Katya took it, with a gesture that was almost solemn, as if, for her, it was a matter of life or death. In silence, building up expectation, she took off her T-shirt, pulling it over her white, voluminous breasts, voluptuous to an extent that was almost absurd. She gave me a fleeting look to check if I, too, was seeing it all. Yes, I saw it, but just like the others I concentrated on her face to avoid staring at those huge naked breasts with their bluish veins. Then slowly, one centimeter at a time, Katya pulled on that yellow sweater, which ended up hanging off her frame ridiculously. Only Il Mammone didn't notice any of this, he was too busy choosing the largest piece of meat of the three or four still left on the platter. But Katya was watching him with a penetrating stare. Katya said, again with solemnity, imposingly, "If only this sweater were a tighter fit!" Il Mammone looked at her absent-mindedly and then, finally realizing what was going on, started to grin, though it was more of a grimace, and then sat his daughter on his lap. The other Italian, Tommaso, red as a beet, quickly changed the subject.

"Not long ago I was thinking about how we Westerners, though we don't even like the place at all, are always focused on what's going on in America. Is that the situation in Russia, too?"

"No," Katya said, without thinking, as if she'd been ready to answer this question for years, "We don't. We've always been different. Russia isn't Europe, but neither does it want to be America. It follows its own path."

Katya said this like a spoiled child calling attention to herself. But all the Russians enthusiastically agreed.

Katya stood up and started to spin herself around across the beach, the yellow sweater down to her knees; she spun on her axis for so long that she lost her balance and fell over, laughing her head off. As I watched her, I noticed that behind her, in the west, the part of the sky that was closest to the sea varied in color from pomegranate-red to violet. Turquoise clouds were chasing each other directly above me.

Il Mammone—his nickname because he was a momma's boy, passing from his mother's tender care into the equally tender arms of his wife—was teaching his daughter to count to ten in Russian. His accent hurt the ears.

"Shall we make a move?" I asked.

"What's that!" Katya exclaimed, concerned, "What, go home to sleep at only half past twelve, when the night is just beginning? First we're going to have tea in Komarovo, but we'll take a detour via the cemetery and visit Anna Akhmatova's grave. Then we're going off to Saint Petersburg to see the bridges being lowered at daybreak," she said, decisively.

So I left and went off on my own.

I ADJUSTED the rearview mirror. The traffic light had changed twice and was now back to red. The woman in the apron, meanwhile, had reached the crossroads, had stopped in front of a mailbox and had taken a letter out of her pocket. After checking both addresses, she put the letter to her lips and only then did she pop it into the slit of the mailbox. I suddenly felt a desire, a strong one, for someone to send me a letter as she had just done.

I crossed the Moyka Canal, lined with neoclassical palaces, and then I crossed the Griboyedov Canal. I parked by the Fontanka Canal; I wanted to walk in the Summer Garden, but it was closed. It's half past one at night, I thought, of course everything's closed. Everything lay under a muffled light. I went into a nearby park, entering through a hole in the railings, and wandered through the twilight toward the Church of Our Saviour. The golden domes of the towers were shining brighter now under the sky the color of fresh violets than they would have done under a summer sun. I thought of our evenings of Russian liturgical music, Mama, those evenings full of memories of Father. I didn't like being in this park; couples were sitting on the grass and on the benches, strolling, hugging, kissing. They looked theatrical. I didn't want to see them, they were distracting.

As I was thinking about my father, I turned down Gagarin Street and walked to the Neva docks, reaching the Hermitage. My father is, or was, from this city, I thought; and I don't even know where he lived. I spent a long while gazing at the transparent waves on the river: Whatever happened to my father? The river flowed solemnly, majestically, carrying away, day after day, all the questions that would never be answered, and with them, all the troubles of the inhabitants of this city, delivering them to the sea that would make silvery fish of them, and shiny seaweed and underwater plants that nobody would ever see.

# VIII

# SYLVA

WE WALKED THROUGH THE CITY IN THE WARTIME BLACK-out. Not a single light pierced the darkness of Nazi-occupied Prague. Malá Strana, where I knew every street and wall and stone, had grown unfamiliar. We walked, lost in the darkened streets, houses were languishing in the shadows . . . houses that came and went, like ocean waves. Andrei had come to see me, from the occupied Sudets all the way to occupied Prague; he had made that dangerous, forbidden journey, just to see me; I couldn't help but think of that, as we walked.

"Have you noticed, Andrei, how intensely one lives in the dark?"

Andrei was silent, immersed in his own world. I explained, "What I mean is, in the dark we experience everything in a deeper way. Maybe that's how blind people live."

Andrei didn't reply. But I needed to hear his voice! So I asked him another question, "They've taken our country away from us. Do you think there'll be a war?"

He remained silent. Hadn't he heard me? After a while he repeated my words as if they were a question.

"Have they taken our country away from us?"

"Yes. It belongs to them by day. And at night they forbid us from seeing it."

Andrei answered in a somewhat illogical fashion, "Can you

see that? That miracle? The starry sky above us, here in this capital city?"

To bring Andrei back to earth, I repeated what I'd said, having held the thought. Andrei answered, "The country and the land have grown bigger."

It struck me that today, as on so many other days, Andrei didn't have both feet on the ground. I just said, "What do you mean, Andrei?"

"The land is reaching upward, look. It is heading upward to the stars!"

We were going up a tree-lined road, Jan Neruda Street, I think it must have been. I couldn't see the passersby, although I knew they were there. We had all turned into shadows. But I heard their voices, which sounded more intimate to me than on other occasions. They were human voices.

We made out a distant echo of thunder. A far-away, continuous thundering, which bode no good. The muffled noise was drawing closer. Soldiers on the march. Soon this strident thunder of military boots started to hurt our ears. The soldiers were marching down the middle of the street, and they too had been turned into shadows. But I did not feel close to these shadows, human though they were.

To the rhythm of their deafening steps, Andrei whispered words of consolation.

Once more we lost ourselves in the winding, dark streets of Malá Strana. But the charm of that night had vanished; at least for me. Andrei solemnly let his eyes wander over the starry firmament. As if something special was about to happen, that he had been expecting for a long time. As if he were about to make a major discovery of some kind.

I walked faster, dragging Andrei after me. We reached the top of the mountain. We were at the castle. Under the starlight

I could just make out the Loreto church. We went down a few steps, surrounded by dark shadows that were pointing at the sky. I knew perfectly well that they were little baroque angels. Andrei had stumbled against one of the steps and if he hadn't fallen over it was because he had grabbed one of those stone angels for support.

IT WAS then. Then it happened . . . For the first time I was witness to . . .

"Look, over there!" Andrei said, "He's coming to me through the sunlight, walking along a pathway of white sand under a hanging garden. The path has a border of white lilies, white Nymphaea are floating in an artificial lake."

"Sunlight?" I exclaimed.

"Easy, girl, don't frighten off Gudea. The fact that this great Sumerian should come to me is a very special honor. I wish to prepare myself properly so as to receive his visit."

His whole face had begun to shine beatifically.

I noticed that, in effect, Andrei was bathed in sunlight, and was now walking as if on a summer's day, although it was a cold, wet December night. Only in the summer do we move with such freedom and ease. I saw that Andrei had no doubts, he knew exactly what was going on. No, that wasn't quite it. I saw that Andrei was looking into the very heart of truth and of all that he found correct and good and beautiful. His lips moved and gave out little sounds, without a doubt he was conversing with someone. He was gesturing broadly, his hands flew hither and thither like a butterfly that knows it has to seek the light. He smiled at the other person, he was getting on like a house on fire with him. He took off his coat and jacket, as he felt so hot on that muggy summer afternoon. I went on watching him: it was clear that that conversation had given Andrei something new, perhaps even essential; some revelation, probably a profound and longed-for truth.

The conversation had lasted an hour, perhaps longer. But it's possible that it had seemed to me to last longer than it really was because I had seen something supernatural, incredible. I was a little afraid.

When Andrei came back from his journey among the ancient Sumerians, he seemed happy and at peace. We were walking slowly over the mountain of Petřín. As dawn broke, I plucked up the courage to ask him, "What did he actually tell you, the Sumerian ruler? Did he give you any personal advice?"

Andrei looked at me, bright-eyed, "Gudea linked my life, my attitudes and my work to his ideals. Everyone must enrich and beautify the world as best he can, and artists more than anyone."

WE HAD breakfast at the Café Louvre; at that hour we were the only customers. We ordered thick coffee with croissants and raspberry jam. Andrei couldn't stop smiling, his mouth open and his eyes sparkling.

Afterward we went home to sleep, or, to be precise, I at least needed a few hours rest. Andrei opened a bottle of wine, and, ensconced in an armchair, sang and whistled and drew the trees and peeling paintwork of the houses he could see from the window.

When I woke up, around midday, I realized at once that Andrei had left. On the bedside table, next to his chair, I noticed the bottle of red wine, half-empty, and an empty cut-glass goblet. The goblet was supporting a sheet of yellow paper covered with a drawing.

I discovered a portrait in the drawing: a man with large, expressive eyes, and an alert, wise face, dressed in a black tunic. His face radiated willpower. He had lucid, almost clairvoyant eyes, prominent cheekbones and a jutting chin, characteristics that marked him as an intense, powerful and spiritually vigorous man. The only accessory worn by this serene figure was a strip of cloth, bound about his head like a turban, and marked with cuneiform inscriptions.

Andrei had never done portraits before. I was absolutely sure of that.

Under the bottle I found a piece of paper. A note addressed to me, I thought. I read:

The name which can be pronounced is no longer a name.
In the absence of the name is the start of heaven and earth,
and the presence of the name is the mother of all things.
If we do not desire to do so, we will become familiar with
its secret,
   whereas if we look for it,
   we will only find its surface.
This is the door that leads to all enigmas.

Who wrote this? Where was Andrei?

How would he get home? A sick man like him? How would he find his house in the mountains? How would he manage to get there, he who didn't live on the earth but in some place beyond? How would he travel if it was forbidden to come from and go to the border areas? I couldn't stop asking myself these and many other questions.

I picked up the newspaper, to give myself a break from these unpleasant thoughts. On the front page of this Czech newspaper I read: "Let us follow the Führer over the Christmas period! Let us follow him through this era which is so important for Germany and the future of our Reich!"

I was overwhelmed by a feeling of loneliness. I too felt abandoned by everything and everybody.

NOT LONG afterward, they presented themselves at the door. Both had smooth, fair hair, combed to one side. They were thin. They looked like brothers. They were a few years older than me. One wore a gray suit, the other was dressed in brown. They spoke to me in German. I invited them into the living room. They were courteous, well-mannered, polite. With expert looks they examined the sheet music on the piano, my German-language leather-bound collection of Greek philosophers. One of them started to talk about Socrates' view of the *Republic*, the other admired—or adored, as he put it—Kant's *Critique of Pure Reason*. After this brief preliminary chat, my two visitors broke off their reflections in mid-sentence, and got down to their essential order of business.

"Forgive our barging in on you like this unannounced, *verehrteste Komtesse*," said the one in the brown suit.

"We come in good faith, you belong to us," said the gray one.

"I belong to you? Me?" I said, alarmed, not understanding a word.

"What I mean is that you are on our side," the gray one said by way of clarification.

I still didn't understand a thing. I decided to wait.

"You're one of us, that is what we wish to let you know, and that is the reason we have come here," the gray one repeated, rubbing his hands in satisfaction.

"When it comes down to it, you are German," the brown one said, smiling as if he could smell his favorite cut of meat roasting in the oven.

"My father was German," I answered cautiously, "My mother isn't."

"We already know that," the gray one said with a scornful grimace that I didn't quite know how to interpret.

"That's good enough," the brown one dryly cut in, "To be

half German, as you are, is to be German as far as we are concerned. Your German father is quite enough to ensure that you can become ..."

Both of them fell silent.

"So that I can become ...?" I said.

"A citizen of the Reich," the gray one said.

"Yes, a citizen of the Reich," the brown one was smiling as if the roast was already carved and served at the table.

"Citizen of the Reich?" I said, surprised.

"Yes, a citizen of the Reich, which is to say officially German, *verehrteste Komtesse*. We are trying to bring the greatest number of Germans possible into our ranks," the gray one explained, unsmiling now, serious, severe.

I began to tremble.

"Think it over, *gnädige Frau*. We do this for your own good. Yours and that of ... the people who are close to you," the brown one said, with a courteous smile on his lips, and a fake diamond gleam in his eyes.

ANDREI DIDN'T come. Christmas, and the New Year, and Epiphany had gone by. Winter was coming to an end. But the newspapers and the radio went on saying the same thing: "The president of the *Böhmen und Mähren* Protectorate has announced that it is now obligatory for all Germans, and, for obvious reasons, all Czechs, to salute the symbols of the Reich, the flag, the anthem, etc., with their hats off and a respectful demeanor. Although it is not obligatory, a raised-arm salute would be appreciated."

ANDREI DIDN'T come.

But those two men, the gray one and the brown one, came back.

I sent them away saying that I didn't feel very well that day. They promised they would be back soon.

"I WANT you in a red dress, like a Gypsy girl. You haven't got one? We'll buy one. Let's go!"

He had come with an armful of daffodils, but he had arrived late, after a long time had gone by, as he always did, in fact.

We were crossing the Charles Bridge. From the rainy, springtime sky the baroque statues greeted us with their heads and arms. Full of enthusiasm, Andrei told me that he had started to do portraits, something he'd never attempted before. He painted the Gypsies who lived in huts and dilapidated carriages at the foot of the mountains. He said he admired the way they communicated with each other by means of folktales. A Gypsy girl had caught his attention because of her fire-colored skirt.

We bought a loose-fitting skirt, red as a sports car, which came down to my knees; black shoes with high, but comfortable, heels; a very wide, black leather belt, and a dark-colored jacket with a red velvet rose on the lapel. Andrei paid for everything. I didn't have that kind of money; two of the three Jewish families who rented flats from me were paying me a lot less now than a couple of years ago. They couldn't afford any more. Andrei laughed as he paid. Back on the street he said to me, "What use is money? I want your beauty to be well-framed, so that it stands out. From now on, we'll buy something once a month. In the summer we'll go to the Vltava baths together; I want to see you in a sky-blue swimsuit: you'll look like one of those *demoiselles* that Ingres used to paint."

"The girls in Ingres's paintings don't wear swimsuits," I protested.

Andrei hugged my shoulders and then, to the rhythm of the spring rain, jumped over the puddles of water.

"Don't they? All right then, you'll be . . . a blue butterfly!"

We were heading back home across the Charles Bridge. The red clothes were swinging between us in a net bag like a smoking censer in a church.

"Blue Butterfly!" Andrei whispered in my ear. There was no logic to his words: my brand new skirt was as red as a stoplight!

"I can already see you in your azure blue swimming costume," he explained, "because I can easily see things in the past and future: I imagine young women when they'll be old ladies who have trouble getting onto the tram, and elderly men I see as good-looking lads, taking roses to their first dates with girls."

It seemed strange to me, his seeing girls as old ladies. But I didn't dwell on it. The wind was lifting up my skirt, playing with it and revealing my thighs. Right in the middle of the bridge we ran into Liza, happy as a lark, and her husband, who had a grumpy look on his face because the wind was also playing with Liza's skirt and uncovering her knees and thighs and more. Liza, playful, naughty, looked to see if there were any men watching and was pleased to find that there were plenty of male eyes focused on her, because nobody wanted to miss the show; Liza, indeed, had long, slim legs, like a ballet dancer's, although her face wasn't so attractive; Liza had small eyes, framed by thick glasses which perched on a nose shaped like a horse's snout; men didn't usually take much notice of her and now they couldn't take their eyes off her. What fun! What an enjoyment! To be the center of attention of all, absolutely all the men, from college students through to stick-wielding grandpas, and Liza, happy as a child, walked on with her scowling husband, yes, he looked like the Japanese god of anger, and he growled to Liza that she should cover herself up if she didn't want to catch a cold, that she should hold her skirt down at the knee, but she didn't even consider listening to him, much less obeying him, her husband's grumbling was inconsequential to her, she, who was exhuberant, enjoying something she'd never experienced before.

When Liza and her husband were some way away, we leaned against a stone balustrade and looked at the river. Andrei was softly singing a song I didn't know:

> Dance and whirl just a little longer
> and breathe the perfumed air,
> even though you have a yoke on your neck!

And then I saw it. The biblical plague. Locusts, clouds of locusts. Locusts with sticking-out knees had chosen Prague to infect it with the plague.

Along the Charles Bridge, between the rows of dancing statues, walked a whole army of pale, serious, solemn-faced children; they had clearly marked partings that separated their fair, Brilliantined hair that was combed to one side; they wore short pants and tall socks that came up to their bony, prominent knees. Those monstrous knees were bending to the rhythm of a Nazi marching song about joining the struggle; this army of children sang it with frightening conviction:

*Die Fahne hoch, die braune Bataillonen, SA marschiert im ruhig festem Schritt . . .*

I put my hands over my ears. Andrei sealed them off with his own hands. I bent over the stone balustrade, leaning over the river. I looked at the brownish water as I had looked at the brown battalions of the marching song.

I SAW them there, they could be made out in the brownish waves.

There were two. The gray one and the brown one. They had come back. One morning, when I was preparing breakfast for Andrei and myself. Had they really turned up at my home, those two men, or was it a nightmare, caused by my worrying, which, in the years thirty-eight and thirty-nine, made me suffer for days at a time? I had a nightmare almost every night. At the chemist's, I had heard that while the Nazis were in power, the Jews and the Russians would suffer most. I was being eaten away by anguish for the future of my mother, of Bruno and of Andrei, and, what's more, my own.

"Have you thought it over, *verehrteste Komtesse?*"

"What are you referring to?"

"To your becoming officially a citizen of the Reich," the gray one said.

"I'm sorry?" I was trying to gain time.

"A citizen of the Reich," the gray one repeated with a smile.

"Yes, a citizen of the Reich, Frau von Stamitz," echoed the brown one.

"Citizen of the Reich?" I said nervously.

"Yes, a citizen of the Reich, that is to say, an official German," the gray one explained, seriously now, in a severe tone.

I began to tremble.

"My husband's still asleep," I said. This statement made no sense at all, I realized.

"Your . . . husband?" laughed the gray one with unconcealed sarcasm.

"That painter of Gypsies is your husband?" said the brown one, looking in the direction of the bedroom.

"Frau von Stamitz!" said the gray one, shaking his head, as if he was talking to a mental retard.

What do they know? How do they know it? Why do they know it? All this went through my mind.

"Think it over. Take your time, dear lady, it is for your own good."

"It is only for your own good, we're not getting anything out of it," said the gray one with a smile, as if imitating his colleague.

"It is for your own good and that of those who are close to you," the brown one repeated as if I were deaf.

At the threshold of the door to my apartment, the brown one said to me in a low voice, almost a whisper, while passing his hand over his lower lip, as if wiping it clean: "Just one last little thing, Frau von Stamitz. The greatest service that a woman can render the human race is to help it perpetuate itself with children who are healthy from a racial point of view."

NOW I saw them in the brownish waters of the Vltava, the gray one, with his white-striped tie, with his small put penetrating eyes, and the brown one with a gold chain in his fob pocket and a golden tooth in his twisted smile. While I vomited into the river, Andrei caressed my hair and dried the sweat from my face with his immaculate handkerchief. The May air was cold and I breathed it in deeply through the tobacco smell given off by Andrei's handkerchief. I rested my head against the stone feet of who knew which saint, like Mary Magdalene. And I longed not to be on the bridge, to not know what was happening, to not have to take any kind of decision, just to be, and nothing else.

I observed the statues, which, a moment ago, had been dancing to the rhythm of the spring; now, black and crude, they grimaced scornfully to remind the passersby of what they already knew: This country is no longer yours! Your national anthem says that this country is your home, but the blonde children with an arrow-straight parting on the sides of their heads, separating their impeccably smooth and Brilliantined hair, with their equally impeccably knotted ties, had camped here, they who knew perfectly well that they were the strongest and the most powerful and the greatest in the world.

I watched the passersby: they crossed the bridge with a weariness apparent in their movements and pace, their eyes empty and indifferent to the fact that that between the tiny drops of rain, rays of spring sunlight were falling. And the phantasmagorical statues were all around us, shaking in a macabre black dance. *Der Totentanz.*

Arm in arm with Andrei, I walked away from the black statues of death toward Kampa, toward the winding streets of Malá Strana. Toward my home.

ONE DAY I was preparing a student for the Music Academy entrance examinations. That day they came back to see me. It was no nightmare. Both men were standing in front of me: the brown one and the gray one.

"Schubert," said the brown one.

"The *Impromptus*," added the gray one.

"Our German music."

"Beethoven, Schubert, Mozart."

"The Czech composers are a match for them," said my student, who still hadn't lost confidence in the possibility of convincing someone with a logical argument.

"The Czech composers have German schools, that is the only reason why they are a match for them," said the gray one wearily.

"And you know it," added the brown one, in an even lazier tone.

I ushered them into another room.

"You are one of us, and that is why we have come," the gray one repeated.

"When all is said and done, you are German, *verehrteste Komtesse*," smiled the brown one.

"And you are about to become a citizen of the Reich," said the gray one, expectantly.

"Yes, a citizen of the Reich," said the brown one.

I began to tremble.

"I have to get back to my student," I said apologetically.

"We'll wait," said the gray one.

That was an order.

I remembered the words of the Minister of Defense that I had heard on the radio, his broken voice, his call to the people: the most important thing is that we remain united. It is vital that we do not allow outside elements to infiltrate us. We will not give in to such confusion. I said firmly, "No. Not today."

"We will be back, we will come and see you another day. Soon."

"We'll be back as soon as we can, *verehrteste Komtesse!*"

They both said this almost simultaneously. Their words sounded solemn. Like the chorus in a Greek tragedy.

I WAS carrying a new swimsuit in my bag, a sky blue, two-piece affair. It had started to drizzle, the men pulled their brims lower over their foreheads, the women covered their heads with their hats or with shopping bags, and were frowning, bent forward. As Andrei and I rode the tram that went along the riverside the sun came out again. Even in the nice weather, people ran about on the riverbank as if pursued by rabid dogs. Some made gestures of irritation, others looked at the paving with indifferent, lusterless eyes. In a Prague chock-full of Nazis, nobody enjoyed a leisurely stroll through town. I remembered one day when I was little, while I was walking with the Carmelite nuns on the quayside, at this very place in front of the National Theater, we encountered two young men: one with the right side of his hair dyed green and the left side yellow, the other with green on the left side and yellow on the right. They walked along with their yellow sides next to each other. People turned to look at them, some indignant, others amused. Later, my grandmother told me that they were brothers, two famous writers. Or maybe they were painters, I can't remember.

But now the sun shone and people still hurried home as if it were hailing.

AT THE Yellow Baths, I put on my blue two-piece swimsuit. We made ourselves comfortable on the yellow-painted wooden floor. Andrei stared out at the waves. I couldn't help noticing that life in the forest had made his body wiry, strong.

I lay on my back; the sun warming me and raising me up from the floor, carrying me off in spoonfuls to a golden space where it is never cold.

I overheard a conversation in German, very close by. It wasn't the smooth, gentle German that the Jewish inhabitants of Prague used to speak: the German that I had once despised but which now struck me as familiar and endearing. The German I could hear now, sounded short, grating, voices accustomed to barking military commands.

Don't think it! I ordered myself.

But the German came closer and closer; it sounded to me like military boots marching on the paving of my conscience. I couldn't help but recall the conversation.

"We have come in confidence, *verehrteste Komtesse*," said the gray one.

"Make yourself a citizen of the Reich," said the gray one, "You have German blood in your veins and you, Frau von Stamitz, will be a good citizen."

"We have brought you papers to sign," said the brown one.

Just then I had a vision: I could see what I was like inside. Arteries and veins and conduits and blood vessels flow into my heart like rivers and streams into the sea. The blood of my father

. . . I saw it as the music composed by Lully for the Sun King. The blood of my mother . . . That was clearly Mahler's *Eighth Symphony*. The blood of my grandmother was music for a solo piano, the little-known and highly intimate piece for piano, "The Consolation" from *Dreams*, written by Bedřich Smetana. All this is me, all these rhythms and tones and spiritual states, all these notes and atmospheres circulate through me and run along my veins and flow together like rivers into the sea.

"We have brought these papers for you to sign."

I looked inside myself again. The blood of my grandmother, then, was Smetana's piece for solo piano. And my dead husband? And Petr? And Andrei? What music were they? Bruno Singer is Janáček's opera *The Makropoulos Affair*, of course. My students are musical instruments. All of this is me . . . but who am I?

The voices were getting mixed up with my fantasizing, or perhaps it was all just a result of my most hidden fears?

"It is your obligation," I heard the gray one's voice say.

"We are telling you that this is an order!" the brown one said while I thought about my veins and blood vessels and arteries.

"It is a moral imperative."

"The moral imperative that Kant talks about in his *Critique of Practical Reason*."

"It is the moral law which is in each of us."

"It is the moral law which is in you."

"There will be a war."

"There will be hunger."

"Your mother has married a man who belongs to the Jewish race."

"There will be a great persecution of the Jews, which will be harsh and rigorous."

"And not only the Jews, but of those related to them."

"And those who help them."

"Those who are the friends of the Jews."

"We will persecute all those who are not with us."

The blood of my mother . . . Mahler's *Eighth*, I said to myself so as not to hear the two voices that were so very insistent. How does Mahler's *Eighth* go? Pam pa pa pa pa pa pam pam . . .

"Those who are not with us are against us," I kept hearing in this nightmare. But then I made out the following words very clearly: "On the other hand, whoever is with us will stand to gain by it."

"If you, Frau von Stamitz, decide to be with us, we can assure you that you will continue to have students."

"And all kinds of advantages."

"And favors."

"You will not lack for food."

"Medical insurance."

"You will not be obliged, as will the Czechs, to work fourteen hours a day in a factory."

"We know how to look after those who serve us. *Verehrteste Komtesse*, we most sincerely recommend that you sign these papers. In fact it's only a mere formality, and in exchange you will be able to live more comfortably and be in a position to help your loved ones."

Then it happened.

The brown one offered me a pen, the gray one pushed the paper toward my right hand. The brown one gave me an encouraging smile.

I reached out to take the pen from his hand.

At the last moment I hesitated. I looked at the other man.

The gray one had a threatening frown on his face.

Frightened, I thought that if they started punishing the Jews and their families, my mother, Bruno, and Andrei would suffer the consequences. As would I myself.

Without a word, I took the pen from the hand of the man dressed in brown.

"Noooooooo!"

I was so horrified I almost fell into the river.

Andrei looked at me, his eyes shining from the brightness of the sun.

I stuck my fingers in my ears. Even so, I still heard his voice ..."What's wrong, Blue Butterfly?" I felt his arms protecting me. His voice hummed Schubert's song in my ear: *Darum Sylvia, tön, o Sang, der holden Sylvia Ehren* . . . We sat in each other's arms like this for quite a while.

It was drizzling again. I took my fingers out of my ears. People were leaving, the conversation in German had vanished.

We continued sitting as before, looking at the river, which was gray with dashes of green.

My sky blue swimsuit, which I wore for the first time that day, got wet in the rain, and stained from the wooden floor.

ANDREI WENT missing. He disappeared. He probably forgot about me in the mountains. When he entered the universe of his visions, he forgot about everything else, even the people closest to him. At those times he knew nothing of me, or indeed nothing of the world at all.

My mother and Bruno Singer also went missing.

One day, I heard an appeal on the radio for citizens to help the tens of thousands of families in the refugee camps, whose survival depended exclusively on charity. I thought of my mother and her husband. I hadn't heard from them in weeks: my phone calls were not answered, and neither was their doorbell. First I went to the bank to withdraw some money, then I headed to the Refugees' Assistance Association, on Karolína Světlá Street. A young man in charge of the office gave me a bright, grateful smile and asked for my ID. Reluctantly, I gave him my new document, that of a citizen of the Reich. The man looked at me now with undisguised disgust, and said in a voice full of disdain, "We're not accepting anything from you."

I WAS headed up Jan Neruda Street toward Prague Castle when I suddenly felt weak and had to lean against a wall in front of the Italian Embassy. The statues loomed up from the baroque palace that housed the embassy, threatening me with their silent cries. They yelled and scolded each other; their stone bodies twisted about in a convulsive, hysterical dance. And one . . . with a raised finger, a forbidding finger of the fanatical Counter-reformist Jesuits. I couldn't walk past them. I went back down, to where I turned left to take another route up: the New Stairs of the castle. Although it was November, I was by now soaked in sweat and took off my dark brown jacket. I remembered the day Andrei and I bought it, that day we were crossing the Charles Bridge; from the rainy, springtime sky, the baroque statues were greeting us with their head and arms . . . That was before the war. Only a few years had gone by, but I feel as if that walk had taken place in another life.

I climbed the stairs to the castle and thought about this morning. In a small café near where I lived I had had a cup of the dirty water that in wartime went by the name of coffee. I picked up a Czech newspaper, which urged the Czechs to "collaborate sincerely with the Germans," I looked at a few more: they all said the same thing in as many words. When I paid, I commented on this to the woman who ran the café, "According to the papers, what does it mean to be Czech? To be a collaborator?"

I will never forget the look she gave me. Never.

She looked at me scornfully. Worse: with disgust. As if she wanted to say: it is not for you—a captivator and collaborator yourself—to talk of such things; you'd better shut up!

I promised myself I would never go to that café again.

No, I couldn't ever go there again, just as I could never go back to the baker's up the street, to the drugstore, or to the greengrocer's on Újezd Street, nor to the Kampa gardens when the students were there. They no longer called me the Silent Woman, as they had after my husband's death. Now on occasion they shouted: you bitch, you evil hag! They spat in front of me.

How have they all found out about my signature? About my signature, and the favors I received from the Germans, from the Nazis? In fact, why had I really signed those forms that day, and agreed to become a citizen of the Reich?

Perhaps because, when I was little, Maman had never tired of repeating that I was a noble, aristocratic orchid, destined to a better life than most people. Yes, in part I had done it because of that. Also because I had never been able to disobey a direct order. Orders must be obeyed, so they had taught me ever since I was small.

But it was not only for these reasons: hearing before the war that it would be the Jews and the Russians who would suffer most, I had thought that, if necessary, I could help my mother, Bruno, and Andrei.

My mother and her Bruno. Bruno Singer, a Jewish businessman, a specialist in the world of finance. Bruno, with his wise, intellectual face, a sensitive, refined man, a perfect gentleman, and a wonderful partner when it came to dancing to jazz music...

The last time I saw her, my mother had told me, "Sylva, they're asking me to leave Bruno, they are demanding it! To spare my life, they are ordering me to divorce him. They have told me that an Aryan woman with a Jewish spouse will be sent to a concentration camp if she doesn't get divorced in time. But

Sylva, if I did such a thing, how could I live with myself? I want to be with him. Nothing else matters."

Here too, my mother outdid me. She always did everything better than me. Always.

What has happened to them? Where had my mother gone? And Bruno? To ask such questions does not mean giving up hope. Not yet.

And what had happened to Petr, my Monsieur Beauvisage? In the thirties, when Masaryk was still in power, he had been the Secretary of the Ministry of Culture and Education of the Government of Czechoslovakia. After Masaryk's death, he retired from politics to become a university professor. My mother had relayed all this to me in front of Bruno, deliberately, coquettishly, "I never did quite manage to fully understand Petr's poems," Maman added, "at home I have a few of his books. The critics praise them to the skies, but I have to confess that the contradictory images that he uses don't say very much to me." Petr's poems didn't resonate very much with Maman, and I hadn't even tried to read them, even though my friends and acquaintances liked them very much. That is to say, my erstwhile friends and acquaintances. Everybody now was keeping their distance from me. But, where was Petr himself? The university had been closed. From the beginning of the protectorate and the war, the Nazis had carried off over twenty thousand people to the concentration camps, mainly members of the Czech intelligentsia. That was how they increased the climate of terror in the country. What had happened to Petr?

No! I said to myself as I climbed the steps. No! I have to concentrate: I turned my attention to other things. Higher and higher up the steps to the castle! I can't, I haven't got the strength to think about . . . that. If only Andrei were here! Why am I going alone? Why is no one with me? So many acquaintances and friends of mine are in concentration camps. And my former students . . . The Jews are in the camps, the Czechs have other things to worry about . . . Those two men, the gray one and the brown one, made sure I had students, they kept their word. "We know how to look after those who serve us," they had said, and they hadn't lied to me, but now I have to welcome those locusts with their socks up to their enormous, bony knees, big as balloons, so that they may play Schubert's *Impromptus* in my home. The boys of the *Hitlerjugend* only play German music, of course. They execute each piece with perfect technique, but do so coldly, mechanically, with severity, without one iota of passion or mystery, and what is art without passion or mystery?

It had been a long while since I last saw Andrei. One day I spotted him in the neighbor's house. When he finished there, he crossed the road to knock on my door. He came with a bouquet of little daisies in hand, of the kind that grow and flower on park lawns, there are loads of them at Kampa. Before the war he used to bring me roses, but who would dare sell roses now with the airplanes whistling over our heads. Who would buy roses if there was no guarantee of getting home safely with them? Andrei used to give me bunches of gladioli in the summer, armfuls of lilacs in the spring, bouquets of chrysanthemums in the autumn, and always lots of roses all year round. Because he never arrived empty handed, he always brought a gift, and that day he brought daisies with buds as tiny as the *halér*, the smallest coin in circulation. He came with a bouquet in his hand and a question on his lips and a greeting in that deep voice of his, but that day I didn't pay any attention to the flowers or the smile or the greeting. All I could think of was that he had been at the neighbor's house. I saw red circles float in front of my eyes, then they grew scarlet and then darkened. I slammed the heavy oak door too, so that Andrei couldn't come in. I heard him ring the bell, then knock with his knuckles and the palm of his hand, and finally scrape at the wood like a little animal while saying my name in a low voice . . . Sylva, Sylva, my love . . . It turned to night and I still hadn't opened the door. I drank cognac and coffee, and when there was nothing left to drink I smoked some cigarettes that Bruno had left in the apartment a long, long time ago, and I remembered the bouquet of little daisies and wanted to go out on the street and look for the one who carried them. But then once again in my mind's eye I saw Andrei with the woman across the street: he was smiling at her, she was saying something to him with great tenderness in her eyes, he whispered in her ear, with passion . . . I fell asleep in the chair and when I woke up I ran out of the house, with just a raincoat on, without a scarf or a hat or gloves, because I had woken up with the image of that bouquet. I had rushed down the stairs as if I might still find him somewhere. Indeed, on the ground floor I saw Andrei on the threshold of the empty apartment from which, some time ago, they had taken away a Jewish family, with the grandfather and the grandchildren and everyone. They hadn't shouted, they had left like shadows, as if they were already no longer there, as if their eyes could no longer see the staircase or the door or the street, as if they were already looking into the heart of horror. Their apartment had been left open. I longed for them to return and told myself again and again that if they left their apartment open, they would come back. The grandfather, dressed in black with a black hat, would return and stroll each day for an hour and a half around the neighborhood as he had before, talking to himself in Prague German, the German the Czech Jews spoke. On Saturdays the whole family would again head off to the synagogue, always on foot, over the Čech Bridge that leads straight to Pařížská Avenue where the Jewish neighborhood is. Yes, all of them together, wearing their very best, the whole family would take part in a Hebrew ceremony, all together. There on the threshold of the Jewish family's apartment I found Andrei, standing with a small, tremulous smile, round as if he were pronouncing the letter U, as if it were a question or a prayer. As before, I imagined him with the woman across the road and watched the projection of this film of mine, and gave Andrei an icy look.

When I arrived under the Charles Bridge, it was still dark and a siren started to wail ayayayayayayayaya . . . ayayayayayayayay! That day the pitiful, and ill-boding sound didn't give me goosebumps, but seemed instead to be the perfect, most suitable musical accompaniment to the way I felt. And as the siren kept warning us—ayayayayayayayaya . . . ayayayayayayayay—that in no time at all the bombs would start to drop, ayayayayayayayaya! I remembered how, not long ago, Andrei had told me that for a long while he had been in debt to Jaroslava and that, finally, he was able to give back the money he owed her, that soon he would pay back the lot and then . . . Andrei had sighed with relief, taken hold of my hands, and led me in a kind of tremulous Russian dance.

The deafening roar of the planes shut off the siren, and my own thoughts. I fled for safety in the direction the river was flowing, warplanes crossing the sky and bellowing among the city's towers. I saw monstrous black birds cawing and flying close to the bridge where I had hidden myself. Which bridge was that? Karlín, maybe? It wasn't providing much shelter, but at least I wasn't alone, lots of mothers had gone there to seek refuge and were hugging their children. You couldn't hear the cries of the infants, just the thundering and the booming and the bombs and the explosions and the detonations . . . I realized that it was I who had caused all this devastation and these detonations, that it was my fault that the streets and squares and alleyways and houses of my city were up in flames, because I was a von Wittenberg like my father and a von Stamitz like my husband, because half my blood was German and because I had publicly admitted that this was so the day I had agreed to become a citizen of the Reich, but I knew now, now that the deafening roar of the planes and the explosions of the bombs had pulled the wool from my eyes, I knew now, all of a sudden, for the first time, that I was not German because I lived among the Czechs, who I respected and loathed at the same time, who I venerated and despised in equal measure, and who I both loved and hated. But I still lived among them, I was one of them, just as Bruno Singer considered himself to be Czech, even though the Czech language was like a jigsaw puzzle for him when he tried to read it, and a tongue twister when he tried to speak it, and he had a terrible time writing business letters in Czech. Yes, for the first time in my life I knew, with absolute certainty and conviction, I saw it as clearly as I saw the earthquake and the volcano of the bombs against the night sky, that I belonged to a specific place: here and now I felt so strong and so firm with my new awareness that I left the shelter, that laughable hiding place, in order to curse the sky that had permitted all that horror and the sky full of black vultures that perpetuated it . . . I ran as fast as my legs could carry me to my Charles Bridge and at the break of dawn I saw the black figures standing out against the pale sky. I saw them threatening that sky, warning it, showing their teeth and nails, raising a finger to a point beyond the evil sky, beyond the sky lit with fury . . . And I calmed down, I knew that I wasn't alone, that perhaps my mother and Bruno Singer had ended up in a concentration camp, that perhaps I had lost Andrei forever, but that for all this I was not alone in my black desperation, my impotence and my helplessness. Those black statues would keep me company, they were with me and would give me shelter. These black statues thought as I did, as, with their fists and fingers, they would threaten that terrible sky . . . above which there was nothing, nothing at all.

Or perhaps there was: hell. For me you will go to the city of suffering, for me you will undergo everlasting pain.

AND NOW it was I who was heading up to that sky, not along Jan Neruda Street, but up the New Stairs of the castle, I was going straight up to the sky, that execrable, evil, abominable sky. At the upper end of the steps I found black stone figures, a gate: they were locked in struggle, trying to murder each other, in a mortal embrace they were stabbing each other with gold daggers.

I avoided them and went on up, higher, infinitely higher until a magnificent palace of white stone blocked my path, a gigantic, white arch, resting on dozens of classical columns. It thundered, don't go on, here is your goal, here is the heart of hell! And before being sucked into its black entrails, I read on the sign hanging at the entrance that it was the Černín Palace, headquarters of the Reich Protector, that fearful, terrifying man, on the stroke of whose pen each and every Czech depended.

. . . Abandon all hope, ye who enter here!

WINTER CAME. Snowflakes fluttered around the gas lamps.

What nonsense! It is impossible to see beauty when you are not feeling well. Anyway, the lamps weren't lit, not the gas lamps nor any others. There was only the howling of the sirens, to warn of the danger of an air raid.

Unlike most people in Prague, I had all the coal I needed to stoke up the baroque stove in my living room. I could eat soft, white bread, just as I liked it before the war. I had students, as I did before the war, and charged my usual fees: thanks also to those gray and brown gentlemen. The boys with prominent knees and the girls in long white socks sat at my piano and played Wagner and Beethoven like well-oiled machines. Their parents had military postings with the Heereswaffe, which had occupied Prague six years ago.

In Prague, there were no longer any stout Jewish matrons, laden with gold chains; there were no longer any Jewish lads with ironic cigarettes hanging from their full lips. There were no longer any Gypsy women clinking their glass bracelets and speaking their guttural language, no longer any skinny Gypsy men giving off the odor of strong tobacco.

Eventually my knobby-kneed students abandoned their classical music lessons at the piano and took to whistling a military march . . . *Die Fahne hoch, die braune Bataillonen* . . .

I WENT out to look for them, starting with my mother and Bruno. I stopped at the city of Kladno, at the home of my mother's sister, to stay the night. During the night I heard a strange noise. Gunshots? I couldn't sleep. There was no way I could get myself to doze off, in that house in Kladno. What was that strange sound I heard all through the night?

It started to get light. I raised the blinds.

The sky was an intense turquoise and the sun was starting to shine. And outside my window some pink, sweet, large cherries were ripening. I stretched myself out on the bed again to look at that miracle. The fruit was bright under that blue sky. I couldn't help but marvel at this prodigy of nature. I spent a long while enjoying that calm, early summer morning. Suddenly in the distance I heard a drawn-out melody, sung by a women's choir. There was something strange about this chanting. I shivered. It was a terrifying melody. The cherries still gleamed in that sunny morning. The melody grew closer and closer. I was filled with horror, I don't know why. I stared at those big, bright cherries through the leaves and branches. The choir moved in my direction, women's voices, that wept and lamented and howled. The door of my room was opened. My aunt said, as if unable to believe herself what she was saying, "The Germans have executed all the men in Lidice, the next village over, and then they burned and razed the houses to the ground."

I didn't have the strength to go through with the journey I'd planned.

When I returned to Prague, it was dark. What could I do for my mother? Me, the frightened orchid who couldn't even make the memory of the dead seem beautiful.

AT A stop in front of the Prague National Museum, I was waiting for the number twenty-two tram when I saw him. Was it him? In the dark I couldn't be sure . . . "Petr, is that you? I'm sorry, sir, I thought . . ."

"Sylva!" His face lit up. "You're not going to be all formal with me, are you?" Finally, I've found a friend, I thought happily. And suddenly I saw that the sparkle in Petr's eyes had gone out, like the lights in an opera house. "No, Madam Sylva," he said coldly, you haven't made a mistake, it's me all right.

He looked at the ground as he said it. So he knew about me too? This man, to whom I still had so much to say, whom I still needed so much. How many things I had to tell him! But he said nothing, he simply stared impatiently at the tracks to see if a tram was coming. "My regards to your mother, Madam Sylva," he said in the end, to break what would otherwise have been a very long silence.

"My mother?" I opened my eyes wide. "She, well, she . . ." Once again, Petr lowered his gaze. Like the statue of Saint Wenceslas's horse right next to us, I thought, and like Saint Wenceslas himself, and everyone in this whole country who had all looked at the ground and their hung heads. "Your mother too?" whispered Petr.

"Yes," I said in a low voice. Petr said, almost inaudibly, "My wife too . . . They took her away too, and she never came back." Then the number twenty-two tram arrived, and Petr got on it. Sylva, how could it be, how could you, how . . ." I read his eyes and his furtive lips. I didn't dare to get on the same tram. I stood in front of the open door and when the tram pulled away, I saw his lips move. Shame on you, I read there. But he probably hadn't said that, he had probably done nothing more than bid me an automatic, courteous goodnight.

THE SHADOWY innards of that palace of white stone ejected me like a white whale spitting out an irritating bone. I was dazzled by the brightness of the day. The Černín Palace, headquarters of the Reich Protector, it read on the sign posted on the white building.

"We know nothing about them, and you would be wise to stop looking for your mother and her Jewish husband. It would be in your own interests. As I told you we don't know anything about them, nothing whatsoever."

I also recalled the words of the young man at the exit, a member of the Gestapo with a face so white he had surely never exposed to wind or sunlight, "Frau von Stamitz," he had said, "since you are a citizen of the Reich, I will do what I can to find out what has become of your mother."

I shut my eyes, so dazzled was I by the white palace that reflected the brilliant sun. Again and again I read the words on the sign.

THE TREES of Petřín Mountain were in bud. The fruit on the trees of Petřín Mountain was growing ripe. Then trees of Petřín

Mountain turned a fiery red. I noticed all this on my walks upward, ever upward, toward that palace of white ice where pale automatons told me time and again that they knew nothing. And I always found one, usually the youngest, who promised, "As you are a citizen of the Reich, we'll try and find your mother."

The trees of Petřín Mountain were in bud. Later, the buds opened, and then they became flowers, then fruit. The fruit fell to the ground. Then the trees blossomed again. Why? Who asked nature to dress up so fancifully, so graciously, when the Nazis were burning villages and taking men and women to nobody knew where?

HOW DID Andrei put it? "To know that I do not know is wisdom. To ignore the fact that I know is a sickness." I knew, but I pretended that I didn't.

I WENT down to the muddy path; the bus was driving away with a rusty, clanking sound.

The footpath, which led from the base of the mountain to the high sierra, was a steep climb. Icy rain fell, and I hid the bag under my raincoat in which I carried the letters addressed to Andrei that had been sent to my house; especially the letter that contained the invitation, the invitation on which I had placed so many hopes.

I made my way up through the undergrowth, stepping over stones and branches as big as the arms of a giant. No one was keeping this path in a reasonable condition. I looked around me at all the houses and chalets and huts and farmhouses, all in ruins. Here, far from the big cities, a war between rats had taken place, the rat families had exterminated each other: first the Czechs against the Germans, then the Germans against the Czechs, and then the Czechs against the Germans again.

Against the greenish sky, I could make out a house with broken windows, holes in the roof, and a half-demolished chimney. The chimney was like a finger pointing to the heavens . . . it's your fault, bloodthirsty sky! I didn't dare enter. I trembled just to think what I might find there.

Bacchic laughter bubbled out of a clearing in the fir trees, something was moving there. Yes, it was heading toward the path. I had asked for directions to Andrei's house. The black figure now twisted and laughed as it ran toward me, and embraced me only to step back a moment later and move away from me. Then the scent of its breath, familiar and perfumed with liquor, came back to me. The figure moved its laughing face closer.

"What are you doing here?" I asked him.

"I'm the guardian," the laughing man sang out.

"The guardian of what?" I asked.

"The guardian of the animals," he sang, "of the boars and the roe deer, of the squirrels, and the mice and the goats. I'm the guardian," sang the giggling man and now he was embracing the narrow waist of a birch tree as he danced a wild polka, and then he vanished once more into the shadow of the forest, jumping and singing and giving out euphoric cries, leaping all over the place . . . When he'd gone, I kept my eye open for that figure dressed in dangling, torn rags, with a bottle of spirits in his hand. I would have liked to have taken a swig, as I did years ago from the bottle of the Gypsy patriarch, on this very bend in the path, I thought, there was his house, already in ruins, then and now abandoned, like everything around me, all this mountain scenery inhabited by a single inebriated man . . . a man who, seeing what atrocities had taken place, had gone mad.

Everything was deserted. There was not a light to be seen. Or a flower on a windowsill. Or a lace curtain flapping at some open window. Only broken glass. No homes now. Only ruin, collapsed. Defeat, death. Homicide, fratricide. Cain and Abel. Abraham and Isaac.

A CAT. And then another, and two more, came out to see me and caressed my legs with their fur. More and more cats, dozens of cats came looking for me from among the holm oaks, dragging themselves along, winding their way through the underbrush, and then suddenly slipping back into the low thickets. I picked one up in my arms, I hadn't felt such tenderness in a long time, my face nuzzling the warm, shivering fur. The cat leaped from my arms. "Cat!" I said, "I'm looking for Andrei, I'm bringing him his mail and a small loaf of bread." The cat understood me, he led me to a house, yes, it was this one, this was his house! He entered the dark interior, the cold humidity smelling of mold and cats.

The house was uninhabited! Where was Andrei? What had happened to him? Had they taken him away too? Or did they murder him, like the others? But he wasn't German, or Czech, or Gypsy. Why, then? He had friends of all nationalities, but he was good friends, very good friends, with the Gypsies . . . The others might hate him for precisely that reason. All of them.

Darkness, damp air, the stink of an uninhabited house. Nothing but cats everywhere. I explored further and further into the house, I ran into all kinds of objects, and hit against a table. Feeling with my hand, I found a box of matches and quickly lit one, and the first thing I saw was a candle. The candle flame flickered—the wick was probably damp—as I crossed the rooms, which this sickly light was unable to illuminate properly. Suddenly, I noticed something on the wall, a dark stain, and I held the candle up to it. Before my eyes was a large painting . . . Gypsy children and a Gypsy couple dancing, all in red and yellow and orange. On the opposite wall was a Gypsy nativity scene, done in blue.

On the third wall I made out an image of male figures, arranged next to each other in a kind of ritual dance or holy ceremony. They wore long, priestly robes and were touching each other with stretched out fingers. All the priests were the same, all looked like that wise ruler of the ancient Sumerians: Gudea. Gudea, who from time to time, visited Andrei. On the fourth wall there was a big, dark stain.

I was in a chapel with frescoes painted on its walls, a chapel in which I was holding up a little flame. I sighed, then cried out. After a moment, I heard, by way of reply, some muffled sounds.

It was probably only some animal from the forest; why should I be afraid? I thought in an attempt to put myself at ease. I crossed the room to the door. The sounds were coming from somewhere to the right, from a small room with a tiny window sunk into the wall.

I noticed the pile of horse blankets on the floor. That was where the sounds were coming from. My fingers trembled and tried to disobey me when I reached out my hands to that pile.

Underneath was a human body.

ANDREI WAS weak. For days he had had nothing to eat or drink. He hadn't even got up in days.

"Why?" I asked him.

"I couldn't."

"Why couldn't you?"

"I just couldn't, not after everything that happened here," he said. After this . . . He made a sweeping gesture with his hand.

On the wall of the room in which Andrei was lying I felt a pair of eyes watching me. There was a painting: a dark man. A man with large, expressive eyes and an alert, wise face, dressed in a black tunic. His only adornment was a strip of cloth, wrapped around his head like a turban, and marked with cuneiform inscriptions.

"At night . . . did the Sumerian ruler come?" I asked with a sigh.

"Yes. And Gudea said, 'The name which can be pronounced is no longer a name. In the absence of the name is the start of heaven and earth, and the presence of the name is the mother of all things.'

And then the Sumerian ruler added, slowly, very seriously, 'The enigma can be glimpsed only when we do not search for it.'"

I understood that this was the vision of a dying man for whom the world had plunged into all the horror it is capable of producing.

I WANTED Andrei to take some food, and the sooner the better. I had brought a little loaf with me, but he wouldn't allow me to give it to him.

"We must celebrate your arrival."

My coming here had given him strength, and he dragged himself along with faltering steps, leaning against the walls. He made me sit down in front of the house while he made preparations for the party.

When he finished Andrei came over to me, took my arm and escorted me inside like the lord of a castle with his beloved. Staggering still, he ushered me into his chapel where he had built a small bonfire, the way he had been shown by the Gypsies, who also built fires on the floors of the half-demolished houses where they lived. The holy fire of the most ancient of the nomadic peoples, as Andrei put it.

On the walls were the three colored frescoes and one dark

one. Now, while the reflections of the flames danced on the walls, I realized that the dark painting represented shadow. Everything was dark, except for the face of the white, illuminated face of a Gypsy woman. She was a moon-woman in the shadowy firmament. I couldn't take my eyes off that painting. The shining Gypsy woman was leading her people far away, nobody knew where.

Andrei threw two cushions onto a ragged mat that was laid out on the floor. I now saw that he had stoked that little bonfire with some chairs that he had broken into pieces. Outside the forest was drenched, the trees were dripping rainwater. On the mat Andrei had put a couple of plates, my loaf of hard bread, a water jug, a bottle of spirits, and two eggs.

"They're rotten, Sylva."

He dusted off the cushion he'd offered me as a seat, and helped me to sit in a cross-legged position.

"It doesn't matter. They're eggs!" I said.

He settled down next to me, so weak he couldn't even cross his legs. He handed me the plate with the two eggs, which he had adorned with a pine sprig.

"Eat them, my love."

When Germany lost the war, I stopped receiving the rations I had been getting as a citizen of the Reich. Famished, I refused the plate offered by Andrei.

"No. Both eggs are for you. You need them more than I do."

Eventually, each of us drank a rotten egg. I doubt if I have ever savored any other food as much in my entire life.

The fire crackled and the golden sheen highlighted the delicate features of Andrei's face. Part of his face shone, the other was submerged in shadow. His pale green eyes glowed, his teeth glimmered above the smooth, gilt hairs of his beard. He spoke in a curious fashion. He said something; his deep voice made it sound important. Then he paused. There was complete silence, and then Andrei, without moving his lips, hummed a melody full of sadness, in a high key that broke at the end to fade away in a deeper tone. It was like the chanting that accompanies traditional Orthodox liturgies. His frescoes too evoked the spiritual atmosphere of a small Orthodox chapel.

With this strange chant, Andrei was telling me that before my arrival he had been convinced that he would never get up again.

"You can't imagine the horror of what went on in these mountains. Sylva, you know that I have already experienced this kind of thing once before. In the Ukraine, twenty-five years ago, remember? But a second time . . . no, I couldn't bear it a second time."

But this time Andrei was different. He wasn't worried about saving his own skin.

I embraced him to calm him down, he couldn't stop shaking. He had the same look in his eyes as when he was suffering one of his attacks of madness. I hugged him close. He resisted. He was stronger. The man from the forest. The madman from the forest. The madman among madmen.

I made an unusual effort. I steeled myself to chat away merrily.

"What about these cats, these dozens of cats?"

"They belonged to the people who lived here in these mountains. With so many . . . well, let's say dying, the cats went wild in order to survive. In the winter, they came to my house to find food and warmth. Until recently each cat belonged to a neighbor, to a home. There were twenty-six, from twenty-six now demolished or half-demolished houses. Now there are only twenty-one cats, I think, although I haven't counted them for some time. I know them as if they were my own children."

He didn't want to talk to me any more about the cats, about the people who had been his neighbors. Those who hadn't died had to forget the dead in order to survive.

I loosened my hold on the man. Andrei had taken my hand in his, and little by little his shivers and convulsions slowly subsided.

We sat looking at the fire. The firewood sang its sad song.

"Sylva, I don't want to stay in these mountains of death."

"We'll go to Prague together."

"I can't live in Prague. You know that."

"Then we'll go to Russia together. Why not?"

From my bag, I took one of the letters I had brought him, which I had already opened in Prague to see if it was urgent.

"They've invited you to the Soviet embassy, to a reception."

"Don't be so naive, Sylva. They're laying a trap for me."

"They just want to talk to you."

"Don't trust them."

"They're counting on you, read it!"

"Sylva, it's a trick."

I told myself: Andrei won't do anything for me. I'm nothing to him. And another sensation imposed itself over this fleeting thought: I needed to cling to something safe, to someone who would take me far from Prague and save me from this destruction.

"It's considerate of them to invite you, Andrei."

"Have you taken leave of your senses, Sylva?"

"Don't you think it's nice of them to offer you an opportunity to start your life over again?"

Andrei kept his mouth shut.

"Say something, Andrei."

"Do you want me to get killed over there?"

"You can't tar all the Soviets with the same brush."

"What are you babbling about, Sylva, my love!"

"What other option is left to us, nowadays?"

"They're after me. I know it."

I caressed his soft hair. In him I saw the fawn from my childhood, fleeing desperately. Andrei grew calmer and calmer, until he became gentle and tender, and, half asleep, he whispered, "When I was fleeing from the Reds, before reaching the Whites, I slept in the forest, in the fields. A Ukrainian peasant took me into his home and dressed my wounds and cured my chilblains. He kept me in his stable. One day he came to see me with a bottle of *zubrovka* in his hand. He told me his story: 'The Whites held me prisoner by mistake. Eventually they let me go. For those six months I was unable to say a word to anyone. Six months without wanting to live because of the humiliation of being held prisoner. Only after six months of living in a black vacuum was I able to return to my life.' That, Sylva, was all the Ukrainian peasant told me. Just that, not one word more. It was the only day he felt like talking, but thanks to his story and then later to my own experiences, I understood there was nothing so terrible or humiliating as lacking freedom."

The house smelled of mold, dampness, and cats.

Andrei whispered in my ear, "I want to be free and unfettered, like a cloud passing through the sky moves without obstacles all its life, desiring nothing, satisfied with everything everywhere. It is nothing in itself, yet roams the whole earth, without leaving a trace. Now, today, it is resting among the mountains, somewhere near us."

At that moment Andrei was transformed into a passing cloud. But he was also the fire warming us, and he was the stone wall against which we were leaning, and the four walls that sheltered us.

The flames crackled and the wood snapped. The light projected reflections on our faces, the forms of exotic flowers and phantasmagorical trees.

Andrei, calm now, murmured, "There is no way home. In these azure-dressed mountains I am far from the world . . . Not even the Gypsy women come to see me anymore, or the inhabitants of the village in the valley. Not even the birds visit me. All I see is the curl of blue smoke from the candle, which I always light thinking of you, Sylva."

Andrei was falling asleep still whistling his words about the clouds and the blue mountains and the valleys, but I wasn't listening to him, I, too, was whispering my version of the truth into his ear, my secret story, like a lullaby . . . "Andrei, there is something I've never told you. I never told you that I became a German citizen of the Reich. Right from the start of the war, Andrei, I was officially German. That's why they didn't send me to a concentration camp, Andrei. The way they did Bruno and my mother. They died there, Andrei, for sure. By contrast, I am still alive. Andrei, this is what I have hidden from you . . . Andrei, now that the war is over, in Prague they will hunt me down and kill me, just as the Czechs expelled or killed the Germans from these mountains. I have to get out, Andrei, I have to flee, to escape to some place, even if it's Russia."

Andrei, half asleep, said, "But Sylva, don't you realize that going to Russia would mean going to our deaths?"

But I didn't listen to him. I could only think about fleeing, I couldn't go on living like a hunted animal. I had a burning stigma on my forehead and I felt that everyone could see it, that everyone was pointing it out. And that wasn't all: I was obsessed with the idea of putting Andrei to a test, the test that would show me once and for all how important I was to him, whether he was capable of doing something for me or not.

In his dreams, Andrei must have seen my furtive and half-formed thoughts because he said in a low voice, "Sylva, you don't know what Soviet Russia is like."

"Maybe now, after the war, after so much misery and losing so many people, maybe things have changed."

Andrei was silent.

"Let's try it, Andrei. If it doesn't work out, we can always come back."

Andrei was silent.

I insisted: "I can't live here now."

Still Andrei remained silent for a long while. Then he said, in a faltering voice, "My love, you are the most important thing to me. I want you to feel happy, and I want to share that happiness with you. If you can't live here, that means that we will have to leave. Today you have saved my life, and this life that you have given me, I wish to spend all of it with you. I will go wherever you say. I will go wherever you wish me to go."

The fire was almost out. Andrei was sleeping deeply now, lulled by my caresses. The embers hissed and barely lit the frescoes on the walls. My eyes wandered from the embers to the painted figures, as if their movement were to have some influence on what was going to happen next in my life.

The next day I took Andrei to Prague.


"GOOD EVENING, Mr. Polonski. We are so happy, dear Andrei Ivanovich, that you have come to spend a few hours with your fellow countrymen and that, as a good patriot, you are interested in the fate of your old motherland, which has suffered so much in the war."

A good start, I thought, giving Andrei an encouraging smile as we headed across the garden toward the main Soviet Embassy building.

"Patriot, fellow countryman, and always motherland, motherland, motherland," Andrei grumbled, frowning.

"What's wrong with that, Andrei?"

"What's wrong with it? Their duplicitous ways, their ubiquitous lies."

Andrei kicked at a little stone on the pathway. The dust sugared his right shoe.

". . . with your fellow countrymen, Mr. Lukov, and as a good patriot, you are so interested in the fate of your old motherland that has suffered so much . . ."

The echoed words of the embassy official sounded strange and absurd.

A dozen waiters in white carried in bottles of vodka and wine and the corresponding glasses and served these with caviar, smoked fish, blini, and bread, along with dozens of other hors d'oeuvres. We all feasted our eyes on such delicacies we hadn't seen for a good seven years. But we still couldn't lay into them. The official who had welcomed us at the entrance, now came into the room and addressed those present, "Ladies and gentlemen, we are delighted that you have accepted our invitation to this little get-together. That you have come here shows that you are good patriots."

Andrei turned to me, "He only says 'ladies and gentlemen' because that is the form of address we exiles would recognize. Otherwise he would simply have said 'comrades.'"

I thought that because of the traumatic experience he had had, Andrei was looking at everything from a negative point of view.

Then the official relinquished the floor to the ambassador, who was also done up in a black suit. He had very thick eyebrows that joined up at the top of his nose, and almond eyes. He gave his speech in a hoarse, nasal voice, "Dear friends, sons and daughters, all of you, of Greater Russia, the same Russia that has generously agreed to protect so many different nations under its wing."

At this point, the ambassador stopped to cough and take a sip of water, as if he had given a long, tiring speech. Andrei took advantage of the pause to whisper in my ear, "He says Russia instead of the Soviet Union because he knows that if he used Soviet terminology with us, he'd spoil everything. You see how crafty they are? I wonder what they want from us, after they've all dressed up to the nines and prepared this banquet fit for a king."

I answered Andrei with a condescending expression. The ambassador wiped his neck, frowned with his bushy, black eyebrows, and was about to go on when he caught a frog in his throat and started to cough. The speech was adjourned, and as if he had just said grace, it was time to eat. Nobody waited to be told: we relieved our bellies of seven years' hardship.

We all devoured those delicacies, all of us except Andrei, who didn't touch a morsel. Neither did he offer me bites of food and drinks, the way he usually did. He acted dumb, as if the food wasn't there.

Next to the window, a singer with a guitar was swaying in time, dressed in a Russian shirt embroidered in bright colors. I took a quick look around the embassy room: there were balalai-kas and mandolins, hand-painted Russian plates and paintings of snow-laden, birch tree forests at twilight hanging from every wall. In the glass cabinets I glimpsed a large matrioshka, disman-tled to form an army of identical dolls that were each smaller and smaller until they vanished altogether. I smiled at the poor taste of this exhibition. The singer was taking his guitar from table to table. Suddenly I found he was standing in front of me, singing:

They have taken everything from me: strength and love.

My body, abandoned in a hostile city,
can no longer enjoy the sun. And I feel how my blood
has turned irreparably cold.

I recognized the verse as one by Anna Akhmatova, a poet I had met in Paris long ago, in another life. Most of the audience were deeply affected, several women were crying, many men had taken out handkerchiefs. I looked at Andrei: he too was impressed. I was astonished to see the frankness with which over three hundred Russians showed their emotions immediately. This was even true of those Russians who had spent twenty-five years here in Prague, where we take care to aristocratically cover up any show of sentimentalism. And this was still true even though most of these Russian exiles came from the old nobility. In contrast, Andrei's eyes were a snowy, Russian pain, over which rolled the ringing laughter of the bells on a troika.

As I watched this scene, I thought of what it meant to live in exile: always hearing a foreign language, being obliged to speak it, to laugh and cry in this language. Or, instead, not to accept it and so condemn yourself voluntarily to a life apart. To see around you, all the time, faces that are still foreign to you, even after decades. What can you do? Stay as you were before, not change at all and run the risk of being misunderstood by most of those around you? Or adapt yourself to the majority at the cost of losing your own personality, your deepest sense of identity? Andrei had solved this dilemma by living far from civilization, well away from Prague's intellectual circles, which he visited infrequently, only to flee quickly back to his mountain solitude like a frightened animal.

What must it be like, to wake up every day far from everything that you feel is truly part of you? I could see it now, written in the faces of these Russian aristocrats, generals, and artists who, at the first puff of a Russian breeze, cast aside their usual restraints, unable to help themselves, like a river overflowing after heavy rainfall. To experience something that was so much theirs, something that smelled of their forests and their rain, that rain with its peculiar drizzle, which left a taste of autumn on country paths, for them it had to be something worth celebrating. And to savor all this collectively, in the company of those who had at some time in the past breathed the same air and drank from the same rivers, must surely have been worth dressing up for.

This was how the gods of Olympus had punished those who had offended them: Tantalus had fruit and water within reach, but as soon as he tried to quench his thirst, they vanished; Sisyphus pushed his rock in front of him toward the summit, but before he got there, the stone slipped from his grasp, rolled back down and he had to start all over again. They punished Ulysses in this fashion for years. And Dante realized one day that he would have to wait fifty moons, fifty months, before he would be free of the difficulties of living in exile.

To disguise my coolness in that emotionally charged atmosphere, I forced myself to eat and drink. But after a couple of blinis, I couldn't take anymore. My stomach was no longer used to banquets.

The ambassador, who had clearly never lacked for anything, chewed away at half a pancake with caviar, and then, after chasing it down with a good swig of vodka, he stood up slowly to finish his speech. He spoke in an uninspired, unamusing fashion, and said nothing clever or interesting. He mumbled his speech in a nasal voice as if he wanted to get it over with, the sooner the better:

"Dear friends, we are all children of Greater Russia, the same Russia that now protects many nations under its wing. We have emerged victorious from a terrible, cruel, and bloody war, in which millions of our sons have given their lives for victory. We know that all of you, who abandoned Russia for different reasons, have always been with us and have done what you could for this victory. Our motherland lies in ruins. We must raise her up. We must put her back on her feet. We must rebuild her. And so . . . Our motherland does not wish to fixate on your pasts. With great joy our motherland will greet with open arms all those who wish to return and take part in the rebirth of Greater Russia. Our Bolshevik revolution has proclaimed the great ideals of humanity: the building of a society in which we are all equal, a classless society, a society without rich or poor, free of hostility and hatred."

Under the table, Andrei grasped my hand.

"Free of hostility and hatred?" he whispered, "Why, Soviet ideology and the Soviet system is based on class struggle, on the struggle against the bourgeois enemy, based on hatred, in other words!"

He was trembling.

I supposed he was right about that, but I remained silent.

"We have won the war," the ambassador went on, "against a terrible evil. Now we are preparing to rebuild our motherland and a society free of hatred. We are waiting for you, my friends, to join us in a brilliant future full of hope."

Andrei squeezed my hand. Like that horse in my childhood, which I hugged after they'd beaten it cruelly, I thought.

"Sylva, come with me, I have to leave. I don't feel well."

I stroked his hand to calm him down, but knew that I could live in Prague no longer and thought that the ambassador's offer would be a way out for both of us. Andrei could go there and see what the possibilities were, and he could either come back to Prague or invite me to move to his country.

I told him of my plan.

When he heard it, he was unable to say a word. He had a bad case of the shivers, like a naked man in a gale. After a long while, he said, "It is not the ambassador who is offering this to us. It is the wish of Stalin himself!"

"Of course. And?"

"There's some evil motive behind it all."

I pressed Andrei's hand, but he didn't stop repeating, "I want to get out of here. I really feel very bad."

A man with a little white beard and an intelligent face, who was sitting at our table, declared that he was going to go back.

"You are?" Andrei asked in surprise.

"Yes," the man said firmly, taking a sip of vodka as if to confirm his decision.

"But this patriotic speech of the ambassador about the merits of the Soviet Union . . ." Andrei said in protest.

"He hasn't even mentioned the Soviet Union," said the man with the beard.

"That makes it even worse," Andrei's eyes were bright. "He's a hypocrite. He's called the country Russia to fool us with a word we might accept. I don't know why they really want us to go back."

"Mr. Polonski," said the man with the white beard, seriously, "it is certainly true that this ambassador is nothing more than a bureaucrat who talks like an ass, but I like what he's saying. A man has to know what he's living for."

"But nobody knows that!" Andrei flew into a tizzy, like a child, "One man convinces himself he's living for his children, another for his novels or his paintings, like myself, still another believes that he's living for the cause of universal peace, but deep down none of us know what we're doing at all!"

"That is a mistake then. We should all make an effort to find out." The man smoothed back his hair and stroked his white beard with his long, pale fingers. "Here in Prague we get by, but in the end where is this life getting us? Do we know what it is we're living for here? Back home in Russia, among our own people, we'll know what we're about, and our life will have meaning once again."

Andrei took a deep breath and started to explain, illustrating his words with sweeping gestures. "Life is a boat on the high seas that carries you to any coast, destinations that you yourself haven't chosen."

"Mr. Polonski," said the man with the white beard, laughing in order to hide his irritation, "you are a painter, but perhaps it would be better if you became a thinker specializing in the philosophy of chance fate. You are André le Fataliste, the Russian version of Diderot's *Jacques le Fataliste*."

Andrei stared at the plate he hadn't touched.

"Andrei," I said gently, "do you really think life is tossing us about on the high seas and we are its victims?"

"We are not always victims."

"So you don't think it's necessary to make any decisions?"

"It is. But from the moment when you told me your story, how you accepted citizenship of the Reich, I haven't stopped thinking about how hard it is to recognize, in difficult times, whether our choice is the correct one or not."

"My story? I have always silently obeyed one order or another. Should we obey orders given by a moral authority over those of our conscience?"

"Our conscience changes according to the times and the circumstances. You, Sylva, are not happy with your choice, but if you had made any other, you would have ended up in a concentration camp—I'm sorry, I didn't want to remind you of that."

"It doesn't matter. Go on."

"In '38, after the European powers had decided in Munich to betray the agreements they had made with Czechoslovakia, the Czech people decided to fight the German occupiers, even though that meant a lot of bloodshed, but the Czech president made a decision to do the opposite in order to avoid the inevitable bloodbaths that would have resulted. From that moment on, the Czechs have hung their heads in shame. The Poles who, guns in hand, a year later offered resistance to the German tanks, now hold their heads up high, but the Nazis killed many Poles, and razed their capital. Which one was the correct decision?"

"To offer resistance."

"To assassinate Heydrich, the cruel Reich Protector in Prague, at the risk of one's own life, was undoubtedly a heroic, honorable, and righteous act. But because of this assassination, the Nazis razed two villages to the ground, installed a reign of absolute terror, and started to deport Czech citizens en masse, as well as the Jews, to the concentration camps, your mother and her husband among them. From this point of view, was it right to assassinate Heydrich? Yes or no?"

"Yes, it was," I answered, "I think so."

"But you're not sure. Take my example. I was convinced the czar's regime in Russia was unjust and that the revolution was in the right. I enlisted voluntarily in the Red Army, and voluntarily I fought for the success of the revolution. With what result? Today the Red Army is doing horrendous things. Now I know that the regime imposed by the revolution is as unjust as, or more unjust than, that of the previous one, that it is itself terror personified. And I also know that the experiences I underwent in that army were so terrible that I almost died because of them. You see? This is another outcome of a decision dictated by one's own conscience."

"So what must one do, then?" I asked.

"Think about the consequences of each step, each decision. Like a game of chess."

"So calculating?"

"Not exactly calculating. Lucid. Rational."

"You, a Russian, are invoking rationality?"

"It's precisely because of that that I have to mention it: to prevent the Russians from spreading further evil around us."

Andrei looked at the ambassador of the USSR, who had tucked his napkin into his collar like a child, and was chewing away enthusiastically. As he observed him, Andrei said gloomily, "You know Sylva, in a period of calm it's easy to make the right decisions. But when the going gets rough, it is difficult to see things clearly. It is easy to make mistakes that you'll regret for the rest of your life."

The singer resumed with his guitar. Again he sang the songs the audience had liked the most:

Inscrutable you are and always new.
And each day I obey you more.
But, cruel friend, your love
is a test of iron and fire.

During the song, Andrei hugged my shoulders and whispered into my ear, "The next decision will be made by you, Blue Butterfly. Shall we live together? If so, where shall we live? You yourself must tell me. I have given you my word, Sylva. And I want to keep my promise. I am aware of your difficulties here. You don't want to go on living in Prague? Then we shall leave here together. Tell me what we must do. I know that your choice will be the correct one."

"And if I say that you should go back to Russia and that I will join you later on?"

"Then I will do as you say. I trust in your good judgement."

I kissed him on the cheek.

# IX

# JAN


THE FOLLOWING DAY, I DIDN'T HAVE ANY NEWS FROM Katya. Nor the day after, nor the one after that. She was probably waiting for me to get in touch with her. I didn't feel like doing so; I no longer found that sort of game amusing.

What should I have done? I realized that for a long time I'd been acting the fool, simply because of a vague feeling, with no basis in any concrete fact, that I had finally found a home. Because of a wish to keep you close, Mama, and because of my memories of silent evenings together and our walks through the parks of Prague, I'd turned into a simpleton. I took the first plane back to the States.

One day I was walking back home from my classes, thinking about an argument that had taken place the evening before at a dinner party with some friends and colleagues. We'd been talking about science and art. Some defended the idea that to search for solutions in an exact science such as mathematics was akin to an adventure. Others disagreed, "What about art? Art, with its magic and enchantment, nothing compares to that! This was why Cicero preferred to make mistakes with Plato rather than be right all the time with Pythagoras." I inclined to this latter viewpoint. Edith, a colleague from my department, didn't agree. "God is in mathematics," she averred, "mathematics is the highest art form there is!"

"It is an art!" I added, "In mathematics, style is just as important as in literature, music, or painting. A stylistically well-structured equation is, for me, an aesthetic experience, more enriching than any other kind."

I was thinking about all this when I got home and checked my mail to see that one of the letters was from Katya: she'd bought an airplane ticket and would be coming over to visit next week. Then I remembered my promise to show her America.

How unfortunate! I had successfully managed to forget about Katya, considering her as I did to be one of my life's minor episodes. But how could I not keep to my promise, especially now that she'd already bought her ticket? In fact, this girl must be seriously interested in me, I told myself again and again, this being an idea I found very attractive.

I rented a small, cozy apartment for Katya right in the middle of the college campus. Before she arrived, I'd placed a bunch of yellow roses in there as a surprise, but when we emerged from there together, Katya, who was wearing a yellow flower bud in her lapel, was silent and sour faced, in a bad mood because she didn't like the apartment. Later she confessed that she found it too small and bare, okay for a student, but not for a grown woman. "I didn't think America was going to be like this," she said, running her pink nails through her blonde curls. As a result, Katya spent a lot of time at my place. She quickly struck up friendships with other Russians who lived in Boston and invited them over. Often when I got back in the evening from school, I found them all partying like crazy. I ended up coming home later and later.

Eventually I broached the subject of Katya's return to Russia. After all, I'd invited her for only a short stay! Katya grew irritated when I asked about her departure. But to be honest, I wasn't sure that I really wanted Katya to go. I didn't much like the company of those Russian émigrés, but neither did I fancy the idea of living as I'd done before, all alone, with only the bare yellow light covered by a lace cloth, and my mathematics for company . . . and the image of Helena playing the violin.

Helena . . . who had disappeared one day, like a grain of sand carried off by the greedy tongue of an ill-disposed wave.

So what choice could I make?

In the end, I didn't have to make a choice. Life made it for me. Katya, like most Russians, would have said it was fate, *sudba*.

WHY, ON the fateful evening, did I seek out Katya's company? I had told her I was through with her, but she still decided she was going to stay in America. At least for as long as her visa lasted, she said. After that we saw each other only very occasionally.

At a dinner with the Boston Russians in a French restaurant, Katya criticized American women, saying they were crude, clumsy, unfeminine, and hypocritical. I didn't agree The American women I'd known were decent, friendly, and natural, whereas Russian women struck me as being calculating and selfish, but I didn't want to come out with any sweeping generalizations, so I kept silent. I knew from my own experience that it was very difficult for an American to get on well with a European. Although we might be similar in appearance and habits, we are different and never seem to fully understand each other, but that was exactly what I liked about the company of Americans.

But Katya still didn't know America, she still hadn't discovered what I still find really surprising: Americans don't believe in nuances, in looking at the gray areas, or in taking a middle path. They want things to be clear-cut, the way they are in sports, where you know who's good and who isn't thanks to measurable criteria, the number of field goals, the number of passes. Americans see the world in black and white terms, everything must be either good or bad, a success or a failure. People too, in their eyes, can be divided into winners or losers. For a moment, I thought that communist regimes don't like nuances either and that their values are equally clear-cut, inasmuch that they make it quite clear what you can and can't do.

Katya left the table a little bit before the other guests; she was followed out by a man called Mikhail. Later, when I left the restaurant with the others, there was a couple in the shadows of the parking lot, quite a distance away from us. The woman's coat was unbuttoned, and under the coat I saw a man's hands, caressing her. Judging from his cap, that man was Mikhail. The woman, without doubt, was Katya.

That night I slept badly. I kept seeing those hands feeling up that voluptuous body. The day after the dinner I gave a student some exam results that weren't, in fact, hers. Fortunately, the girl simply smiled and told me I'd made a mistake.

In the evening, my thirst, my fever grew to an extent that became unbearable. And then I did something that more than anything else shows how irresponsibly and self-destructively irrational I had become.

I phoned Katya.

On the first Saturday after my call, we had dinner together at that same French restaurant. After a long period of keeping each other at a distance, our conversation became animated. Still I couldn't stop myself from seeing those hands feeling up Katya's abundant body.

After dinner, we went out into the parking lot. I headed directly for the spot where only a few days ago Katya had let herself be caressed by Mikhail's hands. For days I had thought of nothing except that moment. I quickly unbuttoned her coat.

Then, when I had a firm hold on her body, I realized that I'd been more excited imagining those alien hands on Katya's body than I was when feeling her up with my own.

ONE AFTERNOON, not long after, I went to her apartment to pick her up and got a surprise. Katya had taken great care with her clothes. A gold chain, high heels. Her hair fell over the generous cleavage of her blouse, practically fondling it. I could see her clearly now: she was like a sip of chilled champagne.

She asked me to sit on the sofa. I looked at my watch, it was half past six. At seven we had to be at Bill and Jills' place, they'd invited us to dinner. Bill came from a farming background and had been a student of mine, but he didn't even finish his first year. He left the university to become a car mechanic. Today he has his own garage and several employees. Still he would call me at the university more than once a week and say, "I'd like to buy you a beer." If he didn't call me, I'm the one who'd suggest that we have a drink together.

Recently, Bill had been putting on weight. I didn't know Bill's wife, all I knew was that her name was Jill, though Bill talked of her often. Bill didn't know Katya either.

At Katya's place, the light of the setting sun fell on a reproduction of a painting with a maritime theme, stuck in a dark, heavy frame, and also on another reproduction of Degas ballerinas and reflected off its gilt frame. There were quite a few gilt objects in Katya's apartment, and now all of them were highlighted in all their pompous phoniness.

Katya placed a bottle of champagne and two tall glasses on the coffee table in front of the sofa. I looked at my watch: it was just past a quarter to seven.

"Katya," I started, but she placed a finger on my lips to shut me up.

In silence, she laid a dish of canapés next to the bottle of champagne. There was red and black Russian caviar.

"Are we celebrating something? I had no idea," I asked, cautiously. I didn't want Katya to see how restless I was, but by now it was getting seriously late. Right there and then we should have been getting in the car, not opening any bottles of champagne.

"Yes, we're celebrating something," she smiled and sat down next to me.

"But . . ." I looked at my watch.

"We're celebrating something," Katya said significantly, as she handed me the bottle of champagne. The cork slid out, as smooth as silk.

Katya picked up a glass, essaying a smile. She probably thought that smiling was the American thing to do. She showed her teeth and gums. Her smile was limited to her facial muscles, it didn't come from within her.

"John," she said, looking at the bubbles. She immediately corrected herself and said my name in Czech, something she never usually did, "Jan."

Call me foolish and gullible, but that little detail won me over.

After a while, Katya said, "I'm . . . you know?"

Now I certainly wasn't expecting that. Had it been me or that man with the hands? How long had it been since . . . I started to calculate.

Katya stared at me. I knew she expected me to say something fitting to the occasion. A toast.

A toast?

Yes, a toast, about us being together for the rest of our lives. That's what she expected of me.

"Is that a Monet?" I asked, pointing to the reproduction with the maritime theme.

"Are you seriously asking me that?" she gave me an expression of infinite scorn, "Can you really not tell the difference between a Monet and a Manet?"

I noticed that some of her lipstick had come off on her teeth.

"Of course I can tell the difference, I just made a mistake, that's all," I tried to explain.

A red stain on white teeth. It went well with the gilt picture frames, I remember thinking.

I didn't say anything to her about that lipstick stain.

So I said a few words, without thinking too hard about them. The fact is, I didn't have anything to mull over: in that instant I knew I had to marry Katya and have the child. And I thought about how, at the age of thirty, or a little less, Katya would be getting married for the fourth time. My thoughts took on a life of their own then, beyond my control: at forty she'd be married for the fifth time, and at fifty, for the sixth. Idiotic thoughts! I ditched them on the spot.

Deep down, I wasn't thinking about anything at all. I said the words, watching myself become a father—a man with a gut and weary, heavy movements, carrying a skateboard and an inflatable mattress in one hand, a howling, screaming child holding my other hand, a huge bag full of cookies and Coca-Cola bottles on my shoulder, and an expression of paternal concern and resignation on my face, my body bent under the weight of my burden and of fate itself. No woman would ever look at me again, and if she did it would be to laugh at that human being turned into a dad. Behind me walked my wife, now on the plump side, looking old and worn out, carrying a little bucket and a toy spade, a big inflatable swan under one arm, a beach ball in the other, and three wet towels hanging off both shoulders. That is how I'd seen parents at the beach, and I had pitied them from the distance afforded me by the conviction that that was never, ever going to happen to me. And now I could see myself becoming a dad.

But right then I could think of nothing except that we were going to arrive really, really late at Bill and Jill's. It irked me.

Katya kissed me.

As I looked at her long, red nails, I heard her voice say, "I dumped Mikhail for you."

I didn't understand. She made an effort to explain, "Mikhail, the one who . . ."

Of course: in my mind's eye I saw a man's hands and the breasts of an Indian goddess.

"Yeah, I dumped him for you. And he isn't just one of your little provincial professors. He's a businessman."

"Katya, it's half past seven, "I said, concerned, "let's go, we were supposed to be there at seven!"

"John! Where do you think you're going? This evening must be for us alone!"

I didn't answer. I handed her her coat.

Katya grumbled. "I knew this would turn out . . ." In a lower voice, she added, "You're a . . ."

In silence, I helped Katya into her coat. It was the same one those male hands had unbuttoned, I remembered it well.

"KATYA, THIS is Jill and Bill. My friends, this is my fiancée, Katya."

Bill wore a checkered shirt and jeans. Jill had put on some white trousers and a pink sweater with a big heart in the middle, made of shiny bits of red plastic. She looked something like Bill. She was obese. In fact, you could only tell them apart by their clothes, they looked so much like each other. The pink sweater tipped you off that Jill was a woman.

"*Hello*," Katya finally managed to say, as wide eyed as if she were at the zoo, looking at some strange and monstrous animals. Katya cultivated her foreign accent like a gardener did a pricy palm tree, but when she spoke in Russian, she always threw in a few American words. She was now shaking Jill's hand, adorned as it was with long, glossy red nails.

We passed into the house. Through the window you could see a huge shopping mall. It was almost dark by now, and I was greeted by the neon words "Woolworth" and "Wallgreens" and "IGA," in red and green and then more red and then yellow. The parking lot was almost empty and I could make out my black Toyota quite clearly. By then, I should have been thinking of it as ours.

I took off my leather jacket, Jill hung it up by the door. Bill helped Katya to take off her coat. Jill was stunned by the sight of Katya's ever so short miniskirt, transparent stockings, and high heels, and ran her fingers through her hair. Katya looked back at her, scared.

Bill patted me on the back and grimaced the way he often did when we had a beer together. He led me to my place at the table. Jill brought Katya. Once we were seated, Katya looked at the walls.

"Are these Madonnas from Florence?" she asked.

Bill scratched the back of his neck. Jill got to work at the stove.

"Florence, Italy, Europe," I explained.

Bill burst out laughing, "There I was thinking Florence, Kentucky, Florence, Illinois, or Florence, Arizona. OK! The Madonnas are from Jill's family. Her mother was from Arizona and they've got Madonnas all over the place down there."

Bill brought over a gigantic bag with red letters dancing across it: Cooler Ranch Bold and Daring Crunchy Chips.

"Want some?" Bill offered the open bag to Katya.

She read the letters and seemed somewhat frightened. Bill took the bag away and in its place offered us a huge bag with a threatening message on it: Grab Your Bag of Tostitos. Crunch into Tostitos.

Jill reassured us, "Don't be afraid, they won't make you fat," and showed us the lettering: Thanks to our Tostitos Chips You Can Allow Yourself More Snacking Fun! Great Taste! No Guilt!

Jill put a lot of plates and platters and bowls and frying pans on the table: mashed potatoes, coleslaw, and a salad made of apples with celery and walnuts. Bill came swaying over to us, bringing more nourishment. "Sweet corn, baked potatoes, hot dogs, for our dinner party!" Jill sang out. Katya grimaced, frowned, then tried to smile, showing her teeth stained with red lipstick.

"These sausages are for you. We're vegetarians," Bill said, as he sat down.

"Our doctor doesn't want our cholesterol level to increase," Jill said in her singsong voice. She stood next to Bill, and stroked his shoulder. She had a tiny nose, teeth like little pearls, and ears that could have belonged to a little girl. The rest of her was simply enormous.

"We have to lose some weight," admitted Bill, pointing at some bananas lying on a platter in one corner of the table. On each banana there was a shiny sticker: No Cholesterol.

"The doctor says we eat too much fatty food," said Jill.

"So we've become vegetarians," Bill added, inserting half a potato covered in sour cream into his mouth.

On her baked potato, Jill added four scoops of a margarine called I Can't Believe It's Not Butter!, and said, "Bill, eat properly. You're supposed to start with the salad."

Bill blushed. "Oh, right, sure, right." When he spoke and ate, he wheezed, as did Jill. When he laughed, it came out as a snore.

We were silent. Only Bill, from time to time, grimaced at me.

Katya put three spoonfuls of salad on her plate. Immediately, Jill passed her a plastic bottle of Thousand Island Fat-Free Dressing.

"The average American puts on six pounds for Christmas and then spends January and February trying to lose weight by going on a low-calorie diet."

Katya poured some of that thick, pink sauce with little green bits floating in it onto her salad and slowly began to mix it all together. She wore her blouse, which was as red as a poisonous toadstool, as were her lips and nails, unbuttoned. She was looking at where Jill had rested her hands on the table.

They were the biggest hands I'd ever seen. They smelled clean, of some kind of special soap. They were vanilla flavored, like the sponge cake you used to make for me for my birthday, Mama, when I was little.

Jill noticed our stares and lowered her eyes.

"This is my wedding band," she said, "and this other one with a shell in it is a gift from when I was being given chemotherapy. That was five years ago. Medal for bravery, huh?" she winked at Bill. Bill winked back, and looked at her as if he were about to sing her a lullaby.

When she saw that, Katya turned to me and kissed me on the lips. Straight away, I followed her kiss with a spoonful of sweet corn and wiped my lips with a paper napkin. I noticed the teddy bears with lace collars around their necks, printed on that napkin. I think I was blushing. Because of the kiss.

Bill smiled at me. When he looked back at his plate, he avoided Katya's eyes.

"In the factory where I work, I have to take my rings off each morning," said Jill, "and when I finish for the day, I put them back on."

"Could I ask you for something to drink?" said Katya in a pleading voice. Then to me, in Russian, she said, "We brought a bottle of French wine with us. Where is it?"

"What do they make at the factory where you work?" I asked Jill.

"Oh, excuse me, I'm a real scatterbrain!" Bill jumped out of his chair, "I forgot. I guess that's because we never drink anything when we eat, do we Jill? So I didn't offer you anything. We've got water, milk, gin, coffee . . . that's about it. And coffee with milk, of course."

"I'll have—" Katya started to say.

"That bottle of wine, we left it back in the car, it's on the back seat," I said to Katya quietly, in English. And it's better that way, I thought to myself.

"What do they make at the factory where you work?" I asked Jill for the second time.

"We drink milk, but only when we've finished eating, right, Jill?" Bill said, as he put a large jug of cold milk on the table.

"I'd love a glass of milk," I said.

"One glass for John!" Bill said, laughing, and poured the milk into a tall glass.

"And where do you work, Katya?" Jill asked, and spooned sour cream onto her baked potato.

"Well, I'll have some coffee, if there's nothing else," said Katya. "I work at a radio station."

"Katya might be able to get a job on a local station that broadcasts programs in Russian for Russian immigrants. If there's a vacancy," I explained.

"So what are you doing meanwhile?" insisted Jill.

"Well, right now, to tell the truth . . ." Katya didn't finish her sentence and gave me a resentful look.

"What do they make at the factory where you work?" I asked Jill.

"Wow, a Russian radio station," said Jill, "So what's going on in Russia these days? The other day they said on the TV that there's democracy over there, like there is here. Is there enough food? Come on, kids, eat away! There's lots of everything!" She pointed at the pots on the stove.

"A radio station, wow!" said Bill, whistling through his teeth, "I guess you'll get to interview the majorettes, and maybe even football players, too, huh?" he glanced at the TV that was switched on.

"I got my rings enlarged, but now they're too small for me again. It's a sign of age, ain't nothing I can do about that!" Jill sighed with a smile.

Bill had forgotten about Katya's coffee. He said, "I'm a Chicago Bulls fan. I'm from, well, not really from Chicago, but from Illinois, from a little town called Rantoul, well, in fact, I'm really from a little farm lost in the cornfields."

"Do you follow American football, Katya?" Jill wanted to know.

"Could I help myself to a little more sweet corn?" I asked.

"Oh sure you can! Finish it all, John, that's what I like to see. What kind of factory do I work in? We make bathroom fittings, bathtubs and basins and showers. Have you been to our bathroom here at home, yet? No? Oh, you gotta go, it's an experience in itself! Hey kids, make sure you leave a little room for dessert, huh?"

"Jill's made a cake that is to die for," Bill said, and brought it over to the table. It was a large cake, decorated with pink icing and a red ribbon made of sugar.

"Hey, hold on there!" Jill told him off, stroking his hand.

"I don't want to wait! I really want them to see this, right now! It's a miracle! It's the best strawberry cake in all of America! And it's been made by my wife!"

Jill grinned.

Bill looked for something in the fridge, then closed it. He solemnly placed a sky blue rose, made out of marzipan, on top of the cake.

Jill clapped.

I joined in.

I looked at Katya, who was sitting with her nose wrinkled up in distaste, stiff, upright, with her head held high and her eyes raised upward, as if she wanted to see what was on top of the furniture that was almost ceiling high. Slowly she reached for my glass of milk and took a sip. Then she was back to being stiff as a statue. The Allegory of Distinction, I thought to myself.

"JEEZ!" KATYA said when we were walking through the parking lot to my car. No, our car.

In one of the display windows in the shopping mall, which was closed now, I saw the essence of American life offered to my eyes in red neon: Snacks . . . Root Beer . . . Newspapers . . . Milkshakes . . . Mango Madness . . . Coca-Cola. It was a completely unpremeditated artistic installation and I looked at it admiringly. There was nobody there, only the low and long and wide buildings of the mall, cold, and, to European eyes, dehumanized, as incomprehensible as America itself.

A European has to get used to the cold beauty of America. I knew this from my own experience. Now I got a kick out of seeing a highway with its colorful gas stations on either side; I enjoyed the sight of the huge empty spaces of the ground-level parking lots, full of cars by day, empty by night. I loved to look at this hidden beauty of America, almost a metaphor for the country itself, where the practical use of a space or a building is more important than how they look.

I took Katya by the shoulders and turned her toward me. She lowered her head, looking down at the concrete, the ground of the parking lot. She probably didn't have any other point of reference. Not even I was a point of reference.

I caressed her shoulders. She didn't move.

I pressed the smooth fabric of her blouse, but I felt no desire. Katya led me to a place that was halfway between two tall street-lights, that was poorly lit. She threw her head back.

I continued caressing her. Katya sighed and moaned with her eyes closed. I was only going through the motions, I didn't feel anything. I pressed my palms up harder against her breasts. Katya bent a little forward at the waist. I unfastened her blouse. Her bra then unfastened at the front. Two full, heavy breasts fell from it.

No desire came.

Pity took the place of desire.

I fastened Katya's blouse. I kissed her hair.

Slowly I took her to the car.

I turned around to see the welcoming yellow light that came from Jill and Bill's house. I thought about them: as they said goodbye and afterward, as Katya and I walked away, when Bill and Jill gave each other a clumsy hug. At a distance, on the lit veranda, they looked like two rag dolls designed to make people laugh and yet feel tender at the same time. Jill and Bill.

WHEN WE stopped in front of Katya's place, she looked at me out of the corner of her eye—in a seductive way? Or was she keeping a careful watch on me?

"Would you like to come in for a glass of wine?" she asked. No, I didn't feel like it. So I said nothing. Katya placed a hand on my thigh.

I remained silent. Katya put my hand on her right breast. I still said nothing. I made a move as if to caress her. Nothing. There was just a breast, nothing else; it might as well have been a chair.

Katya stuck out her lower lip and sang, "Sweet corn, baked potatoes, hot dogs," with her Russian accent. That slightly ridiculous accent. Or sad, even. Pathetic, like my hand on her breast.

"Sweet coooooorn, baked potaaaaatoes, hot dooooogs," sang Katya, a disdainful sneer on her lips. She still had that red stain on her teeth. I knew it, even though I couldn't see it in the dark.

I freed my hand, and turned the key in the ignition.

"Are you sure you don't feel like a glass of wine or champagne?" Katya asked again.

No, I didn't feel like having a glass of wine or champagne with Katya. I don't feel like it, I was about to say. But in the end I replied, "Yes, there's nothing I'd like better, but tomorrow I have to get up early. So I can't."

She left languorously, slowly, with indifference. But I knew she was play-acting. She muttered something in a hoarse voice about Mikhail. Instantly, I saw his hands. But nothing else. I was at peace.


I DROVE, I didn't want to go straight home. I took note of the cold light of the streetlamps as they whooshed past me, each one identical to the other. The same lights, with long breaks between them: always, the same monotony. Always, the same enigma. Sweet corn, baked potatoes, hot dogs. The memory of that evening ran through me like sweet port wine. In front of me, I saw the Chicago Bulls and a few majorettes on a TV screen. And a glass of cold milk. A yellow light in a dark house. I stepped on the gas.

# X

# SYLVA

"IN RUSSIA, YOU WILL MEET TSVETAYAVA. HOW I ENVY you, Andrei."

You were going back to your country, despite your protests, I had got my way. I wanted to follow you, and live peacefully far from Prague where people were making my life impossible.

"Tsvetayava? That would be difficult," you interrupted me, "she killed herself a few years ago, not long after her return to Russia."

Finally! We would live together, far from this poisonous city.

"Then you'll meet Babel, Mandelstam . . ."

"But Sylva, do you really not know that both of them have died in the forced labor camps?"

I had managed to impose my own will, my desires.

"All right, what I mean is, you'll be able to meet important artists and poets, maybe even Anna Akhmatova, and musicians, who knows, maybe Shostakovich, why not?" I told him. I prattled on, talking endlessly just to give myself something to do. "What a great adventure, Andrei! How I envy you!"

I talked my head off to make my inner voice shut up. The voice that had been speaking to me since last night.

Yesterday in the middle of the night I had heard the phone ring. I hadn't woken up. I wasn't asleep. In silence, I picked up the phone.

"I know it's you," said a woman's nervous voice, "You who have Andrei in her power."

"Me?" I'd said, "But Andrei's free to do as he pleases." Silly though it might seem, I felt flattered. The woman's voice was trembling.

"You who do just as you please with Andrei, you who are spinning your little web just the way you want it."

Irritated, I said, "You're the one doing as she pleases, how come you're calling people up at this time of night?" The woman's voice hadn't reacted to my words, she was beside herself: "You're playing with him like a chess player would a pawn. And now you're doing your best to send him to Siberia." "Andrei wants to go back to Russia," I said, and wanted to add, "Of his own free will," but my voice had dried up. So I remained silent, as usual. It was better that way! I didn't have to justify myself. "Pardon me, Madame von Stamitz, for being so forthright. But please, do think things over, there is still time!" The woman was imploring me. Her entreaties made me feel good. "Talk to him, let him have second thoughts," she went on, "You know that he's ill. If he goes to Russia, he's done for. It'd kill him!" In the chill of the night, I felt so cold I was shivering. I had to sit down. "I beg of you," I heard the receiver say. Such hysterics! I told myself, although I knew full well that the woman on the other end of the line was worried sick, that she was desperate. "I beg of you, in the name of your mother, who died in a concentration camp because she wanted to follow her husband even there. Please Madame Sylva, in the name of everything that's sacred, talk to Andrei, he'll listen to you."

I hung up. I felt cold and wanted to get back into my warm bed.

Andrei was sleeping peacefully. I didn't wake him up. There was no reason to. I wouldn't have woken him up for anything in the world, least of all to make him think twice about his trip. And for other reasons, including the fact that I knew perfectly well which woman I'd just been dealing with.

All the same, there was still time . . .

So I talked incessantly, Andrei, just to get rid of the silence that had fallen between us, and to get rid of the phantom thoughts that kept telling me you were going back to Russia because I had willed it, against your own better judgement. I talked and prattled on so much that I managed to convince myself that this trip of yours was a wonderful, enviable thing, that it was a great adventure.

Your return to Russia. To the Soviet Union. The return trip organized by the Soviet embassy. In other words, Stalin himself.

The voice of that woman on the phone went through my mind again and again. She had called to convince me that it would be a fatal mistake if Andrei went back to Russia. But I knew that. I'd known it even before that woman called me.

How had she found out about my mother? Or that I'd asked Andrei to make this trip?

Whatever the case, it was too late to go back. I wouldn't give that neighbor the satisfaction of following her advice. In a short while, Andrei would board a train for Russia. Now that I'd heard how desperate that woman was, I was convinced that Andrei absolutely had to go.

Was it really too late now to backtrack? No . . . there was still time!

On the platform, you looked at me so calmly.

The desperation in the neighbor's voice . . . would I be capable of such deep compassion?

There was still time . . . I had to tell you . . .

Your silence weighed heavily on me, Andrei. It weighed on

me, even though you weren't nervous then, and were simply looking at me.

"Are you looking forward to going back home, Andrei?"

"I'm looking forward to meeting up with you again."

"But not to going back home? We each only have one country we can call our own."

"Why? What does home mean to you?"

"It's something you value. The thing you value most."

"You are my home. I have no other."

"That's a wonderful thing to say, but I'm talking about fields, forests, scents, and colors."

"I've spent the last twenty-two years in the forest, among animals and Gypsies and trees and small flowers. I was happy there, even more so when you came along."

"But Andrei, surely—"

My persuasive chatter broke off. Shattered by the quick movement of the little red flag. By the shriek of the whistle.

Yet there was still time!

You got onto the train, together with other faces that were familiar to me from the party at the Soviet Embassy. Carrying your favorite canvases, you boarded the train, Andrei, too tall and too burly for that narrow door, too elegant for those bureaucrats from the embassy, who made you go deep into the inside of the train; you were too free and too natural—like a creature of the forest—for that prison on wheels.

Andrei, when you got onto that train, I couldn't see you any longer. I just saw a free man who was walking into a cell, it could as easily have been a monasterial cell or a prison cell. A place too dark and narrow for your longings, for your sense of freedom.

You leaned out of the window.

There was still time! I had to tell you . . .

"Andrei, get out," I said in a near whisper.

You burst out laughing, you thought I was joking.

"Andrei, we'll have a child, you'll be by my side."

"Yes, yellow butterfly, I mean Blue Butterfly, of course we'll have children! Of course we will!"

He didn't get it. Yes, we'd have children, because I was already expecting.

I'd put on my sky blue dress, which must have been at least fifteen years old by then. I wanted you to see me like that, in your memories. Dressed in sky blue.

In your memories? Why, we'd be together again very, very soon! And our child would be born there, in those new surroundings where the insufferable atmosphere of Prague wouldn't weigh upon me so. Hatred. Hatred against me, against the mother of Andrei's child.

Lots of people on the platform were crying, and some of those who were leaning out of the windows also had moist eyes. Many others were laughing and waving their handkerchiefs and blowing kisses or arguing and raising their voices—a usual enough scene before the departure of any international train. A feverish atmosphere.

Only you then, Andrei, with your white shirt unbuttoned at the neck, you who had argued against making this trip and had refused to make it, you, who had started at the idea of it like a forest creature when it spots a hunter, only you were looking confident.

You were looking confidently at me. Confident in my correct choice.

Your confidence, your devotion was . . .

I wasn't able to finish the thought. The train moved.

"Andrei, get off the train!"

You didn't hear me. The train was making a lot of noise. I

paid no heed to the hiss of steam from the locomotive, nor to the stationmaster's whistle, nor to the shouts and wails and kisses. All I saw was my own desire, which had appeared before me as clear and prominent as a palm tree in the desert.

I shouted at the top of my lungs, "Andrei, get off the train!"

At that very moment, perhaps too late, my desire was clear.

"Andrei, get off the train!"

Waves of handkerchiefs, waves of tears.

And in the middle of all this hustle and bustle, you whispered.

I heard you through the din of the revolving red and black wheels, through the flames of the women's cries. You were upright in the train, by the window, you didn't feel all those bodies pressing against you. You said, simply, quietly, "Blue Butterfly."


I GOT off the tram in the Prague neighborhood of Vinohrady. I was dragging Jan along by the hand.

Jan, who had just turned five, was looking at the shops on Francouzská Avenue. Unlike our impoverished neighborhood of Malá Strana, here there were long rows of display windows. The shops opened their empty mouths. But the eyes of a child could find, even in that desert, sparkling treasures from lost Pacific Islands.

I pulled Jan away from each one of those temptations; in my left hand I was carrying two heavy bags; in them were Beethoven's quartets, Brahms's sonatas for violin and Mahler's lieder, Janáček's music for piano and Smetana, everything by Smetana. And the Russians, that was something new: Shostakovich's piano trios, Stravinsky's Rites of Spring and Orpheus. And, especially, the song of the angels with golden hair and white wings who carried a flute in their hands—the old liturgical chants—and also contemporary ones, the ones by Balakirov.

I pulled Jan well away from a window displaying caps, of

the type normally worn by building workers. The sign hanging above the caps read: "Throughout our country echoes the voice of hatred and scorn for the gang of spies and traitors in our midst. Death to the agents of imperialism!" I pulled Jan away from the shop windows with my right hand, in my left I was carrying two heavy bags full of records. This music had survived the war declared on me by my first husband, and on the racket made by the Nazi planes and their orders shouted in penetrating voices, like the kicks given by military boots, and now it had survived the shouting of the new leaders of today, the Communists who had taken over by means of a coup d'état. These records had survived the phony euphoria of the workers' festivals with their parades: Schubert and Chopin, Purcell and Schnittke, Martinů and Palestrina . . . Giovanni Pierluigi of Palestrina . . . just his name was music to my ears. In those two shopping bags I carried all my worldly goods, all my treasures.

Jan's treasures consisted of everything he saw in those badly lit shop windows: a wooden train set and a monkey in the toy shop, a string of greenish sausages in a butcher's, a little pot of sickly violets in a florist's.

There were no roses anymore. Roses yellow as sand, roses the color of custard, like the arms of a baroque plaster angel, roses white as clouds in the spring sky. Oh, roses! The color of my Pink Palace in the Malá Strana, which was no longer pink and no longer mine, it was gray and the State had taken it over. Roses red as sealing wax. Roses! You couldn't bring them to me as gifts now, Andrei, those roses in those trembling fingers of yours. What are roses like, those long-stemmed flowers? What do they look like? Jan was eyeing a couple of bluish Vienna rolls in a baker's window. One was covered in rock salt, the other in cumin, and the cumin was green. In the lady's wear shop they were displaying overalls of the kind electricians wear, blue ones:

they were puffed up with pride, like the flag of this new era. I looked inside the shop: apart from four sets of electricians' overalls, there were some navy tracksuits, another sign of the new era.

But Jan was dragging me over to the display in the paper shop, where there were only a few rolls of toilet paper, nothing else. A paper shop, a trunk full of enigmas! Jan asked for a notebook to draw in. As soon as we entered, around me, on all the shelves and on the counter, as in a nightmare, all I could see were rolls of toilet paper. The sales assistant shook his head. "No, we don't have any notebooks. Not one, no. Not white ones, or ones with lines, or little squares. I can give you toilet paper, kid," he said to Jan, "it just came in."

"I'm not blind," Jan replied, but coming from a child it didn't sound provocative. The sales assistant added, "Or maybe you'd like some sandpaper, little man? We've also got some of that."

Chuffed by the success his verbal skills had had, Jan answered, "You're offering me sandpaper in case your toilet paper doesn't work, right?"

I took Jan away, apologizing profusely, but the old sales assistant laughed out loud and gave Jan a sweet wrapped in silver paper, "If you were older, I'd buy you a big jug of beer for answering me like that. So now you know: in a few years' time, it'll be here waiting for you!"

We continued walking along the row of poorly lit displays, and in each shop window there was a kind of red flying carpet with gold letters on it: "With the Soviet Union for eternity. The Soviet Union is the guarantee of world peace. The Soviet Union is the model to follow. The Soviet Union is our future. Together with the Soviet Union, toward a brilliant future."

With Jan's little palm in my right hand, and both heavy bags in my left, I entered house number five on Slovenská Street.

That is where they had sent us after taking the Pink Palace away from me, even the very apartment I lived in, as a punishment for spending my childhood in a Renaissance chateau. I only lived in one part of the building, though, which I shared with my grandmother, I had said by way of a defense, and they laughed in my face and took over the Pink Palace, as well as the Renaissance chateau. They didn't punish me for becoming a citizen of the Reich before the war. During the war my neighbors had made my life impossible with their contempt; after the war, they broke my windows and once, one night in Kampa Park, they beat me up with their fists and sticks. To the new authorities, the Communists, I had become a class enemy, an undesirable being, someone against whom it was necessary to fight until I learned how to share what I had with the people.

Moving house, going to live in a neighborhood that wasn't in the city center, all of this forced on me by the new Communist Party government, was, when all was said and done, a break, a relief for me, even though I was moving to a house that was worse than the last one. More than worse. I knew I was now going to live in poverty. I entered the corridor of the house at number five Slovenská Street, and breathed in the coal-cellar smell. The concierge blocked our path with her fists on her hips, wearing one of those navy-blue tracksuits, which hung in spectacularly loose fashion from her prominent knees and elbows. The concierge, all skin-and-bones, with her head covered in little metal curlers and a checkered apron tied over her tracksuit, stared at me with little eyes that went straight through me. I introduced myself, and I offered my hand; she didn't shake it.

Jan and I walked into an empty apartment. I felt calm, at peace with myself: nobody knew me here, I could go to the baker's and the butcher's and the cobbler's with a clear conscience. Deep inside me I felt Andrei saying in his low voice, "You know,

Sylva, when you're in a period of calm, it's easy to make the right decisions. When the going gets rough, on the other hand, it's difficult to see things clearly and it's easy to make mistakes that you will later regret for the rest of your life." I felt a tremendous sense of inner tranquility.

"Where's the furniture, Mama?" Jan asked. "They'll bring it all tomorrow," I replied. I sized the place up: Would there be enough space for the piano? It would have to go next to the window. The records, my treasures, I placed carefully in a dark corner; they stood there in a multicolored column. In my mind's eye I worked out where the Renaissance suits of armor and the knights' helmets from the Hussite period, and the swords and the lances—those memories of my parents and my childhood—would go. I told myself they would go with the old Chinese tea service, the one from which, as a girl, I had drank hot chocolate, while sitting on a baroque chaise longue. I would place some ornaments on the table, in memory of my grandmother. In this new apartment, I wanted to have a memory of each and every one of my dead. I would carry in Andrei's paintings personally, and put them under my bed.

In the evenings, instead of a lullaby, I read Jan the memoirs of a famous traveller who had crossed the ocean on a raft. Several animals had accompanied the man on that improvised Noah's ark of his, including a monkey so nervous that he padded up and down on the raft. The traveller had tried all kinds of tricks to calm the animal down, all in vain. In the end it occurred to him to build it a little house right there on the raft. Only then did the monkey calm down: what it needed was to feel protected.

"Like a dog needing a kennel," said little Jan, sleepily. He wanted to go on, even as his eyes were closing, "It doesn't matter that we don't have any furniture. We've got a little house just to ourselves, haven't we, Mama?"

EVERYTHING CHANGED. Everything got twisted around. It was like the chaos before the creation of the world. Teachers worked in factories and quarries and sewers. People who often didn't have any qualifications whatsoever, had chairs at the universities. Everybody had to live where the State told them to. There was work for everybody, but you couldn't refuse the work they gave you. There were free schools for children everywhere, but they all went to the same type of school, in which the builders of tomorrow's socialism were trained and indoctrinated. The prisons were filled with innocent people: again. The prisons were chock-full, crammed, bursting at the seams, and their walls eventually collapsed, so thousands of guiltless prisoners were sent into forced labor, to the uranium mines: those who entered even once didn't live past forty. Deep inside me that old voice began to echo, that timeless voice, the voice at the gates of hell, hoarse from repeating the same words so many times . . . For me you will go to the city of suffering, for me you will undergo everlasting pain, for me you will go with the lost people . . . Before me, nothing eternal was created, and I will last forever. Abandon all hope, ye who enter here . . .

Caught up in the maelstrom, my life changed too: I'd lost the Jewish and German pupils who had come to learn to play the piano, I'd lost the possibility of renting an apartment. I found myself, along with little Jan, without any income. Jan had to eat, but there was little food in the shops, and especially little fruit and vegetables, which all children need.

After standing in long queues in front of dozens of offices, in the end they gave me a job: I would work as a librarian in a little library next to the Water Tower in the Vinohrady neighborhood. That political maelstrom also swept away a lot of books: whole truckloads and trainloads took away tons of books that were now banned, reflecting as they did the bourgeois mindset, or showing bourgeois or capitalist or feudal settings, or relaying pessimistic messages. Those trucks carried off the classics of world literature and of Czech literature, and the poets of the international Surrealist movement and Czech poetism, because they were decadent; the Nazis hadn't liked these books, and the current leaders didn't care for them much either. They would permit only works that reflected a spirit of future optimism, and past and present class hatred. If the other lot, ten years ago, had built up their impossible German ideals imagining a world without Jews or Gypsies or intellectuals or artists, the current lot were more or less doing the same thing.

The shelves of the library where I worked were full of the works of new writers, essayists, critics, poets such as František Branislav, Pavel Kohout, and Rudé Pravo.

For two months I walked past the library shelves, pressing my palms against my favorite classics, trembling at the thought that they too might end up in the recycling bin. For two months I caressed those favorites of mine with my fingers; they had so far escaped the eye of the censor, but tomorrow they might be candidates for liquidation. Balzac and Dostoevsky, Tolstoy and Flaubert, Turgenev and Stendhal . . .

And then one day they came. Again, there were two of them: one in a brown suit, the other dressed in gray. These two had puffy faces from all the beer they drank, Slavic faces with high cheekbones. They were even a little more crude and gross than the previous ones. They didn't talk about philosophy or music. "Come and see us," they said, by way of a farewell, "in the Ministry of the Interior!" they added, from the doorway of the library.

I didn't go, but I was troubled by the whole business. During the day I would cross those wide avenues when the traffic light was red; the cars, which barely managed to brake in time, would toot their horns, frantically and furiously.

They came back. "Why didn't you turn up? Aren't you one of us? Aren't you on our side? Do not fail to come and see us. Whoever is not with us, is against us."

I didn't go.

In the evenings, I made an effort to pretend that everything was OK. Little Jan looked at me suspiciously. He knew I was suppressing something, but he didn't ask any questions and stayed on his best behavior. He cut out human shapes from the potato peel, and on Saturday evening he performed a play with potato puppets, just for me.

I couldn't sleep, not even after drinking a tea of lime tree leaves or a cup of chamomile, not even after an unbelievably tiring day, or with sleeping pills. I read Balzac. I'd finished *The Woman of Thirty*, yet couldn't have said what it was about.

The third time, they didn't turn up in person. They sent me a letter. It was an order: Come to the Ministry of the Interior, Day: May 11, at ten o' clock in the morning.

I would have to go, as I'd known I eventually would.

THERE WERE two portraits on the wall: one of Gottwald, and the other, of Stalin.

Abandon all hope, ye who enter here . . .

There was a saucer with some biscuits on the table. "Do help yourself."

They sat me down in front of the saucer. They both sat on the other side: the gray one and the brown one. A character with peroxide blonde hair placed a gilt coffee cup in front of each of us.

Deep inside me, that voice was echoing . . . For me you will go to the city of suffering, for me you will undergo everlasting pain . . . Abandon all hope . . .

"So you finally came, did you? At last."

"Yes."

"You took a hell of a long time to do so, didn't you, Comrade Stamitz?"

"Well..."

"Had to make an effort."

"Well..."

"The important thing is that you're here with us."

"Yes, with us, and that's why we've invited you here," the gray one added after the brown one had said his piece, gleefully rubbing his hands.

"You are Czech, are you not?" asked the brown one, with a smile.

"Czech?" I asked, playing for time, "Only on my mother's side."

"We know that," said the brown one.

"That's good enough," the gray one interrupted him, speaking in a serious tone, "That's good enough for you to join the Communist Party of Czechoslovakia."

"Who, me? Why?"

"Yes, you. That you are Czech is good enough for you to join the Communist Party of Czechoslovakia, without that entailing any further obligations," the gray one explained, without smiling, his face serious.

"Well, with just one tiny little obligation, so little that it's hardly worth mentioning."

"I'm sorry?" I said.

"It's nothing, don't get alarmed. What I mean is, should you see anything, by pure coincidence, by chance..."

"Nothing to it," said the brown one in a nasal voice, "Like falling off a log."

"This way, it'd be easier for you to improve your standing, Comrade Stamitz."

"You see, Comrade, you're in the doghouse."

"During the war, and before it . . . you know what I'm talking about . . ."

"What are you referring to?" I asked in a faint voice, because I knew exactly what he was referring to. And I also knew that now they were going to air my dirty laundry in public.

"You're keeping mum."

"Well . . ."

"Everybody should get what they deserve."

"You went over to the Nazis."

"And you did it even before the war started, that's a fact!"

"And as if that wasn't bad enough, you had been the wife of a tycoon, in other words, an exploiter of the workers."

"That was back then, a long time ago," I tried to say in my defense.

"That doesn't matter. What matters isn't the time, it's the fact in itself," the gray one said.

"You were the wife of an important diplomat, a representative of the bourgeois republic."

"You have aristocratic origins."

"In your family, there hasn't been a single representative of the working class."

"Or of the peasantry."

"So if you want to keep out of trouble . . ."

"Big trouble . . ."

"It'd be very easy for you to improve your standing, Comrade Stamitz. Your current standing is nothing to boast about, you should bear that in mind."

They paused.

The gray one cut to the chase.

"Do you regret all that, Comrade Stamitz?"

"Yes."

I remembered how, fifteen years ago, I had accepted Reich citizenship as if it was a foul communion wafer.

"If you're sorry about having done it, you could make amends."

"Atone for it."

"In a nutshell, make up for it, if you want to."

"How?" I asked, then fell silent.

"Do you want to or don't you?"

"I think so."

"Yes or no?"

"Yes."

"It'll be easy, Comrade."

The brown one rubbed his hands.

"Your head can be held high and your heart be cleansed," said the gray one, finishing his coffee. I didn't touch mine. I was thinking how Andrei, seven years ago, hadn't touched those delicacies provided by the Soviet Embassy.

The brown one cleared his throat.

"And don't look so sour faced. There's nothing to it! You know the other employees at the library, and what's more you've made friends with lots of people who go there to take out books. Very well, this is what your job will consist of: very occasionally, say once a month, you will have a friendly meeting with my colleague," he pointed at the gray one, "and you will tell him that everything is in order at the library. And everything probably will be in order, I'm sure it will, but if there should ever be anything that isn't in order, then you'll let him know, in a friendly manner. In this way, you'll improve you own standing and you'll help others."

"Help?"

"Yes, you'll be helping those who stray from our common path."

"Building up a socialist motherland isn't easy, Comrade Sta-mitz, so we all have to do our bit and report those who wish to see it harmed."

"Do you accept?"

"No."

"Think it over very carefully. You don't have to give us a defi-nite answer today. Think it over and come back here in three days' time."

When I'd already stood up to leave, he continued speaking, "You have a son, don't you?"

"Think it over carefully, Comrade Stamitz," said that Greek choir as I headed for the door.

IN THE library, I watched the people who, exhausted after a full day's work, came looking for books, put them in shopping bags, and took them home. I was starting to get to know them.

When three days had gone by, I didn't go back to the Minis-try of the Interior.

They summoned me there a month later; I refused to collab-orate with them. They didn't pay much attention to my refusal and recommended that I think it over some more.

I was afraid. Really afraid. Jan was having problems at school, and not only there. One day he was attacked in the park. I was sure that they were behind it all; them, the gray one and the brown one. Was I right to be so sure? I really didn't know.

SEVEN YEARS. For seven years, I'd been knocking on the doors of different ministries, asking for news, a snippet of any news, for me, the beggar of news.

For seven years I'd been asking: Where is Andrei?

I was heading toward the sky again.

I was going up the New Castle Stairs right up to the sky, to that foul, evil, abominable sky. At the upper end of the staircase I came across some black stone figures at a gate, figures that were arguing, beating each other, making war. In a mortal embrace they stabbed each other with gold daggers.

I avoided the figures and proceeded to walk up the street, up and ever up, infinitely higher, until a magnificent palace of white stone blocked my path, a gigantic, white arch, resting on dozens of classical columns. Before I was swallowed up in its dark bowels, I was able to read a poster that hung at the entrance, announcing that this was the Černín Palace, headquarters of the Foreign Ministry.

Abandon all hope, ye who enter here!

I stopped to catch my breath. How many times had I already knocked on this door: Please, can you tell me where he is? Tell me, please, I beg of you! Don't shut the door on my hopes, give me just one word of news! Where is he? What's become of him? What have they done to him? Where has he ended up? Where has he disappeared to?

Where is the father of my son? Where is Andrei? Where is Andrei Ivanovich, whose father's name, Jan, I gave to my son? Where is Polonski, the painter?

For seven years I'd been knocking on this door and begging. I beg of you, please tell me, please. That is how I implored them, I, my mother's orchid, I who she wanted to turn into a chocolate cup made of Meissen porcelain.

Is he alive? Just tell me that, nothing else, I just want to know if I can live with some hope. Some hope, no matter how little!

Tell me he's alive.

Tell me he's alive and I will put on iron shoes and I will fill my pockets with iron bread, and I will travel around the world in search of him.

Is he ill? Like Psyche, I will accomplish four impossible tasks.

Just tell me that he is ill, and then I'll know he's alive and I'll go to Tartarus, to the kingdom of the dead, to bring him, as Psyche did, the elixir of life.

For seven years I'd been waiting for a letter from Andrei. For seven years I'd been checking my letterbox five times a day to see if there was a letter from him. Seven years. From the moment when Andrei had left, I hadn't received a single line from him. Silence. Nothing. Seven years of silence. Seven years, seven times three-hundred-and-sixty-five days with nothing to do except wait.

*SVIDENII NE imeem*, we don't know, they'd told me at the Soviet Embassy when, three months after Andrei's departure, I'd gone there to ask for some information about him. We don't know anything about him.

We don't know, the Soviet consul told me four months after Andrei's departure. And after five, six, and seven months he said the exact same thing: *Svidenii ne imeem*. My letters to Moscow, to the Foreign Ministry, and then to the Ministry of the Interior, had gone unanswered.

A letter to Stalin: To the Most Distinguished Mr. Stalin. No answer.

Another letter, a desperate one this time: Comrade Stalin! No answer. Not a single word.

I found myself standing in front of the door that had just been closed behind me. In front of the door of the palace of ice. The door of the Černín Palace, the headquarters of the Foreign Ministry.

Just one thing was echoing in my head, the one thing they'd told me, a single rosary made up of a single sentence repeated as if it were a litany, "We don't know anything. We recommend that you desist from seeking Polonski, the painter, for your own good, although, I repeat, we don't know anything."

THE DAY after my visit to the palace of ice, I received an urgent certified letter informing me that I was to go to the Ministry of the Interior on a matter of the greatest urgency. The brown one and the gray one were waiting for me there.

"Have you thought our proposal over?"

"Yes."

"Do you accept it?"

"No."

"No?"

"No."

"Not at all, not even as an occasional proposal?"

"Not at all. I can't go on living like this. Leave me alone."

They had a good laugh. The brown one slapped his knees, the gray one pressed his hand to his belly.

Suddenly, they fell silent, as if someone had given them a secret signal. They became serious, as if at a funeral.

The gray one said, sadly, "You are in a pickle. Ooooh, what a horrible pickle!"

When the brown one spoke, I saw a stick beating against the table.

"You're playing with us. You have been intimately involved with a Russian, you ask about him all over the office, as if we two here didn't exist."

Did they know something? Hope flared up in my brain like a flaming arrow in the darkness.

The two men fell silent.

"Where is he?" I asked; I couldn't bear it.

They remained silent. I could barely withstand the tension. After a while, the stick hit the table once more.

"You're . . . an enemy of the people!" the brown one said in a tone of infinite disgust.

"Enemy of the people?" I exclaimed. It was all the same to me. Only one thing mattered, "What do you know about him?"

They said nothing. And they grimaced, mixing secrecy with irony, and made sick-sounding noises.

"What do you know about him?" I asked, urgently.

"About Andrei Polonski?" said the gray one, with repugnance, "The painter of perverse scenes and Gypsy orgies?"

They looked as if they were about to throw up.

I made no attempt to disguise the suspense I felt. Nothing mattered to me. I looked at them, humbly. Like a beggar, begging for some news, a bit of information. Whatever it turned out to be.

The gray one spoke in studied tones, drawing out each syllable. That grimace of victorious, mocking superiority remained on the faces of both functionaries, "Mrs. Stamitz, you, who are not a member of the Communist party, who refuse to become one, you, a single mother, which is to say a harmful being in a socialist society, it is you who are asking us for something, and yet you are not prepared to give us anything in return? That is not fair!"

The brown one said, in a low voice, "Comrade Stamitz, whether or not you are a single mother, whether or not you were involved with a degenerate painter and enemy of the people, that doesn't matter. All I want to tell you is that we know how to protect those people who are of service to us."

"I can't do what you ask of me," I said in a faint voice.

"Do you still love him, that enemy of the people? And your son, do you love that son of yours? And does he love his mother?"

"Why are you asking me this?"

"At school tomorrow, the teacher will read out to Jan's class the story of a bad socialist, so that they may learn to despise you. It will be your story, Comrade Stamitz."

I was choking, I couldn't believe what I'd heard, I couldn't believe they could blackmail me in this way.

I shut up and signed.

AT SUPPERTIME, I put on a record of Orthodox Russian liturgies. I made potato rissoles. Jan, having wolfed down twenty of them, asked me, "It's been a long time since you told me about Papa. At school they ask me what my father does and I don't know what to say, so the kids laugh at me because of it."

"He lived with the animals in the forest. He too, was a kind of wild creature that was afraid of people."

"What do you mean? Isn't he alive?"

That was the last straw. The camel's back broke, split, cracked apart.

Jan wiped away my tears with the palm of his hand.

"Papa's got lost in the forest, hasn't he? When I'm grown up, I'm going to find him."

"We'll go together, if you want."

"You'd be afraid. There'll be deer, bears, and maybe even wolves."

"I won't be scared. If you come with me, I'll be brave."

The slate turntable went on turning—here we go again, and again—and filled the little, single-roomed flat with music worthy of the angels, sung by silvery feminine voices and garnet male ones. The kind of voice your father had, I mean has, Jan. Every evening we listened to the Orthodox Russian liturgies, and Jan dreamed about fighting with bears and wolves. Before going to bed, I would tell Jan, by way of a folktale or lullaby, about his father's childhood: how once a week, his parents would take him to church. Spiritual fathers with endless white beards and black tunics that stretched down to the floor would say the words of the Mass in grave, ever-so-melodic voices. When his father left the church, he would find himself in the middle of the stunning white silence of vast Russian solitude, and he would be blinded by sun, snow, and ice.

And Jan would sleep peacefully in the middle of the chanting and the incense, as the candles made the shadows weak.

THE DOOR of the Ministry closed behind me . . . For me you will go to the city of suffering . . . Abandon all hope . . . I took a deep breath, but was short of oxygen all the same. I felt dizzy and had to sit down, but there wasn't a chair or bench in sight. I leaned against the wall, but then I had the sensation that the building's walls were caving in, that I'd be buried under the ruins.

I held the letter with the name of the official to whom I had to supply information, and who would instruct me as to my job. The letter bore as well the time and day of our next appointment: today, in five minutes' time. Now!

Every day I woke up after a sleepless night, with stomach upsets caused by fear. In the library they had fired almost all my colleagues and had replaced them with new people. Why had they got rid of Jana, Jarmila, and Maruška? The rest of us lived in constant fear, like beasts awaiting their turn at the slaughterhouse. It was just like when the Nazis were here. And the meetings . . . Once they accused me of things in the most humiliating way, yet another time they praised me a little so I began to hold my head high and work with pleasure, but not long after they shamed me again and belittled me in front of all the others. They forced me to bow down, more and more until I was unable to hold my head high.

We vegetated, we existed; we weren't living. We tried to turn ourselves into shadows, we dressed in gray, shapeless clothes. Even my hair, which I dyed golden in the summer, was hidden under an old hat. What I wasn't going to tolerate was covering my head with the kind of headscarf used by Russian women working on the *kolkhoz*, or put on a blue tracksuit or overalls, those uniforms of the new era. The concierges, employed by the authorities, kept an eye out and watched everyone like a hawk and knew every step that was taken in the respective houses—they spied and wrote reports. The concierges always appeared everywhere at key moments, they entered the butcher's after you'd been queuing for two hours, and miraculously managed to get their own sausages or half a kilo of meat, and were able to pay for it quickly.

Like everybody else, I dragged myself past the rows of houses like a shadow, so that no one would spot me, so that no one would pay any attention to me, so that no one would spy on me and write a report about me.

Our only pleasure consisted of the absence of any events. We only felt happy when some predictable mishap ended up not happening.

AND NOW they'd asked me, too, to keep an eye on people, to closely observe those around me, to spy on them and write reports about them. That's why they'd summoned me, that's why I'd come to them at the Ministry of the Interior. And afterward . . . afterward perhaps they wouldn't throw me out of my job. Maybe they would let Jan get a place at university. And above all: maybe I could find out what had happened to Andrei.

Where was it I had to go, in fact, in this huge ministry building? I asked myself, full of nausea and loathing.

"Excuse me, sir, is this where I go?" I asked a short man, a visitor like me, and I showed him the name of the official mentioned in the letter.

"Here, on the ground floor? You need to go to the third floor, that's where the top guys are," he said, sniffing loudly, he probably had a cold. "Down here is where you come to collect your money, once you've done your work. You'll see, quite a pretty penny!" He winked at me, sniffing even louder, and added in a low voice, "Today I've made a small fortune!"

Having given me this information, the man felt important; he widened his stance and puffed out his chest.

At that moment I saw myself as if in a mirror; yes, that man, with his wide, orange tie, that man who couldn't stop his loud snot-swallowing and who wet his fingers, counting greedily his banknotes, that man with his self-satisfied smile and his hoarse voice was my mirror image. That is how I was, or would be if I complied.

I didn't pull myself together until I was back on the street, when I'd put some distance between myself and that place, striding away, fleeing as fast as my legs could carry me.

ONE EVENING, when Jan hadn't yet returned home, I sat Andrei's shadow down on the sofa next to me. With his absent self I could chat away as much as I wanted, tell him anything and be sure that he would listen to me, that he wouldn't interrupt me, that he would understand me. I'd never have to repeat myself or explain anything that was inexplicable to him. His absent self would accept my stories and my opinions and my philosophy of life in the way that I wanted him to. He would argue with me, though, for sure. I knew Andrei's replies. They were always unusual, uncommon.

As I listened to the silvery voices of a Russian mass, I told Andrei's shadow, "They came back to the library one day, rude this time, and absolutely furious. They ordered me to go and see them. I told them my intentions: I would not go anywhere and I didn't want to see them ever again. Then, Andrei, they moved us to a tiny cubbyhole. Now we live in an attic room, where it freezes over in winter and is stuffy in the summer. There's a concierge in this house too; this one's fat whereas our previous one was skinny, but as far as everything else is concerned, there's nothing to differentiate between them.

"Jan finished his school year with results that were exaggeratedly bad. At the meetings at work they threaten me and put me down. They've demoted me three times over, which means my salary has been cut by half; it's not enough to live on. My life is fear and defenselessness and terror, but Andrei, my life now really is mine! It belongs to me, to me and nobody else! I've learned to make three dozen different kinds of potato dishes.

"Meanwhile, Jan and I listen to Russian liturgies and plan our move to the forest to live with the deer, the bears, and the wolves. As you yourself once did, Andrei.

"Someone's coming up the stairs now, Andrei, with heavy footsteps, it's Jan, at last. That too, is a kind of happiness."

It wasn't Jan. My eight-year-old son hadn't turned up all day nor that same evening.

I went to the neighborhood police station. They gave me the brush-off. "You're not looking after your son properly, Comrade!"

That's when I started to suspect that the people at the Ministry of the Interior had kidnapped Jan to punish me for not having agreed to work as their spy.

THERE WAS no news of Jan for two whole days.

If he doesn't show up after two days, I thought, I'll go to the Ministry of the Interior and sign everything they ask me to. I'll do anything they want just as long as they give Jan back to me! To stop myself from shaking, I imagined what I'd say to him when he turned up. I'd tell him his favorite folktale; I'd read it when I was his age. It was about a prince who could only be happy in his dreams, and only then if he hadn't previously made his princess sad. The tale finishes with a moral: He who controls the reigns of his beloved's heart should remember that he is in a beautiful dream and should avoid being woken from it! To awake thus, is to fall from a beautiful day into the darkness of night.

Jan hasn't come home now for three days. Where is he?

I berated myself for not having kept a closer eye on him. But

I couldn't very well walk all the way to the school gates with him! I spent all my time in the evenings and on weekends with him only, I rejected the invitations from my new women friends and from my men friends. I remembered my own childhood and didn't want Jan to feel the way I felt then. I remembered my mother, who had often made the trip to Prague to go to a ball or to the theater or to the opera or to a concert. Back then, she would wear her blue coat for going to the theater, with white ermine on the collar and sleeves, and if she were going to a ball, she'd wear the olive lace dress, or the sleeveless pink satin one, with long gloves that stretched to above the elbow. She often didn't even say goodbye to me, but I would wait for her under the big arch of the entrance, beyond the bridge. I used to throw myself at Maman's neck when she reaches where I was waiting. I would smell her pompadour rose perfume and cry my eyes out, shouting at her not to go. Maman always brushed me off coldly, saying, "What a spoiled little girl! Home with you!"

Poor Maman . . .

Four days and Jan still hasn't come home. If he doesn't turn up this evening, I told myself, the next day I'd go first thing to look for those two men and beg them to let me be of service to them in exchange for getting my Jan back.

Monsieur Beauvisage . . . how he'd changed! That night he was sitting on my sofa at home. I'd met him at a drugstore in Zizkov, where I'd been queueing to buy laundry soap and toilet paper, mainly so I wouldn't have to go straight back home after work and resume my exhausting wait.

He'd called out my name when I was in the queue.

"Sylva von Stamitz . . ."

I'd turned around, but hadn't recognized the man who'd said those words, who'd startled me.

"Sylva, it's me, Petr, you used to call me Monsieur Beauvisage."

A man thin as a rake, with just a few white hairs left, but that smile ... yes, it was Petr.

Now he was sitting on my sofa at home, as far as possible from the door. You couldn't talk openly anywhere else, it would be dangerous to do so, Petr said. In a whisper, he told me his story, a persecuted writer who had spent two years in the uranium mines.

That's why I hadn't recognized him. It had been nine years since we'd last met.

"You know how it works, Sylva? The political trials go on and on, so people can see that the class struggle is intensifying. In recent years, this Stalinist doctrine has become the driving force behind the government regime. The secret police look for class enemies wherever they can. Be careful, Sylva. The police themselves invent conspiracies of Western imperialists or emigré traitors. That's what happened to me. Once they've accused someone, they have to give him the works. I know what I'm talking about, and I also know that they use methods that are often worse than those used by the Gestapo. Nobody knows anything about it, nobody can talk about it—only we know about it, we who have been through it all. The police need confessions whether a crime has been committed or not. To obtain them, they tie a bag over your head and chain your hands and feet. Then they blind you with electric light, beat you until you faint, smash your teeth, put you in a bathtub full of excrement. They apply electric shocks to the most susceptible parts of the body, and if you're a man they go for your testicles; this type of torture the police call the 'howl of the calf' or 'tomato purée.' The victims under investigation are made to stand for hours, their faces to the wall, or sometimes quite the opposite, when they are made to walk without stopping. Sometimes there are even fake executions, when they tell the victim to say goodbye to life. And afterward? Those wrecks are no longer human beings: they'll confess to anything, they'll sign whatever needs to be signed. Then they must learn their crimes by heart and recite them before the court. On top of this, they're given drugs before they speak to the court or on the radio so that they lose touch with reality and go on and on about crimes they never committed. Sometimes they even ask for a longer sentence or the death penalty itself."

I began to sink my nails into the sofa, then my whole hand, until it hurt, as if physical pain could throttle a different kind of agony. I thought about Jan, about Andrei, about my mother, about all those noble, feeble beings . . . The torturers had surely never loved anybody, I thought, otherwise they could not carry out their tasks.

"You must be exaggerating, Petr . . ." I said in a muffled voice.

Petr stopped talking. I looked at the signs of pain on his face. He was looking at a corner of the room.

"Innocent people, all of them innocent, I know them, there are thousands of innocent people," he murmured, "What could they be guilty of? The Communists' power is based on making others illegal. They invent guilty charges if and when it suits them. And those affected have no rights, they're completely helpless."

I was only half listening to him. My thoughts were with Jan, I couldn't concentrate on anything else. I told Petr how anxious I was.

"That's simple enough," and he picked up the phone.

He told me that during one interrogation he'd met an old school friend who was now a high-ranking member of the secret police.

"This man still has some scruples left; he felt ashamed in front of me. As if to atone for what he'd done, he told me to call him if I ever had any problem . . . anything specific. He almost begged me to do so, as if I would be doing him a favor; I reckoned he needed it, as a sign of forgiveness. He was red faced and sweating. I wouldn't do this for myself, I'd find it repugnant. But I'll call him for little Jan, and for you, too: if they've started with him, then you're in danger as well."

THAT EVENING, after about two hours, Jan came home. He ran into Petr in the doorway.

"Is this man . . . my father?" he asked, timidly.

"He's an uncle," I told him, taking a firm hold of him, "Uncle Petr."

Before saying goodbye, Petr invited me to a party to celebrate the death of Stalin, which was going to be held in the cellar of a house in a small village near Prague.

I told him I wouldn't be going. "I don't believe anything's going to change. I just don't think that's going to happen."

"I don't believe anything will either. I don't believe in anything at all." Petr said, closing the door behind him.

He started down the stairs, his back bent.

I suddenly remembered something and ran after him. I caught up with him in the street. Jan was running behind me.

"Petr," I said, out of breath, "in a period of calm it's easy to make the right decisions. But when the going gets rough, it's difficult to see things clearly and it's easy to make mistakes that you'll regret for the rest of your life. But you haven't made any, Petr."

With my son beside me, I flew back up to our sixth floor apartment, happy because Jan was back home, alive, and because I'd just met Petr again, alive, and because Petr had forgiven me for the business with the Nazis. I was so pleased that through it all Petr had remained himself.

Jan ate twenty potato rissoles, even though he had a fever.

On the advice of a psychologist friend, I didn't ask my son any questions, so that he might forget what had happened like it was a nightmare and so that it might not turn into a traumatic stumbling block for the rest of his life. I put Jan to bed and in a quiet voice I told him a folktale about Ivan, the son of the czar, and the bird of fire. Jan slept fifteen hours straight that night.

ONE DAY, some five or six years after losing Jan and finding him again with Petr's help, I received a letter with Soviet postmarks and Russian lettering on it. This was a time when I no longer trusted or believed in anything at all.

My heart jumped, but only for a fraction of a second. At first glance, I saw it wasn't Andrei's handwriting.

A friend of his had written to me, a certain Semyon, a fellow inmate in the Siberian gulag.

Almost as soon as he arrived in the USSR, Andrei had been condemned to forced labor.

He must have died in the camp.

Semyon hadn't seen him die with his own eyes, but when he left the camp Andrei was near the end.

When they had said goodbye to each other, Andrei said just one thing to Semyon, "Human life is like foam on the water . . . empty. I have lived for so many decades in the river of life and now, at the end, I am throwing off the burden of skin, of the body. And for the last time I will watch the red circle of the sun, in the west, disappear over the horizon."

Semyon told me in his letter that he would never forget those parting words. Andrei's last wish, the last word he said to Semyon, was this, "Write to Sylva. Write and tell her that she is always with me, day and night. Address it, do not forget this, to the 'Blue Butterfly!'"

Semyon gave me more and more details about Andrei's life

in the USSR. He told me several stories in his letters that passed through the hands of the censor. I didn't find out the whole of these stories until I met Semyon in person, in Moscow. Jan and I took advantage of the 1968 reforms to make the journey that would bring us closer to finding the clues that Andrei had left for us in his wake. So that we might know about his eventual fate.

AS SOON as his train arrived at Moscow station, Andrei was arrested, as were all the other émigrés who had gone back to their country at the invitation of the Soviet ambassador. They housed them in some provisional lean-tos. After a few days they took Andrei off for his interrogation, blindfolded.

When they removed the blindfold, Andrei found himself in a luxurious, carpeted office. He was welcomed by a young man.

"My name is Nikolai Bragin, an art and literature specialist employed by the NKVD, the political police." When he saw where he was, Andrei felt the world collapse around him.

Semyon repeated the story just as it had been told to him by Andrei:

"Don't be nervous, Mr. Polonski, why are you so scared? Stop trembling, I'm not here to chase spies. I completed my studies in the Department of Philosophy, and all I'm trying to do now is have a little conversation with you in a relaxed, friendly atmosphere, and to understand what it is you wish to do, now that you are starting a new life here."

Andrei didn't say a word. He found it difficult to stop shaking and was afraid he might have a seizure.

"What kind of work do you see yourself doing in our Soviet motherland?"

Andrei placed a few canvases in front of the man. He mumbled something about intending to continue along similar lines and develop his style further; he hoped that soon he would be able to have a solo exhibition in Moscow, as he had already had several in Prague, and that if people showed any interest, he could teach at the Academy of Fine Arts.

Bragin looked at the paintings coldly.

"No, this is absolutely no good to us at all. Our country doesn't need this kind of art."

"Why not? I would like to go on adding to what I've already learned from the great Russian artists: Chagall, Tatlin, Goncharova, Malevich."

"All those painters are representatives of decadent western art."

"Western? But they have drawn deeply from the Russian tradition."

"They have been inspired by the bourgeois, depraved West. Many of them have ended up in exile."

"Excuse me, but you're mistaken, Mr. Bragin. All those artists were searching for their Russian roots and for Russian spirituality."

"That was before the revolution. Theirs was a tradition that was not properly in tune with the Russian soul, having been imposed on them since the eighteenth century by French and German artists that the westernized czars invited to Russia so they could get fat on the sweat of our peasants. We, fortunately, have put an end to that particular tradition."

"There is only one cultural tradition, Mr. Bragin, and it can't just be swapped for another."

"Yes it can. We have transformed, and I would almost say regenerated, the bourgeois and aristocratic tradition, and we have replaced the tradition of the drunken, drug-addicted *poètes maudits* with the resilient spirit of the working people."

"The Russian revolution inspired Tatlin and Malevich to create new, revolutionary work."

"What you have just said is in ideological contradiction to the Soviet people as a whole."

"What I have said is simply this: as a person dedicated to creative work, I need freedom."

"If, with your art, you celebrate the freedom, faith, and progress that hold sway over the Soviet Union, then we can reach some kind of agreement."

"I'm talking about freedom, not about ideology. For an artist, freedom is the air he breathes, without freedom, nothing at all can be created."

"You and I are not in complete agreement. Personally, I'm convinced that an artist should not be at liberty to do absolutely anything."

"But if he isn't, how can his work develop?"

"An artist must not be completely free," Bragin said firmly, "because ultimately artists exist to serve the motherland. As with any other worker, their efforts must be aimed at increasing the greatness of the Soviet Union."

"What you are suggesting is that I put myself at the service of the powers that be?"

"The powers that be? No. Of the Motherland. And of the Communist ideal that we are building here."

"The words *Motherland* and *building* are euphemisms for the work of powers that be. What you are offering me is a long, sharp slaughterhouse knife, housed in a sheath of fine, diamond-studded leather."

"Your poetic metaphors are quite out of place here. All I can do is repeat that one of the greatest successes achieved by our country has been the freedom and equality of all those who live in it. And we will not allow this to be torn from our hands."

"Freedom? Equality? Soviet jails and forced labor camps are full to the brim with political prisoners."

"The people who end up in the jails and in the camps are those people who obstruct the creation of a truly free and equal society."

"Freedom means, above all else, the freedom to decide. And that, in this country, is not possible. You and yours decide everything for everybody else."

"Why have you come back, then?" asked Bragin in a low voice.

"Why? To make my country richer."

"No, you have come to be a thorn in our side, to be an obstacle. To demolish what we are building here: our new freedom, a freedom with fair limits."

"A freedom with limits is a prison."

"You may say what you please, but it is a freedom designed with mankind in mind. People cannot bear any more freedom than that which we give them."

"You underestimate mankind."

"On the contrary, we understand mankind. You don't understand it one little bit because you live in an ivory tower, as do so many artists, in fact."

"I don't know if I understand people any better or worse than anyone else, but despite everything, I keep my faith in people. But you, on the other hand—"

"It is not enough to have faith. Deep down, Mr. Polonski, you do not love mankind. That is why you want to make the people suffer by offering them something that they are incapable of understanding, something that is beyond their reach and which will only, in the end, hurt them."

"If anybody is causing hurt, it's you in the NKVD."

"We only punish and banish those who are in our way when it comes to achieving our aim."

"What aim?"

"To conquer and hold power firmly within our grasp, so that from this position of authority we may spread happiness everywhere. As far as conquering goes, we have already achieved that, just as we also now have a firm grip on power. All that is required now is to give people what they need and to impose limits whenever it may be necessary for the people's own good."

"Do you know who you remind me of, Mr. Bragin? Paradoxically, your opinions are rather similar to those held by the Grand Inquisitor, that prototype of an authoritarian ruler described by Dostoevsky in *The Brothers Karamazov.*"

"Paradoxically? Why? Any ruler worth his salt knows that if he wants to stay in power, he must offer something to the people. The Roman emperors offered bread and circuses to their subjects, and the Catholic Church offers a little more: miracles, enigmas, and moral authority. And the Catholic Church was right, that is exactly what the people need. And we will fulfill these needs of the people, following the church's example."

"Following the lead of the Catholic Church?"

"We must offer humanity a unique, clear vision of the world that can serve them as a solid reference in their lives. The church has known how to do that for millennia, and when it was necessary, it used the Inquisition to shore up its position."

"But your struggle is precisely against religion and the church! Your government takes reprisals against the church!"

"Don't interrupt me. We have offered the Soviet people the miracle of electrification, the miracle of armament—thanks to which we shall soon become a world superpower. Very soon we will give people the miracle of interplanetary flights: this country will be the first to fly through the cosmos, I promise you that."

"To the detriment of the bread which the Romans used to go on about."

"The Romans were wrong to do so. The people need miracles more than bread."

"And what are the enigmas you mentioned?"

"Our representatives are enigmatic. Comrade Stalin is inaccessible, and at the same time he is everywhere; photos of him appear in all the newspapers, his image can be found on all the town squares and in all the offices. And on the first of May, you can see him high up on the tribune, flying close to heaven."

"You mentioned the third attribute: authority. You can't tell me, Mr. Bragin, that that also makes people happy."

"It does so more than any of the other attributes. The people need a strong man before them, whom they may bow down to, and they need a moral authority, a moral conscience, if you will, that releases them from their own consciences. The church knew all about that, too."

"True authority is moral authority, precisely, but I don't agree with your view of things: each person must seek that authority within himself, and then perfect it."

"You are a typical intellectual, Mr. Polonski. How many people are capable of doing what you say? I'm talking about the masses and their god. People need a god, and we provide them with one."

"And what if the masses cease to believe in that god, one day? Don't tell me that can't happen. I would say it's probable, even; in fact, I'd say it is absolutely definite!"

"No. If a person needs something on which they can base their existence, they grab onto it with all their might and stop asking questions."

"Under certain conditions, the masses can free themselves of their idols—they can even end up hating them. Even the most untouchable of gods can end up being trod into the ground. Why shouldn't the masses cultivate hostility toward their leader? If he makes the people suffer, Stalin is showing that he is no better than they are, that he is the same as them, or worse."

"Allow me to repeat that you are a typical intellectual, Mr. Polonski. Your noble personal ethics are all right for a few select individuals; but I am talking about the masses! We are building a paradise for everybody!" He added, in a low voice, "Join our ranks, Mr. Polonski. We know how to look after the people who are of service to us."

Andrei had nearly forgotten where he was, and after so many years he was enjoying conversing with someone in his native tongue about a subject that interested him. Maybe this is why he hadn't noticed that for some time now, Bragin had been losing patience with him.

"So what you're saying, Mr. Bragin, is that there are two possibilities: either freedom without happiness, or happiness without freedom, just as the Grand Inquisitor himself believed. Is that right?"

"Something like that, yes," Bragin muttered. He was now looking at Andrei again the way a judge, in an interrogation, observes the detainee.

Andrei, by now relaxed, began to sing, with joyful irony, a song from his Soviet Communist youth days:

Of all the countries which come to mind,
I know of none other than mine
in which all can breathe freely.

At that moment, Bragin grew stern. His transformation from man into bureaucrat was complete; only professional mimes know how to change their expression so quickly.

"This subject is too serious to be made fun of," he said in an official tone, as if he were addressing an audience of comrades. "Too many enemies are threatening our Motherland for us to be able to lower our guard and release our iron grip on the education of our Soviet people."

That was when Andrei understood that further conversation would be pointless. Although he knew there was little hope of success, he had one last try, "Even so, I would like to work in my own particular field. I'm sure that if I did so, I could help our country."

Bragin stood up and coldly replied, "So you say, but this interview is now over."

Bragin's initial friendliness had vanished without a trace.

"Perhaps the best thing I could do is take the first train back to Prague," Andrei said, thoughtful and making an effort to control his inner trembling.

"You have returned from exile and will not be granted permission to travel. You are a citizen of the Soviet Union and the laws of this country now apply to you. According to these laws, nobody is allowed to travel without the approval of the Soviet authorities."

As Bragin accompanied him through the long room to the door, the trembling of Andrei's facial muscles became more and more visible. When he was on the threshold, before they put the blindfold back on him, Andrei stared at Bragin for quite a while. The official stood his ground coolly and said, "What will happen to you after this is beyond my control."

Still staring at him, Andrei asked in a low voice, "Tell me: Why do you do this job?"

Bragin, unmoved, answered firmly, "I am a soldier of the Communist Party and I follow its guidelines. There is no higher honor for a Soviet citizen."

THE NEXT day, they took Andrei to the NKVD examining magistrate. When they removed the blindfold, the judge, in an ominous tone, said, "Come forward, Polonski."

He went on, "We are quite certain that you have come here to promote ideological differences."

Andrei realized that Bragin's report had placed him firmly among the ranks of the enemies of the people.

The NKVD judge said, "We know perfectly well that Czech intelligence has sent you here to carry out espionage work in order to undermine our Soviet Motherland. Here is a paper and pen. Write your confession."

Andrei was trembling visibly, "Me, a spy? This is a mistake!"

"There is only one thing that can lessen your punishment for spying against us: a confession and the names of those who sent you here."

Andrei couldn't stop trembling, he was beside himself.

"What are you talking about? What a load of rubbish! I'm a painter!" he cried, in vain.

"Write your confession."

Andrei became more and more obstinate when he realized there was absolutely nothing he could do.

"Bullshit! I paint, that's all I do!"

"So you refuse to write your confession?"

"Of course I refuse! What do you expect me to confess?"

"Well, then we shall use other methods. The choice is yours."

Even in the state he was in, Andrei remembered that Bragin had said something very similar the day before.

The NKVD judge added, in a metallic voice, "You have just passed sentence on yourself."

HOW DID you manage to avoid having a fit in front of those people, Andrei? You who used to have an episode whenever you were ordered or obliged to do something that was against your will. You were always like that, since the days of the revolution and your days in the Red Army. How did you keep control of yourself in front of those NKVD thugs?

You projected your own film as you endured it. You observed those murderers with the inner eye that enabled you to transform the world around you. Semyon explained it to me as you explained it to him: you imagined them as priests with blood-stained hands, who were officiating at a cold and terrifying ceremony, priests making sacrifices to their bloodthirsty god. Things had been this way since the beginning of time. You saw men dressed in black, with somber faces. All of them with the same expression, all of them saying the same words, the same sentences. They moved through the rooms and corridors of that Palace of Terror, the Holy See of their bloodthirsty cult. You didn't see them in the corridors because you were led along them blindfolded, but you sensed them with your inner vision there in that palace where living men turned into condemned ones, as has happened so often in the history of mankind, when some impose a single truth upon others, and, if necessary, condemn them to death.

To death: because the gulag meant almost certain death.


SEMYON, WHO was also a painter, told me Andrei's story, although he knew that to do so was dangerous both for the speaker and the listener.

Both painters spent ten years in the same forced labor camp in Siberia. Ten years. Semyon was sentenced to the camp for being Jewish: they accused him of cosmopolitanism. They condemned Andrei, so they claimed, for having spent twenty years working for the intelligence service of a foreign enemy.

For ten years in the camp Andrei and Semyon survived as best they could, helping each other out, more through friendship than with the meager physical means at their disposal. When in the first winter after his arrival Andrei caught pneumonia,

Semyon, helped by other prisoners, loaded him onto a sled and covered him with a thick layer of fir branches. In this way, he avoided death.

Semyon said to me in a low voice, "Deep down, what saved Andrei were his visions of the Ancient World, his hallucinations of the arrival of the Sumerian ruler, Gudea."

I encouraged Semyon to tell me more.

"'Gudea is coming to meet me,' Andrei whispered to me one evening when all the other prisoners were asleep," Semyon said. "He was smiling at the unseen person who had come to meet him, and was enthusiastic about this interview. I watched him: it was clear that that conversation provided Andrei with something new, and some crucial thought that was of vital importance; some revelation, perhaps of a profound truth. The next day, Andrei woke up, energetic and full of life. That's what he was like, Sylva: during the day Andrei suffered along with the rest of us, but unlike us, he had his nighttime life where he sought refuge."

But his health, in the end, was affected. When he no longer had any powers of resistance, he succumbed to exhaustion and sickness. Ten years in the gulag: Andrei's health couldn't cope with it.

Two years after the death of Stalin, Semyon was given reparations for having been unjustly imprisoned, and he left the work camp. The authorities sent him to live in a small Siberian town. In 1957 they allowed him to leave the town, and he returned to Moscow. Then he started to look for me to give me the news of Andrei's assumed death and to pass on his last message, "The ambitions of an entire lifetime, and all the innumerable mundane affairs: I am throwing it all away, chucking it away, into the transparent mirror of a long Siberian river."

And a few words by way of a signing off, "You kept me company in this world, and you will keep me company in the next one, my Blue Butterfly."

I AM at the opening of an exhibition by Semyon, in Moscow. For the occasion I put on my best dress: lace and pearl white, with a skirt that reached to just above my knee. At my sixty-something years—in 1968—my hair was as blonde as when I was young, with just a few wisps of white hair making it a touch lighter. I wore my hair loose: it hung down to my shoulders.

Semyon took my arm and introduced me as a most welcome foreign guest. Jan was on my right.

Jan . . . When he was still only a little boy in Prague, he insisted that he wanted to come with me to Moscow to look for his father. Getting the visa to visit the USSR wasn't easy at all; they didn't give it to me until after many years of visits back and forth to the Soviet embassy. And when they did give it to me, it came with a long list of conditions: one of them was that I wasn't to see or talk to anyone except the person who had extended the invitation.

Jan, by that time, had finished university; the political authorities hadn't allowed him to enter the Academy of Music because of his family origins. It's a short step from musical theory and *solfeggio* to mathematics, said Jan. Later, from mathematics he progressed to cybernetics. With that, he got his first job in a scientific research institute and on his first holiday from that job, he'd wanted to discover the country where his father had been born. "And where he must have died," I was about to add, but I kept silent.

BACK IN Prague, Jan had insisted that I go and see him at his new job; he was proud of it. This was his first year as a professional scientist.

I entered the scientific institute where Jan worked. Most of the tables were unmanned. After glancing at me without interest, the people working in the building had bent their heads back over their work. Jan told me that just before my visit, one of the women scientists, Hana, had burst into the room to announce that in the House of Fashion, they'd received a consignment of coats made of artificial fur. If they all hurried up, maybe they could still get their hands on a few. "What an opportunity, fur coats!" Hana shouted. "It's not often that that happens!" Immediately, eight scientists had headed off in pursuit of the coats.

Jan took me on my tour of the institute. When the eight missing scientists returned from their coat hunting, Jan tried to introduce me to his female colleagues. None paid any attention to him, though, and one of them had even shouted at him, "Are you still wet behind the ears or what? We're busy here!" She threw herself, as did the rest of the women, at their prey, those huge packages, like hunters who managed to bag an especially large boar. Seven women unwrapping seven packages, the wrapping paper scattered all over the room, until finally they managed to remove their booty from their boxes. Seven women stared rapturously at seven coats made of obviously ersatz fur—they waved them about, so that seven coats floated over the scientific institute's desk, each with a hood. All seven were white, not a salt-and-pepper white, not off-white or ivory, no, these coats were as white as recently drawn milk, white as hospital walls, or a bridal gown. The eighth lady, Květa, hadn't been so lucky: there had only been seven fur coats left. Seven women of a certain age tried on the coats made of artificial fur, one of them raised up the collar or straightened the hood of one of the others, and fastened or unfastened the little hooks at the neck.

"Květa, isn't it a bit too tight?" a plump lady with lacquered hair asked Mrs. Květa, who was standing with her hands on her hips, admiring her quicker and luckier colleagues with envy.

"No way! It's perfect. Fits you like a glove! You look like a school girl!"

"But, Květa, aren't I too old to wear a white coat? As you know, there weren't any other colors—"

"Nonsense! Don't be so soppy! This white color suits you. In that coat, you could pass for Snow White!"

"I'll wear my white boots, then I'll be white all over!" said the lady with the lacquered hair.

Seven women in fur coats, seven Snow Whites twirling around the desks of the Prague Scientific Institute, seven Snow Whites with not a dwarf between them, who touched each other's coats and patted each other's backs, and admired each other from close up and from a distance, seven Snow Whites who made decisions as to where and when they would wear their new coats and who they would surprise with this new gear.

As I was leaving, one of the seven Snow Whites flapped the wide, white sleeves of her coat by way of a farewell.

WHAT WAS I thinking about before the Snow Whites made me lose track? Oh, yes, about Moscow and the opening of Semyon's exhibition. I put on my best dress and carefully combed my hair down.

However, I had problems getting to the opening. With the high-heeled shoes I'd worn, I kept treading in the mud and getting stuck time and again. Whenever they saw that I was about to topple over and fall flat on my face, Jan and Semyon helped me to walk straight. "The Moscow outskirts are unpaved," Semyon said, quietly. The cars parked in front of the identical blocks of flats were wrapped in newspaper and plastic.

Semyon had given me a bunch of white chrysanthemums and I attached one of them to my dress. For the whole journey,

Jan never stopped watching me, inquisitively. I'd spent that afternoon alone with Semyon, and hadn't allowed Jan to stay with us. I was hoping that Semyon would give me some further details of Andrei's life, as well as the names of his executioners. I didn't want Jan to hear those names; I was afraid he'd try to avenge his father, and destroy his own life in the process. As Andrei had destroyed his.

No, it was I who destroyed Andrei's life.

"Mama," Jan interrupted my thoughts as we made our way to Semyon's opening, "did you find anything out about my father's life? Where is he, in which work camp?"

I said nothing.

Jan didn't understand. Probably, deep down, he hadn't expected me to react differently.

"At least, do you know," Jan asked in a strained voice, "the names of the people who sent Father to Siberia?"

"No. I don't think there's any way of finding that out."

Jan accepted my lie in silence, even though he knew that I hadn't told him the truth. He respected my wish not to give away any names and didn't insist any further.

Semyon was walking alongside us. I got the impression that he wasn't listening, that he didn't understand Czech, perhaps because of the fast way we spoke. He was humming some tune.

Then he took me by the arm to lead me into the gallery and introduce me to people as his guest from abroad. Jan was on my right, maybe just half a step behind me. I was expecting a white, spacious, light-filled art gallery, like the ones I had known in Prague. On the contrary, this was a hole-in-the-wall, a kind of workshop or garage in a block of flats on the outskirts of the city, transformed for that evening into a gallery. The place was lit only by a couple of weak, flickering lightbulbs. Those present applauded us when we walked in. At that moment, I felt young again, as I had when I was twenty years old, dazzling all the men and conversing with ministers and diplomats and President Masaryk himself at receptions at the Prague Castle and in Paris.

When I'd recovered from my initial impression I realized that I'd walked into a party that was completely different from what I'd expected.

I was surrounded by human wrecks. Men and women with pale, yellowy faces, with the odd eye or ear or set of teeth and almost always the hair missing, engraved with a complex network of wrinkles and scars and marks and stigmata, from the eyes in which all hope and optimism—that is to say, life itself— had been thrust by extreme suffering; elderly creatures, these were, each with a cane or crutches, some missing a hand or an arm or a leg, with broken noses, distended bellies, with one or two stumps, with their slumped shoulders, with hunchbacks.

I sneaked a look at the paintings on display. There were drawings done with pencil and Chinese ink, and what I saw there was what I also saw around me in the gallery itself: fearful shadows dragging themselves along a barbed-wire fence.

"Semyon, this is horrible!" I said, unable to stop myself.

"No. This is my life. That is what I have seen in my life. An artist draws what he's seen."

"Semyon, tell me something. Did Andrei also draw these . . ." I was going to say corpses, but corrected myself in time, "people like this?"

"Andrei? He was always drawing, even though it was strictly prohibited. He took a great risk whenever he drew. In the beginning, he sketched firebirds and nymphs, princesses riding gray wolves and heroes fighting dragons; he often drew the sweetest children, who felt drawn in by monsters, and wild beings, I don't know why. He also drew deer and squirrels, bear cubs, butterflies, and frogs, trees and bushes, clouds and mountains. He gave his drawings away to his fellow prisoners, who hid them between their blankets. It was one of the few things that made us happy there. That was at the beginning. Later . . . later Andrei too grew apathetic, listless. I could see that he was losing more and more energy every day. He concentrated on controlling his fits, but was not always successful. Only at night did he come alive again, living in his dreams where he was visited by a wise man from the Ancient World. Sometimes he talked in his sleep or when just barely awake, saying strange strings of words that sounded like poems."

"Have any of his drawings survived?" I asked hopefully, "Could they be bought somewhere, or from somebody?"

"Survived . . . Bought . . . ? I don't understand what it is that you're asking," Semyon said, taken aback.

I realized that when something horrifies us, we come up with banal comments, as if being superficial could save us from our terrifying leap into the abyss.

"I'm sorry," I said, "I don't think I've really grasped the situation."

In order to fully understand a situation, above all if it's a tragedy of some kind, you have to have been there in person, to have seen it with your own eyes. Just as when one hears of other people's misfortunes, one can only feel true horror if one imagines them happening to someone close, someone loved, or oneself. Right then, I was unable to do that.

"You're lucky," Semyon said, "not to comprehend it. All of those who were there with us, they grasp it only too well."

At which point, Semyon turned to greet a prematurely aged woman with red eyes and gray skin, who had come up to say hello.

I scanned the room for Jan. An elderly man with white hair had dropped his cane and Jan was picking it up off the floor and handing it back to him with a smile. The elderly man—he looked like Tiresias, the blind prophet of Greek mythology—stared at him with eyes full of sadness, as if from some shadowy tomb he had spotted a ray of sunlight. He had looked at me, too, in that same way, just a moment earlier; I'd felt his eyes on my face. Seeing that I was watching him, the elderly man lowered his gray lashes and, leaning on his cane, turned to the wall to examine some of the artwork.

Semyon invited Jan and me over to the table where there stood two solitary bottles of vodka. Jan and I remembered the openings that we'd been to in Prague, with a choice of white and red wine, and tables laden with colorful *canapés* and pastries.

"Semyon, you're a great artist, why don't you exhibit in normal galleries?"

He looked at me as if I'd spoken to him in a Chinese mountain dialect about the best way to milk a cow.

"In normal galleries? Me? The only ones who can exhibit there are the apparatchiks! I've been sidelined, Sylva! I'm Jewish and what's more I used to be a political prisoner!"

How could I have asked such a stupid question! I was angry with myself, but a glass of vodka soon had me asking more questions.

"Semyon, why are there no young people at this opening? Why does everybody here look as if they'd just arrived from the depths of hell for a brief visit to Earth before going back to where they came from?"

"I can best answer you by telling you a story. When I returned from Siberia, I left my wife. I abandoned her, even though she'd waited for me faithfully for all those years."

"That's terrible! How could you do that?"

"When I got back, I'd changed; I'd changed completely. Day-to-day life with its day-to-day pleasures no longer meant anything to me. I can't explain it, you have to experience it for yourself. My wife and I tried to make everything between us just the way it was before, but we lived alongside each other like two deaf-mute people. The same thing happened with our children, who I found to be like two strangers from a country whose language I didn't speak. I hardly ever see them now, maybe just a couple of times a year to celebrate their birthdays. After what I'd been through, their concerns and interests are trivial to me."

"Have you tried to express yourself to them?"

"I can do so, at least a little, through my drawings. Sylva, a man who has survived the gulag—or a Nazi concentration camp—ends up being incapable not only of making friends, but even of understanding anybody who hasn't shared a similar experience. One option is to kill yourself, as a few of us have done. We survivors can only live with those who have been through the same thing, who live in the world as strange, incomprehensible beings to others. Those who have survived the gulag or any other such attempt to exterminate mankind, are scarred for life. For us, living in this world is like living in exile, and it is humiliating for us; we are permanently humiliated. And humiliation is as painful as the physical torture of interrogation, it is merely a different kind of pain. We have been exiled a second time, but now we are exiles in freedom."

He stopped talking. I said nothing. Once again, that Tiresias with his cane turned his knowing, blind eyes to us. He was breathing fast, excitedly, as if he wanted to say something but couldn't get the words out. His eyes were shot through with pain. When he looked into my eyes, he lowered his gray lashes.

ON THE way back to the hotel, Jan and I were silent.

Jan didn't feel like talking the flight back to Prague either. He stared at things without seeing them. He couldn't imagine how grateful I was for his silence.

On that journey back to Prague, I seemed to hear what I heard more than twenty years ago; through the racket made by the wheels of the departing train, you Andrei, whispered, simply and full of confidence, "Blue Butterfly!"

# XI

# JAN

"HERE YOU ARE, GENTLEMEN, THREE KEBABS, ONE WITH french fries, two with rice pilaf. The wine's on its way!" chanted the waiter in his heavy foreign accent. He had enough experience waiting tables to know that the rice dishes were for the adults and the one with french fries was for the kid.

I'd chosen that Persian restaurant on Seventy-Second Street and Second Avenue in Manhattan for our little private party. That afternoon, we'd been to see a puppet-show version of *Hamlet*. Our son, Peter, whose ninth birthday it was, lapped up the show from close up, seated at a corner of the stage with a few other kids. His mother, Katya, was sitting in the seats without even having bothered to take off the fur coat she'd wanted for so long, and which I'd given to her recently for her thirty-seventh birthday.

Peter . . . Does that name ring a bell, Mama? It makes me sad that Peter, my son, wasn't born while you were still alive. I named him after that friend from your youth, that man who, half a century ago, calmed me down after the police had released me. "Peter," you said to him back then, "in a period of calm it's easy to make the right decisions, but when the going gets rough, it's difficult to see things clearly and it's easy to make mistakes that you'll regret for the rest of your life." I didn't understand them then, but I have remembered those words of yours as if they were engraved in my memory. From time to time I'd think about them, and each time I came to the conclusion that people should always be on the alert so that they don't make the wrong decisions, ones they will later regret. I haven't lived through anything like the experiences you've had, Mama. You once told me that gentleman, Uncle Peter, had saved my life. I don't know anything more about that, we never spoke of it again, but I wanted my son to bear that name, in honor of the man you told me had done so much for me.

That Persian restaurant . . . Now I am walking along a long airport corridor and the flight I've been waiting for still hasn't landed. Flight OK 2901 from Prague to New York has been delayed by approximately two hours, that's the information I have been able to glean from the rather cryptic messages on the airport arrivals screen, and I'm racking my brain for the address of that restaurant so that you can imagine what kind of place it is, Mama. But what am I babbling on about? You never traveled to New York.

It was Saturday evening, the restaurant was chock-full of people wanting to have fun and eat well and laugh and joke and tell stories about their lives. At one of the tables, there was a married couple whose son was eating reluctantly, the woman never stopped talking into her cell, and the man made feeble efforts to cover up his boredom, trying repeatedly to start up a conversation that wasn't going to happen. It was my family and me.

My wife, Katya, was complaining about the American way of life, above all as it was lived in our little university town full of professors and scientists who weren't at all worldly, and among whom she had no admirers. To some extent, I felt sorry for Katya, she who always looked as if she had just stepped out of the pages of a fashion magazine, always dressed up. When Katya recited her litanies of complaints, I usually kept silent. I love this country because of all it has to offer me, things I could never find in the city where I was born. American law guarantees the freedom of the individual. This country full of powerful lawyers with their endless court cases—a country, to be sure, often criticized for its puritanism and materialism—works well in social terms because the law holds sway over the powerful at all levels, and everyone is equal before the law.

That solitary husband, although surrounded as he was by his family, removed a piece of meat from its skewer and reflected back on a scene that had repeated itself several times in the course of his life.

I WAS sitting at a table with two men who were showing their whiter-than-white, perfectly aligned teeth as they laughed and took bites of their sandwiches, rinsing each mouthful down with milk and Coke, respectively, as they patted me on the back and shoulders and emitted little sounds of pleasure.

Suddenly, the tanned one said:

"Let's talk about the possibility of you working for Ford."

"In the future, is what we mean," said the sporty one.

"Not right now," said the tanned one.

"But in the future, hell, why not!" said the sporty one, grinning and raising his glass of milk.

I didn't say anything. I waited.

They watched me carefully.

I remained silent. There was nothing for me to think over, so I simply waited to see what would happen next.

"John, we're talking about a chance for you to work with us."

"I have no intention of leaving the university or my academic work."

They looked at me as if I were some kind of unusual animal.

The tanned one said, in a low voice, "I guess you realize, John, that with Ford your salary would be way higher than what you're getting at the university."

I was silent for a while. Then I repeated, "I do not intend to abandon the university and the research I'm doing there."

The sporty one reeled off a figure in the hundreds of thousands of dollars. It struck me as being so fantastic, so out of proportion, that I couldn't even make the connection between it and myself. I didn't understand what was really going on, so decided to say nothing.

But later, I said no again. Running through my head were those verses you'd taught me, Mama: "Whoever refuses does not regret it. If they ask him again, he'll say no once more. Yet, despite everything, that 'no'—which is exactly what had to be said—will terrify him all his life." I repeated these verses to myself, and thought about Helena and wondered what she would have said about all of this. I think she'd have been proud of me.

"Think about it long and hard, John. It'd be crazy not to accept an offer that even the ten greatest universities in the world could never, ever beat."

KATYA WAS talking on her cell, Peter was playing with his french fries, which had long since grown cold. I pretended that I was eating with enthusiasm, while letting myself be carried away by the torrent of my own thoughts. All my life I'd been working with mathematics, either pure or applied, in other words, I'd been working with an exact science. From the start I'd known that the very structure of the exact sciences offered hope, not to mention security—the results of scientific research were objective, objectively valid, applicable, and capable of being objectively valued. The starting point of the exact sciences is a collection of axioms, the correctness of which is beyond any doubt. The exact sciences operate within parameters that are absolutely verifiable.

Yet little by little, I was starting to have doubts. A new discovery? To what extent can any discovery really be called new? After all, any new development has been based on long-accepted axioms and can only exist on that basis! The acceptance of the axioms as truth is based on long and exhaustive research, and only afterward can they been accepted as established fact, as if they were the Ten Commandments. But I was thinking about the laws of Newton, those axioms of physics: in some cases they had since become invalid, until Einstein turned up and made some small corrections to them, but by correcting them he founded a new branch of science. Doubting as I was, I thought about medicine: in medical journals I had read that medicine isn't a science but rather an empirical collection of facts, which is why it is unable to guarantee a cure that is absolutely one hundred percent.

So in what way is science infallible?

There among the laughter and liveliness of the restaurant, I suddenly glimpsed a blue memory. Yes, that letter had been written on paper of a sky-blue color. That was not long after having dinner at Jill and Bill's place. Peter hadn't been born yet, but he was on his way and Katya and I were planning to marry soon. That morning, Katya was in the shower when I glanced over the handwritten lines; the letter was written in Russian. I shouldn't be doing this, I told myself, but went on reading anyway. It was a draft of a letter and, without a doubt, Katya would later write a neat version of it, and then send it. Behind me I heard the splashing of the shower as I read this letter, the first page of which was missing:

DO YOU remember, Sasha, the day you burst into my home shouting: "We've got to split up!" I looked you up and down, coldly, "Don't make a scene. Go away. Come back in three days' time and we'll talk about it then." And I added, "That is, if I still feel like seeing you in three days' time." Then and there you sent me crashing to the floor, Sasha, and if I forgave you it was because of the things that happened right there, on the floor. Do you remember? I had never been with you that way before, and we went on, in the shower, on the sofa, on the balcony, until nightfall, do you remember? I don't know what your wife said to you that day. And do you remember that evening, too, when you threw me onto the snow on your way back from a restaurant near Moscow? With you things were always stormy, passionate. Every time we saw each other you told me you couldn't stand the situation we were in, that you would get a divorce the very next day. You repeated these words to me a thousand and one times and like that you made it impossible for me to discover other men . . . discoveries that were more than possible, as I'd found out. I met an Italian who lived in Saint Petersburg, who everyone called Il Mammone, above all I met a Russian emigré in the United States named Mikhail, a businessman, and not a gangster like you. And then there was an American. Yes, him. The one I told you about, during my last visit to Moscow, as I kissed your sportsman's thighs, hard, yet tender. I kissed your thighs, starting at the knees and working my way upward, and you Sasha, repeated, first in a whisper and then shouting and panting, that you loved me and were going to marry me.

Now that I'm writing to you, I remember your body, without a gram of fat on it . . . those arms that lifted me up as if I were a feather, that muscular belly that I so liked to caress . . .

But let's get back to the facts: there we were, stretched out on the floor, and I was kissing those magnificent thighs of yours, moving higher and higher, and then, just at that moment, I raised my head and said quietly, "You say that you love me? You're not the only one. I have a lover who wants to marry me." And you,

you slapped me hard and left. I loved you with passion for that, Sasha, because it was proof of your erotic frenzy for me. But I won't marry you even if you did really get a divorce. No Sasha, I don't want to marry a Russian, not even a rich one like you. It's not that I'm bothered about how you earn your money, no, that's your business. I simply do not want a Russian. I don't trust Russians. I don't trust them because I know them, I know myself, I know there is nothing solid inside us. We all lead potentially doomed existences, like the characters in a Dostoevsky novel.

You say that you aren't doomed? Not yet you aren't, but we'll see. I simply don't believe you.

Sasha, please understand. I'm not doing this for myself. You know that I want to have a child, you've always known that. I want to have a child in the best possible conditions: I want to give him everything, I want him to grow up in a civilized, Western country, with good schools and even better teachers, as well as the best possible health care.

I want to be a housewife and look after a family. Even though my American is of Czech extraction, which is rather a pity, I'll soon have him forgetting about his roots. At home we'll speak in English only, and I'll learn to cook American dishes. We will be an American family. We'll be winners, the kind of people who have nothing but opportunities ahead of them and live exactly as they please, and not the kind who end up being life's slaves.

My American isn't a smart operator like you, Sasha. He's a bit of a wimp when it comes to making money, and in other aspects too, but I'll change him, you can bet on that. I've already started. For a long time he didn't want to make any decision as far as our relationship was concerned, so I've made him take one now. What's more, I've discovered that he has a chance of earning a lot more money than he does at the moment. Why doesn't he do it? Because he's a typical intellectual and says that he has to dedicate himself to what he calls his mission. But when our son is born, I'll make sure he takes good care of him! I'll force him to earn some real money, and I know that you know I mean business, because you do know me, you certainly do!

You ask me to come and see you again in Moscow, you say that you'll run to me carrying anything I should ask of you between your teeth. Every night, yes, every single one of all the many nights that make up the year, I long for your ancient warrior's body. I dream of what I would do with you: I'd begin right where I left off the last time, with your hard, muscular thighs, covered in golden hairs. I would kiss you, my tongue would caress you, higher and higher . . . But I'm not going to do it, Sasha. I've decided to be faithful to my husband. He doesn't know anything about you. He will never know. I don't want to make any mistakes. But Sasha, my love, promise me just one thing . . .

THE SPLASHING of the shower came to an end. I quickly put the sheet of paper back in its place, and locked myself in my study.

Once Katya had left the house, I went back into the bedroom to finish reading the letter, but all I found was the polished wood surface of the bedside table. The sky-blue letter had disappeared.

I dismissed the whole thing with a wave of my hand. What did the bedtime adventures of Katya's histrionic ex-lovers mean to me! Indeed, I felt relief at not having to choose between my curiosity and a deeper sense of decency, which ordered me not to read letters that aren't addressed to me.

But on that day I had certainly committed a grave error: I should have learned something from what I'd read. If I'd done so, I could have foreseen many of the things that happened later.

I had slowly been eating the Persian kebab and was thinking

about another dinner, one that took place not long before I read Katya's letter, when she and I were eating in a restaurant, planning our wedding. That memory is salmon colored, as were the walls of that small, poorly lit restaurant.

I had little interest in talking about the details of our future wedding ceremony. I took advantage of a break in the conversation to recite some verses that had influenced me greatly:

> For certain men the day still comes
> in which they have to say the big Yes or the big No.
> It's instantly clear which one is ready with his Yes,
> and as soon as he says it he moves forward
> to honor and conviction.
>
> Whoever refuses does not regret it. If they ask him again,
> "No," he'll say once more.
> Yet, despite everything, that "no"
> —which is exactly what had to be said—
> will terrify him all his life.

KATYA DIDN'T get it. The poem probably wasn't very clear. I boasted to her then that from time to time I received visits from two men who were trying to persuade me to work for them at the Ford Motor Company.

Katya stared at me with wide-open eyes.

"You have to accept this offer," she said, breathlessly.

By way of an answer I gave a little giggle.

"You have to accept this offer," Katya repeated, as if hypnotized, "Remember we're going to have a baby, John!"

At night, I dreamed that the sporty one and the tanned one, those two men who had never known the meaning of failure, were sitting at a table with Katya, who also looked tanned and sporty, and wore the happy smile of a woman who knew that she had been born for success. They sat at the restaurant with the salmon-colored walls, opening their mouths wide to take bites out of their multilayered sandwiches. They talked like conspirators and laughed and patted each others' backs, drinking milk and giggling with pleasure.

Throughout this I was sitting at a table in the corner, and I wasn't looking at all sporty. I was pale, joyless, with graying hair, slumped over and resting my cheeks in my hands. I was drinking red wine and whispering to myself, "He who refuses does not regret it."

I'd had that dream more than once. Did you also have dreams that came back to you again and again, Mama?

My father had them . . . I think I owe you an explanation, Mama. For a long time I wasn't sure what had happened to my father. I only managed to get an idea after your death.

Based on what you'd told me about my father's fits whenever he was given an order, I sought to understand his psychological condition. My colleagues who were specialists in this field told me what you and I already knew: that he had been traumatized by his wartime experiences. As for his hallucinations, they were the result of a kind of mystic ecstasy. The emotional shock my father had experienced as a young man during the Russian Civil War, had shifted his brain in such a way that he found it easy to reach states of ecstasy, mystic states. That is why my father was a brilliant painter: people who are able to have mystic experiences know how to take their art further than others do.

But the most important thing they told me was this: thanks to this ability to see the world in a different way, such people are able to weather the most terrible suffering, more than most could cope with. In their vision-filled ecstasies, in that world into which they are able to escape, they can create their own paradise that nobody, not even their jailers or torturers, can tear away from them.

What happened to my father, Mama? Did he survive the gulag or didn't he? And what was the name of that high-ranking NKVD man who signed his verdict? I'm sure that you found out when we travelled to Moscow together in the late sixties. You never wanted to tell me, you hid that information from me so that I would not seek vengeance and so ruin my life. What was the name of that man, Mama?

But what does it matter now, that name! It would be of no significance if my wife's father turned out to be my father's murderer; the important thing is that he very well might have been. And I have joined his world voluntarily. Now at last I understand those words of yours, Mama: "In a period of calm it's easy to make the right decisions, but when the going gets rough, it's difficult, and many people make wrong decisions." Solitude and exile can also be rough going.

Who is my father's murderer, Mama?

Revenge: how many times have I thought about it! In order to punish evil or just to vent my anger? Vengeance can relieve pain, remove frustration, and give satisfaction to the one who has taken justice into his own hands. But who knows where justice lies? By killing a wrongdoer, would I bring justice to the world? Or would I add to the evil that is already there?

PETER SAID, "I would like to eat nothing but potatoes, like Papa did when he was little, and draw endless pictures on toilet paper, like Papa's papa. And your father, Mama, what does he do?"

I was watching Katya: she looked at a loss, so Russian in a foreign country she just couldn't understand and which didn't understand her. In the US, Katya applied the principles of her native land, which, in this new context, just didn't work. What's more, the language cut her off from American society: in the shops, the sales assistants couldn't understand her properly, and Katya never completely got what they were saying to her, just as she never really understood the advice that they gave her in banks and post offices.

"My father worked in the highest echelons of the Russian Communist Party," Katya said.

I interrupted her, I couldn't help it. The subject was too painful to me.

"Katya, your father worked for the NKVD and then the KGB. Why?"

"He was doing his duty."

"His duty to whom?"

"To those who had ordered him to do so."

"I don't understand what you're saying."

"My father believed in the party and in the aims of the Bolshevik revolution. When he was able to join the party, he gave it everything he had. At home, he told us eagerly about the laws and the decisions they made that would lead us into a better future, which is why it was so important to watch out for and imprison all those who were opposed to it. My father always said that he was a soldier of the Motherland, who obeyed orders."

I picked up my glass of water and took a couple of long sips. Peter watched me. I counted to ten, and took a long time to reach it. I followed Peter's gaze: my hand was trembling. Peter held it in his.

What had I been thinking when I started this futile conversation that was going to lead nowhere? I'd been thinking about happiness. Happiness is when somebody understands us, Bill had said to me once.

"Peter, what is happiness?" I put my son to the test.

"Are we at school or what?" Peter put on a cross face.

"Tell me, what comes into your head when somebody says the word 'happiness?'" I went on.

"I know when a hamster's happy: when he escapes from his cage. Remember?"

"Remember what?"

"That one day we went away for the weekend and we forgot to close the door of the cage, and the hamster got out and spent three days playing with the edge of the carpet and roamed all over the place. And he preferred nibbling at the carpet than eating all that really nice hamster food we'd put especially for him in his cage."

"And what else is happiness, Peter?"

"I'm telling you. Happiness is being a hamster. He doesn't do anything, he spends the whole day lying around, and when he gets fed up he takes a little walk, nibbles things here and there, then plays and goes back to sleep. Me, every morning, I have to go to school, then I have a French lesson in the afternoon, then a drawing class and a violin class, and there's no time left for me to play. Being a man's a waste of time. I don't want to be a man."

"And what's happiness, not for a hamster but for a man?"

"For a man, I don't know ... maybe ..."

"Seeing a puppet show? *Hamlet*?"

"Yes, and when you come over to see me and stay sitting with me on the floor of the stage and you don't care that the rest of the audience are kids and you hold my hand and laugh with the kids, not with the grown-ups."

"What else is happiness, Peter?"

"Well ... Hamlet with the gravediggers."

"Hamlet with the gravediggers?"

"Yeah. With them he's got stuff to talk about. Not like with that soppy Ophelia, he's got nothing to say to her. Not to the king, either, or to all those nobles."

I quietly returned to my rice pilaf so as to get the idea of my own happiness out of my head. I wanted to think about freedom. My freedom is my son, I thought, the fact that I can bring him up and live in his world. And my freedom lies too in my big No, I thought to myself. In order to divert my thoughts before they started to dwell on the role of tenderness and understanding in my life, I took a swig of wine and went on eating. And remembering . . .

IT WAS August 20, 1968. Helena and I had shared a kebab similar to the one I was eating now, in one of those little cobblestone squares in Sarajevo, under some trees the name of which I didn't know. Trees, or maybe they were climbing vines with purple flowers. From a window in one corner of the square came a melancholy tune, full of affliction. A *sevdalinka*, Helen had told me. The *sevdalinka*, sad and unhurried, is a traditional Bosnian song about something, or someone, that has been lost. These songs are about paradise lost, when it comes down to it.

After dinner, we finished the wine that was left in the bottle and langorously let ourselves be caressed by the breeze, which in the evenings flowed through the narrow streets of Sarajevo's Turkish district. A family had sat at a long table on the far side of the little square. Helena and I were silent, intent on listening to the newcomers' laughter. One of the women started to sing, the kids had joined in, and then one of the men, and after him, yet another. They all sang in soft voices, almost in whispers, a nostalgic song in their Slavic language, of which we could make out the odd word, like ping-pong balls being bounced our way. Earlier that evening, in a theater surrounded by a garden, Helena had performed Bach's "Concerto in B-minor."

During the performance, it seemed to me that her violin was trembling with hidden grief. Helena played with lowered eyes, her chestnut hair falling freely over her shoulders. Helena played, and her music and my thoughts became enmeshed with the call of the muezzin that came from one of the surrounding villages, or maybe a Muslim mother was singing a Turkish song while she darned some socks. This oriental melody, whatever its source, caressed the Bach concerto with its white wing.

That evening I saw Helena for the last time.

At the break of dawn the radio announced that the Soviet army had crossed into the borders of Czechoslovakia. Helena wasn't in her room. I looked for her all day, in vain. Desperate as I now was, that evening I clambered up the mountains that surround Sarajevo, looking for her. I walked nervously along the paths I'd previously taken with her. In that twilight perfumed by pinecones and moss, a few dogs came after me, growling and showing their teeth, but there was no sign of Helena. I searched for her in vain for days on end, looking everywhere. After I left, I plunged into my academic life in the United States, but never ceased to long for her, to look for her in all the women I met. For the woman who simply disappeared one day from the banks of the Bosnia river, like sea foam on sand, abandoned there by the waves.

But that night I searched for her. At first light, I hurried through the streets of Bascharsha, Sarajevo's Muslim neighborhood. People were going to work, and I kept bumping into them by accident. By the time the sun had covered the city, I had collapsed into a café chair, exhausted, fighting off my dizziness. A woman brought me some coffee so thick you could bite into it. A young man put a piece of baklava in front of me, that ever so sweet Balkan dessert, along with a glass of water. I couldn't make out the passersby. I saw only gray shadows walking absurdly ahead. I know only one thing for certain: Helena was not among them.

Sarajevo, I said to myself as I drank that Turkish coffee, this city so full of the steeples of Catholic and Orthodox churches, and dozens of synagogues decorated with Hebrew letters written in gold, and Turkish mosques with thin towers, white as sails on the sea. In the evenings, when Helena was rehearsing, I would order a glass of earthy red wine that gave off a smell of holm oak barrels and of melancholy nights, and sip it with the starry sky above me. Those nights were humdrum yet unforgettable, like the inhabitants of that country. I became lost in thought observing the mirror image of that street—a fragment of the world, my entire world right at that moment—reflected in the cupola of the mosque opposite. I had no sense of the passing of time. When the shadows passing in and out of the café started to order grilled meat for lunch, I stood up and left a few coins on the table by way of a tip. The woman in charge gave them back to me, laughing. She too, was one of the shadows.

The best place to look for Helena was Ilidza Park: my girlfriend must have gone to the source of the Bosnia River, that place that was sacred to Bosnians, to tell of her sorrow at the assault on her country to the river's springs. I wasn't allowed into the park as night was already falling, but I had to find Helena! After dark, I jumped over the fence. The water from the springs fell onto the stones and grew wide as other streams fed into it, then sang its song in the middle of the night, a litany of grief.

I spent the next few days looking for Helena in Sarajevo and the surrounding area. All in vain.

Then I realized that, immersed as I had been in my own anguish, I had forgotten about the grieving for my own country invaded by Soviet tanks. I felt I was a selfish person who didn't have the right to share that sorrow with my countrymen. But I had to make an effort to believe this self-confession of mine, which I supposed noble, like all confessions.

Two days after all that had occurred to me, I joined the queue in front of the American Embassy in the Yugoslav capital, Belgrade, where I asked for political asylum in the United States. As I was a young scientist and had obtained good professional qualifications in Prague, after a considerable wait, my request was granted.


KATYA WAS back on her phone. I signaled to her that I'd like to talk to her. She closed the clamshell.

Perhaps in order to express my enthusiasm before starting this conversation with Katya, I gestured in a rather rough way and knocked over my glass of wine. Peter smiled. Katya leaped off her seat and began to brush herself with the napkin as if she'd been engulfed by an entire swarm of furious bees. Peter put his napkin over the red wine that had spilled onto the white tablecloth. The waiter turned up in an instant with a clean glass, filled it, tidied up the table a little, and everything was just as it had been before. Except that Katya was still on her feet and all the restaurant's customers were staring at her in astonishment. I blushed. Calmly and decisively, Peter said, "Sit down, Mama, what's wrong? Why are you standing up?"

But Katya stayed as she was: a statue built of indignation.

Peter, with his innocent, ten-year-old's voice, said, "Do you want everyone to stare at you, Mama?"

When the place filled once more with the buzz of laughter and voices, Katya sat down. I agreed with Peter: Katya made that scene to become the center of everybody's attention. It had been her minute of glory. But I didn't have time to think this through, because Katya immediately removed Peter's napkin in order to reveal the full horror of the wine stain.

"You always find a way to put me in a bad mood!" she said,

contemptuously, without looking at me, and went on rubbing her thigh as if she were putting soap on a huge wine stain.

She was referring to another dinner, this one with some friends from my department. Back then, Katya had said those very same words to me in front of my colleague and his wife, "You always find a way to put me in a bad mood!" My American friends were left speechless by that bitter sentiment, spoken by my wife in front of other people. From that moment on, my colleague's wife eyed her with abhorrence. Only when we were saying goodbye did she allow her back into her good graces, it seemed: Katya talked about our son Peter and how much he took after me.

That evening, when we got back home, Katya told me a few stories, laughing easily as if she were a completely different person. I immediately forgave her previous lousy mood and hugged her.

"Now I have the right to ask for three wishes, but I'll stick to just one," she'd said, laughing. "I'm a modest girl."

Once again, she flashed those white teeth of hers at me. That happened so rarely that I promised Katya to grant her a wish.

She whispered in my ear, "You will take that job at the Ford Motor Company. For Peter's sake, I'm not thinking of myself. We have a son, John, remember that!"

NOT LONG afterward, they came to see me: the tanned one and the sporty one, both in their best, impeccable dark suits. They invited me for a meal in a French restaurant.

When we'd taken our seats, the tanned one said in a low voice, "I guess you realize, John, that with Ford, your salary would be incomparably higher than the one you're getting at the university."

Maybe if I stayed on at the university, I thought, and did something for Ford at the same time, I wouldn't have to go back on my big No, I wouldn't have to betray myself.

"John, what if you decided to work for us from your office at the university?" It was as if the tanned one had read my thoughts.

"You'd be earning a good salary with us," said the sporty one, finishing the sentence.

"You'd make your wife happy." The tanned one winked at me.

"We'd make sure you had an experimental research center at your disposal," the sporty one said, temptingly.

"An electrical motor and two measuring devices, a salary for a technician, or two, if you need them."

"And then there'd be your salary . . . Wow!"

"It'd include frequent trips to our main office in Detroit."

"Your salary . . . Wow! It'd be finger lickin' good! Good enough to lick those fingers twice!" exclaimed the tanned one.

For some men a time comes when they have to give a big Yes or a big No. Over and over, I told myself: No. But then I thought to myself that if I worked for the Ford Motor Company from my university, I wouldn't be betraying my big No, and Katya would stop her nagging.

I nodded, "OK. Fine. I'm in."

# XII

# SYLVA

AT NIGHT I WAS WOKEN UP BY THE RINGING OF HUGE bells, the kind I used to hear when I was little at my parents' house; the sound came from a nearby village. Bells. They didn't augur well. They sounded very close, and rang without a break, one after the other . . . Bells? No! This was the thunder of the gods, the *Dies Irae*.

I got up and from my attic window in the Vinohrady district, I watched the river of huge metal objects that was flooding Francouzská Avenue. The clamor of those hellish monsters silenced people's fear, their cries and moans. All you could hear were the blows and their echo, the blows of metal against the stone of the street; those monsters were the absolute masters of sleepy Prague, of the city that was now waking up with a shock in the middle of the night amid the roar of those savage metallic beasts. Those iron beasts were bursting into the circus into which our city was being turned, so that its inhabitants could become a source of amusement for a depraved emperor. *Morituri te salutant, Caesar!*

I picked up the phone, finally hearing its ringing in between the passing of one iron monster and the arrival of another. I could hardly hear anything that was being said over the line, the racket on the street was drowning everything out. I was sure that it was Jan who was calling. My son, who was in Sarajevo, wanted to know what was happening, and how I was, how we all were. And he wanted to tell me . . . to tell me something that, although I couldn't make it out, I knew what it was, yes, I heard it all right . . . "Mama, I won't return to a humiliated country, I can't live in a country that from this moment on will be trembling forever under the heel of a foreign power, more than it has ever done before." And I knew that Jan was right, and I knew I was signing my own death sentence when I said, "Jan, my child, don't come back." Yes, I was signing my own death sentence because I would never see my son again, because I wouldn't be able to leave the country to see him, and he wouldn't be allowed to come here to see me. All this I knew perfectly well, as I said those prophetic words . . .

"Life here will be impossible, Jan."

I COULDN'T spend any more time at home; that nightmare had me running out onto the street. The sun had been up for a few hours.

The tanks were pushing their way through the crowds, and people dodged them. Young men circled the tanks on motorbikes at incredible speed, they rode through the spaces between one tank and the next. I closed my eyes: I thought a man in a red T-shirt was going to fall with his bike under the metal tracks of a tank. Finally he shot off to the right, out of the path of the armored vehicle.

Cameras were focusing on the tanks and clicking away. Movie cameras hummed. I shut my eyes. When I opened them again, down there on the street, there was a little boy, holding a stone in his raised hand. He was about to throw it. At the tanks? He was very young, still a child. There was no hatred in his eyes. Only excitement. And tension. He was carried away by the overall atmosphere, by the intoxication of the moment. He was looking forward to an adventure, that little boy holding a big stone in his hand. He was strong. He raised his hand some more. Any moment now he was going to throw it. It was heavy, too heavy to reach the top of a tank. The boy was getting himself all worked up: he made a violent grimace and stuck out his free arm to prepare his aim. He drew back his other arm, to gain momentum and was aiming at the upper part of the tank. The tank officer aimed his machine gun at the boy. To frighten him, only to threaten him, I told myself. Then the boy drew his arm back a fraction. He was getting ready to attack. Or was he? Couldn't his arm simply have dropped back a little under the weight of that rock? The tank would withstand his attack, even supposing he went ahead with it. They were strong, they were armed to the teeth, but the tank kept on coming and the boy didn't step out of its way. Step away! I wanted to shout from my vantage point. I wanted to yell: Stop the tank! Stop it! But I couldn't get a word out. Too late. I shut my eyes.

When I opened them again, there was a flurry of activity in the crowd. The officer was putting the machine gun inside the tank. I saw people's eyes were wide with horror. I didn't understand. My brain wouldn't obey me. I was thinking of only one thing: That was Jan! My little Jan! Where is Jan? Some women were howling, others were crying. Men were tearing up paving stones. The women, too, were throwing stones.

The column of tanks moved away from that place.

Jan!

I gave out a cry that was inaudible, but everybody was screaming and roaring, and I was going away, staggering, far from those swarms of people, I needed to wake up from this nightmare and feel sure that boy wasn't Jan. Jan had called just that same morning. Jan wasn't a boy anymore. Jan was abroad, free from danger . . .

But Jan wouldn't be coming home.

That thought stuck its beak into my stomach. Jan wouldn't be coming back. I wouldn't see him again. I couldn't go and see him; the borders had been sealed off, or would be soon. The cage door had closed once again. I would never see him again.

I watched the desperate crowds, but felt sorry only for myself. The rest were nothing but props for my own grief. I looked at the statue of Saint Wenceslas on his horse: both horse and rider had bowed heads. The horse was moving forward bit by bit, reluctantly. It wasn't trotting, it was stumbling. Everything was sad in Prague. Jan had left and would never be coming back. For the first time, I had understood something that I would have once disagreed with: that a personal concern could be stronger than a collective affliction. On the day of the Soviet invasion, I understood it for the second time.

ONCE AGAIN, they forced me to move, this time to a one-room apartment in a prefab building on the outskirts of Prague. In the library, I'd been relegated practically to the status of pensioner, with the lowest possible salary. So that I, who had lived in Paris, I, who had been addressed as Madame l'Ambassadrice, I, who had conversed with President Masaryk, now lived alone and removed from everything, and only rarely had guests at home, inviting them only so that the four walls in which I lived might be gently touched by human voices and not just by my memories, which were forever floating in the stuffy air of my modest room.

I saw myself . . . I was Sylva, the silent woman whose hair was now white. Since Jan had gone into exile in the United States, my hair had turned the color of milk. Not the Nazi occupation, nor the war, nor the loss of my beloved, nor the terror of the Stalinist years had been able to make my hair snow colored; only the loss of my son had managed to do that.

I HAVEN'T seen Jan for five years.

Five years . . . What are five years when compared to an entire lifetime? What are they, sub specie aeternitatis?

No. Five years are an eternity for a mother.

And Andrei? Twenty, twenty-five, twenty-seven years have gone by without seeing my Andrei. Twenty-seven years that stretch into infinity.

I was gazing through the window of my apartment on the outskirts of the city. When the rays of the setting sun had reached the highest flats and stopped dazzling me, I looked out at the surrounding buildings: what uniformity, not a bit of imagination, just insignificance, grayness, and boredom, Communist buildings! Beauty says nothing to the Communists, they never seek any kind of artistic pleasure. For them, the yearning for creative beauty and aesthetic feeling are the marks of a decadent bourgeoisie and aristocracy, that is to say, their class enemies. The other day in the library, I was leafing through a book on the history of art, and, remembering Andrei and his dreams of Sumerian sages, I took a close look at the Gate of Babylon, which is now housed in Berlin's Pergamon Museum. The writing, in cuneiform script, on one side of the door, says more or less the following: "I am constructing a building of monumental beauty so that its solemn splendor may remain for all time in the memory of the people, so that all humanity may forever admire its sublime magnificence." By contrast, the Communists have never bothered with this kind of beauty, as if they were afraid of it—just as they fear humor and irony—because they don't understand it. They aren't interested in building anything lasting, on the contrary, they tear down monuments dedicated to their own leaders as soon as one disgraces himself. Perhaps nothing will remain of the Communist regime, in a few centuries' time. Only a few thousand uniform buildings, dull and uninspired, with a provisional feel to them, will bear witness to future generations of the bitterness of so many soulless lives.

Then I saw a red geranium on the windowsill. It rose, content, after the rain, stretching itself lazily, and shaking its branches, aware of its charm. It stood out against the background of gray buildings like a light among shadows.

Five years. Twenty-seven years. Does it make any sense to go on living?

Does it?

Yes, it does. To live for the memory of my son and for the memory of the man who was my great love, to live for my memories like the red geranium in the middle of a street of gray houses.

And, if no memory remained, no recollection, it would be necessary to live for the flower alone.

TWILIGHT WAS falling. I saw myself reflected in the suddenly darkened window; I saw Sylva with her white hair: the woman whose son and beloved were in exile, each in a different exile. I watched her, that woman who had conversed with President Masaryk, who had lived in Paris, she, Madame l'Ambassadrice.

I watched Sylva as she placed a candle in the dead center of the table, thinking as she did so about another candle, a long time ago, in the Café Louvre in Prague. I watched Sylva as she placed the new candle next to the vase with its red flower. The flame flickered; like the wings of a newborn fly, thought Sylva, smiling because the Café Louvre kept coming back to her, time and again. Then a gust of wind reminded her that she still had to take in the washing if she didn't want it to freeze during the night.

The clothes were still soaking wet. And icy now. Sylva briskly closed the window. She'd attend to the clothes in a little while. The candle's flame had settled down so now it radiated peace and tranquillity. That day in the Café Louvre, they were sitting at a round table, Sylva recalled, her eyes fixed on the icy darkness on the other side of the window. Whoosh! A gust of wind had shoved the window open, angrily blowing the candle out.

Sylva took in the clothes that had been hung out on the line, throwing them, wet, into a tub. She closed the window and, moving automatically, put the tub away under the bathroom sink. She checked her watch: she still had time, before the arrival of . . . It didn't matter who turned up, as it wasn't going to be Andrei. She turned to the window. It was now completely dark and a few dogs were barking in the street. The sound of barking dogs that she had so much enjoyed hearing in the villages near her parents' chateau, here, in this block of prefabricated flats, reminded her of the muddy, lonely streets of those bleak outskirts.

What had the dogs been like, in that remote epoch, in Prague of the twenties, that was once so elegant, avant-garde, and free? Sylva made an effort to think of more agreeable memories . . . Another howl of a dog—this time, the neighbor's lapdog, followed by the shrieks of its hysterical mistress, screaming at it until she was hoarse. Tired out. Like me, Sylva thought, feeling as she did like roaring the way her neighbor did, or even better, howling like that dog. Standing on the linoleum floor, she imagined she was sinking into mud with her shoes on and all, just as she did every morning when she hurried to catch the bus that took her to the last station on the metro line, which took her to the tram station, where she took a tram to the library.

She picked up a box of matches. This was her daily ceremony: hand . . . match . . . flame. Candle . . . flower . . . glass.

THE TELEPHONE, I must pick it up, Sylva thought, darkly, hearing that piercing ring. If only she could finish her daydream, and mentally project herself to its end, she thought, putting her hands over her ears. The man had said such-and-such and then . . . no. The telephone had broken her dream into little pieces. She would have to put them back together . . .

"Hello? Oh, good afternoon, Monsieur Beauvisage. Are you on your way? No, no I haven't forgotten, how could I! Really, Petr, supper is almost ready! Well, you could bring a bottle of wine if you wanted . . . From Mělník? Absolutely not! Yes, I told you, of course I'm expecting you."

Why had she said the supper was almost ready if that wasn't true? To get him off the phone, of course. Sylva took a board with three or four types of cheese on it, among which there reigned a French camembert with its fabulous cape of ermine, white as snow on a mountain peak.

Sixty-seven years old now. In five or six years, she would retire for good. Would life end then? What would be left of her, she who had lived in Paris working as a cultural ambassador, she who had been able to play the piano like an angel? No one would weep over her grave, no desperate husband. She would leave behind no book of poems, no oil painting of a mimosa bouquet. Just a few candles at the bottom of a dustbin, candles that served as witnesses to her evenings with nothing but the barking of dogs for company.

Quickly, I must get dressed! she thought. Sylva put on a black skirt. For whom was she dressing with so much care? For herself. She released a sigh. She gave herself the once over: Wasn't the skirt too tight? Not at all! Not for nothing did she practice yoga. On the first day, the teacher had said to them: "Those adept at yoga must always remain calm, relaxed, and also ensure they are on friendly terms with both themselves and others." When she heard that, Sylva knew she was going to continue practicing yoga. She knew of no other place in Prague where people were so relaxed and friendly. Everybody—with their lack of any kind of future prospects—carried their portion of concern, envy, worry, fear, and boredom with them to work and on the metro, as if they were carrying an eggroll wrapped in aluminium paper. Sylva, on the other hand, went off to do yoga every Wednesday evening with people who were making an effort to turn themselves into calm, friendly souls as they attempted the Cobra Position, the Lotus, or the Dancing Lord Position.

The doorbell. With a final glance at the mirror, Sylva smoothed her thick, dark eyebrows. She looked through the spyhole. Petr was standing in front of her door, frowning and touching his gray hair with nervous eagerness. Sylva opened the door. Petr gave her a hug, looking at her with his round eyes that still had a touch of ingenuity in them; and his face lit up.

"It's so dark in here! Are you meditating or something?" Petr asked as he walked in, already looking for a light switch. "Can I put on a light?"

"No!"

Sylva took the bottle from him and looked at the label: a young wine from Mělník.

"There wasn't anything better," Petr said by way of an excuse, noticing her stern expression. She said nothing.

Sylva shook her head, smiling as if she were forgiving someone she considered inferior. Suddenly, a bird started to flutter about inside her, then it opened its beak and ... Sylva felt a tremendous urge to drink wine, glass after glass, to drink and laugh and find herself in Paris—a twenty-year-old pianist again with a brilliant future. She wanted to forget the mud of the Prague outskirts, the solemn faces that accompanied her daily on the bus, the metro, the tram, and in the streets, to drink with a musician, a violinist, of course, to raise a toast and gaze out on the lit-up Parisian boulevards from a first-floor restaurant, to clink glasses happily amid the lights of the metropolis. She picked up a corkscrew and a bottle of Tokay. As for the other bottle, they would wait and see.

"Let's travel!" Petr said, taking Sylva's glass away from her and opening up a travel brochure. "How about a trip to Spain? We might be able to get visas."

The blackbird inside her opened its beak once more. In her mind's eye, Sylva saw the golden clouds of mimosa cuttings which her colleagues sometimes gave to her on the eighth of March, International Women's Day. But now she was imagining an entire mimosa tree, the golden fleece of the Argonauts, a forest in Paradise comprised only of mimosa trees, lit up by the sun.

"Are there mimosa forests in Spain, like the fir forests here?" she asked.

"Maybe, I couldn't really say, but I'm sure there are forests of palm trees."

"And why go to Spain, why not to Paris?"

"I want to see the Costa Brava, to sleep in a white hotel listening to the sound of the waves. And then later, to have a whole day with nothing but sun."

His teeth shone in the candlelight, as if the southern sun had already given him a tan. Behind him, Salvador Dalí was lifting up the edge of the sea to discover what lay underneath. The Costa Brava . . . She would go to Dalí's house, and touch it with her fingertips. The walls would be baking hot from so much sun. Sylva would place the palm of her hand on a white wall and let herself be filled with all that sweet heat, so that she would never feel cold, ever again, not even when she got up in the morning when it was still dark and hurried over the puddlesto the bus stop, her hair still a mess, or in the evening, when she took the same route back and finally opened the door of her damp little apartment on the outskirts of the city. She took a long sip of wine.

PETR GOT up and began to stride back and forth: two paces here, two paces there, at one point, feeling a helmet that had once protected the head of a knight, or tapping the torso of a suit of armor. On the chair next to the window were a few sheets of paper. Petr bent down to read them, more out of whimsy than any real interest:

> The era of imposed oblivion, the dark era of forced blindness, the era of having to walk blind and deaf and dumb among the shadows, has arrived.

As he read, Petr remembered that Sylva had told him that a woman doctor the authorities allowed, very rarely, to take part in certain scientific conferences in western Europe, had offered to smuggle out a letter from Sylva to Jan, which the doctor would post to America from somewhere abroad. As he read, Petr realized she had searched with some difficulty for the most suitable words, that with a considerable effort she had composed these sentences to describe her situation and everybody else's, now, five years after the Soviet invasion. Petr felt that Sylva had written all of this reluctantly: she was aware of the extent of the tragedy affecting all Czechs, she didn't want her son to suffer on her behalf, and, nonetheless, she tried to give her son the most precise information possible.

> As you probably know, Jan—the new Communist authorities, the neo-Stalinists, are setting culture back twenty years, back to the depths of the fifties. Many Czech writers have gone into exile abroad, as have the most important musicians, painters, film directors, and scientists. There has been an entire Czech exodus. The other day I read these words in a samizdat publication: "Before

forcing him to drink a cup of poison in punishment for having offended the local deities, they offered Socrates the possibility of exile. The philosopher said that he preferred to take heed of the laws of his own city, where he has lived up until now as a citizen of the world, and only afterward would he go into exile, through the Greek sky, off to the cosmos."

Son, I feel something similar. Despite which, I am deeply grateful to you for your offer to join you in America and to remain with you there. I don't know if I will be able to express my thoughts clearly enough. My whole life long, I have obeyed orders, I have satisfied other people's wishes, and so it was that I gradually lost touch with myself. I didn't know who I was, what I was like, or what it was I had to do. With this disjointed way of going about things, I hurt myself, but above all I caused a great deal of pain to those around me. If only you knew what I have been guilty of! My first husband killed himself; it was my fault that your father was sent to the Siberian gulag; during the war I betrayed my country. And all because I obeyed the dictates of those who were not the people I should have listened to. I married a man I didn't love, I made your father go back to Russia to prove that he loved me and I became a citizen of the Reich out of fear because I lacked the courage to realize what it was I had to do at that time, the kind of courage that my mother had in spades. Now, at last, it would seem that I have found myself. I firmly believe that no one will ever be able to order me to kill that which I love most.

I have taken refuge within myself, Jan. Of my own free will I have distanced myself from my friends and colleagues, and from the political and cultural debates and discussions that the dissidents organize in the strictest secrecy. Perhaps you will criticize me for this. But the fact is I only have faith in what I can do by myself, I take pleasure only in little, everyday things. I have dug myself in, here in my solitude on the outskirts of Prague. Like someone seeking sanctuary in a monastery, I have fled from a world to which I am not bound, at a time when hypocrisy reigns mightier than ever. During the darkest periods of our recent history, the times of Hitler and Stalin, our moral values began to deteriorate. That process is continuing now, nobody knows the difference between good and evil. In Moscow, Mr. Semyon—you remember him, don't you, Jan?—told me that a man who survives the gulag or any other system involving the extermination of men by other men, remains devastated by the experience. The world around him becomes a place of exile. It becomes a humiliation that lasts forever, and humiliation is as painful as physical torture during an interrogation. From a world that humiliates me, that humiliates all of us who live in this country, I have taken refuge in myself, as if I were my own convent. I lack for nothing, I depend on myself and myself alone, the gray, rainy autumn sky is as appealing to me as a wonderful sunny day. I lack for nothing . . . No, I won't lie to you. There is something I do find lacking. I lack tenderness . . .

"WHAT IS your son doing now, Sylva?" Petr asked.

Sylva said nothing.

"What is your son doing now?" Petr insisted.

"He lives in America, where he is a prestigious mathematician specializing in cybernetics. He's doing research into electric cars now," Sylva said, matter-of-factly.

"An exile," Petr sighed.

"Yes, an exile," Sylva repeated in the same weary voice.

"There are so many emigrants ... when is the stream of people who smuggle themselves out of the country every day, going to stop?"

"I understand them," Sylva said, thoughtfully, "They want to live as they please, not according to someone else's whim, and here, they can't do that."

"They are weakening us."

Sylva didn't answer. With her nails, she traced shapes in the wax that had fallen from the candle onto the plate.

"This exodus is weakening us. Don't you feel weaker, Sylva?"

With her nails, Sylva drew a flower, a four-leaf clover, a teddy bear with round ears. In her mind, she had gone beyond the conversation. The flame in the dark was whipping at her thoughts.

"You've probably had supper, haven't you, Sylvette? So I'll gobble all this down on my own," Petr said, without waiting for Sylva's reaction.

His job as a parking lot attendant has changed him, Sylva thought, he's Monsieur Beauvisage no longer, elegant as he was, with that air of *poète maudit* about him. The atmosphere in which we live has changed all of us.

"Don't you think, that with all these exiled people, we have grown weaker? Don't you feel weaker, Sylvette?" Petr toyed with the last morsel of camembert on his fork, before popping it into his mouth. "Yummy!" he said.

Sylva wanted to leave. Where was her handbag? And her coat?

But she was in her own home! She couldn't run away. She had to stick it out, no matter what. How can a person change so much? she asked herself again.

"How much did it cost you, this French cheese that I've gobbled up in no time? Two hundred crowns? How many hours would I need to work to earn this ephemeral piece of food that has only lasted me a couple of minutes?"

Petr picked up a pencil and, drawing highly complex equations in the margins of a page of the newspaper, worked out how long he would have to work in order to earn two minutes of gastronomic pleasure, how many days, how many hours, and probably how many seconds.

"You know, Petr, whoever can, gets away from here, flees from this deathly atmosphere as if from the plague."

"We don't have any incentives, or any freedom, that's for sure, but so what? You can take pleasure in what you find within yourself."

"That's not good enough for everyone, Petr. Who can be interested in what you do, if nobody, in the end, cares whether you work or not? How can anyone live like that, especially young people?"

"It's good enough for me."

"For you, maybe it is, but a young person needs to face up to the outside world, just in order to know himself. The more there is to face up to, the better."

"This country is good enough for our dissidents. They write their novels and their philosophical essays here. And even if they're not allowed to publish, they make an effort to keep a smile on their faces."

"Petr, making an effort to seem happy has nothing to do with real happiness. It is nothing but a contrived grimace."

"They are bound by friendship, and loyalty."

"Who is bound?" Sylva smiled wearily.

"The dissidents."

"Friendship, certainly, now that they have a common enemy. But if they lived in freedom, you'd soon see just how well they'd get along with one another."

"You're a pessimist. You can't deny that these are people who know how to love, who feel that love is an incentive."

"In the dissidents' ghetto, promiscuity is a substitute for freedom of expression."

"You paint everything gray, no, black, Sylvette," Petr said, shaking his head.

"I know these dissidents of yours well enough. Helena was a young violinist who lost her job in an orchestra because she's a dissident. She was a friend of Jan's. There is just as much sadness among the dissidents as there is among the rest of us; sadness and boredom and ennui."

"Sadness? Are you sure? I would say rather that they share a tragic spirit, a common sense of tragedy."

"No, Petr. You're sugarcoating it. Tragedy is energy, flight, zest, pathos, dignity. We live in a dull vacuum with nothing glorious about it at all."

"You talk as if you were the victim of an injustice, Sylva."

"No, it's not that," Sylva watched the wax circle spread as the candle kept dripping onto the plate, "My fate has not been unjust to me. I look back without regret at all those years of humiliation, first because of the Nazis, and now, for the last quarter century, because of the Communists."

"Sylva, it is good to regret the negative parts of our lives."

Sylva didn't answer until after a long pause. She did so with a cry, albeit one in the form of a whisper.

"If I were to regret all those years . . . what would be left of my life?"

Petr raised an objection, but Sylva paid it no more heed than if it had been distant rustle of tree branches. She looked at the flame, and her thoughts toyed with another evening, long ago.

"Do you still do some accounting, Petr?" she said, smiling at the edges of the sheet of newspaper, packed with equations.

Petr pushed away the newspaper and the pencil. He took Sylva by the arm. His eyes rested on her lips.

"That's right, I'm always doing sums of some kind. It's a professional drawback that comes from spending every day charging people for parking spaces. But I also count all the obstacles I will have to cope with before I can have you . . . the way I want to. Like this."

Petr hugged her with both arms. Sylva saw that he was emotional.

She, on the other hand, was anything but. She dwelled on very different images.

Sylva released herself from Petr's embrace.

"You always say our, our . . ." she said, "Our dissidents, our country, our nation. Humph!"

Sylva wrinkled up her nose. Was she capable of loving a nation, a country, a collective? Suddenly, she heard herself say, "Spare me your groups, your collectives. I want to live! I want them to let me live, to breathe! I want to be me!"

"I'm sorry?"

"I want to be me, nothing more than that!"

"I most definitely believe in working for the good of a collective."

Sylva told herself that she liked this Monsieur Beauvisage she saw now, with his shining eyes as they were then, in that remote time, in that remote chateau.

"We live in a cemetery, Petr, can't you see that?"

"What will become of us?"

"You're like an actor in a tragedy," Sylva gave a tired laugh.

"No, I mean it. What will become of us?"

Sylva took a long sip of wine. She walked over to the window and looked into the darkness, saying more to herself than anyone else, "It is our fear that allows them to subdue us."

"Fear?"

"By playing on our fear, they keep us in a state of constant panic. We're afraid they'll punish us for a crime or misdemeanour we haven't committed. We know we haven't committed it and still we're afraid."

Petr stared at Sylva's glass without seeing it.

"Sure, I'm afraid, me too, but I know I should stop feeling this way. I should get rid of such an obstacle to inner peace."

"You won't manage to do it, Petr. Everybody's afraid. Whatever we do, we always act under the influence of fear. And that's what is humiliating."

Petr blinked several times, uncontrollably, violently. Sylva thought that maybe this was a nervous tic left over from his time spent in a Stalinist prison.

"But don't you think that . . . "

"Come on, Petr, don't kid yourself. Our life is nothing but humiliation with a capital H."

"But, perhaps you can just ignore it and . . . "

"Ignore what? Ignore that at any moment they can take the few things you have left? Ignore that they have managed to grind you down, to shame you? That they've won?"

"What do you mean that they've won? They haven't as far as I'm concerned, Sylva."

"They have, Petr. They have turned us into exactly the type of people they wanted us to become: run-of-the-mill citizens, bothered only about day-to-day problems, without any grand ideals, or anything to look forward to. We're capable of denying ourselves everything for months and months because we're dying to get hold of some Spanish entry visas. Have you any idea of the wasted energy that that entails? When we worry about such things, we're unable to spend time on things which really matter."

"Sylva, there's something you need to know. You'll have a go at me, I know you'll say it's trite, but to be honest it's what I feel: even in prison, one can be free."

"That's a pretty-sounding thing to say. Just try it, Monsieur Beauvisage."

"You're a spiteful woman, I knew it. I don't need to try it, I do it all the time. My work consists of taking people's money so they can park their cars. Do you know what I like best about this modest little job?"

"I've no idea. I mean you're out there in the freezing cold, they haven't even given you a shelter!"

"What I like best about the job is that I don't have to put up a front. If I want to speak ill of the regime, I do so. In your line of work, of course, things are different."

Sylva looked at the cast iron helmet, staring the armed knight in the eye. The light of the candle's flame danced over it: the knight had come back to life. Sylva addressed her reply to him, "Yes, everybody pretends to believe in Communism, those at the bottom and those at the top. I don't. They've taken everything I had, they've dispossessed me completely. I haven't got a thing, which is why I feel free."

"I don't see the logic of what you're saying, Sylva."

Sylva addressed herself once more to one of the resuscitated knights who were trembling to the rhythm of the candle's edgy flame.

"They took everything away from me, even the piano. They've made it impossible for me to move, to travel, they have taken my son and the man I loved. There is nothing else for them to take away. I am nothing, I have nothing, I desire nothing. I'm free. Maybe that's the irony that lies behind this regime: they take everything away from you and by doing so they liberate you."

Sylva gave a melancholy smile and went on, "Petr, the other

day, in this cupboard here, I found a photo album. There's not much of a chance I'd run into many of the people in those photos in the streets or concert halls of Prague these days. My mother and my father and my grandmother and even Mama's second husband, are all dead. Jan and his closest friends are in exile in the United States and Canada and Switzerland. The only one left to me is Helena, Jan's ex-girlfriend, a woman whose life has been very different from mine. With the photos on my lap, I started daydreaming: I had ended up on the seashore, where there was nothing but black willow trees and black sand under a dark gray sky. I dug a ditch in that sand and filled it with the blood of the dead animals that were lying close by. Then the souls of unknown dead people appeared, along with the souls of others who I knew and will never see again. Those shadows wandered around the ditch full of blood. The inhabitants of the kingdom of shadows, the inhabitants of Tartarus, were coming toward me: figures in white and black and gray, that could barely be made out against the black sand and the black rocks that enclosed the bay. In that strange procession I recognized my father, my mother, and Bruno Singer, my first husband and all the friends and loved ones I had lost. As the shadows of the dead were passing by, my mother stopped, 'You have brought the wrath of the gods upon yourself, daughter of mine.'

"My mother's shadow looked at the horizon, as did Tiresias, the blind fortune-teller, who was there as well, not very far from my mother. And the Black Lips—Maman—slowly pronounced their verdict, accompanied by an echo from the grave, or so it seemed to me, 'You have brought the wrath of the gods upon yourself, daughter of mine, because you never used your own head, but allowed yourself to be swayed by the opinions of others.'

"'What can I do to make up for my errors, Maman?'

"But my mother wasn't listening. The Black Lips went on weaving their oracular spell, 'Andrei, the father of your son, has not ceased waiting and hoping that he will see you again; he often weeps for you. Your son is fulfilling his destiny, but he is alone. Alone, daughter of mine, he seeks solace in feverish work and has gained worldwide prestige. And I? My longing to see you and my grief upon discovering that you had forgotten me when I was suffering in the Terezín concentration camp, cut my life short.'

"My mother walked away, and with her the other shadows also wandered off. Those people who knew me waved when they passed by, and immediately disappeared into the mist.

"Only the shadow of my first husband passed in silence, his head bowed. Even dead, he resented me and would never forgive me."

"I understand you, Sylva," Petr said, although he didn't understand a thing, or precisely because of that. He couldn't understand her because he was thinking about something else. After a moment of silence, he told her about his idea, "In *The Charterhouse of Parma* Stendhal talks about Fabrizzio, who, when he's imprisoned in the tower, is happier than when he was free."

"That's a novel. Don't tell me you're influenced by rubbish like that. Freedom is a synonym for happiness, at least it is so for the great spirits."

"I am indeed influenced by it, and am happy to be so. Fabrizzio was happy because his love was also in the tower, Sylva."

"Not a love, an illusion. Don't be naive, Monsieur Beauvisage, it's been a long while since you were twenty years old."

Petr got up and approached Sylva. He bowed over her.

"Sylva, would you . . . ? Would you want to marry me?" he said in an uncertain voice.

Sylva didn't move a muscle. She thought that Petr now looked just as he did a long time ago at the chateau, in a similar situation.

"After fifty years, Sylvette!" Petr added. So he too has been thinking about events back then, thought Sylva. Petr gave a little laugh to cover up the catch in his throat.

Sylva moved away from him, threw her head back, and sank into the darkness of the past, lit up by the lampposts in the park of the chateau.

Once again, she released herself from Petr's embrace and sat down at the table.

"Sylvette," she repeated.

The only reply was the sound of a dog barking and then howling. The window trembled from the gusts of wind. "Sylvette," she said, quietly. The wind was whistling on the far side of the window, as if threatening her. Sylva took a long look at the candle flame, until spots began to dance before her eyes.

Slowly, she brought her face closer to the candle. She took a breath and released it with a puff.

The candle went out.

Sylva went over to Petr.

"My name is not Sylvette," she said in a metallic voice, in the middle of the dark. And she added, in the same tone: "Yes, I'll marry you, Petr."

Untethered, she ran through the shadows.

A dog howled on the street. Gray light heralded the dawn.

After a short while, the first morning bus passed by, sounding its horn, and, for a fraction of a second, it lit up the wall of the room.

# XIII

# JAN

"DID YOU ENJOY THE KEBAB AND THE PILAF?" THE WAITER asked, hurrying on his way past us to the part of the restaurant furthest away.

I nodded, trying to smile with my mouth full.

"How about the wine, did you like our shiraz? Would you care for another bottle?"

The waiter's accent was foreign to me; it sounded like he was talking in Persian.

Again, I answered in the affirmative.

Katya went on talking offhandedly into the phone. It was becoming more and more obvious to me that she might never get used to life in the United States. I thought about her and the cake she'd baked for my birthday, on which she'd placed six symbolic candles; Katya, who for Christmas always filled the house with red plants and colorful decorations; Katya, who went shopping at the supermarket and prepared meals and cleaned dishes; Katya, who did the laundry and hung it out to dry and ironed it afterward; Katya, who told Peter to be quiet when I was working in my study at home; Katya, who on my toughest days massaged the soles of my feet to calm me down.

She looked good. Men noticed her; she noticed them and watched them through half-closed eyes. Katya was smiling at me now. No, her smile wasn't for me. Her coquettish laugh accompanied the words, "I don't believe a word you've said," spoken into the phone.

I never asked my wife or family to come with me when I went to scientific conferences; I went everywhere alone. Alone! That word that had scared me so before, now felt like some exquisite fruit from the garden of earthly delights.

Not long ago, I'd even gone to Prague alone. You'd told me about Prague and its cafés so often, Mama, about the cloakrooms with long winter coats hanging down to the parquet flooring. I'd gone to Prague to enjoy the various ambiences that spring up around the different café tables, and, above all, to imagine the piano teacher Sylva von Stamitz seated there: a cigarette in a long holder in one hand, and before her, a tall glass half-full of glittering, pomegranate-colored wine.

IN PRAGUE I, too, went to the cafés to pass the time, because there I could be alone and enjoy it, without feeling the least bit lonely. Perhaps you, too, searched for a crowded solitude surrounded by people's conversations and emotions. Perhaps you, too, had become a stranger in your own land.

Anyhow, one day I dropped by a café, which had on one wall a picture of a naked green nymph sitting at a gentleman's table. Looking at the picture, I thought of something completely different: Aesop's fable about the jackdaw and the crows. A jackdaw who was bigger than the other jackdaws decided to go and live with the crows. By way of an explanation to the jackdaws he was leaving for good, he said that only the crows were worthy of his company. But the crows didn't like the jackdaw, and thought that his feathers were ugly and his voice disagreeable, and they attacked him with their beaks. In the end, the jackdaw wanted to go back to the other jackdaws; but they didn't want to have anything to do with him. So the jackdaw ended up without anyone who would accept him as he was. He was a stranger wherever he went and fell ill from loneliness.

That is a feeling I personally know rather well.

Is it arrogant, though, to search for freer climes? Is it a kind of cowardice, to abandon your country when it's going through a difficult time?

So I sat there in the café, with that picture of a nymph and a gentleman in a dress coat in front of me. I took my eyes off the picture and looked around to see if I might find Helena somewhere on the premises. Then I noticed three white-haired men sitting at the table next to mine. Two of them were almost bald, and the third had a flowing mane of hair. Two of them . . . seemed to me to have once been my colleagues at work. Exactly thirty-five years had gone by, but I was sure I still recognized them. They were older than I was, and in their elegant suits and ties they still cut handsome figures. In this café, the three of them looked as if they'd stepped out of another world, an old, outmoded world, maybe that of Prague between the wars. I sampled the white wine in my glass, and let myself be carried away by their voices: the voices of Antonín, Pavel, and Dušan.

"In Holland they've discovered how to retain the consciousness of recently deceased people."

Pavel took a sip of his cognac, and stroked his baldpate as if he were smoothing back an unruly fringe, and looked at the others to ascertain whether what he'd said had the desired effect on his friends.

It was obvious that it hadn't made any impression whatsoever on Dušan. He stared first at the naked green nymph, then looked over at the curtain—a lace curtain turned gray by café smoke, which Prague's spring breeze was fluttering in the open window.

"Retain the consciousness of the dead?" Dušan said in a low

voice, more to himself than to anyone else. "That's all the dead need. Not to be able to forget. What a load of nonsense!"

A fit of coughing shut him up. When it was over, Dušan gave his companions an apologetic look, but in that noisy café they didn't seem to have noticed his coughing and probably hadn't heard what he'd said before it, either.

"It's not exactly the way you've described it," Antonín stopped reading the newspaper editorial and energetically flicked the ash off the tip of his cigar. "In Holland they haven't discovered a way of retaining the consciousness of the recently deceased. No, all they've done is study what happens after death. What they've discovered is that consciousness doesn't disappear immediately. I've read about it too."

Antonín tapped his knuckles against the final authority, the newspaper.

Maybe to cover for his weak memory, Pavel reached a hand out in the direction of the waiter and pointed to his glass to indicate he wanted another cognac.

"I'm thinking about a particular death," Dušan said all of a sudden, while looking at the flapping curtain, which was spreading tiny flecks of dust into the air, visible only in the rays of sunlight. "I am remembering the death of somebody who had the same name as me, Dušan, and whose father was also called Dušan. The Russians have a word for this kind of double name-sake: *tiozka*."

A fresh attack of coughing shook Dušan's body; he turned his face away from his friends. When he stopped coughing, he stayed quite still for a moment to get his breath back. He took deep breaths and watched the curtain as it billowed out and the flecks of dust that floated all around it.

"Do you want me to close the window?" Pavel suggested.

"No need, the fresh spring air is just fine!" Dušan said.

"He was seventy years old, that *tiozka* of mine. At our institute one of our colleagues was called Koči. Before he called himself Koči, he'd had a long German surname, but had changed it for a shorter, Czech one. Friend Koči wasn't a complete dunce, but he wasn't that smart either: mediocre from tip to toe, he was. Right at the start of our teamwork at the institute it was obvious that for his scientific work—if his patchwork mish-mash could be described as such—our colleague Koči was drawing inspiration from texts published by my namesake. As happened all over the place during the Communist regime, meetings were organized pretty frequently at our institute to debate all kinds of matters, always from the point of view of the One True Ideology. You all know this, of course. One day, at one of these meetings, our colleague Koči said, in reference to my *tiozka*: 'Comrades, in my opinion, we should demote Comrade XY'—my *tiozka*, in other words—'to a position involving less responsibility. In our managing body, we should avoid people who are not members of the party, and who, moreover, do not actively respect our current political regime or ideology.' Nobody protested: that was unthinkable, naturally! We were, of course, afraid. To protest would have meant putting our jobs, our futures as scientific researchers, and our children's welfare on the line. You're right, Pavel, that's no excuse, it really isn't. But in that era we did so many things that . . . Who can say of himself that he bears no guilt? My *tiozka*. That's who. After Koči's little speech, they forced him to step down from his position as co-director, and after the 1968 Soviet invasion, they sacked him altogether. My *tiozka* went on researching and writing articles, and I don't really know how but he managed to keep up with the latest scientific trends in the West. How did he earn his living? He worked laying pipelines through the northern Bohemian mountains, but in the evenings, in a trailer, he studied and wrote. Since he was unable to publish, he passed his scientific articles on to me, and he probably passed them on to other people as well, because soon his reflections and analyses began to appear, incorporated into the otherwise worthless, supposedly scientific articles written by our colleague Koči. And the director of the institute, ask me who our director was! Have you guessed? After the 1968 invasion, our colleague Koči himself became the institute's director, of course he did! Anyhow, to go on: after a short while, our colleague Koči started to insert whole sections of my *tiozka's* research into his own articles for publication, without any kind of acknowledgement, it goes without saying.

"After democracy," Dušan went on, "our colleague Koči stayed on in his job, of course, but he had to allow my *tiozka* to return to the institute. That's right, the new authorities forced Koči to invite my *tiozka* back to his job. Afterward, Koči continually berated my *tiozka* for having lost touch with the scientific world when he was doing all that manual work, so that his scientific methods were now outdated and useless. But despite all this, he still took my *tiozka's* articles and stuffed them away in a drawer for years. Without publishing them, of course. So my *tiozka* continued to write with no hope of publication, with the only difference that before the fall of the Berlin Wall his work was, from time to time, plundered by somebody else and publicized, whereas now under democracy, he was writing only so that his work could be put in somebody else's drawer, where he had no access to it. My *tiozka* understood what was going on, and grew ill from the frustration of it. But why am I telling you all this? What were we talking about?"

"I think you'd started to tell us about the death of your namesake," Antonín said.

"We were talking about life after death, that's right. Thank you." Dušan smiled and cleared his throat. "At my *tiozka's* funeral, the director of the institute, our colleague Koči, gave a speech in front of the coffin. At length, in detail, and with great pomposity he praised the highly commendable life of the deceased. People were crying, I saw their tears."

Antonín's spectacles flickered in Dušan's direction, and he scratched his forehead. "What a cheek! Didn't his friends, his acquaintances, his family, didn't anyone protest at all?"

Dušan looked again at the curtain, the gray edge of which had just caressed the head of a man seated next to the window. He took a deep breath and his voice was hoarse when he said, "The deceased's wife, my *tiozka*'s wife, was sitting in front of me. She only sighed loudly and said: 'What a beautiful speech!'"

The waiter brought the bill to the three customers, asking them to pay now because his shift was over. They paid, Antonín then resumed reading the newspaper column and stroking his bald head. Dušan watched the gray curtain flutter.

WHAT WERE we talking about, Mama, before I remembered that conversation between the three men? Oh yes, the *emigré*'s loneliness in a new country. My friend Bill told me that happiness is when we find somebody who understands us.

In Prague, I visited old friends, and had supper with former colleagues and schoolmates. Everything I saw there struck me as being old, as if it belonged to another life; can you understand that, Mama? My acquaintances told me about their lives, about those twenty years of putrefaction that had my native country in its grip after the Soviet invasion: a gray, dull, humiliating time, everywhere, in shops and on trams, in offices and during the holidays, at work and in restaurants. I wanted to know more details; they answered, "You didn't live through it the way we did, you can have no idea what it was like."

I think everyone I spoke to wanted me to feel guilty. My

acquaintances didn't want to hear about the loneliness of an exile, of his marginalization, or of his paralysis due to his poor knowledge of both the language and the cultural background of his new country. They didn't want to hear that becoming an exile is an incurable illness. My acquaintances had got into the habit of thinking themselves superior, as men who had become exceptional because they'd been victims of a merciless dictatorship and had survived it, left to fend for themselves, while the West grew richer and richer. They were the great victims of the twentieth century, and now they waited for history to do them justice. So in silence I let them talk, without asking any questions, nodding at their stories because they really did interest me.

In Prague, I had tried to solve the mystery of your sudden death, Mama. At just over seventy, your death was premature; indeed, every death is premature. I was told that an unfortunate accident befell you: you inhaled toxic gas from a heating system, and had died together with a male friend of yours. Nobody could give me any further details. I liked knowing that during your last days, you had a man friend. Who was he? I imagine a slim, distinguished gentleman with white hair, the one you introduced me to once when I was little: Uncle Petr, you'd called him. Was it him, Mama? Or could it have been my father? I wish it had been my father there with you, but I'll never know.

No sooner did I arrive in Prague than I realized I didn't have any place to go, because you were nowhere to be found, Mama. Up until then, I'd imagined, from my solitary desk in the United States, that all I had to do was go to Prague in order to hear your voice and see your caring eyes, Mama, which never lost any time in discovering the feelings I'd hide behind an impenetrable façade. Since then, nobody has shown any interest in pulling the mask off of the prestigious researcher and happy husband. On the evening I arrived, I went to the apartment where you and

I had lived; now a man was living there who didn't want to let me in. Only then did I start to understand that if I wanted to be with you again, the only option was to do so by means of an internal monologue. I also traveled to the chateau of your childhood, where a guide was showing a group of tourists your Venetian colored-glass chandeliers, your Bohemian cut-glass wine goblets, the silver cutlery, and the Japanese cabinets that had belonged to your father's grandmother. In that old chateau, the image I had of you took on a kind of solemnity, a grandiloquence, a distant, almost foreign beauty. I saw you standing there in the dead center of those rooms, their walls covered by the paintings of Dutch Old Masters. You, noble, distant, untouchable. You were filled with the atmosphere of that old chateau, which, like everything that belongs to a remote past, one conceives of as something unquestionable, absolute, full of a lost, impenetrable wisdom.

Did you commit suicide, Mama? I'll never know for sure. You were a strong-willed woman. You must have been to raise a son on your own under Stalinism, and to accept that your old age would be lived in solitude, without the support and devotion of your son. You must have had the most extraordinary willpower. So perhaps you were also strong in death, if you yourself chose its time and manner.

On that Friday afternoon, an afternoon like so many others, as I was heading off from your chateau in the direction of Prague, while the sun could just be glimpsed through the low, leaden clouds, I instantly realized that for me, one life was coming to an end and another was about to begin. Yes, Mama, even at age fifty, one life can end and another begin. I was returning to Prague in a rented car, driving along narrow roads flanked by apple trees, and I felt reborn, not into a better life necessarily but definitely into a different one, one in which you would no longer be there. It was with an almost painful nostalgia. I was deluged by the perfumes, tastes, and ambiences I associated with you: the cup of hot chocolate on Sundays, and the steam coming off it, which I used to imagine would eventually join the heavy-looking clouds beyond the window. Our walks on Petřín mountain, with its carpets of leaves, as you would hum a tune from Janáček, I think from that series that has to do with a path laden with grass. On Sunday afternoons, there would be our visits to that oddly preserved little world of the homes of your mother's friends, where I as a little boy discovered the charm of Prague between the wars: the fragile steps taken by the elderly ladies rendered silent by the thick Persian carpets, the polite gestures used by those present, the Sèvres porcelain tea set, the amber liquid that made a singing sound when it was poured into my cup, blending into the majestic melodies of Schubert's *Fantasias*, which somebody was always playing on the piano.

I drove along the narrow roads, leaving behind those little villages with their melancholically beautiful names. I realized that the life into which I had just been born, the one in which you would have no part, would nonetheless be filled with the smells and tastes and ambiences that we had lived through together. I realized that for one to be able to evoke one's most deeply buried sensations, a certain distance is required: distance in both space and time, to be sure. But above all, it is most profoundly called forth by the distance that death interposes between the present and the past.

BUT LET us get back to the present. Peter was thumbing his nose at me and sticking his tongue out at me, making sure his mother couldn't see him. Not long ago, Katya had seen a photo of Helena, and she'd pulled a face too. With an indifferent grimace and a superior manner, she'd pushed the photo away.

That photo had dropped out of an envelope that had arrived shortly after my return from Prague. It contained a letter, or rather a note in a handwriting that I knew only too well and that I read with much fondness.

"I know you've been in Prague. Word travels fast! Why didn't you let me know, damn you? Apart from anything else, I've got a present for you: a kind of journal or memoir your mother entrusted to my keeping not long before her death, asking me to pass it on to you."

In the same envelope there was also a newspaper clipping with a photo of Helena playing—once again—in Sarajevo. "Does this photo jog your memory?" Helena had written in the margin.

It was just then that Katya, issuing a sneer, had said, "So this . . . is the one?" as if she was staring at some sort of monster. To thirty-seven-year-old Katya's eyes, did a woman aged fifty-six look like some kind of *Homo neanderthalensis?* I thought just the opposite. Helena hadn't changed: at fifty-six, she was no longer a Spring Girl, but rather a Summer Woman, the Goddess of the Harvest. Helena was the woman of a hundred smiles, the lady of the thousand looks, the violinist of ten thousand melodies.

Helena told me that soon the quartet she played in would be traveling to the United States and that she personally would bring me your memoirs, Mama. When I read this, a tree sprung up in the barren field of my mind and dozens of green leaves sprouted from it.

I decided to go to New York City, to the JFK airport, to pick up Helena in person. On my own. With a flower.

KATYA ISN'T happy, not even now, after . . .

From the start she'd taken me to task for refusing to work for the automobile industry, where I would have a far higher salary, and punished me with a stubborn silence that sometimes went on for days at a time. And I was stubborn too, as far as that particular subject was concerned, I wasn't about to give in.

Was I so stubborn really? Because in the end I did finally agree to sell my services, even if only in part.

Still I hadn't left the university, I hadn't betrayed myself! Even so the work for the automobile industry took up so much of my time that only with a tremendous mental and physical effort could I ensure that I was still on the cutting edge of my scientific field. I could tell that I wasn't going to be able to keep this up forever. Katya insisted that she needed more money.

And then, one day . . .


"NEXT STOP, Detroit!"

The pilot's voice woke Katya in the airplane that was flying the Midwest route.

Danielle was a colleague from Paris; her eyes passed from one person to another; at this reception, organized by the Ford Motor Company, she had discovered more than one influential person with whom she wished to get in touch. I spotted Katya across the room. If she'd come with me to the reception, then how could I have completely forgotten she was there? She was wearing a leopard-skin patterned mini-skirt. It would have suited her if she hadn't worn it with a skin-tight white blouse and transparent stockings. Katya had also festooned herself with a huge pearl necklace. Her rather artificial appearance contrasted with the simpler style of the Parisian woman in a long gray dress with a fuchsia silk foulard. Katya was having fun with a couple of men, glancing flirtatiously up at the ceiling, down at the floor, or at the lips or eyes of one or other of the men. Katya was holding a stack of papers, which she showed, laughing, to the two men. When Danielle started chatting to the CEO's wife, I managed to sneak a quick look at the sheets in Katya's hands. They looked like architects' drawings.

The tanned one, who was one of the two men talking to Katya, called out to me.

"Having a good time, John?"

The sporty one slapped me on the back.

"Great party, huh, John?"

"It sure is. John's having a whale of a time, we can all see that," said Katya, slowly, coldly.

"These canapés are yummy, huh, John?"

"Have you tried the curry-flavored nacho chips?" asked the sporty one, interrupting the other guy.

"Bullshit, they're wasabi flavored," said the tanned one.

"Having fun, huh, John?" the sporty one asked, slapping me on the back.

"More or less. One of your colleagues was just telling me about all the adventures he'd been having in my country," I said, while trying as best I could to see what was in the architects' drawings that Katya was putting away into a folder.

"My country? Did you say 'my country'?" asked the tanned one.

"Even now you still talk about 'your country'!" said the sporty one in amazement.

"In my country—wow!" the tanned one said again, "I thought your country was right here in the United States of America."

"What's the matter with the States? Why can't this be your country now?" the sporty one asked, dumbstruck.

"Nothing. There's nothing the matter with them, it's just that I didn't grow up here. And my mother never came here. That's why." I was trying to clarify my own feelings.

"So let it go! That country you were born in, just let it go and be an American like the rest of us. C'mon! Join the club!

We'd be only too happy to accept you," said the sporty one, laughing.

I smiled and winked at Katya, but my wife didn't wink back.

"Tell you what," the sporty one said to the tanned one, "now that John's got a home and a country, I reckon we can tell him our secret, whaddya think?"

"John," said the sporty one in a solemn tone of voice.

"In your new life with a home and a country, you're also going to have . . ." the tanned one said, pausing to mull over what he wanted to say.

The sporty one helped out:

"You'll be the owner of . . ."

"As befits your status . . ."

I had the feeling I was in some kind of fantasy movie. A terrible suspicion was creeping up on me.

"John! You're going to have one big house!" exclaimed the sporty one.

"With a pool!"

"You can invite us over!"

"A yard!"

"Ideal for barbecues!"

I felt a knot in my throat.

"You've got a whole new life ahead of you!"

"A *vita nuova*. Isn't that how you say it over in Europe? Did I get that right?"

"Cut that out, he's an American now, the hell with that bullshit!"

"It's just the beer talking. A *vita nuova*, John! A magnificent house, the envy of your neighbors!"

"And me too, no kidding!"

"Just as well my wife hasn't seen it; otherwise she'd want one just like it."

"Yeah, my wife would too."

"John, today is a special day in your life. You've got a new home! To pay for it, the bank's just given you a twenty-five year mortgage."

"If you're lucky, you'll be able to pay for it before you kick the bucket!" the tanned one said, laughing.

"Your wife's prepared a little surprise for you, John. The drawings! Yes, the architects' drawings of your new home that is being built as we speak!"

"You don't have to worry about a thing. Everything's in place."

"We've got another surprise for you, John, too!" the sporty one was beaming. "We've got a contract here that'll make it possible for you to work right here, at Ford's Detroit headquarters!"

The sporty one announced this as if he were the president of the Swedish Academy awarding me a Nobel Prize.

Katya took out the drawings and the contracts and the two men spread them out in front of me.

I took a sip of champagne.

A fuchsia foulard cut through the thick air of the party and suddenly vanished.

WHEN THE Ford reception was over, we headed for a taxi stand.

"Did you have fun, Katya?"

No reply.

"Are you tired?"

Silence.

"Don't you feel well?"

This question also remained unanswered. Knowing Katya, this kind of silence meant that I'd somehow put my foot in it.

"Have you got a headache, maybe?"

No answer.

"Is there something I can do?"

Again, silence.

We were in a taxi, headed for the Hyatt Regency. Silence sat between us like a Japanese sumo wrestler. Not for the first time.

The next day, I awoke in the wee hours. Katya was still asleep. I went over to the window. The frost had drawn miniature Chinese images on the pane: pine-topped cliffs, knotty branches covered in flowers. I looked at this marvel, this drawing done with white ink on rice paper. I'd lost sight of so many day-to-day details when concentrating on the so-called important tasks!

In the gray-white sky with a golden tint courtesy of Detroit's ambient light, the snowflakes made curves and arches as they fell. I imagined a winter forest and a Russian snowstorm; I saw a window framed in painted wood in the middle of a fir wood and in the window looking out were a woman's gray eyes, searching for someone . . . Where had all the Russian heroines gone, all those Tatianas and Natashas, all the Sonias and Dunyas, the female heroins of Pushkin and Turgenev, Tolstoy and Dostoyevsky, women that men could not help but worship? Where were those women, transparent as snowflakes, who had sung Orthodox liturgies like the angels in Renaissance paintings? The snowflakes outside were falling fast like hundreds of ballerinas on an immense stage. So many Russian heroes had ended up finding peace. What did I have to do to find some tranquillity? Did I have to be hard and unbending, or soft and pliant? A rigid tree can be broken by the wind, so you used to tell me, Mama.

I solved this dilemma in accordance with my nature: if Katya decided to remain obstinately silent this morning, then I would stick to my guns no matter what. If, on the contrary, she woke up in a sweet, talkative mood, I would try and satisfy her needs.

Over the breakfast I ordered from room service, Katya ended up mentioning that, the previous day, I had almost forgotten about her, distracted as I'd been by another woman. The fuchsia foulard had cut through the room, to stop, finally, in the middle, where it fell to the floor.

I felt tired.

I was so lethargic that when Katya placed several forms that needed to be signed in front of me, I took the pen from her and signed all the contracts, the ones for the house and the mortgage, and the one concerning the fulltime job with the Ford Motor Company. I longed for some peace of mind, the peace of the exile who simply does what his new country tells him to do.

Katya looked visibly relieved, but after a little while her face returned to its usual bored expression. In silence, we ate bacon and eggs, washed down with lukewarm coffee. The morning was growing dark, or was it nighttime already? The snowflakes weren't dancing anymore; they were waterlogged and fell straight to the ground, as if weighted. But I wasn't looking at them, I merely sensed them, because I was flicking through the *Detroit Free Press*.

IN THIS Persian restaurant in Manhattan, Katya got out of her chair and went to the bathroom. Her face proclaimed: *I am a victim. Before, women were victims of violence; now, in this civilized world of ours, we are victims of a brutal indifference as well as violence. I, who am a remarkable woman, born to dedicate myself to higher ideals, I am now a martyr. Yes, a martyr to my husband's apathy and that of all the gluttonous men who invented Western civilization. And a martyr as well to my son's future.*

And Katya was right.

I took the job at the Ford Motor Company. I agreed to do that which, for decades, I had refused to do. The tanned one and the sporty one were rubbing their hands in satisfaction and applauding themselves like little kids. My capitulation had probably earned them the congratulations of their bosses and some kind of reward.

So, I now work for Ford. We have a brand new house with a swimming pool. Katya has covered the walls with reproductions of Monet and Manet in the gilt frames she prefers. On the shelves and in the glass cabinets there isn't an inch of free space, there are gold-colored objects everywhere, as well as enamelled Russian boxes, miniature icons, embroidered doilies, painted plates, and dozens of photographs: Katya swimming in Lake Placid wearing an orange bikini; Katya skiing in Vermont; Katya in an evening dress at New York's Metropolitan Opera House; Katya in the pool with Peter; Katya at a Washington, DC reception, hanging on my arm; Katya waterskiing on Lake George; Katya playing golf in Cape Cod; Katya in a summer dress, yellow as a butterfly's wings.

The waiter served us some oriental sweetmeats, which looked really rich, and then filled our glasses with a wine that was almost black. Katya turned up clasping her cell phone to her ear.

These days, Mama, when I retire to my study, I don't think much about my research anymore. Sometimes I think about my life, about my being rooted in my solitude, about being a foreigner no matter where I go. In America I can live in a comfortable but not very interesting way; I feel no strong ties to the place. I couldn't live in Prague because I feel such a strong emotional bond to the city and sense gross injustice there, with every step I take.

You ask about my work? If I am deeply involved in my work? Don't even mention it to me, Mama, I beg of you.

I'll tell you about something that happened to me the other day.

At an international convention in Los Angeles, I ran into the prestigious mathematician Kenneth McMasters, of the Massachusetts Institute of Technology, whose current research I admire more than just about anybody else's. As soon as he saw me, a glass of champagne in his hand, the professor left the group of people he was standing with.

"My good Professor Stamitz," he said as he quickly headed over to me, "what a pleasure to see you here! I know all about the research you carried out in the seventies and eighties, with regard to the discontinuous function of coordinates. After those first steps you took many of us have continued researching this field, which now looks so promising. Forgive me, perhaps I simply haven't seen them, but recently I've been missing your articles in our journals. The fault is probably mine. I'd be interested in hearing about your most recent results."

McMasters took a sip of champagne, automatically, without noticing he'd done so because he was so focused on our conversation, and went on, "I'd like to share the information with my colleagues. How would you feel about giving a series of lectures at our institute?"

His invitation struck me as a very attractive one and I began telling Professor McMasters about the most recent developments in my work: I had discovered that my theories had many practical applications, such as my theory of control that I had adapted to electric automobile motors, all of this for the Ford Motor Company. Another interesting application I'd developed was the automatic control of diesel motors; this involved a non-linear model, of an elevated order and with many uncertainties.

Professor McMasters stared at me as if he didn't recognize me anymore. I thought that what I'd explained hadn't satisfied him, so I added climatic control on commercial automobiles.

"I'd be happy to talk about these matters with you and your colleagues, any time you wanted," I suggested.

The distinguished professor cut me off, "Thank you, but . . ."

There was a lengthy pause. Then he finished this sentence, "But . . . I was referring to a quite different sort of thing. I don't know if I've made myself clear."

I didn't know what to say. The professor had already changed the subject: Hadn't the president of the convention been exaggerating, yesterday, about the methods of simulation?

"The methods of simulation?" I didn't understand him, "Which ones? Well, yes, I suppose in the end, maybe you're right. Look . . ."

But McMasters was already saying goodbye.

"I'm pleased that you've settled down in your new, industrial working environment. If you ever publish a scientific article again, please do let me know."

And he was off. I no longer interested him, because industry didn't interest him. He is a scientist, a researcher, just as I had once been.

WHO AM I? Someone who has gone to the extreme of rejecting his last refuge: his scientific work, the fortification of his big No.

I'd married a woman who turned out to be a good wife, maybe; and a good mother, a good housewife, the daughter of a high-ranking KGB official, who has hundreds, perhaps thousands, of human lives on his conscience: all the people he sent to the Siberian gulags, innocent people, people like my father. Man is capable of just about anything in order not to feel alone!

Katya dreamed of her lost lover, just as I dreamed of my beloved from long ago. We are two solitudes chained to one another by weakness.

HERE IN the JFK airport there are so many greetings and fare-wells, hugs and tears and kisses. I should go and look at the arrivals screen; Helena's plane might be about to land.

I've hurt my hand on a rose thorn. Helena used to like dark red roses, the kind that smell like aged wine, or nighttime gardens in the summer, and the secret places of a loved woman.

Finally, I too am waiting for someone, for a woman! How I envied the man to whom a woman on the outskirts of Saint Petersburg had written a letter and kissed before posting it. How I envy Bill and his plump Jill!

Only now, after so much time, have I realized that you, Helena, you who never wanted to emigrate, who always said that a person has only one home, that you vanished that day from Sarajevo to make it easier for me to decide if I wanted to go back to Prague or to emigrate. That's why you disappeared, Helena. That's why you vanished like a grain of sand on the beach: to allow me the freedom to choose. And having done that, you preserved my longing, my desire for you, which has always been with me and without which my life would have been like an endless winter journey.

I head for the arrivals screen. Just a few more steps, and I'll find out if Helena's plane has landed.

The letters glow with green light, announcing FLIGHT OK 2901 FROM PRAGUE TO NEW YORK HAS BEEN DELAYED INDEFINITELY.

# XIV

# SYLVA

A FEW DAYS AFTER THE DINNER AT MY PLACE DURING which Monsieur Beauvisage had first gobbled up all the cheese and then asked me to be his wife, someone I didn't know delivered a large brown envelope.

"Madame Sylva von Stamitz?" he asked. "This envelope is for you, Madame." And added, in a low voice, in Russian: "It's from Moscow." Then he disappeared.

In the envelope, I found a little pile of torn newspaper, toilet paper, a napkin, a paper cone: all these were covered in closely packed, penciled writing that was blurred and mostly illegible. After sifting through all the different components, I found a small piece of notepaper. My mysterious correspondent, who hadn't signed his package—something that didn't surprise me one little bit: who wouldn't be afraid of sending banned material?—had written a few lines by way of explanation. Using a trusted messenger, he had sent me the clandestine notes Andrei had taken in the fifties, in the forced labor camp where he'd been imprisoned. Andrei wrote them in Siberia, taken by a strange mood: after Stalin's death he'd thought that some of his fellow prisoners would leave the camp and could smuggle his clandestine jottings out and send them to my address. All those notes were addressed to me. Which is why the *von* in my proper name had been put on the envelope, which indicated my aristocratic origins, and a name that I hadn't used since the end of the war. The mysterious sender—Semyon, perhaps?—didn't say how the notes had come into his possession, and I knew that any questioning on my part would be met by silence.

Letters from Andrei! I couldn't wait. I was burning with impatience, so I picked up a handful to take to the library. There I ran into Helena, who had come to return some books. When there was nobody nearby, she said, in a quiet voice, as if casually, "What are you up to, Sylva? Reading clandestine material? Have the Communists thrown someone you know in jail?"

She winked at me.

I blushed with shame at my unforgiveable naivety and my dismay. I quickly hid the notes in my bag.

I suddenly had an idea that I felt had to be tried out immediately. Balancing the receiver between my mouth and shoulder, with my left hand resting on Helena's arm, I dialed a number.

After a little while, Helena listened as I spoke into the receiver in a warm, but firm, voice, "Good afternoon, Monsieur Beauvisage. Petr, forgive me if you can for what I'm about to say. I acted too hastily when I gave you my answer the other day. Yes, that's right: I won't marry you. Forgive me for being so skittish. Even though . . . what I've done is unforgiveable, I know."

And I hung up.

"Helena, for the first time in my life, or maybe for the second time, I have freely made a decision on my own."

"What are you talking about?" Helena stared at me, wide eyed.

"Up until now, I've always followed other people's orders."

"You let others order you about?" Helena interrupted me, looking at me as if she were seeing me for the first time. "I wouldn't have imagined that possible! Never!"

"They used to call me the Silent Woman. Only once did I

have enough presence of mind to make a decision on my own, and it ended in disaster. Before and after that, I always did other people's bidding. Today I have exercised my own free will."

Helena said nothing. Then, "I'm proud of you. Even though, from what I believe I overheard, you must have really upset someone."

THAT EVENING I spread the smuggled notes out on the kitchen table; they made a yellow-gray collage. Some words, sometimes whole sentences, had been completely erased. After a month or two, as if in a kaleidoscope, the story of Andrei's life just before he must have died began to take shape, becoming clearer and clearer. In my mind's eye, I projected these scenes from the end of Andrei's life on the wall of my refuge on the outskirts of Prague, on library walls, and on the dirty, gray windows of the public transport in which I spent an hour and sometimes two, every day. In the end, I was able to piece together an entire film, with sound and in color.

LEILA SAT with two other nurses in the camp hospital. The three women were drinking tea around a table.

"If you don't want to tell us his name, at least tell us what he's like," Nadya insisted.

"Good looking and—"

"Oh, I'm sure he's good looking," said the shameless Olga, spitefully.

Without meaning to, the two women looked at Leila's huge nose, the hooter that was the first thing anyone saw when they caught sight of that bony, unattractive Georgian woman.

"Good looking and strong and—"

"Come on, here in the camp they reduce the lot of them to skeletons fit for anatomy classes," said Olga, laughing.

"Here they turn them into petals, into autumn leaves, you blow at them and they're off, gone!" Nadya grimaced, scornfully.

"Maybe he isn't a prisoner, Nadya," Olga reminded her colleague.

Nadya looked at her incredulously. She clearly couldn't believe that Leila had a handsome, muscular lover. Nadya didn't want Leila to have a strong, good-looking lover who could protect her and . . . and, well, whatever.

But Leila stuck to her guns.

"He's flabbergasting! And gentle. He's an artist!"

"When are we going to meet him?" Olga asked, dryly.

"I'll have to think about that."

"Are you going to bring him here?" Nadya asked, with feigned indifference.

"Yeah, we want to take a look at him," Olga repeated off-handedly and sipped at her watered-down tea.

Leila played her cards close to her chest. She wanted to draw out this little scene that gave her such pleasure, and gave a self-satisfied smile. She, gray and mediocre, was now the center of interest. Maybe the others even envied her as well. What was more, it was easy for her to talk on and on about the man who was uppermost in her thoughts.

Leila looked over at a corner in which there was a broom and dustpan full of rubbish. In the middle of that rubbish, she saw a shining golden head. She would have liked to have presented it to her colleague by way of proof. She, Salomé, wrapped up in several guazy veils, would approach them, dancing on tiptoe, with Saint John's golden head on a tray. Yes, on a silver tray, not on a rubbish-laden dustpan, absolutely not!

"You bring him over in a week's time, all right?" said Olga, winking, refusing to believe that Leila had a beau.

"I want to see him tomorrow without fail!" Nadya banged

her fist on the table. She added, ungracefully, "I'm off to see that man with a broken spine. They called me an hour ago!"

"Tomorrow, sure!" Leila shouted, as Nadya closed the door behind her.

THE NEXT day, there was a man sitting in Leila's chair.

Olga and Nadya knew him from the hospital, but they felt that today they were seeing him for the first time. They stared at him, they observed him. No, that isn't the right choice of words. They ate him up with their eyes: this was Leila's lover! He was, indeed, a man, beyond any doubt he was a live man, sitting there, in the flesh. A man!

After a routine exchange of greetings, nobody felt like saying very much.

"Can I go now?" the man asked.

Leila, who was seated next to him, shot him a filthy look. The man shuddered, and remained seated. And he went on shuddering, neurotically, like someone deranged.

Olga and Nadya said goodbye. At the door they turned to Leila; judging by their expression they seemed to think: a prisoner, hah! A nonentity!

But the bitter twist of their lips bore witness to the fact that they hadn't been able to secure even that. And they'd have liked to, oh, how they would've liked to get what Leila had!

Leila knew it. Leila was glowing.

She, the soppy one who'd become a star. The envy of her colleagues. They envied her man, a man as handsome as . . . sin. He was a vice! Leila was as drunk on her success, as if she'd been drinking strong wine.

And if he wasn't handsome—that, after ten years of forced labor in the mines, would have been asking too much—he was, when all was said and done, a man.

Leila gazed at him with protective affection and with a pride that was partly maternal. But there was something else in her look. Sensuality. The sensuality that Leila kept painfully, shamefully hidden.

"You're getting bored," Leila said, to break the silence.

"Me, bored? With three pretty women around?" the man smiled slowly, tormentedly.

He gradually stopped shaking.

Leila went red. "Me, pretty? You're having me on!"

Nobody had ever before said anything like that to her. On the contrary, her father had always called her a scarecrow!

The man said nothing then. Leila remembered the drawing he had given her one day. She had barely recognized herself: the drawing of a pleasant-looking woman who, even if she couldn't be called beautiful, certainly looked interesting, original, and smart. There was no trace of her hooked nose: what stood out were a pair of lips as sensual as the waves of a summer sea. Leila had pinned her portrait to the wall next to her bed. In the evenings she stared at it with passion, and promised herself over and over that she would keep the man, who was able to see her in this light, by her side, no matter what the cost.

Suddenly, Leila realized that the man had spoken not of one but of three pretty women. The nurse trembled with rage, both at him and her more attractive colleagues.

"Have you been working on our project?" she asked him.

"I had to go to the mine, because The Whip turned up."

"What's that to me? I don't care! Don't spin any of your yarns with me, dammit, you filthy miner, you traitor to the Motherland! Do you think I'm keeping you in the hospital so that you can live like a pasha? When are you going to finally cut the crap, you liar?"

The man went pale and made as if to leave, leaning on the table for support. The paler he got, the more excited Leila became and the more she bared her teeth, as if she'd sucked the energy out of him, "Show me what you've done, you third-rate artist, you useless loafer!"

Leila looked at the photographs of Siberian *kolkoz* workers and compared them with the portraits that this artist had done of them. With the money that Leila got from selling the portraits, she usually prepared some kind of informal meal.

"Why are you goggling at me like that? Give me the latest of those crappy portraits and get the hell out of here, you slob! I don't feel like keeping you here in the hospital, like some kind of big softie. As far as I'm concerned, you can break your back down in the mine, the way that wily mate of yours did this morning."

"I'm sorry? Could you say that again? Who did that happen to?"

"What do you care? Buzz off, you pompous know-it-all!"

"I'm sorry, but have I insulted you in any way?" said the man, after a moment.

"Insult me? What are you going on about? I make all these sacrifices for you like the soppy fool I am, and what do you do? You go after the first woman who crosses your path!"

"Me, go after someone? After who?" The man stared at her with wide, pleading eyes that softened Leila on the spot. She locked the door.

"Leila, please, tell me who got hurt down the mine."

"Later."

"Please, I beg of you."

"Now's the time for something else. Look! Look what I brought you!"

On the table, Leila laid out a bruised apple and two poison-red sweets, which nobody, not even an infant in nappies, would have touched with a bargepole. The man's eyes lit up. He reached out as if to grab something much sought after that might disappear at any moment, but then thought better of it. He pushed away the sweets, offering them instead back to Leila.

"I don't want them, thank you, Miss Leila."

"You filthy snob! Even when you're starving to death you can't help showing how noble you are. How superior you are to the rest of us, we're just common fools, then, the vulgar proles!"

Leila removed the wrapper to put the sweet into the man's mouth.

Leila picked up the apple and brought it to the man's lips. While he chewed on it, she rose and positioned his head so that it rested on her bony body. She caressed his short hair, his neck, his chest.

The man made an effort to escape the clutches of those passionate, wandering hands, but Leila wouldn't let him go. She pressed against him even harder, stroking his cheeks, his shoulders. As her hands were busy, Leila gave little sensuous moans, signs of a pleasure she had never known until now, when she was fifty-five. Leila trilled, cooed, chirped, and whistled in delight, like a mother cradling a newborn babe.

"Miss Leila, some of the inmates here have been allowed to leave the camp after many years. Do you think they'll let me go one day?"

"You're sick, Andrei, first we have to make you better, my love," Leila said with a languorous sigh.

"But after that, they'll let me go?"

Leila sighed again.

At that moment, her whole body wanted to cry out: Let you go? Over my dead body!

THE YOUNG doctor finished the man's examination.

"Did you go to the mine today?"

"Yes."

"Do you spit blood when you cough?"

"Yes."

"Do you know that your sickness is incurable?"

"My cough? You don't think that . . . perhaps in the summer . . ."

"I'm not talking about your cough. That's nothing! But about . . . the other sickness. It seems to me that here, with the forced labor, it's grown worse."

"I know that . . ."

Nurse Leila, breathless, came into the infirmary.

The man signaled to her, but she didn't see him. Her attention was concentrated solely on the doctor. The doctor himself hadn't even noticed her presence. No, he had indeed noticed it: now that she was here, the doctor's compassionate voice had taken on a gray, unfriendly tone.

"Exactly, your original sickness has got worse."

The man asked, in a weak voice, "Doctor, what does that mean in terms of my case?"

"I'm not sure that you can cure yourself on your own."

"You won't be attending to me anymore?"

"That's right."

The doctor didn't see, because he couldn't have, that Leila had placed herself behind him so as to catch every word.

"Are you leaving here, doctor?"

"Me? No," the doctor laughed, "on the contrary, it's you that will be leaving."

"Me?" The man couldn't believe his ears. "Me? How come? Doctor, for the love of God, don't make fun of me."

The patient was trembling, a tear fell down his cheek, followed by another.

The doctor rested a hand on the man's shoulder: he, too, was moved.

"How come, you ask, Mr. Polonski? The time for your political rehabilitation has arrived. Colonel Tertz informed me of it this morning. He asked me if it was possible, as far as your health was concerned, to set you free. And he gave me strict orders not to tell you anything," the doctor shrugged, "but I couldn't resist the temptation to share this happy news with you. So it only remains for me to wish you the very best of luck once you are free."

The two men embraced. The patient muttered words of gratitude, and wet the doctor's coat with his tears.

Nurse Leila took a few steps forward and stood in front of the doctor so firmly and energetically that he couldn't go on pretending to ignore her.

"No!" Leila said, menacingly, "We are not going to do that, doctor. We're not going to send this man to his death."

"Who's talking about death? We're talking about freedom," said the doctor, looking away from her in disgust. Leila looked like an old, doddering doe in heat, thought the doctor.

"For him, freedom means death. We'll keep him here and cure him, doctor. This patient needs care as badly as the bread he eats."

"In these conditions? In Siberia? In a concentration camp? You're a . . . " the doctor could barely contain himself.

"What am I? A scarecrow?"

"What I wanted to say was that this suggestion of yours is sheer madness. Here, this man will die."

"Our duty is to cure him. He's a schizophrenic."

"He's been rehabilitated!"

"We'll do this together, you and I. Colonel Tertz has asked for your professional opinion. You will tell him the truth: that the prisoner Andrei Polonski is gravely ill, his attacks of schizophrenia are so frequent and dangerous that you cannot allow him to be removed from our care."

"Nurse Leila, patient Polonski is not a schizophrenic. Don't forget that I'm the doctor around here!"

"Exactly. You're the doctor and you have revealed a political secret to a prisoner. Unfortunately, I am obliged to report your conduct through the proper channels. And I will do so, should you refuse to cooperate with me."

The young doctor's face went pale. "This man has the right to leave the camp. We shall do whatever is required to facilitate his return to freedom."

Leila's bony body stretched, soldierlike, to its full height in front of the doctor. In a loud, clear voice, Leila said, "Over my dead body."

"YOU, MY love, my only love," Leila's lips whispered, as, for just a moment, she leaned in close to the patient's burning forehead.

From the sick man's half-open mouth came a hoarse sigh, "Blue Butterfly!"

The tenderness vanished in an instant from Leila's face. To whom was he addressing those beautiful words? Not to her. No way! Nobody had ever, ever said anything like that to her.

"Who are you talking about when you come on with that blue butterfly stuff?"

Instead of an answer, only sighs could be heard from the man she'd just woken up.

"Who is Blue Butterfly, Andrei?" Leila asked in the same inquisitorial tone, with an insistent edge to her voice.

"My wife," came the faint voice from the pillow.

Leila said nothing, as if refusing to believe what she'd just heard. Immediately, hardening her voice to a threatening tone, "Your wife! Well, look at you! Why on earth am I, idiot that I am, acting as your mother and your maid, your doctor and your nurse? I dedicate myself to you. I lose sleep and slave away so hard I can't even describe it. But that doesn't mean a damn thing to you, does it? You just keep on, you don't have to go to the mine every day, you don't care that I'm making myself sick with worry for you, while you there, you ingrate, just go on about your wife!"

Leila was shaking with fury.

The sick man could barely get his words out, "It's been fifteen years since I last saw my wife, you see, Miss Leila. I've had no news of her for fifteen years. It's easy enough to say fifteen years, Miss Leila, but . . ."

His face became pale. Weakened, the patient fell into an uneasy sleep.

Leila looked fiercely at his face. Once she was sure her patient was in a deep sleep, she got up.

She went over to the window, and opened it wide. Icy gusts of Siberian wind flew into the room.

The nurse uncovered the sick man's body. As she did so, she looked at the patient with eyes that were once more filled with tenderness.

"My love, my love, finally, you're all mine," she said with passion, and watched the man's shivering body, and his lips that were turning blue from the cold. Gently, lovingly, she pressed her dry lips to his.

"Now, finally, you belong to me, my love."

Suddenly she heard footsteps in the corridor. She quickly covered up the sick man and closed the window.

The young doctor opened the door, "My God, it's cold in here!"

"I need to put some more wood in the stove," Leila said sharply, her eyes fixed on the floor.

"You've ventilated the room. You should never do that. It'd kill the patient; what he needs is warmth, energy."

Leila went on staring at the none-too-clean floor; she looked as if she were grieving. Nonetheless, flames of hatred leaped up behind her half-closed eyelids.

The young doctor, whom life had not yet discouraged from seeing the positive sides of others, saw nothing amiss in the nurse's posture other than a feeling of guilt indicated by her lowered eyelids.

Kindly, he said, "Put more wood in the stove, Miss Leila, and go to bed. The patient is resting and you need to catch a few hours of sleep as well."

But now the doctor couldn't ignore the open hostility in Leila's eyes. The nurse answered in a low, metallic voice, "I can look after myself, Doctor, don't worry about me."

The doctor, a Russian, closed the door thinking he'd never manage to understand that nurse. She's a Georgian, who knows what's going on in her head, he said to himself. Georgia, he repeated to himself, is a culture that's so very different from ours.

The nurse sat at the head of the bed and frenetically, deliriously, caressed the patient's cheeks and forehead, staring avidly at his barely open lips. "Rest, my love, my only love. I don't want to make you suffer, I'm only making sure that you never leave me, that you don't desert me. All I want is for you to be mine. Mine, no matter what it takes, my love."

The ends justify the means, Leila thought as she continued to mull over the situation. Who'd said that? Lenin, maybe? Or perhaps it was Marx? Somebody wrote it down and now I consider it mine: the ends justify the means. And Leila remembered that a long time ago, when Andrei was just a political prisoner like any other, without the privilege of rest stays in the camp hospital, Leila had found the means to make it possible for her to protect and adopt this man. He had struck her as being more sensitive and more delicate than almost any other person she'd met.

She had taken notice of a stocky guard, who everyone in the camp called The Whip. He was from Georgia, like her. They spoke the same language, shared similar customs, and they quickly struck up a friendship and got along well, to the extent that they were practically able to communicate without the use of words.

The Whip came from the Georgian mountains and, although he was the son of a kulak, he admired the Russian Revolution and blindly followed the Soviet creed. When he was young, he'd been informed that the people he'd be guarding in the work camp were political prisoners, in other words, enemies of Soviet power. He, The Whip, who lived and breathed the Communist dream, truly loathed the prisoners he had to watch over; he felt so much rancour toward them, it was as if they were his personal enemies. In the mine, The Whip rained blows on the belly of anyone he imagined wasn't working hard enough, and on their return from work, he would shoot at those exhausted men who were so worn out they staggered or tottered.

This was the man into whose care Leila had entrusted her beloved.

The Whip spat derisively.

"Listen brother, this Polonski, this aristo, deserves The Whip's iron hand. But don't kill him," laughed the nurse, with a glint in her eye.

The Whip got the message.

After two or three days of The Whip's iron hand, after a few kicks in the belly from The Whip's military boots, Andrei was unable to get up. They took him to the camp hospital.

At last!

At last, Leila could be with him twenty-four hours a day.

Now she was caressing his head, his sweaty forehead, her hand slid seductively over his neck and chest.

"Rest, my darling, be at peace. Your Leila is with you, my love," she whispered into his ear, her eyes moist.

From time to time, her patient would open his eyes, look at Leila as if he were a faithful dog, then close them again.

"Your Leila is with you, my love. Your faithful Leila loves you."

The next day, when the patient fell asleep, Leila first made sure that everyone else was sleeping. Only then did she open the window wide to offer up the sick body of her beloved to the icy Siberian cold. As for her, she loved those icy gusts: only they could keep her beloved just as she wanted him: here, bedridden, dependent on her.

Suddenly the door swung open and the young doctor appeared at the threshold. Today, he wasn't smiling.

"What is the meaning of this?"

The nurse got over her shock in an instant.

"Perhaps you had better explain to me, doctor, what you think you're doing bursting into the room of a seriously ill patient!"

"I forbade you to open the window like that. That could kill him!"

"The only thing that could kill him is his own crazy behavior. As a nurse, I know perfectly well when the room has to be aired."

Leila realized, however, that she wouldn't get anywhere by quarrelling with the doctor, so she quickly covered the sick man with a blanket and closed the window.

"There, you see, doctor, I'm following your instructions to the letter."

The doctor left. His forehead creased in a worried frown.

AFTER A few days, when the doctor came to examine the sick man, he found that Leila's patient had grown so weak he couldn't even sit up in bed.

"What is this . . . this isn't normal!" the doctor grumbled as he listened to the patient's chest.

There was little light that day; the patient barely recognized him.

"Mr. Polonski, what medication is nurse Leila giving you?"

The patient kept his mouth shut. The doctor saw that he wouldn't get anything out of him. He asked, "Which Russian painters have influenced you the most?"

Andrei perked up, "Malevich, Tatlin, Jawlensky, Kandinsky, but above all, the great Chagall."

The doctor was unfamiliar with the work of Tatlin and Malevich; on the other hand, he was enthusiastic about the paintings Chagall had done of his native Vitebsk and about the way he'd painted the Russian Revolution.

"Tell me, Andrei, what medication is Nurse Leila giving you?"

The patient gestured toward some small bottles on the chair next to the bed.

The doctor examined them one by one, from the outside and then sniffing the contents.

"All this is as it should be. Is she giving you anything else?"

"Doctor, if you knew everything that Miss Leila is doing for me!" sobbed the sick man, "She is so selfless, so unselfish! What would I do without her?"

The next day, the doctor came back; the patient wasn't showing any signs of improvement.

"Is this the only medication she's giving you? Try to remember, please, Andrei."

"Well, if you want to know everything, then . . . But it's not at all important."

"What isn't at all important?"

"After washing her hands in the bowl, nurse Leila always takes something from the medicine cupboard, the one where the bandages are kept. She puts a few drops of it into my water glass."

The doctor jumped up and went to the medicine cupboard. He took out several small bottles, and examined their contents.

"That's it!" he shouted, "What the hell are these doing in the medicine cupboard?"

"Doctor, promise me that . . ." the patient begged, but the doctor had gone.

HE GAVE Leila a stern warning that to disobey a doctor and independently administer medication to a patient was a grave breach of conduct. Without mentioning Nurse Leila by name, the doctor recommended to the authorities in charge of the labor camp that they free Andrei Polonski, so that he could get better by himself.

Leila, who had been eavesdropping from behind the door and overheard the conversation about art, called her ally, the camp guard. The Whip reported the young doctor to the military authorities. His line of reasoning was clear enough: the doctor was spreading anti-Soviet propaganda by talking to the patient Polonski about bourgeois art done by émigrés and traitors to the Motherland.

The camp authorities gave the doctor a choice: either he could accept a transfer, by way of punishment, to another camp, located on a small island in the Pacific Ocean, in the Far East, with conditions even harsher than in this one, or he would get a stamp in his work book declaring that he was unfit to serve as a doctor, and as a result, he would never be able to find work anywhere, ever again.

The former political prisoner Polonski left the camp before he was properly cured. They sent him off to the Siberian town of Tomsk for a couple of years, and then to a small town seventy miles away from Moscow, where he worked as a boiler stoker.

TODAY IS the day! Today!

I got up earlier than usual in order to polish the antique silver cutlery and to buff the cut-glass wine glasses until they shone, to clean everything that had come from the chateau. I bought a bottle of Tokaj wine and another of Rhine wine, and put them in the fridge. I washed the Chinese tea set thoroughly, even though it was perfectly clean. And as I polished and rubbed and buffed these beautiful antique objects, in the shining surface of a knife I caught the reflection of a photograph from my child-hood, or rather my adolescence, framed and hung on the wall. In the photo, I was dancing with an extremely good-looking young man, Monsieur Beauvisage. Petr. He has forgiven me my recent skittishness, that loyal and lifelong friend.

This morning, when I left the building where I live, the wall of prefabricated buildings across the street, which was usually as threatening as a row of heavily armed gray warriors, was hidden under a gray veil of mist. It was drizzling gently, so I sat down on my bench. The red one. A sparrow immediately came over to me.

A sparrow!

On that other day, a bird had also come over to me, yes, I think it was a sparrow too. That day, not so long ago, maybe two years, when in my letterbox I found a note from the post office, telling me that I had to pick up a telegram that had just been sent to me.

My first thought was Jan! With trembling legs I hurried to the post office.

It was closed.

All night, purple visions of car accidents alternated with white scenes of hospital rooms.

In the morning, the post office delivered the telegram. I ripped it open in a flash.

It had nothing to do with Jan, but nothing else was important to me.

In the telegram there was just a single sentence, written in French:

*JE SUIS VEUF, JE SUIS SEUL, ET SUR MOI LE SOIR TOMBE.*

No signature. I recognized the verse by Victor Hugo. "I'm a widower, I'm alone, and the evening is falling upon me," I translated the beautiful Alexandrine line into my own language.

Who had sent me this mysterious telegram? I couldn't fathom it.

Back at the post office, the clerk flicked through a large book for a moment. When she'd finished, she announced, in her tired, official voice:

"This telegram was sent from Moscow, madam."

SOMETIME LATER, I received a letter. It must have been some six months ago. Somebody was looking for me. A man. I sent him a dispassionate reply; I didn't want him to know my innermost thoughts. And he answered me back.

Dear Sylva,
I am so pleased that you answered my letter! Your answer has given me reason to believe you also remember me and the happiness that we shared such a long time ago. "Dear," this standard term of endearment strikes me as so

wonderful when coming from you, or rather from your pen. When I read the word, I felt a kind of physical warmth.

You mentioned memories. For my part, I assure you that the times I spent with you were the most beautiful I have ever experienced in my life. Back then, I thought I would always feel as good as I did during those moments.

Do you remember the present you offered me? You don't? I'll tell you about it: One evening, in a café, the Café Louvre in Prague's city center, I was admiring your black lace glove, and you too as you toyed with it. For many years I have kept that glove which was my only possession; over many decades, whenever I felt like it, I took out your long, black lace glove with its bloodstained fingers, and laid it out before me. Whenever I see that bloodstained black lace, I hear you, Sylva, I see you and feel your presence.

I would like to know about your life in more detail, and, of course, I hope to see you again. I would meet you anywhere, no matter how far I had to travel.

Please do not get lost again. I beseech you with all my heart.

Yours,
The Old Tree


P.S. The old tree no longer has any leaves or branches, and yet the spring winds have shaken its roots and it has flowered. Both the red flowers and the yellow ones will soon disappear without a trace.

When I read these words, a white flower budded in the royal garden of my old age.

Half a year ago I followed his second letter with my reply, my doubts, and then, his third letter came. In the fourth, you wrote to me, my love (by then you had started to use the familiar form of address), that from a distance you had followed the lives of your fellow inmates in the forced labor camps. That you didn't go out much, you didn't see anybody, you lived in a little den, and at night you stoked boilers. You wrote that you weren't looking for anyone, and no one was looking for you, that you didn't have any friends. But you did keep up with people you felt close to, and you knew how Semyon's artwork was progressing.

You wrote in one of your letters about an art exhibition of Semyon's in Moscow. You wrote about the dozens of people, or rather, the human wrecks who attended the opening:

Men and women with pallid faces, all of them were my twin brothers and sisters. Just then Semyon came in, leading a young woman into the gallery. At least, she seemed young to me. She wore an ivory dress that came down to her knees, and her golden curls fell freely over her shoulders. That woman wore pearl earrings. I knew those pearls well. It was as if a ray of afternoon sunlight had broken into that dark basement where we, the gray shadows, were living, as if a ray of sunlight had broken through to show us that life exists. A young man in his twenties accompanied the woman. Her son. I approached her, in order to look at the pearl earrings she wore. Those were the ones: my last gift to you, Sylva. Your son has your hair, your golden skin, your lips. But he has my build; I used to be like that, before, when I lived in the forest. And your son has my eyes. You, Sylva, didn't recognize me. I'm not surprised. You weren't expecting to see me, you thought I was dead. What's more, you couldn't have recognized me. I was one of those human wrecks.

Which of those devastated men could have been Andrei? The old man that looked like Tiresias, the blind seer of Greek mythology? Could that have been Andrei? No, for God's sake! Andrei, the forest hero who hunted firebirds!

But how will I recognize him today? After so many years, so many decades of suffering . . . Had that been him?

AT SEVENTY, your life is over.

Or does a new one begin? I am trembling in this steam-filled station. It's cold, it's been raining nonstop and this cold wind has been blowing for three days. But if I'm cold, it is, above all, just because I'm here waiting.

At home, everything has been left ready: the antiques are shining, even the helmets and lances, the medieval suits of armor and the cut-glass goblets, everything that I have known since my childhood in that elegant, spacious chateau in northern Bohemia, all those objects now piled up uselessly in my little hidey-hole on the outskirts. I've polished everything, I've dusted the plants and I've brightened up the room with a few white lilac stems that give off the perfume of spring, which is late this year. I have adorned the table with a book, just one, the one that says . . . in all the terrible periods of human history, in a corner somewhere there is a man who has dedicated himself to his calligraphy and to the stringing together of unusual and exquisite words. Yes, I have chosen that book, because that person is myself. It is I who is sitting in a silent corner, and history gallops past me, as I busy myself with the rosary beads of words and the pearls of musical notes.

Yes, this is my daily route, this is my life, this is my daily trip to the library. Recently I've been going on foot from home to the tram stop and from the tram stop back home, indeed I've been dragging out the walk as much as I can because when I do so, I see all kinds of admirable and marvelous things, I see the light and colors and shadows on people's features, each face is a symphonic poem or a quartet or a sonata or a trio. In those faces I read, or rather listen, through them, to the fierce passions of Mahler and Beethovens' symphonies, from other faces come the tensions and anguish of Shostakovich's chamber music or the profound grief of Dvořák's *Stabat Mater*. On occasion I'm lucky enough to fall into the tender, autumnal melancholy of Schubert's *lieder*, and only rarely do I have the good fortune to overhear Mozart's exultant glee. And so I walk and listen to the music that people release and let flow, I who had once owned a Pleyel piano, a box in the National Theater and the German Theater, and the very best recordings on disc. Now I have nothing, but music plays on inside me in a way that is clearer and cleaner than before. I only have to go out into the street and I can already hear an entire concert, spontaneous and unexpected and unusual, I do not need to look for music in the concert halls, I don't need to go to Prague's old city center, with its self-evident charm: I prefer to discover beauty and music and poetry there where we normally do not expect it. In the morning I walk under the gray walls of prefab panel houses and the laundry drying on lines that tells me what its owners are like. The clotheslines sway to the rhythm of Lully's Versaillesque marches, and the tempo of the fairy steps in Purcell's operas. When I pass those same walls again in the evening, the windows lit up in different colors allow me once more to imagine the people who live and love and suffer behind those blue and ochre and green and yellow panes. As I do, I am accompanied, as he plays his magnificent compositions on the violin, by Johann Sebastian Bach himself.

I no longer need to look at the Vltava River from Charles Bridge in order to search its waters for Smetana's symphonic poem. I have only to look at a tree trunk, here on the outskirts, or a blade of dry grass. I need only catch sight of a muddy puddle and a rusty length of pipe to hear the symphonic poem *Vltava* in them, to hear the piano and the violin of the river of my life, and I can even hear the infrequently pressed pedal of the piano, the violin's broken string, the cello's wrong note, all those false sounds that have formed and still form part of the flow of my river. They cannot ever cease to belong to the symphony of my life.

EVERYTHING IS ready, the wine and the cheese canapés garnished with tiny pieces of carefully sliced tomatoes and cucumbers. I have showered again and put on perfume, and I dried my hair slowly, bit by bit, so that it would come out soft, my white hair that he's never seen. The last time, at Semyon's exhibition, he must have seen my hair as it used to be, that light chestnut color, which with the aid of some chamomile, would turn golden . . . My hair that went gray after Jan left. Jan went away and he won't be able to come back because his home no longer exists, his home has ceased to exist because it has changed so much, into a strange, alien place. He who abandons his home becomes an eternal globetrotter, a stranger with one wish in his heart, a longing that can never be satisfied. He turns into a foreigner whose home is everywhere . . . and yet everywhere means nowhere.

My hair is as white as milk, my face is a finely spun web, a skin of thin snakes covers my hands, Andrei. You have never seen me like this, my love, you won't know me, I'm not me any longer, this woman is not the Sylva who lived in Paris, where they addressed her as Madame l'Ambassadrice. No, she is no longer the Surrealists's inspiration, she is no longer Mnemosyne, the goddess of the muses and the deity of beauty, that Sylva whom the painter Semyon and his friends called *Solnyshko* in Russian, meaning little sun. The seventy-year-old Sylva, whose age pretty much coincides with that of the century, is somebody else now. Who is this solitary woman with a handful of white narcissi on her head, with lace thickly woven by a spider and then engraved deeply on her face?

Sylva is no longer your blue butterfly, her hair is covered now with a layer of frost and her skin is like a blank page on which someone has spilled dry tea leaves. But inside Sylva there is now a garden full of green fruit in the middle of which there shines a single, white, perfumed apple. That apple ripened when I found out you were alive, my love.

Andrei, at home the soft, fresh smell of white lilac awaits you . . . At home, Andrei, where is your home? Where is home for you? The forest in the Czech mountains? The streets of Moscow? Among the coats of arms that cover the low walls of my swallows' nest on the outskirts of Prague? Maybe it's in that squirrel burrow, in the middle of which there is a vase full of lilac, tender and white as old age, and next to which there are two candles, one a little shorter, the other just a tiny bit taller, two lit candles, golden, searing, two candles and two flames, our lives, and those two candles will burn and two people will get to know each other again by looking into each other's eyes. The river of our affection and our compassion and our desire, and the river of our understanding will be different now. It will be a river of old age, a river of shared silence, a quiet, white-waved river.

I HEAD for the station exit. I am leaving this place. I don't want to see you, I don't want to be a witness to the change wrought in you. And I don't want to see my own transformation mirrored in your eyes.

No, that's not right, my inner voice tells me. You're deluding yourself. This isn't right!

So what is it, then? I ask, in a weak voice.

This: that you're ashamed. Not because your hair has gone gray. You are so shame faced because you are guilty.

A moment ago, through the window of the station café, I was secretly watching the people who were greeting the passengers on your train: I saw everything. I even saw the pillar where we'd agreed to meet. But I didn't see you, Andrei. I didn't want to see you, that's why I didn't go over to the train, nor did I go up to the pillar, our meeting place . . . in order not to see my man of the forest, weakened, wrinkled, wan.

All because of me.

To the exit! Get out of here! As far away as possible!

Rain and yet more rain is flooding the street, white rain, alluvium swallowing me up. I have to walk, always forward, for a long time, then drop into the first café to have a glass of wine, yes, a good glass of wine, white as the rain, to celebrate the definitive entry that I have just made into the empire of solitude. And when I've done that I will walk some more, never turning around, going ahead without staggering, trotting at an even pace, for a long time, and then even more, until weariness settles in. Why am I going, if I came here with such hope, expectation, longing? I don't know. I only know that I have to do this. I have to go. To flee, fast!

And what about him, what will he do when I go? Has he gone to the pillar, our meeting place?

But surely even now, at seventy, life can begin again! There's still time! Life has trembled in me like a blackbird in spring, it's shaken itself like a sparrow in a puddle of water, and it has opened its beak. I go back to the station, I head for the platform. I walk over to the café where we were supposed to meet, where we must meet, by the pillar. I lean on the café's closed door. I look at the pillar: Is it the same one in front of which Andrei said goodbye to me thirty years ago? I think of the brook on Andrei's mountains; I am the stone, he, the water. The stone remains, the water, in its eternal movement, goes back to where it came from. Just a furtive glance, just to see Andrei, and I'll go. Just one look, like Lot's wife. One single look, and I'll be turned into a pillar of salt!

I shouldn't do it. I can't. I can't think it over, I only know that I have to leave. To flee, fast!

It's raining, it's pouring down, the rain is black now, people are restless, pushing and shoving each other with elbows and umbrellas as if they were medieval weapons. What would have happened if I'd stayed at the station? I see myself, looking at our pillar . . . I see myself, leaning against the wall, looking at the pillar with its peeling paint, I watch it as if my life depended on it. A pillar, which stretches vainly up into the sky, because nobody's leaning against it. It supports the entire vaulted roof of the station, the vault that shelters dozens of platforms from the elements. A simple, bare, old pillar. A pillar to which somebody has walked up, and waited a long time, before leaving. A solitary pillar.

Now that I am moving away from you once and for all, Andrei, in my mind's eye I see, between the drops of black rain and the lilac-colored ones which the sky never ceases to pour, another look. I see eyes staring at the pillar. From a corner full of cobwebs, an old man is watching the column. His lips are parched and his eyes, sunken. But on his eyelashes, waiting and resignation, uncertainty and hope. And the glow of the last ember of life left burning. The old man's look, edged by white lashes, is fixed on the old pillar as if it were a goddess to whom he had come to make an offering. A look like the white wings of a seagull. A look like the flame of the candle in the Café Louvre. A look like the flame reflected in the glass from which we both once drank. As I make my way through the heavy, lilac curtain of the rain, I see myself in the station . . . I am not taking my eyes off that pillar either; then they settle on the old man. Our eyes meet. We don't move, we don't breathe. And, finally, on our lips appears a barely perceptible smile . . .

That might have been the case, if I hadn't left the station. But I had no alternative.

The canapés, prepared for him, garnished for him, are getting dry. In vain did I polish and buff everything, in vain did I put on my pearl earrings. In vain did he pack his luggage, and search for gifts and buy the ticket. In vain did he take such a long journey. Now he must be sitting there on the platform, two heavy suitcases in his hands, full of gifts that he has been choosing for a long time. I see him in my mind's eye: an old man on the station, rubbing at his eyes, thinking that this is impossible. Where are you, Blue Butterfly? No. Sylva isn't there. Sylva hasn't come. He is alone.

Alone, forever.

As am I. Two solitudes. Two rivers that flow separately. Two candles that have gone out.

Heavy black drops are falling, drops of tar. I am dripping wet. Where's my umbrella? Could I have left it at the station? No. It's in my hand, still rolled up. It doesn't matter. It doesn't matter that I am soaked through if he is stuck on the platform, alone, disappointed, desperate.

Far away!

The Feminist Press promotes voices on the margins of dominant culture and publishes feminist works from around the world, inspiring personal transformation and social justice. We believe that books have the power to shift culture, and create a society free of violence, sexism, homophobia, racism, cis-supremacy, classism, sizeism, ableism and other forms of dehumanization. Our books and programs engage, educate, and entertain.

See our complete list of books at
**feministpress.org**

**THE FEMINIST PRESS**
AT THE CITY UNIVERSITY OF NEW YORK
**FEMINISTPRESS.ORG**